PRAISE F

Follow Her Down

"*Follow Her Down* is compulsively readable and surprisingly moving—with a twist that knocked me off my seat. This one will burrow deep into your muscle."

—Jess Lourey, Edgar Award–nominated author of *The Taken Ones*

"Victoria Helen Stone delivers an emotional gut punch of secrets, betrayal, and unresolved trauma in this gritty revenge thriller. You'll cheer for Elise as her life unravels when she's forced to confront the one thing she wants to forget—the murder of her sister. The tension in *Follow Her Down* builds until you're desperate to see how the pieces fit together—and secretly hoping this won't be the only book in this world."

—Darby Kane, internationally bestselling author of *Pretty Little Wife* *and The Engagement Party*

"*Follow Her Down* pulled me into a tangled web I didn't want to get out of! Like any good true crime devotee, I couldn't help but binge this story and heed Stone's bidding to 'follow her down' a path of distrust, denial, and intrigue all stemming from a decades-old mystery that's suddenly found new life. Fellow fans of true crime will be spellbound by Stone's tense, empathetic writing and fascinated by the window she provides into the long-lasting effects on a family that's found themselves at the center of one of these tragic but enthralling stories."

—Emily Bleeker, *Wall Street Journal* bestselling author of *When I'm Gone*

"A simply riveting novel of suspense... a complex and deftly crafted story built upon decades of doubt, fear, and suspicion that will not allow a woman overcome her trauma at the unexplained loss of her sister and the mysterious and possibly linked death of her ex-husband. Original and fascinating from start to finish, "Follow Her Down" is a strongly recommended pick for personal reading lists and community library conspiracy suspense/thriller fiction collections."

—Midwest Book Review

"A must-read for romantic suspense fans, Follow Her Down delivers nonstop tension and a mind-bending twist. You'll root for Elise to overcome the traumatic past she's desperate to escape."

—Melinda Leigh, *Wall Street Journal* bestselling author

At the Quiet Edge

"The plot's many twists and turns will stun and surprise readers. Suspense fans will get their money's worth."

—*Publishers Weekly*

"Sharp and sophisticated, *At the Quiet Edge* commanded my attention from the captivating first chapter to the electrifying ending."

—Minka Kent, *Washington Post* bestselling author

"An utterly compelling blend of family drama and suspense, *At the Quiet Edge* pulled me in and didn't let go. I read this riveting, twisty book in one sitting. Not to be missed."

—A. J. Banner, #1 Amazon, *USA Today*, and *Publishers Weekly* bestselling author

"I raced through the pages of *At the Quiet Edge*. This propulsive story places you inside a world of secrets, and locks you inside. And like our heroine Lily and her son Everett, it's hard to know who to trust. This is taut, heart-pounding suspense."

—Kaira Rouda, *USA Today* and Amazon Charts bestselling author of *The Next Wife* and *Somebody's Home*

"As a single mom, I couldn't help but identify with the complex dynamics between mother and son as each protected the other in this gripping thriller. It is a thrilling game of cat and mouse that kept me guessing all the way up to the jaw-dropping conclusion."

—Lucinda Berry, bestselling author of *The Best of Friends* and *The Perfect Child*

Evelyn, After

"Hands down, the best book I've read this year. Brilliant, compelling, and haunting."

—Suzanne Brockmann, *New York Times* bestselling author

"Readers will cheer on Evelyn when the power dynamic with her lying, cheating husband shifts, even while they watch her flirting with disaster in her steamy affair with Noah. A solid choice for Liane Moriarty readers."

—*Library Journal*

"Stone (a nom de plume of romance writer Victoria Dahl) . . . ably switches to darker suspense in a compelling story exploring what lurks behind a seemingly perfect life."

—*Booklist*

"Stone pens a great story that will have readers wondering what will happen next to the characters involved in this mysterious tale . . . Fascinating tale told by a talented storyteller!"

—*RT Book Reviews*

"Victoria Helen Stone renders the obsessions and weaknesses of her characters with scorching insight. Her sterling prose creates a seamless atmosphere of anticipation and dread, while delivering devastating truths about the nature of sex, relationships, and lies, often with a humor that's rapier-sharp. *Evelyn, After* reads like *Gone Girl* with a bigger heart and a stronger moral core."

—Christopher Rice, *New York Times* bestselling author

Half Past

"A gripping, haunting exploration of the lengths to which we'll go to belong, *Half Past* will hold you in its thrall until the very last page. Stone's expert storytelling, vivid characterizations, and tantalizing dropping of clues left me utterly breathless, longing for more—and a newly minted Victoria Helen Stone fan!"

—Emily Carpenter, bestselling author of *Burying the Honeysuckle Girls* and *The Weight of Lies*

"A captivating, suspenseful tale of love and lies, mystery and self-discovery, *Half Past* kept me flipping the pages through the final, startling twist."

—A. J. Banner, #1 Amazon and *USA Today* bestselling author of *The Good Neighbor* and *The Twilight Wife*

"What would you do if you found out that your mother wasn't your biological mother? Would you go looking for the answer to how that happened if she couldn't provide an explanation? That's the intriguing question at the heart of *Half Past*, Stone's strong follow-up to *Evelyn, After*. [It's] both a mystery and an exploration of what family really means. Fans of Jodi Picoult will race through this."

—Catherine McKenzie, bestselling author of *Hidden* and *The Good Liar*

Jane Doe

"Stone does a masterful job of creating in Jane a complex character, making her both scary and more than a little appealing . . . This beautifully balanced thriller will keep readers tense, surprised, pleased, and surprised again as a master manipulator unfolds her plan of revenge."

—*Kirkus Reviews* (starred review)

"Revenge drives this fascinating thriller . . . Stone keeps the suspense high throughout. Readers will relish Jane's Machiavellian maneuvers to even the score with the unlikable Steven."

—*Publishers Weekly*

"Crafty, interesting, and vengeful."

—*Novelgossip*

"Crazy great book!"

—*Good Life Family Magazine*

"Stone skillfully, deviously, and gleefully leads the reader down a garden path to a knockout WHAM-O of an ending. *Jane Doe* will not disappoint."

—*New York Journal of Books*

"*Jane Doe* is a riveting, engrossing story about a man who screws over the wrong woman, with a picture-perfect ending that's the equivalent of a big red bow on a shiny new car. It's that good. Ladies, we finally have the revenge story we've always deserved."

—*Criminal Element*

"Jane, the self-described sociopath at the center of Victoria Helen Stone's novel, [is] filling a hole in storytelling that we've long been waiting for."

—Bitch Media

"We loved being propelled into the complicated mind of Jane, intrigued as she bobbed and weaved her way through life with the knowledge she's just a little bit different. You'll be debating whether to make Jane your new best friend or lock your door and hide from her in fear. Both incredibly insightful and tautly suspenseful, *Jane Doe* is a must-read!"

—Liz Fenton and Lisa Steinke, bestselling authors of *The Good Widow*

"With biting wit and a complete disregard for societal double standards, Victoria Helen Stone's antihero will slice a path through your expectations and leave you begging for more. Make room in the darkest corner of your heart for Jane Doe."

—Eliza Maxwell, bestselling author of *The Unremembered Girl*

"If revenge is a dish best served cold, Jane Doe is Julia Child. Though Jane's a heroine who claims to be a sociopath, Jane's heart and soul shine through in this addicting, suspenseful tale of love, loss, and justice."

—Wendy Webb, bestselling author of *The End of Temperance Dare*

"One word: wow. This novel is compelling from the first sentence. An emotional ride with a deliciously vengeful narrator, Jane's tale keeps readers on the edge without the security of knowing who the good guy really is. Honest, cutting, and at times even humorous, this is one powerhouse of a read!"

—Brandi Reeds, bestselling author of *Trespassing*

False Step

"[A] cleverly plotted thriller . . . Danger and savage emotions surface as [Veronica] discovers that she's not the only one whose life is built on secrets and lies. Stone keeps the reader guessing to the end."

—*Publishers Weekly*

"Intense and chilling, *False Step* wickedly rewards thriller fans with a compulsive read that'll leave readers wondering how well they know their loved ones. I was riveted!"

—Kerry Lonsdale, Amazon Charts and *Wall Street Journal* bestselling author

Problem Child

"Outstanding . . . Readers will find vicarious joy in Jane's petty vengeances and unabashed meanness to anyone who tries to take advantage of her. Stone turns some very dark material into an upbeat tale."

—*Publishers Weekly* (starred review)

"This installment is highly recommended for fans of edgier psychological fiction."

—*Library Journal*

The Last One Home

"Stone gradually reveals her multifaceted characters' secrets as the intricate, fast-paced plot builds to a surprising conclusion. Fans of dark, twisted tales of dysfunctional families will be satisfied."

—*Publishers Weekly*

"The story gives just enough detail in each chapter to keep the reader intrigued about where it is going to go next . . . family secrets will never be looked at the same."

—*The Parkersburg News and Sentinel*

"A slow burner . . . *The Last One Home* takes its time to set the scene for the twists and revelations that will come in the last chapters of the book."

—*Mystery & Suspense Magazine*

"*The Last One Home* is elegant and chilling, an indelible novel of family secrets. I couldn't put it down until I learned the truth about these finely drawn characters—the ending left me absolutely shocked and amazed, and I can't stop thinking about it."

—Luanne Rice, *New York Times* bestselling author of *The Shadow Box*

"Gripping and relentless, *The Last One Home* stalks you like the serial killer within its pages: you know danger is right around the corner, but you don't know when it'll strike. And just when you think you have the story figured out, Victoria Helen Stone rips the rug right out from under your feet. Highly recommended!"

—Avery Bishop, author of *Girl Gone Mad*

"In *The Last One Home*, Victoria Helen Stone weaves another sure-handed story, this one about mothers, the fierce love they have for their children, and just how far they will go to protect their progeny. This is a suspense novel that's in part a love story, as well as a chilling mystery. But it's the kind of tale that sneaks up on you, revealing discoveries in the last scorching chapters that flip the whole narrative on its head. Full of shifting family loyalties and recollections of the past, and creepy, alone-in-the-countryside vibes, this book held me, start to finish, in its mesmerizing thrall."

—Emily Carpenter, author of *Reviving the Hawthorn Sisters*

BALD-
FACED
LIAR

ALSO BY VICTORIA HELEN STONE

Follow Her Down

The Hook

At the Quiet Edge

Evelyn, After

Half Past

Jane Doe

False Step

Problem Child

The Last One Home

BALD-FACED LIAR

A NOVEL

VICTORIA HELEN STONE

LAKE UNION
PUBLISHING

This is a work of fiction. Names, characters, organizations, places, events, and incidents are either products of the author's imagination or are used fictitiously. Otherwise, any resemblance to actual persons, living or dead, is purely coincidental.

Published by Lake Union Publishing, Seattle

www.apub.com

EU product safety contact:
Amazon Media EU S. à r.l.
38, avenue John F. Kennedy, L-1855 Luxembourg
amazonpublishing-gpsr@amazon.com

ISBN-13: 9781662514616 (paperback)
ISBN-13: 9781662514623 (digital)

Cover design by Caroline Teagle Johnson
Cover image: © Peter Dazeley / Getty

Printed in the United States of America

This book is for everyone still fighting back.

CHAPTER 1

The woman on the other side of the privacy fence is sobbing in great, wrenching coughs. The cries emerge half-muffled as if she's making an attempt to hide the noise with a hand, but it's a hopeless gesture. She sounds like a dying animal.

I lean closer, pressing my forehead to the rough gray wood to get a better angle even as splinters brush my nose. When my eye finds the widest space of the gap, I finally see her. Julia. I heard her introducing herself on a phone call yesterday.

I'm behind her, a stalker peering down at the arms she's curled around her legs as she presses her pretty face against the bones of her knees. Above her shoulder, my hand is splayed wide on the fence, and less than an inch of wood separates my fingers from her spine and the smooth, tan skin stretched over her back. Dappled sunlight shifts against her shoulder blades as her body heaves with the stress of holding in sobs.

She is one of the beautiful people, thin and fit, her blond hair always tousled by the breeze as if God's own hand had styled it. They'd arrived at the beach bungalow four days earlier, Julia and her husband and little baby Sheila.

Sheila. Isn't that an odd name for a baby? But I guess every Sheila, Roger, and Bernice started out as an infant with an adult name.

Baby Sheila was born four or five months ago, but Julia's belly is flat as a pancake already. Just this morning I'd still been sprawled in bed when I heard a quick, steady jog carry the young mother past my window and back to her rental at half past seven. She's dedicated to fitness or maybe just to appearance, I'm not sure.

My own stomach is curved and soft even though I've never had kids. Granted, I'm almost forty, but I imagine this woman separated from me by a bit of wood plank will have the same body in ten years, whether through sheer force of will or surgery or both.

But her life isn't perfect. No one's is. I've come to learn that here in my little beach hideaway, and it's why I stay. This hiding place is the best medicine for what ails me. I can be involved in others' lives even while I stay safely invisible.

A door squeaks open on the other side of the fence. The crying woman gulps down a gasp and goes quiet, but it's too late. Her husband is already there, his face a jumble of confusion and annoyance under a backward-facing ball cap. He'd fit in perfectly on the set of *The Bachelorette*, one of those white men I can't keep track of, hard-jawed handsome, with blue eyes balanced over a respectably masculine nose.

"Babe?" he ventures. "You okay? What are you doing out here?"

"I'm good!" she croaks, the words scraped from her strangling throat, and I see in his uncertain smile that he's desperate to accept the lie. He wants to give her a thumbs-up and escape back to the soccer match blaring inside.

His chin dips in a nod. His hand curls around the handle of the door.

But he pauses, then after one quick glance back toward the screen of the huge TV mounted on the wall of the bungalow, he pushes the door wider and steps out. "Hey," he croons. "What's wrong, babe?"

"Nothing." She tries to offer a laugh, but it bubbles with snot. "Nothing. I'm sorry. It's the hormones."

"Aw. My poor girl."

Before I can think to draw back, he's only two feet from me, crouched down in front of his wife, and I'm staring directly into his face. I'm afraid to even blink for fear he'll see the movement between the slats and glance up to lock eyes.

Shit. My back twinges with the realization that I'm twisted awkwardly in my chair and I'll have to hold this pose for a long while.

"Tell me what's going on," he says, reaching out to hold her hands when she tries to hide her face again. He's so close I can see a stripe of scruff on his chiseled jaw where he missed a spot shaving. I have no idea what his name is. Julia only refers to him as "sweetie" when she's talking to him and "Daddy" when she speaks to her daughter.

"I'm just overwhelmed," she squeaks out before her voice breaks again. "With . . . you know . . . everything."

"Your doctor said it's totally normal to feel that way, right?" I assume he's dismissing her, but then he hunkers down a little lower and kisses her knuckles. "You've gone through a lot. The C-section, the mastitis."

He looks like such a bro I'm surprised by his soft understanding. Surprised, but relieved for her sake.

"And hey . . ." He nudges her knee with his. "Sheila will be fine. She won't even know she started out life as a dork."

Julia manages a mucousy laugh. Their daughter wears a cranial helmet to reshape her skull. An alarming look for a baby, but the kid will be fine in no time at all. I wonder if she needed it or if her head just looked a bit bulbous for Instagram photos.

The husband is even closer to me now, and my eyes are dry and burning as I try not to blink. Imagine if he looks up and realizes there's a stranger's eyeball staring right through a crack in the fence. So creepy.

I breathe out as softly as I can, focusing on a small scar at the bottom of his chin. I imagine a childhood trampoline accident. "You're taking your meds?" he asks.

She nods.

"And . . ." When he hesitates, she dips her head down as if she knows which words are coming. I hold my breath and wait as his face twists into discomfort. He clears his throat. "And you haven't been talking to her?"

Her? I accidentally blink in surprise, but it doesn't draw his attention.

"No!" she declares. "I promised I wouldn't. I'm not."

"She's not good for you. Or us."

"I know. I said I'm not talking to her. It's over."

It's over? *What's* over? A muscle I didn't even know I had begins to cramp in my waist, but I'm not backing off now that stuff is getting deep.

"Babe," he says, "I'm not saying never. But not *her*."

At first I'd thought he might be referring to a toxic mother, but now? Is this an open marriage? Accommodation for her sexuality? Or just some intense friendship drama?

I desperately need to know more, but the cramp is getting worse, so when he leans in to press his forehead against Julia's, I break free from the trap and ease back into my chair. After muting my phone, I open the security app and tap the patio camera to watch the couple from above.

Don't worry. I'm allowed. The external cameras are written into the rental contract whether they noticed it or not.

Now I can see the outdoor dining set and the husband's broad back, but Julia is nearly hidden from view. A bird's-eye view isn't all it's cracked up to be. Disappointing.

"You miss her," the husband says, the words flat and weary, and my skin prickles with anticipation.

"No!" Julia protests. "No, I'm just tired. It's not like that at all."

"Right." We can all hear the resignation in his voice, poor guy.

"I'm sorry," she whispers so softly I find my ear brushing the wood again. Then disaster strikes. My foot slips against the brick patio, and I swear to God, not only has the soccer game gone quiet, but the constant road noise in front of the house has dipped into silence at that exact moment too.

I freeze, they freeze. My mouth twisting in a horrified grimace, I watch the husband's tiny head ease up on the screen of my phone. He looks around. I grimace harder.

But it's *my* patio. I have a right to sit out here in a chair pulled too close to the fence. It's not my fault they decided to have this conversation six inches from my favorite spot. They might be creeped out if they peer over the fence and discover that they've assumed a privacy they don't have, but I haven't done anything wrong.

Still, I take precautions and slip in my favorite camouflage: earbuds. If I see him stand to look over the fence, I'll lean back, close my eyes, and bop my head along to nonexistent music. Get your shit together, Julia and Company. You're staying in a crowded area!

But I'm saved by the bell of little Sheila's sudden, piercing cry. The tension breaks. The husband looks back at his wife. "She's awake," he says, prompting a laugh from Julia.

"She certainly is."

"I'll get her. You take a break."

"No, I'm fine. And I'm already leaking."

I watch as he helps her to her feet. She dusts off her shorts, then presses her hands to both breasts to hold in milk as she follows him inside.

My relief over not getting caught trips quickly into sinking disappointment. I need to know who this other woman is. Julia and her husband shared a bottle of wine on the patio the night before, so hopefully they'll do the same tonight and spill more details. I've heard them discuss their departure tomorrow, so it's now or never.

In the meantime I open Instagram to check once more for recent posts to #SantaCruz. And finally, *finally*, there she is. Julia MacAttack, clearly not her real name, but that's her real face. The husband, it turns out, is named Jamie. Jamie and Julia. How perfect. I'm surprised they didn't pick a *J* name for baby Sheila, but maybe that trend isn't cute anymore.

Ignoring that I should have started work an hour ago, I stretch out my legs and begin to pick my way through Julia's camera-ready universe. No one is as careful about privacy as they should be, and that means I'm never lonely no matter how alone I am.

CHAPTER 2

Screams really carry here. Everything gets quieter in the offseason, but during summer the ocean breeze carries the cries of people dropping down the big hills of the roller coaster, the squeals of children rocketing past on scooters, the screech of seagulls fighting over fries. I like the noise, the life, the humanity drifting toward me, so I can experience all of it.

Some people only live one life. I have no idea how they do it. I can live as many as I want, remaking myself and pulling from others. People are like books for me, and I wander the world like it's a library, plucking out whatever catches my interest.

There's the rental upstairs from me, empty today but usually busy with guests coming and going, and then there's the beach bungalow next door where Julia's staying.

Other than that . . . well, almost everyone is a stranger in this town, and they leave bits of their stories with me, whether they mean to or not. Most people have no idea how exposed they are these days.

For example, no one blinks an eye at the doorbell or patio cameras. I've witnessed more than one couple have sex right there on-screen. My most scandalized moment was seeing a man go down on the family nanny after the wife and kids were asleep. I slapped my hand over my mouth to smother my shocked guffaws, but she was a little less successful at hiding her noise. The wife either didn't hear or didn't care, I'm not sure.

Ah, humans. We're truly fascinating.

Speaking of, Julia's entire life with her husband is now available to me, from their adorable dating selfies to their new house and the wedding and the pregnancy and, oh look, there's tiny newborn Sheila! What a cutie.

There's another blond woman with them in many of the prebaby photos on Instagram. She's older than Julia, with bold, striking features and an intense gaze that eats through the camera lens. They don't look like sisters. Could this be the unnamed troublemaker?

The username tagged in the photo isn't helpful: Chromospheric1—some sort of astronomical term—and her account is private.

I pause over a shot of the other woman with her arms wrapped around Julia from behind. Both women are pink-cheeked and laughing while Jamie stands six inches away flashing a smile that doesn't reach his eyes. I build a whole story for them as I scroll through, watching Julia's belly grow as the other blonde appears less and less often.

Letting my creativity run wild, I imagine Jamie told his wife he was totally comfortable with her *special friend* . . . until he wasn't anymore. Until the competition intensified and the inside jokes got to be too much. And then they were having a baby, and wouldn't the baby be confused by her—

The vibration of an alarm interrupts me, and I sit up straight with a muffled curse. That was supposed to be my alarm for break time, but I haven't even started working yet. Oops. Time to transform myself into Eliza May, nurse extraordinaire.

People really like that name. When I was working hands-on in hospitals, it always made my patients feel comfortable, like I was an innocent farm girl fresh out of the Midwest. And really, I was. I'd never lived on a farm, but plenty of my classmates back in Fair Isle, Iowa, had. I'd even raised rabbits for 4-H, though I'd mostly been in it for the excuse to spend hours in the backyard, away from everyone who knew me.

Maybe that's what I'm doing with this job too? Spending hours in my backyard, away from everyone who knows me? Probably. I miss the day-to-day interactions I got in hospitals, but I'm so anonymous here. Safe and comfortable and surrounded by strangers and casual acquaintances.

Though I step inside to drop into my desk chair, it's positioned right next to the open patio doors so I won't miss any delicious tidbits because of work.

But don't worry, work offers plenty of tidbits too.

Two messages await me when I sign in, and both are related to my juiciest file. I've really dug into this one, cheering on the patient as she progressed from an ER visit for a mysterious fever to hospital admission for kidney failure, and on and on until she was in the ICU for six full days and veered close to death twice.

Mrs. Washington is a fighter, and I was breathless the first time I waded through her charts, relieved to find notes from nurses about the extensive questions posed by her son and daughter. Both of her kids have been right by her side through all this. Despite that she's eighty-five, Mrs. Washington hasn't given up, and neither has her family. I love them all, and I felt nothing but relief when I got to her discharge paperwork and knew she was at home and on the mend. But medicine is a business in this country, and everyone expects documentation and payment, which is where I shine.

Her nephrologist took several days to answer my questions about the medical coding, but he's given me a lot to work with. I can definitely press Medicare for the maximum allowable payment, and that makes me, the hospital, and everyone involved happy. Mrs. Washington has done it again!

I add the latest notes to her file, then go through the same process with the information provided by a lab supervisor. Wrapping up this case is a triumph, but I'm a little sad to let it go. I miss being fully immersed in patient drama, the ups and downs of a life-and-death struggle, but—like so many health care professionals—I burned out badly during the pandemic, so last year I walked away from nursing to become a clinical documentation specialist. Nursing is always there waiting if I want it, but I'm lazy as a cat now in my little place near the beach.

And hey, new files arrive every day. I crack open a fresh one and rub my hands together, ready to lose myself in every detail of this stranger's life.

I'm not really a stalker. I'm not! It's not like that.

Then again, isn't that just what a stalker would tell herself? *I'm not bad, I'm just misunderstood.* No one thinks they're the villain of their own story.

"Not true," I mutter to myself. I've been the villain since I was five years old, an enfant terrible who helped destroy an entire family and ruin several careers. No one back home ever let me forget, and it sticks with me no matter how far I run.

CHAPTER 3

"This dumb bitch," I mutter, absolutely furious with Dr. Dwayne Wubbles, orthopedic goober extraordinaire. He's a preening ass, likely a side effect of living every day with the name Dwayne Wubbles. Worse than that, he's married to the woman in charge of coding in his office, and Madam Wubbles is an absolute shitshow. These people pop up in my life at least once a month, probably because their charts are fresh poop blended with dried poop, like the world's grossest smoothie. You'd think the guy was a gastroenterologist.

And now he's pushing back on my expertise? Pfft. I'm going to query every note in this chart and watch him fume. It's almost quitting time, and this is my last chart of the day, so I'm going to make it count. My keyboard clacks loudly as I bang out a response to his snide answer to my latest query, but I pause when I hear a loud thump outside my front door.

My head rises in interest.

Another car door slams, voices explode in anger, and then a herd of elephants stomps up the stairs that angle over my entry to the door placed artlessly above mine. The staircase really ruins the pretty facade of this beach cottage. Or beach-*adjacent* cottage, if you don't count the eight blocks between the house and the boardwalk.

I switch on the doorbell camera for the unit upstairs and see a very young white couple. She's wearing a tiny crop top and has wrapped her arms around her middle as she bounces. "It's cooold!" I hear her complain over the speaker. "How are we even supposed to go to the beach?"

"I don't control the weather, *Karen*," the man sneers as he hunches over the keypad. I can't see much more of him than a brightly-dyed blue crew cut.

"If you call me that again, I'm going to punch you right in the face," she snarls.

"Do it, and I'll call the cops." When he stands up, they disappear into the rental, and I practically vibrate in anticipation of their clearly messy relationship.

Eyes on the wood-plank ceiling, I follow their footsteps through the living area. I can picture their movements perfectly since I lived in the upstairs unit for a year, and the layout is just a smaller version of my place.

They drop their bags by the door before the heavy tread of boots moves across creaky laminate flooring. They approach the long counter that masquerades as a kitchen, then draw nearer my position as they enter the living area at the back of the house to look around. Within a minute, they've opened the sliding door right above my head.

"Seriously?" he huffs. "That's the view? Jesus, what a shitty neighborhood. How much are we paying?"

My mouth drops open in silent outrage. This isn't a shitty neighborhood. It's busy and crowded like most of Santa Cruz, but it's cozy. I hope he's used to living in the quiet suburbs, because tomorrow is trash day, and the truck will perform its cacophonous ballet at exactly 6:32 a.m. and ruin this asshole's morning.

"We both picked this place on the website!" the girl upstairs screams. "You're not putting this on me!"

When I glance at the clock, my mood immediately skyrockets. It's finally quitting time, and I have big plans for my evening: dinner out with a book and a cocktail. I drop back into my chair to log out, but when I see a waiting email, my mood inches even higher. It's from my boss, and she's asked if I'm available to come by her office at 10:00 a.m. tomorrow.

Now listen, mornings aren't my favorite, and the main hospital is a forty-five-minute drive from here, but I have reason to believe I might be up for a bit of a raise, so I'm pretty excited. I've been in this position for just over a year, and I've kept careful track of how profitable my exploits have been.

The hospital touts my work as a way to improve patient outcomes and make confusing records sing with clarity for our team of health care angels, but really it's about clarifying our need to increase profit and decrease liability. Fair enough. I still improve patient outcomes.

I confirm the meeting time with a click and a little wiggle of happiness as the lovebirds upstairs start snapping at each other about dinner plans. I hope they have a few cocktails while they're out, because I can tell these people are human fireworks ready to put on a good show.

After brushing a few tangles from my newly refreshed chestnut hair and slipping on my favorite flip-flops, I grab a sweater and step out into a perfect Santa Cruz evening: seventy-five degrees and peppered with the gentle sounds of traffic and pigeons. Gorgeous.

"Hi, Liz!" my neighbor calls from across the road. His grandson echoes the greeting with a fat-fingered little wave.

"Hello, Mr. Sanchez! Hi, Roberto! Babysitting duty tonight?"

"She's got late shifts this month, so we're having grandpa time." He grins beneath the flower crown perched on his head.

"You should post a picture online!" I call. "You look beautiful, and your daughter will love it." Mr. Sanchez's wife died a few years ago, and he's been so much happier since he started babysitting. Honestly, I think he was depressed when I first moved in, but now he's getting outside more, and seeing them together always brightens my day.

He also doesn't ask many questions about my life, which makes him a great neighbor. "Have fun, Roberto!" I yell as I take off for one of my favorite restaurants four blocks to the west. "Bye, Mr. Sanchez. I'm off to dinner!"

I've only just reached the first corner when I slow to watch a man on the next block haul a suitcase from the trunk of a sedan. He gets out his phone and looks from the screen to a house and back again, clearly checking for instructions on how to get in. I've seen this dance a hundred times, but I can't help but study him in his dark jeans and worn flannel shirt.

He's cute. Average height, dark hair. Not gorgeous, but definitely cute, and the look of confusion on his face is adorable. But more than that, he's actually somewhere around my age. Maybe a few years older. Forty-three? Forty-five? His pale skin marks him as a visitor, but he was smart enough to wear flannel instead of shorts and a T-shirt for the evening. Or maybe he just landed from Alaska? Hot.

I cross the street and approach. "Hey there," I coo. "Need some help?"

He jumps in surprise, hazel-green eyes huge behind wire-rimmed glasses as he looks up. His thick eyebrows rise in such an expressive way they remind me of a puppy's. Then he smiles a goofy, self-conscious smile that melts my knees. Or something.

"Is it that obvious?" he asks, shoving a hand through brown hair that doesn't look long enough for that kind of gesture. Judging by the neat edges, he just got it cut, and the look adds to his lost-schoolboy appeal. His features are a bit too large in his thin face, but I've never been one for pretty-boy looks. He's just the right amount of quirky, so I smile back for a moment longer than I should.

"This address doesn't seem to exist?" he says in a question.

I lean toward him, and he shows me his phone. "Probably a garage apartment. People use every square inch of space here. Are there any instructions?"

"That's what I was just looking for . . ."

While he studies his phone, I glance up and spot a hedge that isn't quite square with the fence at the edge of this lot. Abandoning him to his phone, I head toward the big bushes. "Aha!" I call when I spot the opening. "There's a walkway here that goes around to the side."

"Is it stone? This says something about a stone path."

"This is it!" I glow with pride. Being able to offer local expertise is still a novel treat for me.

After adjusting his backpack, the man hauls up his suitcase and hurries over to join me. "Thanks for stopping to help."

"No problem. I'm only one block down, so I'm sure I'll see you around again. I'm Beth, by the way."

"Mike," he offers as he takes the hand I've extended. "It's a pleasure to meet you, Beth."

Wow. Adorable with nice manners and a firm, warm grip? I'll be sure to take a couple of walks by his place in the next few days. Just in case he needs a local's touch. "I'm off to dinner." I point west and give him a wink. "Wavy Gravy is a few blocks down if you're on the hunt for good food tonight. If you see me sitting outside, you'll know you're in the right place."

"Oh!" He looks surprised, those abrupt eyebrows flying high again. "Sure. Thank you so much."

"Any time, Mike. Welcome to Santa Cruz." I float down the sidewalk with a self-satisfied smile. I haven't flexed my flirting muscles much lately, and he's exactly my type. Cute, a little awkward, and very temporary. The Elizabeth May trifecta. Maybe I'll get a chance to exercise a few more underused muscles before he leaves town.

By the time I reach Wavy Gravy, I'm practically strutting. The patio is crowded, as it always is during tourist season, but there are several spots available at the bench seating that overlooks the sidewalk, and that's exactly what I want. It's the ideal location for people watching.

The hostess gives me a thumbs-up when I wave, and I know she'll put in an order for a mai tai before I even sit down. The rumbles and squeals of raucous conversation enfold me like a hug as I edge between tables. I slide into an empty chair at the simple bar of wood where I've dined dozens of times, and settle in to listen.

A child is whining behind me about a scrape he got at the beach today. Another counters that she was stung by a jellyfish even though the teen sitting next to her yells that there isn't a mark anywhere so it clearly wasn't a jellyfish. Their parents are ignoring them to bicker at each other in quiet resignation.

"It's my vacation too," the woman is saying. "If I want another tequila shot, I'm going to have another tequila shot. We're all supposed to be having *fun*, right?"

"I just don't—"

She immediately cuts him off. "Am I allowed to relax after planning every moment of this trip and packing every suitcase and buying every bag of groceries so everyone else can have *fun*?"

Amen, sister. My mai tai arrives, and I turn to raise it toward her in solidarity. When she looks up, she only frowns at me, so I shrug and leave her to her family fun.

After snapping a pic of my gorgeous concoction, I post it on Instagram under the SantaCruz hashtag. Just another Thursday night in paradise! I fantasize about it popping up on Julia's feed and smile wistfully over this little connection between us she'll never recognize.

My Instagram profile says I'm a twenty-five-year-old yoga instructor living at the beach, which is why I never post pics of my face. Or my decidedly unmuscled arms. But I post lots of inspirational beach shots, pictures of my meals and drinks, and an occasional snap of a cute pedicure.

After a sip of my drink, I offer hearts to a few tourist snapshots and one local chiropractor I've flirted with online. He's fifty-five and should be ashamed of hitting the like button on every one of my pedicure photos. My profile is thirty years younger than his! Regardless, I grin every time I pass his office. Cheeky monkey.

Once my online presence is sorted, I order the chile verde enchiladas, open my book, and settle in with my cocktail. Tonight the book is a prop, but don't get me wrong, I love reading and I visit the library at least once a week. But during tourist season there's too much life here to ignore, so my eyes scan the sidewalk in front of me, picking out interesting people as my joints melt with the first rush of alcohol.

Everyone is interesting here, really. Rich or poor, local or tourist, they all have a story. Look at me. I'm a thirty-nine-year-old average white woman walking around with an after-school-special past I'll never tell, yet people's eyes glide right over me. I'm not young enough to be perky, not stylish enough to stand out. Really, I'm a background extra.

When I was younger, I had to work at that. At disappearing. Once I became a traveling nurse, I moved every few months, hopping from state to state, creating vignettes of life in each one. I got to meet new people, be part of a workplace, enjoy an unknown neighborhood, all while in a protective bubble of impermanence. That worked perfectly for me for almost fifteen years before I hopped into another supposedly short-term gig here in Santa Cruz.

It's strange that I've been here for two years now. Scary, even. But so many people move through this town that I can create a hundred vignettes without ever leaving. Plus my shady Romanian landlord gives me a nice discount for the work I've done for him since I arrived.

It's comforting to hold this place while everyone moves around me, a strange anchoring I've never felt before, a sense of belonging.

Will I leave soon? Sometimes I think I will. Sometimes I feel a target on my back when familiar faces call out a greeting or a neighbor brings up something I told them a year ago. I'm not used to it, and the connective tissue beneath my skin goes tight at this evidence that they *know* me. That I'm vulnerable. It wants me to bristle and run, abandon my burrow and dig a new one far away to keep my tender insides safe.

But the truth is no one truly knows me, and I can always calm my crawling dread by reminding myself of that. No one knows me, so I don't have to leave this place.

Santa Cruz isn't very big, but it's nothing like the tiny town where I grew up, where you couldn't avoid awful familiar faces, the knowing smiles and eagle eyes. I'll never go back there.

My older brother lives in Minnesota, and my parents retired to Arizona, not that I'd want to see their dour faces anyway. We existed peacefully together until I left for college, but for most of my childhood, we carved wary paths around each other, carrying our uncertainty and stubbornness like shields.

They tried their best. I know that. But if that was their best? Well . . . better for us all to move on. I send a card at Christmas and include a few quick, fun notes about my life. But I always reference a town I've already left behind. I want them to know I'm okay. That I'm doing just fine. But I don't want them to have my address. If they can't reach out, I won't know if they choose not to, right? Right.

They have my brother, Nathan, anyway, and he's given them a lovely stay-at-home daughter-in-law and three adorably rambunctious boys.

In the pictures I see online, my dad looks different with the grandkids than he did with his own children. He smiles sometimes. My mom, though, still bustles around solemnly in the background, always finding a chore in the middle of any fun.

I insist on fun. I wallow in it. Speaking of . . .

Across the street a gray-haired man in several layers of clothing opens a guitar case and sets it on the sidewalk before lifting out the instrument. When he straightens up, I grimace.

"Oh God," I groan. It's Rosco, the absolute worst busker in town. Equal parts tone deaf and confident, he either enjoys torturing onlookers or has lost a lot of his hearing over the years. This is not a serenade I'll enjoy.

Damn it, Rosco.

I glance around for my server, hoping to order my dessert mai tai early so I don't have to listen to that caterwauling for more than half an hour, but she's dealing with an eight-top, and I can tell it will be a while.

Sighing, I twist back around to face Rosco, then yelp when I find someone standing directly in front of me, blocking the view.

"Sorry!" he says quickly, holding up both hands, but I'm already laughing. It's my new friend Mike.

"Mike!" I exclaim. "You're here! How's the rental?"

"It's really nice, actually. Small but lots of windows."

I point to the chair next to me. "There's an empty seat if you came to see me."

His face glows with an immediate blush that lights me up inside. I love a cute guy who doesn't know how cute he is, and it's easy to tease and flirt when everything is so temporary. What's the worst that could happen? I embarrass myself in front of a guy I'll never see again? Anonymity is the ultimate freedom.

He swipes his hand through his short hair again without responding, and I wrinkle my nose. "Hey, if you just came to eat alone, don't let me bully you." I lift my book. "I came prepared for solitude myself."

He glances at the empty seat, then back to me. "But I wouldn't be intruding?"

"No way. Still, I have to warn you that Rosco is about to start singing—if that's what you want to call it—and you might wish you were sitting inside."

His smile is crooked with confusion, but he skirts around the barrier and weaves through tables to join me. I snag a menu left a little farther down the bar and point out my favorites just before the server finally returns.

"Another mai tai?" she asks, and I give an enthusiastic yes, then grin when Mike orders one for himself. Either he's a man who loves fruity drinks, which is nice, or he wants to be part of my little club, which is even nicer.

"Are you a Santa Cruz native?" he asks. "I've never been before."

"Oh no. I've only lived here a couple of years, so I'm in middle territory. Not a visitor, but not quite a local yet. Are you here for work or fun?"

"Work. I'm helping with an ocean-monitoring project along the coast. I'm an environmental chemist."

"Wow, that sounds cool."

"Yeah, I dreamed of being a marine biologist when I was a kid, but turns out I get seriously seasick."

"Oh no!" I try and fail to cover my impolite laughter, but he joins in. "That's awful!"

"It is. I can handle quick jaunts out to sea to take samples, but weeks of field research on a boat would be beyond me. How about you? What do you do?"

He's asking about me, which would be appealing to most women, but that simply isn't my comfort zone, so I shut it down the best way I know how. "I'm an accountant," I say.

And that's the end of that conversation.

CHAPTER 4

There was another round of mai tais as Mike ate, but we didn't really have a choice once Rosco started singing, did we? It was either more alcohol or a retreat to my lair.

In the end we did both.

I didn't mean for Mike to spend the whole night, and I'm regretting it now as I carefully unwind my limbs from his and attempt to ooze out of bed like a snail. We walked for almost an hour after dinner as I showed him all the local secrets and pointed out the best spots for food, shopping, and drinks.

When we slowed to a halt in front of my place, it was only natural to invite him inside. Only natural to open a bottle of wine. Only natural to make out like a pair of horny teenagers on the couch, then fall into a deep sleep in my bed after sex that was damn impressive for a first time. Not perfect, but I had a great orgasm, and that's never guaranteed, is it? Sometimes it's not even hinted at.

All in all it was quite a treat, but now I just want Mike gone so I can prepare for my meeting. I stare down at his one visible arm and his mussed hair as I pull on a sweater and leggings against the morning chill.

He's appealingly furry in a lumberjack kind of way, but I was wrong. Despite his pale skin and flannel shirt, he's not from Alaska. He's from Tacoma, Washington. But I went on an Alaskan cruise once, and the coastlines look the same to me, so I'll call that a good guess.

Should I open the curtains? Smooth a finger over his adorable puppy eyebrows? Make coffee and gently bring him a cup like the sweetest little one-night stand he's ever met? No, that's not my style.

When I was young, if I stared hard enough from the foot of my parents' bed, my mom would jerk awake in a panic to ask what was wrong. I realize now that this was just some animal awareness tickling at my mother's brain, but I thought it was proof I truly was touched by demons, just as people said. Regardless, my stare isn't working on Mike; his breathing remains deep and slow. He's not the motherly type, I guess.

A car door slams nearby, and I hurry to the window to look out with a sad sigh. Julia and Jamie are loading up their SUV to hit the road, and now I'll never learn their secret. "Crap," I whisper as I watch her shift little Sheila in her arms. The unwieldy pink helmet rests awkwardly against Julia's clavicle, but she gazes down at her baby's face with sweet wonder, and I have a sudden, fierce hope that these crazy kids make it.

Speaking of crazy kids, I still have the drama upstairs to look forward to, so that's something. If they argued last night, I was too distracted by Mike to notice.

"Hey," he croaks behind me, his voice a weary rumble. "Good morning."

"Oh, heyyy." I swing around to see his furry chest half-exposed. His eyes are narrowed against the light, but he's smiling. "I'm glad you're up! I've got to leave for a meeting in an hour, so I was about to slide you off the bed and out the door. But it'll be much easier with you awake."

His laugh is genuine and unoffended. "Okay, got it. No breakfast in bed."

"Not a chance, mister." But when he sits up and exposes his whole naked torso, I'm tempted to at least grace him with a quickie.

No. I shake my head and back out of the room, easing myself farther from temptation. We had a great night, but it's time for him to disappear into his real life and leave me to my fake one. "I'll let you get dressed."

I use the bathroom, wash my hands, and then gesture him in when he emerges fully clothed from my bedroom, carrying his shoes. I'll start coffee after he leaves so we won't have to navigate that exchange. By the time he joins me in the living room, I've got the blinds open and the heater turned up to seventy.

"Can I get your number?" he asks. He already has his phone out, so I have a moment to try for the perfect answer while he's staring at it. Do I want to hook up again before he leaves? I'm not sure, so I try for lightness.

"Planning to call the next time you're in town?"

"Ha! Yes. But I thought maybe I'd call about dinner in a few days after I get settled in." He glances up, and his smile drops at my expression. "Unless you don't want to?"

Settled in? My neck prickles. "Wait. How long are you staying?"

"At least six months. Maybe more."

"Six months?" I don't mean to shout the words, I swear. But this is *not* what I signed up for. "You said you were heading to Cambria next week!"

"Yes, but just for two days. Santa Cruz will be my home base through this whole project."

My jaw muscles give up the ghost, and I stare at him like an idiot for quite a few seconds before I manage to close my mouth with an audible gulp. My skin crawls with discomfort, like someone just lifted a rock and found me without my shell. *Six months.*

"Uh," I manage.

Mike is astute enough to realize things have taken a turn. I watch his face close down, but not before I glimpse disappointment. "Hey, no pressure. I'll see you around, I'm sure."

"Yeah," I say dumbly, my mind working back through what I've told him. *Beth, accountant, thirty-nine.* Nothing too disastrous. Not many neighbors know I'm a nurse, and Liz and Beth are both nicknames. But

I don't like people fucking up my different compartments. Why didn't I just tell him my name was Liz?

What a disaster. I watch impatiently as he ties his trail shoes, trying not to glare as I remember the way he talked about heading to Cambria next week. He'd implied he was going to disappear into the fog of the coastline like a misty sex dream, hadn't he? What a betrayal.

"Thanks, Mike," I say breezily before he even straightens.

He frowns at that, like it's weird that I thanked him. Fine. Get out if you want to have a bad attitude about good manners.

But he takes the hint, at least, and heads immediately for the front door, adding a polite "Have a good meeting" as I rush forward to twist open both locks and throw the door wide.

"Thank you!" I close the door behind him as soon as he's through it, and that's that. Hopefully.

"Everything's fine," I murmur as I rush to the kitchen to start the coffee. "No big deal." Forty minutes later, I'm in my car, sporting clean hair, a pair of non-Lycra pants, and my favorite travel mug filled with perfectly creamed and sugared coffee.

Time for some good news to wash away this bad morning.

CHAPTER 5

God, this coffee is good. Nothing fancy. I'm a simple girl. But I finally found a low-acid brew I like. Poor Mike really missed out, but he clearly didn't deserve my expensive beans.

"How was your girls' trip?" asks Mary, the billing support specialist whose desk is three feet from my boss's door. She's sweet and a little dowdy for being in her twenties, which makes me like her more. I hope she finds a nice partner who loves her handknit sweaters and big glasses.

I throw my hands wide in surprise as I try to recall what I told her. "Oh my God, the trip was great! Thank you for asking!"

"I can't imagine trying to organize something like that with seven friends. And in a foreign country?"

Ah-ha. "Mexico is pretty easy to navigate, especially the touristy parts like Cancún. We had a blast. Cold margaritas, a hot beach, and just catching up, you know?"

"Ugh, I'm so jealous."

So am I. Though she's right. I wouldn't actually want to organize a vacation with that large a group. It could be fun, though. If I ever have to go back to hands-on care, it might be a nice treat to insert myself into a group of friends and tag along to a wine-tasting weekend or something. Maybe right before I leave for a different post. We could be close for a few weeks, and then I'd extricate myself. All the fun with none of the vulnerability. It's a possibility.

I'm still thinking about it when my boss's office door opens. "Hi, Chen!" I say, jumping to my feet.

Her black hair is shorter than it was during our last meeting, a shaggy style that looks fun and carefree. She, however, does not look fun and carefree. She's normally efficient and unobtrusive—the perfect boss—but today Chen seems downright dour. I ignore the twinge of warning in my gut and widen my smile.

"Ms. May," she says as she directs me into her dreary box of an office.

Hm. She normally calls me Eliza. I hold tight to my smile as I take a seat in one of the metal-framed chairs in front of her desk. The air smells of an expensive essential-oil blend, and her dress is crisply tailored. But in this light, Chen's eyes look tired, and now I'm not sure if the new haircut is supposed to be shaggy or if she tossed and turned all night.

"We received an email yesterday," she says.

Aw, poop. This isn't about a raise at all. This is about that insufferable Dwayne Wubbles. Whatever. I can handle him. But my shoulders still slump. "Dr. Wubbles has been insisting that—"

"Are you active online?" She glances at her monitor as she interrupts me. "On a subreddit called CDS?"

"Uh." I'm speechless for the second time this morning, though now I manage to keep a little dignity and stop my jaw from dropping. CDS. The subreddit for clinical documentation specialists. There are hundreds of users on that forum, if not thousands, most asking what the job is like, what kind of pay to expect, if they have the right qualifications. There's been a surge of nurses looking to get out of direct patient care since the pandemic. Too much trauma, too much bullshit.

My mind races through my recent posts. Then my not-so-recent posts. Nothing worrisome comes to mind. "I've been on it, sure. I asked questions about the CDS role before I took the job. Now I answer other people's questions about the work." Okay, I might have cracked a few jokes since then too, but . . . No, I can't think of anything *bad* bad.

My shoulders straighten. What kind of Big Brother crap is this anyway? They're *monitoring* me? That's definitely not something I'm willing to tolerate in my life.

She continues on, her hands clasped tightly together. "Is your username MayTNurse?"

Now I really am indignant. "I'm sorry, I don't understand why you're asking these questions." It's none of her business what my personal username is. Even if I weren't such a private person, they didn't purchase my whole life with their average salary and middle-of-the-road benefits.

"The administration received an email yesterday with screenshots and links to the CDS subreddit pointing out several posts from you. Apparently you've been badmouthing the hospital and administration on this forum. What you do in your free time is your business, but that kind of talk is the hospital's business. Literally. And I'm personally embarrassed that someone in my department chose this route."

My mind spins. "I'm sorry, what? What are you talking about?"

"If you're having issues with your employment here, I'd ask you to come to me instead of publicly embarrassing—"

"Wait! No! No, I have never posted anything like that. Never." What kind of idiot would openly badmouth an employer on a professional forum? Not *this* kind of idiot, that's for sure.

"Is this you?" She tilts her monitor to show me a screenshot, and I see my little icon, a grumpy cat wearing a nurse's cap. "I . . . Yes. But I didn't post those things. I must have been hacked!"

"Hm" is all Chen offers in response. She hasn't even looked up at me, conveying her fury in the most dignified way possible. "If you've been hacked, I'm going to need proof of that."

"Hold on." I fumble to get my phone out of my pocket in these ridiculously unstretchy pants. After opening a browser to check my account, I'm able to log in just fine, so the password hasn't changed. "I'd never do anything like this," I insist, feeling like a spineless butt kisser, but . . . desperate times. My whole job now is reporting to administration, so I'd better pucker up and slather on the lip balm.

"I really don't understand," I mutter, still clicking frantically around and only growing more confused. "I haven't posted at all since last month, and that was just a congratulations to someone who had a baby. These screenshots must be fake."

"No, I made sure to check," Chen insists, "and I'm looking at a comment on the forum right now. It's under a post about average pay and benefits in a big city."

I scramble over to the front page of the forum and scroll desperately through. When I see the post asking what benefits and starting pay are normal in a large West Coast city, I click on the comments and glance through. There I am.

> Whatever you do, don't ask anyone from Community Trust Health. Our benefits are laughable and the pay is crap. I'm looking for a new job right now. This company is the worst I've ever worked for, and I can't wait to get the hell out of here. Nothing but corporate ghouls leeching off the bodies of patients. My boss is the worst of all.

"I didn't . . ." I fade into shocked silence, gawking at my phone. As my forehead crumples, my eyes burn with the beginning of panicked tears. I blink them back and shake my head. "Hold on." I open another tab and check my profile, then look at the damning quote again. Relief rushes through me before it crashes into a wall of new shock.

"That's not me. I'm MayTNurse underscore, not MayT underscore Nurse. It stands for May the Traveling Nurse. I was a traveling nurse for so long, and it really helps to—Whatever, that doesn't matter. But it's not me. You can look me up! The one with the underscore at the end is me."

Chen begins typing away, now frowning just as hard as I am. Why would someone do this to me? It's obviously deliberate. They even used my avatar. Goose bumps cascade down my arms.

Who the hell have I pissed off? Dr. Wubbles is surely too busy being a terrible doctor. Maybe it's his wife?

The metal of the chair digs into my lower back, and Chen is still reading. I panic at the way she's squinting angrily at whatever she sees, and an old, familiar weight presses down on my head. *You're a liar. She won't believe you. Even when you're not lying, you're a freak and no one likes you.*

"I'm not looking for another position," I insist past the rising fear. "I love this job. I thought we were meeting about . . ." God. Even if she believes me, that raise isn't going to come anytime soon now. And if she doesn't believe me? "I thought I was doing a good job," I finish quietly.

"Someone's impersonating you?" she asks, and despite the skepticism in her tone, I almost groan with relief, because I have a chance.

"Apparently. Because that is *not* me."

"Hm."

"Why would I post that publicly? Or—" I jump in with an immediate correction. "Or ever, I mean. Everything is good. I feel like I've really settled into the work and stepped up, and . . ." When I trail off, I hope she'll volunteer some praise.

She doesn't.

"A disgruntled former colleague?" I propose.

"I don't see any personnel issues in your file." She must have checked that first thing this morning.

"No, I really haven't had any conflicts, but I guess you never know if you've stepped on toes. Maybe someone else wanted this position?"

"Hm. Maybe."

I nod. "I assume a lot of other people applied. It's a great opportunity!" I try another smile, but it feels like a grimace, so I drop it. "This is very disturbing, and I'm so sorry if it's caused trouble for you. I'll look into it and see if I can find any clues, but I'm just as shocked as you are. More, probably."

She finally looks straight at me, one eyebrow lowered in what looks like admonishment, even though I didn't do anything wrong. "Perhaps you should refrain from participating in this forum for now." *Or ever* is implied but unspoken.

"Sure," I answer, "of course," but for once, I have no intention of running away without a fight.

Because who the hell could guess that was my username in the first place? And what other secrets do they know?

CHAPTER 6

Who is this?

I decide to face the problem head-on with a straightforward message as soon as I'm through my front door. Whoever this person is, they started posting only three weeks ago. There are seven comments in total, and all of them are trashing my employer. They don't care about employees. Cut corners with patient care. Our recordkeeping is a lie. Worse yet, the account profile lists my work name: Eliza May.

It has to be some medical professional I've angered. But who would've connected me to this Reddit account? I've never posted a picture of myself or even mentioned my employer. I'm careful because I don't want anyone connecting me to my real name, to my hometown, even to my ex-husband. In fact, I've hardly posted at all this year, though in the past I was pretty active on the r/travelingnurse forum and even made some virtual friends.

Speaking of friends . . . I go to my phone to text Tristan. Emergency!!! Someone is impersonating me on Reddit!!! My fricken boss called me in!!!

After burning up with anger during my sunny drive home, I'm chilled now in my still-cool living room. I reach for the throw blanket draped across my couch, then lean the other way and push open my patio doors. I doubt the couple upstairs is awake yet, but I'll appreciate the distraction when they finally start sniping at each other. I don't want to sink too deep into my own thoughts. Don't want to get trapped in here with my guilt.

Tristan isn't responding quickly, but that's not unusual. He's a nurse too, and his hours vary.

Trying to think past my churning brain, I open my work account and stare at the files. Then I toggle back to my private messages. Nothing there. But doesn't bad luck come in threes? What the hell else is waiting for me today?

I'm feeling violated. I purposefully don't let people into my life, and now two people have invaded my carefully controlled world. I've relaxed too much in this place, let myself feel at home. Was staying here so long a mistake?

I fled Iowa seventeen years ago, and I've carried my life with me ever since like a turtle. A super-cool turtle, though. But I must have dropped too many hints on Reddit, breadcrumbs for someone to follow.

Should I think about moving on? Perhaps a big city would be a nice change. Or something more extreme like Alaska. Would it be better to hide myself in crowds or in vast spaces?

But I look out my back door to see two hummingbirds dueling in front of a blooming angel's trumpet bush, more flowers than I might see in a whole garden in other places. I love Santa Cruz so much. I can walk through the woods, to the beach, to the store. I can find solitude or bustling crowds. All the walking makes me strong, and for the first time ever, I feel grounded.

I don't want to leave and go back to being a stupid turtle.

When I arrived here, it was the same plan as always: Stay for a few months or a year, and then move on down the line. Knowing my time would be divided between San Jose and a smaller hospital in Monterey, I decided to live it up and move to the beach. I got the place upstairs at a bargain, because my landlord wanted a nurse nearby for his mother, Doina. She'd been the occupant of this downstairs unit for the first year I lived here, and he'd listed the upstairs apartment on a traveling nurse rental site.

The situation worked out perfectly. I checked in on Doina every morning and every night, and on my days off I'd even make her lunch and sit on the patio with her. She didn't speak much English, but that made it more relaxing for me. I didn't have to lie; I could just *be*.

I was home the night she got up to go to the bathroom and fell. I heard her calling out from beneath me, her voice weak and high, the words a jumble of Romanian I couldn't understand. But I could understand the sound of pain and fear, more familiar to me than any other cry after all my years in nursing.

Using the lock code her son had given me, I found Doina on the floor just inside the bathroom, trembling like a bird with a broken wing. Her wrist had snapped, yes, but her hip had fractured too. After I called 911 and then Grigore, she never returned home, though she lived for three more months at a care facility.

Poor Doina. She'd lost decades in her confusion, speaking only in Romanian and weeping quietly for hours at a time. I'd visited, but she didn't know me. But I was used to that. The story of my life.

After she died I'd planned to move on. I made good money as a traveling nurse, after all. Then Grigore—big, hulking Grigore with his craggy face, dyed black hair, and cauliflower ears—had hugged me, weeping pitifully as he thanked me for saving his dear mother from rotting on the floor like an animal.

"You'll always have a home with me, Miss Elizabeth. You are family now."

I can't deny that a warm rush of hope and acceptance had cascaded through my body. My real family had rejected me, after all. Not because of my testimony in a Satanic Panic trial that put innocent people behind bars, but because I'd later recanted and exposed my lies and the community's failures. I'd embarrassed my parents in front of people they'd known their whole lives.

But now Grigore wanted to be family? Frankly, I wasn't sure that was safe. Grigore's business ventures are varied and . . . opaque. He invests in properties, yes, but not so many that he should have a new hundred-thousand-dollar vehicle every year. He wears a lot of gold jewelry, and no matter how long Grigore's visits with his mother lasted, he'd often had an "associate" with him who waited in the vehicle the whole time.

Shady, very shady. But when he said he meant to renovate both apartments and I could move into the larger one downstairs for only one hundred dollars more a month, I decided we could be cousins at least.

Since then, things have evolved. I took this new job with a slight decrease in pay, and Grigore cut that hundred dollars off my rent to keep an eye on the apartment upstairs and the cottage next door, since I'm home all day.

If I turn back into a nomad, everything will change. I'll have to go back to the ER and all the aggression and conspiracy theories it comes with these days, and I'll have to leave my perfect little beach nest. The thought drains me. I'm out of the habit of running and hiding. The appeal of it has finally begun to fade.

"This is bullshit," I mutter as I check my phone again. I'm going to have to delete my Reddit account. I clearly got complacent. Maybe someone who wanted the CDS job and knew I'd been a traveling nurse before connected the dots. It's time to tighten things up.

Still, there's no reason to let any of this ruin my life. I've dealt with both problems that popped up this morning, and I live in paradise. It's time to turn this frown upside down and do what I do best: Walk away from my problems.

CHAPTER 7

The trek down to this beach is a long one, and I had to park far from the sand dune trail because it's a gorgeous day. Warm—well, seventy-seven on the water, which is warm for here—with big, smooth swells that surfers love.

I hike the chair strap higher on my shoulder and step/slide my way down the path to the beach below, the aluminum frame clanging awkwardly against my hip.

There's a jumble of people on the sand when I finally hit the flat cove. Couples, gangs of teenagers, and families with screaming children, all of them packed close to the water on the south side of the long beach. Angling my wide-brimmed hat a little lower to fight the sun, I keep hiking toward the jutting rocks at the north side, where the tourists rarely venture.

Every step takes me further from the morning's worries. I'll spend an hour or two in the sun and breeze, and then I'll be in the perfect place to forget that violation and get some work done. This is why I live here, isn't it?

By the time I reach the stony outcrop bordered by a swath of sand that curves around it, there's only one other person near me, a man walking toward the south, his towel, beach chair, and bag all hanging from his arms. I wave, but he ducks his head. Rude.

The moment I escape the shadow of the triangle of rock, the beach expands into a second little cove embraced by steep cliff faces. There's a lot of shade available, but a lot of falling rocks too, so everyone gathers near the center.

I draw close to the first towel and spy a man's bare ass. The exposed skin is as dark as the rest of his body, so he obviously goes nude frequently. I aim my eyes straight ahead and keep walking.

Skirting a big boulder, I nearly stumble over the next sunbather. He's face up, genitals completely hairless and glistening with oil, and he's stretched his penis up to lay on his taut belly.

"Oh!" I yelp. "So sorry! I didn't see you!" He barely glances away from his phone despite that a stranger nearly fell face first onto his naked, shiny groin. "Sorry," I mutter again as I stumble through the gauntlet, trying not to kick sand.

I look up to see yet another completely naked man standing thirty feet ahead, a hand raised to shield his eyes as he peers toward me. I squint against the glare of sunlight off his oiled body. A gray-haired woman sits up and looks toward me as well, her tanned breasts resting against a soft and dimpled tummy.

"Hey!" the man shouts as I get closer. "Hey, Betty! Over here!"

Grinning, I rush the last twenty feet as the older woman waves. "Betty!" she calls, and I feel a rush of pleasure at the welcome.

"I'm here!" I say as I drop my gear onto the sand and whip my sundress over my head. The ocean breeze curls over my naked skin and whisks away the sweat I've worked up on the walk. What a perfect feeling.

"Finally," Gerald says. "It's been weeks."

"You know I can't get my white ass out in the sun too often."

"Wouldn't be so white if you put some effort into it," the woman, Opal, offers.

I laugh because she's right, but I'm trying to straddle two worlds here. One is the wicked fun of being naked outside, and the other is the promise of lifelong skin damage. If I came out as often as Opal does, my skin would look like jerky in a few years. But I have to admit, Opal does look happy beneath her wrinkles and sun spots.

The wind presses against my body as I turn to gaze out at the breaking waves. Despite the cold turbulence, a naked middle-aged couple eases deeper into the water, holding hands and laughing. He squeals in a high pitch when a wave surges up his pale hips. They're both grinning like naughty kids splashing in a puddle, and I wonder if this is their first visit to this side of the beach. I hope they wore sunscreen.

"Come on," says Gerald. "I made space for your chair when I saw you coming. This is Bob and Bob." He points to a naked man and woman who look to be in their seventies, and each raise a hand in greeting. They're both white with long gray hair, and the man sports an unruly beard that whips in the wind.

Gerald shifts his pointing finger toward a Black woman who looks retirement age also. "And that's Jackie over there knitting."

"It's crocheting!" she yells back without looking up.

"This is Betty Disco," Gerald says with a gesture at me.

"Just Betty," I correct with a roll of my eyes. He calls me Disco because I have a full bush like a girl from the seventies. I'm not retro; I just have no reason to try to impress anyone with labor-intensive grooming. And I figure it gives my tourist flings a thrill. Santa Cruz is known as a hippie town, after all.

It's easy to have confidence when no one knows you. Easy to do what you want without fear.

I put my hat back on, plop down into my beach chair, and stretch out my legs with a contented sigh. This is the life. How could I possibly leave all these little Santa Cruz treats behind?

Gerald is handing me an ice-cold juice box from his cooler when my phone chimes. It's Tristan, finally!

What the hell? Someone's IMPERSONATING you? Why? How?

I pop the straw into my box and text him the fake username. Look it up. I messaged this clown but no answer. They're badmouthing my employer and pretending to be me!

Whoa. How did you find out?

From my BOSS, unfortunately. Someone sent the company screenshots! Trying to get me fired?!?

Who???

No idea. I've been working from home for a year. If I pissed off a coworker, they've been simmering for a while. Or someone who wants my job? Or maybe it's someone in billing who hates me?

Hey, maybe I should message the impostor. Pretend I think it's you?

It's sweet that he wants to help.

Gerald bumps my knee. "What are you smiling about over there? Got a new man?"

I shrug and smile harder. Tristan isn't my man, but he does feel like a real friend, and I'm always happy when he texts. I've never really had that before.

He checks in a lot just to see how I'm doing . . . almost like he cares. He's the only person in my life like that. Because he's not real. He's digital. We've emailed and texted, but I won't ever run into him on the street, and he doesn't know my real name. He's perfect.

A sudden impulse washes over me. What if I told Tristan where I am right now? What would he think? I know he's single and in his forties, and I think he's straight. He's sent me a couple of pictures, and he seems cute enough beneath his sunglasses and hat.

Would he think nude sunbathing was funny or weird? Would he think it was sexy? Regardless, he'd definitely be trying to picture me naked. Do I want that?

I'm tempted. I feel close to him in a strange way because he's not real, not really, so it feels safe to let my guard down. But if we start flirting, everything could change. There'd be calls. Pictures. Phone sex. And then? A trip? Real life?

Ugh. No, I don't want that. Sex is cheap and easy to source, and I need Tristan there to talk to. There on the other side of the country, far away and very much not part of my real world.

That's sweet, I type back. I guess it couldn't hurt.

That's the moment I realize the more insidious issue. I met Tristan on Reddit. Could he be the impostor?

God, it's possible. But why? We met nine months ago when he asked Reddit for advice about a hospital where I'd previously worked. He lived in Florida, but he'd gotten a job offer and wanted to know if anyone had insight. I did, so I gave him some of the pros and cons of working there and we just . . . hit it off.

He was raised in Wisconsin and got all my nineties Midwestern jokes. And from the tidbits he's shared about his family, they sound a bit like mine: a lot of hardworking values and not much nurturing. He'd fled Wisconsin for Florida after high school, eager to escape the cold of both winter and his upbringing, and boy, did I understand that. It was nice to share commonality with someone since I'm not truthful about my past with anyone.

But mostly he was just *kind*. A little flirtatious but not pushy about it.

We're friends. So why the hell would he target me? And how would he know my real name? It makes no sense. Still, I frown and wait to say more.

Okay, he responds. I'll message the impostor just to ask how she's doing and what's going on to make work so bad? I'll let you know if she answers.

I hesitate for a moment before setting my fears aside. His plan won't hurt anything. Thank you, Tristan. That would be great.

When he responds with a cute blushing emoji, I smile despite my paranoia.

"Does this mean you got laid?" Opal asks.

My smile snaps to a frown. "Actually I *did*. And then the guy ruined everything by revealing he *lives* here. I signed up for a fun weekend, not a permanent resident!"

Opal shakes her head. "Men."

"Men," Gerald agrees.

Men. No, thank you. Love isn't part of my story. Not because I'm a monster or even a weirdo. But I could never, ever trust someone with my most secret feelings. I can't even trust myself.

CHAPTER 8

When I get home, I push work even further back on the burner—probably not the best idea considering I'm currently in hot water—and open a browser window instead of my work log so I can google myself. Sand is all over the floor beneath my feet, and there's sunscreen on my chair, but the thought occurred to me on the long hike back up the cliffs, and I couldn't dislodge it.

What else is floating around about me?

I try my work name first: Eliza May. Nothing alarming pops up. Instead there are only the usual hits: a few public thank-yous from patients at different hospitals for my work as a nurse, and one newspaper story that I heartily wish would go away. There's a captioned picture of me and everything.

Five years ago, I'd been working as an ER nurse in Las Vegas, and a car had crashed right in front of the hospital. A man had tried to drive himself to the ER during a stroke, and he'd eventually drifted through a red light and been T-boned. I'd been one of the many staff who'd rushed out to help, and unfortunately a coworker had given a photojournalist my name and position. There I was, "ER nurse Eliza May," pointing toward the stretcher, my face turned directly to the camera.

I hate it, but it's been out there for years, and there's nothing I can do.

Happily, the man survived against all odds, so it was a newsworthy story. I can't fight what the people want. But yes, I quit that job almost immediately after, worried someone would translate Eliza to Elizabeth. It never happened.

After a few more seconds of scanning, I start over and search my full name—Elizabeth Mary May, just as I used to be introduced to church congregations—and I brace myself for the results. Holding my breath, I scan the first page, then the second, then the third. Nothing. There's nothing new. My breath floods out on a long whoosh of relief.

All the news stories naming me are ancient. Back in the nineties reporters might identify a five-year-old witness with zero qualms, but that's not tolerated these days, not even if she later recanted her story as a seven-year-old. But a lot of things happened back then that simply wouldn't occur today.

Actually, maybe I'm wrong about that. There are tons of bullshit conspiracy theories today too, especially surrounding children. The next Satanic Panic is always right around the corner.

It comes in waves like that, like the devil can only be chased away for so long. In the sixties it was roving gangs of devil-worshipping hippies out for blood. Then came movies like *Rosemary's Baby* and *The Exorcist*, ginning up a terror of demons in the seventies. There was the moral panic over D&D and metal rock in the early eighties. And then my time to shine arrived with a bang in 1991. Yeehaw.

Logically I know it wasn't really my fault. I ruined several lives, but I was just a little girl. Granted, even when young, someone with more confidence and conviction might have resisted the draw of telling a story everyone demanded to hear, but still . . . I was a baby. It's not that I think I did something unforgivable. It's that everyone else did.

My parents. Therapists and psychologists. The police. Social workers. The DA's office. The older girl I looked up to. The press. My church. Even the doctors. And yes, I should've been better too.

But honestly, it's not that I can't forgive any of them. It's that I can't *forget*. I was failed by everybody and everything in my life for years. And then I was tortured by those failures for so many more. Who the hell could I ever trust after a childhood defined by false memories and community hysteria?

I'm shaking just thinking about it, so I push the thoughts away. It's my only coping mechanism. Deny, deny, deny. I can't go to a therapist, after all, because I'm painfully aware that mental health professionals are just flawed and fucked-up humans like the rest of us. The social workers and psychologists were always bright-eyed with excitement at my stories. At least they have Yelp reviews these days, I suppose.

On the next page of old news results, I glimpse a picture of the Hoffholders leaving a courtroom, their hands clasped and their eyes terrified, and I cringe away with a violent jerk.

"Damn it." Squinting my eyes half-closed to avoid another peek, I exit the window and slap my laptop shut. This has nothing to do with *that*. I shouldn't have even looked. My past is firmly locked away and always will be.

I barely notice the muffled shouting at first. I'm used to rowdy teens and the occasional loud confrontation out on the street in front of my home. This is a bustling, crowded town. But when the shouting moves closer to my door, my first thought is that the kids upstairs are fighting again.

I'm about to rub my hands together like a cartoon villain when a sledgehammer hits my door.

"Ah!" I scream, rocketing up to my feet. The office chair barrels into my couch with a crash as I twist to face the door.

When it rattles with more pounding blows, I realize it's not a sledgehammer; it's a fist. "I know you're in there!" a man yells.

Me? What did I do? Is this the person masquerading as me on Reddit?

I don't recognize his voice. I need my phone, need to call the cops, but I'm frozen with alarm, hoping if I don't move, he'll just go away.

More booming blows echo through my small house as he bangs again. I force my fists to unclench and lower one hand slowly, slowly toward my desk to feel blindly around for my phone, but all I find are papers and pens and a water bottle that teeters when I accidentally brush it.

"I want my money!" the man yells.

"Money?" I mutter. I don't owe anyone money. Maybe it's a random drug user on the prowl.

My shoulders inch down from my ears. This guy must have the wrong place. Like I said, it's a crowded area.

Once I find my phone, I stride to the window next to the door and crank up the blinds with a thwack loud enough to stop the man mid-knock. He glances around in confusion, his shaved head gleaming in the sunlight.

He's white or Latino, I can't tell, with an unruly black beard, a pug nose, and squinty eyes.

"Wrong house!" I yell through the window. His gaze snaps to me, finally locating me in the dim light of my home. "I don't know what you're looking for," I call, "but it's not here."

"Fuck you!" he yells, holding up his phone as if I can read the screen. I shrug, but he doesn't notice. "Where's Grigore?"

Oh no. Seriously? He doesn't have the wrong house at all. But at least he's not after me. "Grigore doesn't live here!"

"Bullshit! I've got the address right here."

I point toward the door he's been assaulting. "This is a rental. See the keypad? He owns a few properties. I have no idea where he lives. He's just my landlord!"

The guy looks from me to the keypad, then back again. Then he glances toward the stairs that rise above my door.

"That's another rental!" I call.

"You tell Grigore to stop fucking me over or I'll be back. Got it?"

"Okay, sure. What's your na—?"

He kicks the door before I can finish, then stomps down the driveway toward the black Camaro parked halfway over the sidewalk.

Yikes. I press a hand to my galloping heart. Shady, Grigore. Very shady indeed.

As soon as the Camaro pulls away—with a showy squeal of the tires, of course—I open the door to assess any damage. The wood looks fine. It's either an original hardwood door or Grigore invested in something very solid for his mom's safety. But the dark-blue paint is scraped near the bottom, revealing a tan color beneath.

I'm not going down for the damage. I snap a picture and text Grigore. Someone came by looking for you. He seemed dangerous.

My phone rings a few seconds later. "What happened?" Grigore asks in his graveled accent.

I describe the man who pounded on the door. "Bald guy, black beard. He said to tell you to stop fucking him over and he wants his money. He drives a black Camaro. Do you know who he is?"

Grigore's voice grows muffled as he speaks Romanian to someone.

"Grigore?" I ask after a few seconds.

"Yes, no problem. I know who he is. Sorry."

"Am I in danger?" I squeak before he can hang up.

"No, no danger. I'll take care of it. No worries. He won't be back."

He sounds so confident that I think I believe him. "You're sure?"

"I'm sure, Elizabeth. I'll repaint the door next month. You pick color, all right?"

"Well . . . all right." I have been a bit jealous of a bright-yellow door I pass on my walks, and this house is gray and white, so it would go just fine.

I hang up and realize I'm mostly feeling relieved this had nothing to do with that online impersonator. After all, this isn't the first time a scary man has yelled at me. It happened quite often with combative patients in the ER, and I've experienced it a few times on the street in Santa Cruz.

Frankly the guy must be an idiot. I certainly wouldn't want an angry Grigore looking for me. Nodding, I close the blinds. I've got nothing to worry about, and I need to reclaim my day and get some work done.

Another yell snaps me back to attention, though. I turn back to the window, then realize the yelling is coming from upstairs. After living downstairs for a year, my ears tune out most of the creaking and footsteps above my head, but now that I'm listening, there's suddenly a lot of movement. Clomping, stomping, pacing. The guy upstairs speaks loudly. The girl screeches back at him.

I quietly open my patio doors so I can eavesdrop on the soothing sounds of the argument above.

"You promised you wouldn't be a cheap asshole this time!" the girl screams.

"Those places on the water are just taking advantage of stupid tourists! We can walk out there after dinner, okay? I'll buy you ice cream. But I made a reservation at a nice place that's half the price."

"I want to eat dinner on the water, Kevin!"

"You just want to take fucking pictures for fucking Instagram!"

"You didn't mind those pictures when you DMed me to ask if I was single!"

Nice. I should be in my happy place now, quietly listening to their antics. But something doesn't feel quite right. There's an itch at the back of my brain letting me know that my world isn't settled. Someone out there is looking at me, and I don't like it.

After checking my Reddit messages one more time and finding nothing, I sigh and close the patio doors like an adult. I need to get my work done before anything else hits the fan. Because what if bad luck actually comes in fours?

CHAPTER 9

I did it. I crammed all my work into six frantic hours, and I'm free!

I treat myself to a late dinner at a hole-in-the-wall restaurant I'm sure Mike won't come to. I can't believe I pointed out all my favorite spots to that invader. Next time I pick up a tourist, I'll try to pull my gaze away from his cute forearms long enough to be cautious.

But my world feels softer now after an amazing eggplant parmesan and a glass of red wine. I saunter home through the streetlights, watching chilled tourists wrapped in beach towels hurry by, trailing the scent of sunscreen.

I wave to Joanna, a cellist busker who's legitimately amazing. When I get to the river, I hand a few dollars to Lucy, a woman who's usually camped near the banks, but I have to haul ass when her shitty boyfriend yells at me from their tent. He's always hyped up on something that happens to bring out his raging misogyny.

After grabbing a few necessities at the corner store, I get home and stop at the mailbox before I go inside. Junk mail, junk mail, a bill, and . . . two letters festooned with real stamps and my name and address written out by hand. The first envelope is from a hospital I don't recognize in Los Angeles.

A job offer?

"Ooo." I'm not looking for a new job, but it's always nice to be wanted.

I rip it open beneath the streetlight that lurks at the end of my driveway and quickly scan the letter wrapped around a brochure. "Inpatient care?" I mutter as my hopeful eyes narrow into confusion. I squint harder.

It's a letter addressed *to me* touting their inpatient psychiatric facility. They aren't offering a place to work; they're offering their services. What the hell? Some sort of bizarre database mix-up, I guess.

Frowning, I open the second letter. That's when my shopping bag drops to the ground with a crack of breaking glass.

Adrenaline floods my body even as I freeze. Goose bumps race over my skin as I blink away my blurry vision long enough to confirm the contents. The form letter is welcoming me to a group I've never heard of, yet I understand what it means immediately. Someone has signed me up for Liars Anonymous.

My rapid breaths flutter the paper before the brochure slips free of my fingers and flips end over end to the ground. When it lands, a white woman stares up at me with a slightly rueful smile and kind eyes. A smiling Black man has his hand on her shoulder, supporting her through this trying time of being a fucking psycho who lies to everyone around her. Just the way I do.

"Beth?"

Oh God, now she's talking to me. This is it. I've buried myself so deep beneath layers of fictional stories that I've finally lost it.

"Beth, are you okay?"

I jerk my head up to spot Mike on the other side of the street, already stepping off the curb to come toward me. I crush the letter to my chest, then realize I'm hiding the wrong thing since the brochure on the ground screams **LIARS ANONYMOUS!** across the top.

Dropping to a crouch, I snatch it up, dragging my fingers through the dark-green liquid of the smoothie spilling from a broken bottle. The nauseating liquid snakes down the sidewalk to fill a jagged crack, black in the ugly light of the streetlamp.

I gather up the brochure and the bag and hug it all tight to my body as I stand.

"Hey, let me help," he offers as he tugs out an earbud.

"No! No, I'm fine." I scramble back, suddenly suspicious that this all has something to do with him. All this bullshit started when he appeared in my life, after all.

But surely not. I spotted him only yesterday, and these letters must have been mailed a couple of days ago. This probably has nothing to do with him. *Probably.*

I'm scrambling back, but he keeps walking, then kneels down to pick up a small rectangle. "Here. You missed this."

A business card. Oh Christ, what does it say?

Intending to snatch it from him, I dart quickly forward, but my fingers are busy clutching at a million things, and there's green goo sliding under my top and into my bra and—

He slips the card between two of my fingers, then ducks his head to try to meet my gaze. "Are you sure you're okay?"

"I'm great!" I yelp in a tone that clearly belies that lie—yet another lie—as I turn to jog awkwardly toward my doorway.

"I'll close the mailbox?" he offers as I hunch over to punch in my code. I shove through the door and slam it shut without answering him.

Somebody knows. Somebody *knows.*

When I lean back to rest my weight against the door, my legs give way, and I slide down, letting go my death grip so everything rains down with me. The letters, the envelopes, the brochures, the groceries, and juice the color of the bile rising in my stomach. My breath is hitching, hitching, depriving me of oxygen.

They know. Everyone knows about me.

Knows what? a calm voice in my head chimes in. *That you're a liar?*

Yes.

Who cares? Because you are *a liar, aren't you?*

That's true. I am a liar. In fact, I like it. I *love* it. Lying is power. It's a tool and a trick and security, and it makes me happy that no one really knows anything about me. It feels *good.*

That's right, the little voice adds. *So what does it matter if someone knows you lie about your name?*

"That's not a lie," I whisper. Elizabeth has a thousand nicknames, and all of them are rightfully mine.

Okay, so someone found out that you lie about your job and your hobbies. And your past is no one's business but yours. Big whoop. This is some weird busybody shit.

The voice in my head is right. This is middle-school-level bullying. And I should know, because I saw that bullying in all its original nineties glory. Less because of what I'd done as a kid, more because of the miasma that followed me like a cloud. I'd started out as an outcast, so I was always an outcast. It was that simple. I had to live with it, had to endure.

My breath is still fast and rough, so I concentrate on calming it down, drawing in more air and letting it out slowly. I'm okay.

Yes, someone has pierced my superpower, but I don't have any injuries.

Still, what if it's one of the neighbors? What if it's Mr. Sanchez or Carol or—

No, I assure myself. No, this isn't like my life before. I'm an adult now, and I can walk away whenever I like. I'm not trapped here, I'm not stuck in one spot, locked into a tiny town with three thousand people who know everything about me and despise me for it.

I'm fine. I'm safe.

"Sure," I say, looking down at the ruin of my favorite button-down shirt. The dark jeans will wash clean, but the pale-yellow cotton isn't going to come back from this. But I will. I'll be fine, despite the nonstop drama that keeps dropping into my life uninvited. And despite the voice talking from inside my head. Everyone has an internal voice, right?

Right, she answers.

My phone dings. I brace myself for what's next, what kind of psycho shit I'm going to deal with now, but it's just Tristan.

The account is gone.

I know what he's texting about, but I still stare dumbly at the message for a full minute until he follows up.

She probably got spooked when I started messaging her.

I wipe off my right hand and type back, wanting to engage with this good news. My fingers shake so badly that predictive text comes up with a random word: Jedi. I erase and try again, and this time the correct letters appear.

Her?

Oh. I guess that's sexist. I just assumed it was a woman pulling this crap. Sorry.

Probably sexist, but I realize I was picturing a woman too. A competitor or someone jealous or . . . Shit, I don't know. But what am I supposed to think now? Because this must all be related.

What if I unwittingly slept with a married guy on a boys' trip and his wife found out and is determined to ruin my life? What if she—but no. Surely posting quietly on a message board would be quite a long con for simple revenge.

I met Tristan on Reddit, so he's still a possibility for those posts. But how the hell would he find out my address without my real name? He knows I'm in California, but I've told him I work in San Jose, and he thinks my first name is May. I might open up to him sometimes, but not like *that.*

So it must be someone at my job. Or a neighbor who discovered my multiple personas. Or maybe . . . No. No, it couldn't be.

But I still find myself whispering his name. *"Frank?"* My face scrunches up into a tight knot of distaste.

Frank Doukas doesn't even make for a good story. He was just a patient who got weird after I helped save him during a heart attack. The brief period of stalking wasn't the best time of my life, but it was hardly shocking. Frank stared into the dark eye of death, he pulled through, and then he transferred his overwhelming feelings to me.

It had started as simple gratitude. Two weeks after he flatlined at age forty-two, he returned to the emergency room in Denver with flowers and some homemade Greek food for me. My mistake was agreeing to sit with him at an outdoor table with the souvlaki and rice. His mistake was losing his damn mind over the next month, insisting we were obviously destined to be together forever.

Had Frank tracked me down?

My phone dings again. You should let your boss know the account is gone.

That's a good idea, and probably not something my stalker would suggest. But I'm still not volunteering more information, especially not about the strange mail scattered on my floor. Yeah, I'll let her know. Thanks for helping.

Of course! Everything else going ok?

With a glance around at my splayed legs and the crumpled letters and stained clothes, I finally laugh.

Sure! I answer. All good. How about you?

Same stupid family stuff.

We discussed our traditional, repressive families a little once we got past the first weeks of chatting about work stuff. It's been so nice to have someone to commiserate with. I'm sorry, I offer.

Eh, it's fine, Tristan texts. At least no one is stalking me online, right?

I laugh again, but the giggle is cut off by a sudden thump on the door behind me. I choke on a squeal and fumble my phone, managing to steady it before it drops into a puddle of green juice. When the knock repeats, I realize it's coming from a bit farther above my head.

Those crazy kids upstairs. Okay, good. I pounce on the distraction and open the feed to the doorbell camera. This is exactly what I need, someone else's glorious mess to pull me out of mine.

"Come on!" the guy shouts from the small landing at the top of the stairs. "This isn't funny! Unlock it!"

"Not until you let me see your phone," I hear in a more muffled voice from behind the door.

I watch his skinny neck cord with stress as he throws his head back, blue hair glinting in the porch light. "Oh my God! If I were cheating on you, I'd have deleted everything by now, wouldn't I? This is so stupid!"

"So you have it all planned out, huh?"

"Babe, come on! We're late to dinner! And I already changed it to that expensive place, so let's go. You can look at my phone. I don't give a shit."

The door opens, and she comes out like nothing is happening. They even share a quick kiss before she toddles toward the stairs on stiletto heels. She doesn't bother asking for his phone, so I guess the concession was all she wanted. Wow, some people really love being exhausted by drama all the time.

I mean, not that I'm one to speak, but at least I can turn off the camera at any point. But to live with emotional chaos every moment? No way. Being on my own is peaceful. Mostly peaceful. And occasionally a tiny bit unnerving.

I push to my feet to check every window lock just to be sure. The one major disadvantage of being alone is, of course, being alone. But it's still the best way to stay safe.

CHAPTER 10

"Hi, Lizzie!"

I can barely see anyone behind all the animal pictures on the counter as the glass door swings shut behind me. I hurry closer to peer down at the curly-haired woman at the desk. "Esmerelda! Oh my God, you're back! How are the babies?"

She beams up from the reception desk, her eyes disappearing into chubby cheeks. She's so cute. "They're wonderful! Both boys are sleeping through the night, and it only took three months! Can you believe it?"

"My cousin had twins," I lie. "It took almost a year for her, so you are killing it. That's so impressive. But we all knew you'd be a great mom since you're the puppy whisperer around here."

Giggling, she holds up her phone and lets me scroll through a dozen pictures of her sweet boys. Is there anything better than fat babies? I don't think so. "Look at those beautiful brown eyes. Just perfect. I know they're fraternal, but they really look identical to me."

"Right? I can tell them apart, but most people can't. Rafael has bigger ears and only one dimple."

"Give them both kisses from me. I hope you're planning to bring them to the autumn adopt-a-thon. We all need to meet them!"

"I will, I promise. Hey, how's the new book coming?"

"Great!"

She scoots closer and lowers her voice. "If you tell me who you ghostwrite for, I swear I won't breathe a word."

"I can't!" I protest with a laugh. "I could lose my job! But . . ." I lean over the tall counter and lower my voice to match hers. "This time I'm working for a big recording artist."

Esmerelda's eyes light up. "Is it someone I know?"

"Definitely." I offer a conspiratorial wink before I head into the bowels of the pet shelter.

For the first time in a long while, I feel guilt for what I've just said. No, not guilt. I feel *exposed*. Does Esmerelda know I'm lying? But how could she? And look how happy I made her.

I know lying isn't technically right, and yes, some people have a damaging relationship with it, but my lies hurt no one. I offered a nice woman a little boost about her parenting and brought a bit of excitement to both our days. That's it. And shelter workers don't care who I am as long as I can help.

Happily, neither do the dogs.

"Where's Cocoa?" I'm cooing before I even make it through the heavy soundproof door. Today is Cocoa's morning for a walk. I have to walk her alone, because she loves chasing squirrels, so I need to concentrate. The only thing she hates more than a squirrel is a bicycle, and there are too many around for my comfort. Or hers. I don't know what a bike did to her, but she's determined to make them all pay.

"Cocoa!" I cry as I reach her cage. I spot a man sitting on the floor at the far end of the kennels. I glimpse only his back and a bright-pink leash coiled next to him, and that's all I have time for since Cocoa is barking with delight and hopping against the kennel door. "Hey, girl. How's my pretty girl?"

I grab a leash from a hook and pop the lock, bracing myself just in time for sixty pounds of excited chocolate lab. Cocoa is so sweet, but she has no manners. None. She's a slobbering mess of scratching nails and stinky breath. Still, I'd take her home if I could, but even family doesn't get to break the no-pet rule at Grigore's properties.

I step forward into her enthusiastic jumping and order her to sit. It takes only five commands, and I clip her in once she's still. She's improving.

"Let's go!" When I stop mid-step, Cocoa nearly knocks me over, but that's not why my heart jumps with alarm. It's because the man gawking up at me from the floor is none other than Mike, fake tourist extraordinaire.

I grunt out a weird little gasp, and his lips move as he speaks, but I can't hear him over the dozen dogs barking. How can he be here? This can't be a coincidence.

"What are you doing here?" I yell.

"I miss my dog!" he calls out.

I shake my head because what does that have to do with anything? I need to know if he's the one messing with my life for reasons beyond my comprehension.

Mike stands up. "My dog is with my ex while I'm stationed here, so I thought I'd drop in and help walk some pups."

Okay, I didn't tell him about the shelter, so he couldn't have planned this. And he was here when I walked in, so he couldn't have followed me. Right?

He offers a half smile. "I drove by yesterday and couldn't resist the painting on the side of the building."

"Oh," I say. "Right. That." I'd forgotten about the big dog mural that reads **FREE WALKIES!** in huge white letters. That was how I found the place too. Filled out a form, showed my ID, and I was walking a dog within a few minutes.

"I'm supposed to take Chompers out," Mike says with a gesture toward the farthest kennel, "but he's really scared."

"Chompers?" How the hell am I supposed to resist that? I ease forward, and Cocoa happily bounces along with me. Mike backs up to make room for me to lean over and take a peek.

"Oh, poor baby," I sigh. Chompers is a tiny terrier mix who's cowering in the corner, his little fangs sticking out at funny angles around his protruding tongue. "Chomperrrs," I croon.

"That's him. He's terrified, but they say it'll help his anxiety to get out of here for a bit."

"I'm sure." Cocoa wedges her body in between ours and sticks her head into the kennel. "No," I say firmly, trying to tug her back. But Chompers actually perks up, and I spot one brief, pitiful tail wag.

When I let Cocoa push farther in, Chompers is suddenly up and sniffing, his tail now a blur of eagerness. "Maybe Cocoa can help." I ease Cocoa back, and the other dog follows. "Little guy needs some dog company to help him feel safe."

"Hey, that's how I feel too," Mike says, and a surprised giggle pops from my mouth.

I'm still angry with him, and I'm on edge about all this strange shit going down, but Chompers and Cocoa look so happy sniffing and dancing around each other that I can't walk away.

"I guess we're walking together," I say with a gesture toward the back door.

"My plan is working perfectly," Mike says.

I shoot him a glare, my frayed nerves already too tight with suspicion. "What the hell does that mean?"

His smile drops like a lead balloon. "Nothing. Sorry. Just a bad joke."

"Yeah," I agree, and he follows me out, properly chastened, as I grab a poop bag from the dispenser and direct him to do the same.

The dogs immediately stop to check out a patch of grass just past the door.

"I'm sorry," Mike says quietly. "I really didn't mean to turn up in the same spot as you. I couldn't bring my dog here with me, so . . ."

I shrug, trying to play it cool, but I can't pass up a pet story. "What's your dog's name?"

His cheeks go a bit pink. "Princess."

"Princess? That's so sweet!"

"She had that name when we adopted her, and it seemed wrong to spring a new one on her."

"Didn't the rescue people just make it up, though?"

"I don't think so. She was surrendered by someone going into hospice care, so they knew her name."

"Ah. That's sad. But I've always thought it would be fun to be the one who names the stray animals." I glance down at the tiny scrap of fur pawing the ground. "Chompers."

"Poor little guy."

"He's adorably ugly. I bet he'll get adopted quickly. People love that. No!" Mike startles next to me as I tug Cocoa away from a big rock she's trying to chew. "Drop it."

She does not, of course, drop it, so I spend thirty seconds prying the rock from her mouth before she lets it go. "All right, let's get moving before she wreaks more havoc. She really needs to burn off some energy."

Surprisingly, Chompers keeps up with a fast pace, his little legs moving at warp speed to stay near his new friend. "This will be good for him," I say. "More confidence will get him adopted more quickly." I slide Mike a look. "So Princess is with your ex-wife?"

"Yeah. We separated a few years ago. The cat worked better for her new condo, so Princess stayed with me."

"Sounds like you kept things reasonable."

"Absolutely. We're still friends. We got married in college, and things just didn't quite work out in the end. No kids. How about you?"

"No kids," I say quickly.

"And no pets at your place either?"

"No, unfortunately." We stop while the dogs sniff their way around a huge oak.

Mike clears his throat. "I was a little worried about you last night. You looked upset. Bad news?"

"It was nothing," I answer immediately. "A mix-up."

"Oh, okay. Good."

I tug Cocoa along to resume the walk, and Chompers follows happily, but before we reach the next block, his tiny strides have slowed. Probably hasn't gotten much exercise lately. But Cocoa is picking up speed as we near a small park.

Mike leans down and scoops up Chompers to carry him like a football. When they catch up with me and Cocoa, Chompers's eyes are half-closed in bliss.

Mike offers another throat clearing as we walk. "Beth, did I do something wrong? I hate to think I . . . I mean, did I overstep in some way? Because I had a great time, and it seems like you didn't, which is not good."

His words cool my wariness into regret. It's not his fault I hoard secrets like treasure. Mike seems like a decent guy, and he's asking straightforward questions like a mature adult. He'd be a perfect catch for a woman who's throwing out lines, but I'm very much not.

"It's not that," I admit. "I had a great time too. It's just . . ." Now I'm clearing my throat, trying to soften how I say this. "I'm really only interested in short term."

"Perfect. I'm only here for six months."

"Uh, I meant more like six *days*."

He chokes on something, air or surprise, and stops to face me, his hand softly stroking Chompers, who's fully asleep now. "Okay. I see. So you're, like, *in a relationship*?"

"No!" The word bursts out on a laugh. "No way. It's not that."

"Oh." He only looks more confused, so I smooth things over with a lie, of course.

"I just went through a bitter divorce, so I don't ever plan on being in a relationship again. Hence, the short-term requirement." That's not exactly false. I did go through a divorce, but it was a long time ago. I met my ex at my first nursing job out of college. I still believed I was only running from Iowa and my family, so I thought it'd be safe to fall in love and settle down in Dallas, where my hometown was far enough away to fade into nothing.

I was wrong. My husband had been an X-ray tech at the same hospital where I worked in the ER. I loved the job, the fast pace and quick decision-making. Turns out I'm good under pressure.

Well. Some types of pressure. We got married quickly because I thought I'd finally found a home. My own place, my own heart, my own safe arms. And it was nice for a year or so.

But my husband was screwed up in his own ways, and the poison of his dad's emotional abuse began to leak out of his pores. That's what happens. I barely even blame him for it at this point. We were young and dumb, and our individual dysfunctions lined up wonderfully when times were good. But when times were not good? Well, I discovered I could hear my childhood bullies in his cruel words. And he learned I'd walk out and disappear for days at the drop of a hat, leaving him scared and betrayed.

Our neuroses brought out the worst in each other, and we separated. We got back together, then separated again. Finally, we divorced.

My ex had been in Dallas for a decade, so all our friends were his old friends. My work buddies were his work buddies. They all believed what he said about me. That I was unstable and crazy and probably cheating. That I was a fucked-up freak.

By the time I truly walked away, I'd dissolved into a broken-down mess. The awful, ugly years of my life seemed to fall on me all at once. Because if people call you a liar even when you're telling the truth, if that can follow you all the way from Iowa to Texas, from childhood to marriage, what's the point in showing anyone your real self?

So I ran, I found I liked running, and I've never stopped. No one gets hurt this way. Especially not me.

"I've never had a one-night stand before," Mike blurts out, shaking me from my dark thoughts, thank God. "It's just . . . not really my thing."

"Oh." I didn't mean to make Mike into a slut. My bad. "I'm sorry about that. I didn't know."

Cocoa winds around my legs a few times, trying to catch a scent. I spin around to free myself of the leash before coming face-to-face with Mike's gaze. He tries for a careful smile.

"So if your limit is six days," he says, "maybe we could go out once a month while I'm here?"

"Ha!" I honestly can't feel threatened by the guy while he's standing there with such a weird little dog cradled in his arms like a baby. Chompers obviously trusts him. "Was it that good, Mike? You simply can't stay away?"

His blushes are truly adorable, and this time warm feelings tighten around me instead of the leash. "I had a nice time," he says, blushing harder. And I bet he did. "Can I get your number at least?"

"Hmm." I look him up and down, then guide Cocoa around him toward the direction of the shelter. "How about you give me your number instead, and maybe I'll call next month."

"I can work with that."

It's possible Mike could be a nice new hobby. A guarantee of good sex once a month for the next little while? It might be worth any awkwardness of having him just down the block, if I can manage to keep him separate from the rest of my life.

If things settle down, I just might give it a chance.

CHAPTER 11

Things have settled down!

I hum my way through the aisles of the big store where I buy bulk packs of paper towels and other essentials. I finished work early, which is unusual for me. I like to take my mornings slow and easy, but I woke up with a ton of energy today.

My boss informed me that no other weird email has shown up. Though her tone was still cool, she said she noted in my HR file that my Reddit account doesn't match that of the impostor. In response to that small olive branch, I deleted my Reddit account and let her know. Better to be safe than sorry.

I also informed her of my suspicions about Frank Doukas. He'd managed to track me down before, after all.

In Denver, after he left a couple of fairly innocuous notes on my car at work, I'd asked security to contact Frank and politely request that he stay off hospital grounds. That worked for a couple of weeks. Then I "ran into him" at a burrito place around the corner from my apartment. That was bad enough, but after he taped a note to my actual apartment door, explaining his deep feelings for me, I decided it was time to pack up and move along.

I made the mistake of telling my coworkers about the gig I'd picked up in Austin, and yep, Frank mailed a letter there too. Just one letter, but still. When I left Austin six months later, I didn't tell a soul where

I was going. I haven't thought about Frank since then, but maybe that was a mistake.

Why can't men just be normal? Ugh. Sorry I was nice to you, Frank!

But there is good news. One of the patients whose files I've been working through had been heading toward hospice, but suddenly showed promising results from a new chemo treatment. God, I do miss the day-to-day involvement in patient lives. The constant human contact. As a nurse, I became an intimate part of people's families, just for a moment. I still get a little of that through the files, but not as much.

Is that why I've been thinking a lot about calling Mike? Am I craving more intimate connection?

I smile just thinking about his nerdy glasses and blushing cheeks. Despite everything, I am joy and positivity today. I am floating.

Actually I'm not really floating, because my shopping cart has a wonky front wheel, but even a noisy pull to the right can't burst my bubble. I put a piece of chocolate cake into the basket to celebrate, then add a pack of carrot sticks I'll inevitably neglect before throwing in the trash. We all have our private battles.

Should I actually call Mike? I haven't run into him since our walk four days ago, but I think he was in Cambria. Still, it's reassuring that he didn't show up for my dental cleaning or for my weekly lunch out on the wharf. I can keep him at a distance.

Now that he's not in my sights, it's hard to resist pulling him back in. Forbidden fruit and all that. I whistle my way through the last aisle.

After a nice, long chat with the checkout woman about the upcoming end of tourist season, I wrangle my cart out to the car and start loading shopping bags into the trunk. Each bag has an iconic image of one of the places I've lived. The bat bridge in Austin, the Grand Ole Opry in Nashville, and so on. The little collection makes me happy every time I shop. I might live life on the run, but it's an adventure, isn't it?

When I get to the bag from Denver with the painting of Red Rocks, I stutter over the sight of soft red fabric wedged between the apple crisp oatmeal and a bunch of bananas. Puzzled, I reach in and tug out the mystery item I don't remember buying.

A moment stretches out before it hits me. A few heartbeats where all I see is a cute little stuffed toy. Fuzzy red fabric, adorable pointy horns, the small swoosh of an evil smile, and the even smaller curls of eyelashes. She holds a felt pitchfork in hands instead of hooves, but there's no mistaking what she is. A devil girl.

The devil girl. Me.

My vision narrows into a small, vivid circle. I see only my hand holding this thing above the bananas, everything else gone black. I hear barks of laughter, snorts of derision. I feel so much shame that it's a solid thing inside me, a hot, burning worm that winds and twists, tugging at my aorta and lungs and guts.

White sparkles begin to strobe. My blood is an ocean against my eardrums, roaring and pounding.

When my throat finally unlocks, my chest expands to suck in a huge, wheezing breath. I back up until my hip hits the car, my eyes sliding desperately left and right as I search for my attacker.

Because this is an attack. A monster has crawled out of my past with dripping fangs and scraping claws, and it's hunting me.

Who is it? *Who?*

That man crouched in the grass on the corner, watching me as he lights a cigarette? The woman returning a cart to the store? The guy sitting behind the wheel of that parked truck one row over? Any one of them could be stalking me.

As the shock dissipates, I tell myself this gift might mean nothing. It's the end of August. The Halloween crap is in stores already. A kid could have picked it up and carried it around, and somehow it ended up in—

But no. This isn't a bizarre coincidence. My classmates started calling me Devil Girl in third grade, and it didn't stop until I left town nine years later. Some of them weren't even bullying me. It was just my commonly known nickname. Devil Girl. Satan's Spawn if they wanted to get more sophisticated. It was open season on a liar like me who made up creepy sex stuff about parties with demons. Fair Isle was swept up in the Satanic Panic like so many other communities across the country. When the flood receded, I was left behind, a part of the ruins.

Hey, Elizabeth, did the devil put his dick in you? Did you love it?

Ew. That's the girl who had sex with Satan. She probably has herpes!

Yo, Devil Girl, want to party with me? I like it freaky.

It wasn't every day or every person. But it was more than enough to leave scars on every inch of my soul. It was bad enough that I sat alone at lunch, got picked last in gym, was never asked to dances, dreaded each day of school. The featured traumas of teen movies.

Even when a classmate was nice, I couldn't take it as friendship, couldn't trust that it was real and honest. Because what was? Not me, not my parents, not the world.

And no, Devil Girl did not want to party. She wanted to stay locked in her room with a book or hiding in the backyard with her rabbits. She wanted to be invisible.

And I did it. I've been invisible for decades.

But not anymore, because someone here sees me. "Nooo," I whisper as I turn in a slow circle, scanning again. But looking for what? Who?

I pitch the last two bags into my car along with the plush toy, slam the trunk, and shove the cart out of the way. My skin burns with the hot weight of watching eyes, and when I hurry to open the door and slide into my seat, I'm terrified that a hand will reach from under the car and grab my ankle.

I pull my foot in, slam the door and lock it, then immediately hit the ignition and shift into reverse, not even taking the time to put on my seat belt.

Once I'm on the road, my panic recedes a bit, but the dread stays. Yes, I escaped the store, but I won't be safe at home either. They have my address. And whoever this person is, they walked right up behind me in line. I'd been putting each bag into the basket as it was loaded, and for one of those moments as I turned to chat with the cashier, a nightmare was at my back.

Had I seen them? I bare my teeth, straining to think, but I can't picture anyone, just a general mill of bodies flowing past.

Oh God. How has the past caught up to me? And *why*?

I've minded my own business since I escaped my hometown. I haven't hurt anyone else. I just want to be left alone. Please. *Please.*

I try to blend in with the traffic before making a hard left across a bridge I normally don't take, then I turn right as soon as I'm over the river. No one follows that I can see. Then again, why would they need to? They know where I live.

The dread sharpens to fear again.

Because they know where I live, where I work, where I shop, what kind of car I drive. And that means my years of hiding are over.

CHAPTER 12

It's not until I'm locked inside my own home again that I start to question my sanity. Maybe I finally broke wide open.

It's not impossible. I certainly could have picked up the stuffed devil on my own. I could have signed up for Liars Anonymous or requested information about an inpatient stay. Maybe the weight of carrying around my memories and guilt finally snapped the frayed threads that hold me in place.

There are dangers to stuffing all your bad feelings down as deep as you can. I know that. But I also know the dangers of opening up and letting your control fall into the hands of others.

My lying wasn't even purposeful at first. When I met my husband, I was just Elizabeth May from Iowa. I didn't talk about my past, but I didn't hide it. But after my marriage, after his shouting that there was something wrong with me, that I was screwed up and crazy and not normal and very broken . . . well, I guess I decided he was right.

Once I left and moved to a new place, my social anxiety vanished when I told that first big lie. I wasn't from Iowa anymore; I was from Kansas. I wasn't really Elizabeth; I preferred Eliza. And no, my parents weren't stoic and silent; they were the kindest old farm couple you'd ever meet. We used to have a corn maze and a pumpkin patch. I was on the pep squad. I hosted sleepovers every Friday!

Okay, yes, I have *felt* crazy at times. I have wondered if my ex was right.

In school I'd been more like a zoo animal than a person. My brain and my soul had both been bundles of such awful confusion because I wasn't a devil girl or a freak or a scandal. I was just a kid like the rest of them, with fears and dreams and pains and hopes. But if everyone saw me as something different, maybe I was the one who was wrong.

God, for a brief moment during my marriage, I'd been just like everyone else. So blessedly average and normal. A newlywed in love, a newbie nurse with a promising future in an adopted hometown I chose to call my own. And yet in reality, I'd been nothing but sharp edges, cutting up everything around me. I'd failed at normal life and found myself alone and shaking again.

And now? Now I'm a liar. A freak. Just as they'd always named me.

The old shame gnaws at me, but I *need* my lies. They connect me to people in a way no one ever wanted to connect with Elizabeth Mary May. No one had anything in common with that girl. No one was like her or wanted anything to do with her.

With my lies, I found I could tie myself to people with pretty little ribbons in any arrangement I chose. Dog lover with this one, cat lover with another. Share my amazing parents with the devout Evangelical Christian, lament my absent father with the emo guy in pediatrics. I'm a vegetarian with the pierced, tattooed woman at the gas station and a barbecue fiend with the owner of Smokey's Haven at the farmers' market.

These connections are as ephemeral as spiders' silk, but taken altogether, they hold me tight and keep me from drifting away. Or they always did before. What if I'm now sinking so slowly I can't feel it? What if I'm already lost?

My phone dings. A text from Tristan. Just found out I lost a patient. A young mom. So sad.

Oh no. That poor woman. And poor Tristan. My problems aren't so bad compared with other people's, are they?

Assuring myself that a stupid stuffed toy isn't that scary, I ignore the shopping bags dropped in a heap next to the door, and I curl onto a chair to grab this faint lifeline and hold tight. Oh no! What happened?

A woman who got a lung transplant last year. It's been nothing but complications since, but she was so young. Only thirty-four.

God that's awful. I'm sorry, Tristan.

I just keep thinking about her children. Trying to decide if I should go to the funeral.

How heartbreaking. Sometimes you really need closure.

Yeah. I knew you'd understand. I don't suppose . . .

I wait for the next text and eye the bags of groceries. I should put everything away, but I'm afraid something else could be hidden in there.

Hey, he texts, could I call you?

"Oh!" We've only spoken once before. He asked if we could game out some strategy for a job interview. I agreed because my phone number is an Illinois area code and reveals nothing about me.

I expect the discomfort that prickles through me at the idea, but I'm surprised that it's tinged with relief. It'd be really nice to have company while I try to pick up the pieces of my day. Or my whole life, whichever. I'm already feeling less scared just messaging him.

And in the back of my mind, that internal voice says, *And if you talk, you can be sure he's not Frank.*

I blink hard. I hadn't entertained that thought before, but now it rises up and trembles inside me. I don't remember Tristan's voice at all. Months ago, Frank hadn't been on my mind anymore, so I could have missed it.

But could Frank really have discovered my past? Could he be using it to torment me and even masquerading as a fellow nurse? It's possible. I'm pretty damn familiar with how easy it is to track strangers online.

Sure, I type. Give me a call.

My phone trills almost immediately. A nervous smile twists my mouth as I answer. "Tristan?"

"Hey," he says a little darkly, "nice to hear your voice again." My heart aches with both sympathy and relief. It's not Frank's gruff wheedle; it's just a normal, unremarkable voice.

"It's good to talk to you," I say. "I'm sorry you're going through it, though."

"I'll be okay. You know how it is. I thought she was improving, and then . . . Well, you understand."

"Sometimes everything just starts breaking down at once."

"Yeah. It's really rough. Her kids are only four and six. I can't imagine losing a parent so young. But I'd better stop talking about it or I'll break down. So tell me how you're doing. No more creepy stalkers?"

Oh shit, he's already asking the important question, and I don't know what I want to say. "Uh. The work thing settled down. I think things are okay."

"That's good. But . . . ?"

This is so weird. We've texted four or five times a week for months, but his voice makes him a stranger. Funny that I have no trouble sleeping with men I don't know, but speaking to this guy about my real life? Wow. My hands are shaking. But I really, really need someone to talk to.

"I don't know," I finally say, not yet committing to this. "Things are still strange."

"How so?"

"Just . . ." I get up to face the bags, but no. I can't tell him that part. "Someone had some strange mail sent to my house. Brochures that make it look like I'm interested in . . . inpatient treatment."

"Holy cow! That's definitely creepy. Like rehab?"

"Yeah." I wipe my sweating palm on my jeans, then switch hands to wipe the other. "I'm freaked out that this stalker apparently has my address."

"Oh crap," he whispers. "You're right. That's bad."

"It's not great."

"That's truly disturbing," he says. "Have you called the cops?"

"No, I don't think they can do anything."

"Maybe, but you might want to get this on the record in case it escalates. It couldn't hurt, could it?"

Oh, it could. I know that from my own experience. The cops can definitely make things worse.

"This person could be dangerous, May. You should put the police on notice. They might drive by once a day at least."

"I'll think about it." The cops here in Santa Cruz would just roll their eyes at me, I'm sure, but maybe he doesn't understand that.

"You should tell your boss too, just in case."

I'm relaxed enough now that I can get up and deal with the groceries. "If you hear me moving around, I'm putting stuff away. I just got back from the store."

"Yeah?" His voice gets more cheery. "What are you making for dinner tonight? Did you get any treats?"

Laughing, I dig into the bags. "I got myself a piece of chocolate cake, actually." I'd forgotten about that. I search around until I find it, then put it on the coffee table. No point in waiting until later. I've earned this. "And tonight I'm making stir-fry."

Tristan tells me about the new grill he bought, and after we talk about food for a while everything feels so normal. So nice.

I'm not losing my mind. I just needed a friend to talk me down. That's what normal people do, right? They talk to friends to feel better.

And Tristan is proof that I can have friendship if it's safe enough. But that's a really big if, isn't it.

CHAPTER 13

Now that I'm full of chocolate cake and my heart rate has slowed, I'm thinking more clearly. If this is Frank Doukas, how could he possibly know about my schoolyard nickname in Iowa? Has my story been posted online recently? Are people from Fair Isle making nasty comments?

I sit down at my computer to dig deeper. I'd searched for my own name earlier, but I hadn't looked into the root of the problem: the Satanic tornado that hit my little town in 1991.

We were slow to take up the craze, as we were slow to everything, including the realization that naming a landlocked town "Fair Isle" would set up disappointment for centuries to come. What a start.

The McMartin Preschool nightmare began in 1983, and it eventually blazed into the longest series of criminal trials in America. Seven people were accused of child abuse involving rape, power drills, Satan worshipping, witches, underground tunnels, and even a hot-air balloon, all somehow originating in a small neighborhood preschool run by a local family. The hysteria from that case bubbled up and up like crude oil until terror covered the entire country in a sticky film. By the time the McMartin case finally wrapped up in California in 1990—with no convictions—the Midwest was just hitting its stride.

I type in *Hoffholder daycare* and *Fair Isle* and see all the articles that circulated back then. But when I sort by date, something shiny and new pops up: a big article in the *Des Moines Register* that dropped almost three years ago: "When the Devil Came to Iowa."

"Shit," I bark. "What the hell?" Why would anyone be revisiting the case now? The thirtieth anniversary was over four years ago. I know because I'd been dreading the press taking it up again, but they'd been silent. The Hoffholder case only involved two defendants, so it hadn't blossomed into a huge mess. It was a minor blip in the Satanic Panic but a nuclear explosion in our town.

Before reading the story, I hold my breath and run a quick query for my name. Nothing. It's not there. I knew that already, since it hadn't come up during my last search, but I still exhale a shaky sigh of relief.

The article begins as all of them do, with the origins of McMartin and other bigger cases, but it quickly moves on to recapping exactly what led to the Hoffholders being arrested and convicted of child abuse and sexual assault.

> On May 1, 1991, an eleven-year-old girl showed up for her after-school job at Hoffholder Haus, a home daycare at the rural outskirts of the tiny farming community of Fair Isle. It seemed to be a day like any other. She rode the bus after school straight to the Hoffholders' to earn $2 an hour helping with dishes, giving bottles to babies, and sometimes doing crafts with the older children. But on May 1 when she returned home to the rambling farmhouse where she lived with her parents and sister, she told her mom about the awful things she'd seen during her six months of working for Linda and Mitchell Hoffholder.

I can picture eleven-year-old Lauren Jensen perfectly. I'd only just turned five, but I'd felt far too old to be sent to daycare for the three days a week my mom worked at a local insurance office.

Most of the other kids were toddlers and babies, so I'd been overjoyed when Lauren would ask me to help pick up toys and entertain the smaller kids. She'd elevated me above the babies to her peer. Her helper. At eleven, she hadn't been a teenager, but she'd seemed like one to me. Fun and friendly and tall, with long blond hair and a freckled nose. She was so alive, unlike my somber family. She laughed loudly and wore big hair bows and sparkly nail polish. I'd suffered a bad case of hero worship and wanted to be just like her.

That was my downfall.

I scan the next few paragraphs quickly, as I'm intimately familiar with the story. Lauren's claims were backed up by the Hoffholders' thirteen-year-old son, Jacob. The article hasn't mentioned me yet, but I was the third, crucial witness. I stepped forward because Lauren asked me to lie. She'd "revealed" the horrible things she and Jacob had seen and gave me a few details, saying I needed to help them save the babies in daycare.

I'd repeated her tales to the police, but after those first basic lies, the rest of the story had been pushed on me by interviewers until I'd started to believe them.

Yes, of course I'd seen red robes and black candles. Crystal goblets full of blood. A skull with symbols drawn on it.

Yes, I'd also seen a baby's throat slit. No, I didn't know which baby. In fact, there might have been more than one.

Yes, the Hoffholders touched me, both of them. Sure, I can show you where on this doll. Right here. There? I don't know, I can't remember. Maybe. Yes! It hurt, and they said they'd murder me and all the other kids if I said anything. Said they'd cut us up like they cut up that baby and made us watch as they fed it to pigs.

No, I don't know where the pigs were. Maybe another house? Wait, maybe the pigs were in a cave. They made us go there and take off our clothes. The devil was there. I saw him! Black eyes, red skin. He touched us too. He hurt us.

And on and on and on and on. It sounds like a mad fantasy now. Of course it does. The prosecutions were patently absurd, but a feverish contagion had infected the country, and innocent daycare workers were railroaded in many different states. The grasping fingers of paranoia even reached into Canada.

For months, the authorities asked me questions and asked them again. The police, the prosecutors, the therapists. They showed me scary pictures, then asked me to draw my own. I was examined, interrogated, hypnotized, guided, and prayed over. The scenes were a horror movie on repeat in my brain, and after dark the nightmares swooped down to claw at me. It all became real. I *remembered* the pain, the fear, the torture. I relived it in my dreams every night.

In the end, it was abuse; it just wasn't the Hoffholders who did it.

I skip over the black words crawling like ants across the screen until I reach a picture of the house and wince. There it is. Just a white two-story farmhouse like any other but for the wooden sign hanging from a frame in the front yard. The big bubble letters spell out "Hoffholder Haus." It's a black-and-white picture, but I remember the sky blue of the background, the white letters surrounded by red, yellow, and green balloons.

The sign was more cheerful than Mrs. Hoffholder had ever been, and Mr. Hoffholder had hardly been around at all.

> By the time a primary witness stepped forward to recant, more than a year after the convictions of the Hoffholders, the terror had faded and the Satanic Panic had begun to cool. A new county attorney looked at the evidence and felt horror, not at the alleged Satanism, but at the lack of physical evidence. "It read like spooky stories being told around a campfire," he said. "There were literally two pieces of physical evidence, and one of the key witnesses revealed they'd been planted."

That key witness was Lauren. She revealed that Jacob, two years older, had manipulated her and persuaded her to lie. Lauren said that he'd touched her, and he'd talked her into touching him. She'd thought they were in love and would get married, but first he needed to get away from his cruel, abusive parents. She'd been eager to save the tortured boy she loved.

In 1993 when the case was overturned and the Hoffholders were released from prison, the story twisted in on itself, and Jacob emerged as a bad seed. A teenage boy jealous of the attention his mom gave to other children. An evil adolescent lashing out at the rules and expectations of his family. He'd apparently seen a tabloid cover about Satanic abuse, read the story, and plotted revenge on his strict parents.

> Once the parents were free, their teenage son was removed from the foster home where he'd lived for two years and returned to the care of his family. Court records show his troubles continued into the next decade. He dropped out of high school and was convicted of robbery at age twenty. He served a short sentence in county jail.
>
> Records are scarce after that. Mitchell Hoffholder died in 2018, and no one in the Hoffholder family agreed to give an interview or a statement for this article.

Wow. I don't remember Jacob well, as he rarely made an appearance around "the brats," as he called us. He'd been small for a thirteen-year-old, and always sullen and sneering.

He'd disappeared after the original allegations, apparently swept away to a foster home. I'd heard he came back two years later, but he was so much older that I never saw him again.

That had been the end of Jacob Hoffholder in my life. I'd seen Lauren occasionally, but we'd run in different circles. I was ostracized from such a young age that I'd never broken out of that cage. But Lauren was pretty and vivacious, and she'd already had large groups of friends before the scandal. We'd moved on different trajectories in Fair Isle. The article doesn't mention what became of her later.

Miracle of miracles, when I reach the end of the piece, I realize that not only is my name not mentioned, but my existence isn't even hinted at. Not as "another witness" or "a five-year-old" or even just a daycare kid. Instead of rehashing the whole investigation and the trial, the article delves into an examination of the societal trends and family fears that grew these terrors, and how those same insecurities manifest today.

What a broken, confusing world we live in.

"Jacob Hoffholder," I murmur, opening another window to search for his name. All the same old news links come up, and that's about it. Whatever Jacob is up to now, he's keeping a low profile. I'm sure we all are.

Knowing Lauren's name is likely too common, I still try searching for "Lauren Jensen." As I expect, there are far too many. The Midwest is teeming with Jensens, and most of them are blond. A dozen different women smile at me from my laptop. There's a very good chance she's been married at least once, and the odds seem likely she'd want to get rid of her maiden name. So I give up.

I hope they both found some peace, though Jacob's problems clearly continued. Lauren always seemed like she'd turn out fine, though. She rose above it even as a teenager. She had charisma and boldness. All I had was confusion.

"But you're all right too," I say, nodding to help it sink in. "You're fine."

My phone chimes. Did you call the police? Tristan asks.

I have friends in my own way. Or at least one. Tristan is worried about me, and if he were my stalker or even just the impostor on Reddit, he wouldn't tell me to go to the police, would he? I'm not as alone as I think I am.

After drawing a deep breath I tell the truth. I can't go to them. It's too much to explain. I'm sorry. But I feel so much better since we talked. Thank you!

Ok but I'm worried about you.

I'm good, I swear! It's all kind of silly when you think about it, isn't it? Don't worry!!!

I put on shoes and grab a sweater. This day was awful for a moment. Really awful. But interacting with Tristan has made clear that I need to be around people tonight. My fear will only get worse with isolation. I may not have friends, but I have plenty of acquaintances and so many strangers to watch.

I wave goodbye to the fridge packed with healthy groceries and head out to another favorite watering hole for a summer spritz with a side of mozzarella sticks and the bustling comfort of crowds.

I've managed to make a good life for myself, and that glimpse into my past makes me feel thankful I pulled myself out of it. I'm not that girl anymore, and I'll never let myself be her again.

CHAPTER 14

I'm dividing my attention between a side salad and the mozzarella sticks when someone sits down next to me at the bar. Glancing over quickly, I establish that it's not Mike. Or Frank. Or any other stalker. It's just Beret.

That's not his real name. He never says a word, not even to introduce himself. I have no idea if he speaks English.

Beret looks to be in his seventies, with brown, fantastically wrinkled skin and a red beret always pulled over the straight white hair that brushes his shoulders like drifting moss.

"Hey, how's it going?" I ask.

Beret lifts his chin in acknowledgment, then does the same toward the bartender who's already bringing over a Tsingtao beer. Beret never speaks, but he's a fixture here, though he only comes Tuesday through Friday. Why then? No idea.

When I lift my summer spritz toward him, he clinks his bottle against it, and we drink. "Nice day today," I offer, and Beret nods.

Maybe it's the spritz I've almost finished, but suddenly the story is bubbling up in me, the awful feelings I couldn't share even with Tristan. The bartender is at the other end of the counter, so I let my lips part, and the words spill out.

"I got really scared today," I confess. "I think someone is stalking me."

I draw hard on my straw, the bittersweet bubbles popping on my tongue as Beret waits silently for more.

I nod as if he's made an observation. "It doesn't make any sense, though. It has to do with something that happened when I was just a little kid, you know? I was *five*. So why would someone care about that now?"

That internal voice pipes up inside my brain with some thoughts. *Because you ruined lives. You ruined Mrs. Hoffholder's life. Maybe it's her.*

It could be, I suppose. The news article said Mitchell had died, which likely means Linda Hoffholder is still alive.

I sit up a little straighter and glance around to look for an older woman. She was chubby and gray-haired even back then, and today she'd be around eighty. I don't spot anyone in the right age range.

And what about Jacob? Whatever evil plan he'd had, I'd helped to mess it up. Actually, now that I think about it, I remember hearing a few stories during my school years. That he'd lived with a rich family with a pool. That he did it all out of greed because his parents were poor. That maybe he'd paid off me and Lauren to lie so he could live in luxury.

Ridiculous, but if there was any truth to that at all, could he still be bitter after thirty-some years? It's possible. And frightening. Because I can't figure out how Frank Doukas could have tracked me all the way back to Iowa. May is such a common name. It could be him, but more likely it's someone from Fair Isle.

Sighing, I rest my chin on my hand and shake my head. "It wasn't just today either," I continue. "Somebody tried to get me fired last week. And they signed me up for Liars Anonymous." I steal a sidelong glance to see if Beret has recoiled. But no, he's looking down at his bottle, one thumbnail lifting an edge of the label. He's reserved about it, just easing it up. I'd have already torn off a long strip and destroyed the paper.

"And I do lie sometimes. I admit that. But doesn't everyone?" He doesn't respond, and I pause to watch him work at the label for long seconds before I snap back to myself, scared that I've said anything at all.

Shit. I'm already regretting it.

"Sorry. I don't know why I told you all that." I pluck the magenta umbrella from my glass, eat the maraschino cherry, and tuck the umbrella into the hair above my ear. My gaze slides desperately around, searching for a distraction to toss Beret's way. I pop up straight when I spot it. "Oh my God, look at that girl's sunburn."

Beret and I stare at a college-age girl wearing a tube top that looks like it has white straps crisscrossing over her red shoulders, but the stripes aren't fabric. They're lines from a swimsuit she must have worn earlier at the beach. "Ouch," I say, "that looks painful," and Beret toasts me again. I take a final sip, getting nothing but ice melt before I set the glass down too hard.

"I guess that's a sign that I should get going." The hair on the back of my neck is standing, letting me know I've exposed too much of myself. I look around to be sure no one else heard my story before I signal the bartender for my bill.

Crowds of people are still walking by outside the open door, and I know I'll feel safer out there, lost in the shuffle. Maybe I'll walk through the amusement park and take my time, because I'm already dreading the tension of stepping into my empty house. The loud young couple checked out yesterday, and I'll be alone with my fears.

When my bill arrives, I sign with an angry flourish, suddenly pissed that this stalker is messing up my life. A week ago I was perfectly content and totally unintimidated by solitude. Now I can feel the muscles in my shoulders straining with tension, even after my cocktail. "See you next week," I say to my companion, not bothering to wait for an answer.

Beret is a lot like me, I think, but instead of lying about who he is, he never even pretends to give a clue. It's a good strategy, but I'm way too chatty to pull it off. Still, I might run out of words one day. Or run out of lies, at least. And then I'll be the silent old person nursing a beer and hearing others' secrets instead of hoarding my own.

I pause in the doorway, and a dozen strangers rush by, leaving nothing behind but hints at who they could be. Nobody even glances toward me.

It's another beautiful night, of course. That's why people come here. A huge pack of wild tweens flows by, and I hang back, no more willing to thrust myself into a crowd of pubescents now than I was at their age. They're little meat sacks of chaotic energy, the girls squealing in high laughs, the boys shoving each other. One of them whips off his shirt and snaps another with it, which shifts the whole pack like a writhing amoeba.

I stay put, wanting no part of it. "Tannerrrrr!" one of the girls cries. "Stop being a dick!"

"You want my dick?" he yells back, and the gang hoots and hollers before they finally ooze through a nearby doorway into an ice cream shop. Oof. Those poor workers.

I step out into the flow and leave my sudden confession to Beret behind. It was a clear sign of my distress, and I regret it, but now I'm part of the crowd, another tourist enjoying the magic of this place. The lights of the boardwalk, the screams from the roller coaster, the guttural echo of sea lions, the twin scents of cotton candy and buttered popcorn. Pigeons bob around tables and trash cans, pecking at leftovers and dodging seagulls. A bike flies by only inches from my elbow before the shirtless rider bounces down the curb and careens into traffic.

The crowd around me slows as we reach a busy intersection being serenaded by a beautiful girl with a violin and an amp. She's fiddling away with a talent that leaves me in awe. I have zero musical skills, and when a busker is really good, I feel like I'm watching a magic show.

What is she doing here, this tall Asian woman who's got half the crowd hypnotized with her art? Shouldn't she be on a big stage? Or playing on one of those TV talent shows? I drop a couple of bills into her violin case and squeeze through the pedestrians to the edge of the crowd. By the time I reach the curb, the light has turned red, so I have to wait.

Tapping my foot along with the music, I stare out toward the boardwalk and the slow spin of the Dream Wheel. It's mesmerizing, and I like to try to imagine the stories of the people floating up there. When a plane flies overhead, I glance up, wondering about their stories too. I want to know them all.

Someone touches my back, and I try to shift forward a bit, but suddenly I'm flying just like that plane.

No, not flying. I'm falling, the touch on my back turned into a hard shove, and I float for one second, just for one panicked gasp, before a red Ford becomes my whole world.

My hands fly out, bracing for the ground or for the looming grille of the car, as if I have the power to stop either. My mouth opens and my lips stretch wide for a scream that won't come in time, as I wonder if I'll take all my secrets with me once and for all.

CHAPTER 15

My left wrist jolts with a hard pain, but my body keeps falling as my elbows give way. I can see my face about to smash, to scrape, can see it like a movie. My nose will get the brunt of this or maybe my whole skull if the screeching tires fail to catch hold. Blood will fly. Bones will crack. As a nurse, I know exactly the shape my ruined skull will take.

Then everything goes still. Not silent, though. The fiddle keeps fiddling, and the coaster keeps coasting, and the crowd is abuzz. There's a belated scream behind me, then a rising murmur. But I'm stock still, and so is the red Ford a foot from my left ear.

I whimper, moan, a tiny drop of spit falls from my lip to the cracked asphalt three inches beneath it.

"You okay?"

Hands touch my shoulder, careful this time.

"Ma'am?"

More hands. Are these the hands that just tried to kill me?

I try to lift my torso, and two people help as I attempt to stand on legs turned to trembling sludge. "Someone pushed me," I rasp.

"What? Are you all right?"

I turn to the teenage boy next to me, whose eyes are wide with shock. The red Ford slides by, the driver's mouth a dark O of surprise or outrage. This will be a story they tell someone in a few minutes, a few hours.

"Someone pushed me," I say again. "Did you see it?"

The kid scrubs a hand over his short-cropped black curls. "I was watching the girl playing violin."

My hands burn. I turn them over to see that my palms are bleeding and peppered with sand and pebbles. Still in shock, I look dumbly up, searching for a guilty expression or a known face. But there are only strangers looking back at me, some of them worried, some embarrassed.

"Thanks," I whisper as the crowd begins to flow around us. The light has changed, and the nice teenager pats my shoulder before easing away. I'm left standing stupidly, staring at the backs of the violinist's audience.

Somebody tried to push me into traffic. It wasn't jostling or impatience. My shoulder blades still burn with the phantom palmprints of those hands, the ten spread fingers covering nearly the whole width of me. An assault, not a joke.

"Someone pushed me," I repeat, louder now as clawing fear finally takes hold.

No one cares. A few people turn to throw me wary glances, perhaps assuming I'm one of the many troubled people who wander these streets every day. When I curse aloud, they turn away.

My knees are so weak I'm not sure I can walk, but I point my feet to the left and shuffle away from the corner to a quieter patch of sidewalk. I should do something. But what? I want to flee, but I can barely move, my body stiff and clumsy with shock.

Someone pushed me. Someone is *following* me.

That's when I spot the cop across the street. He's emerging from an art gallery, and his appearance must be a sign, so I raise my arms and wave frantically before I can chicken out and remember that I don't like cops. They're just as fallible as other humans. They believed all the spooky Satanic stories a small child told them, didn't they? Yet they have more power to wield than the rest of us.

The cop spots me, frowns, and starts across the street. "Can I help you, ma'am?" he calls.

I show him my bloody palms as he reaches my side of the road. "Someone shoved me into traffic."

He frowns, and deep wrinkles appear on his face. He's older than I thought, an Asian man with a closely shaved head and eyes that narrow with concern. Or maybe it's suspicion. "Are you sure?"

"What? Yes! I was standing there waiting for the light to change, and someone pushed me."

"An accident?"

"No."

"It's pretty busy over there." He tips his head toward the corner ten feet away like I wasn't just standing there. "Someone probably bumped into you."

"It wasn't an accident!" I'm trying to control my voice, but adrenaline is pushing it higher. "Someone *pushed* me!"

I can see the switch, the click of his face shutting down into flat professionalism. "Ma'am, please calm down."

"I am calm!" No, I don't say this calmly.

"It's a crowded intersection, and no one else seems alarmed. Do you need medical assistance? Should I call a paramedic?"

"No, I'm . . . No, I don't need medical assistance, but there must be cameras around here. Can you see who has video?"

"Ma'am, if you don't need medical attention, the best thing would be to move along. Accidents tend to happen when you're out having fun and your guard is down. If you don't want an ambulance, maybe head home, clean up, and drink some water."

"What? Why would I drink water?"

The officer's eyes shift to my right ear, and when I reach up, my fingers dislodge something. The magenta umbrella spins lazily to the ground like it's dancing.

"I'm not drunk!" I protest just as loudly as a drunk person would. I see more of the crowd turning to look at me, so I clear my throat and try to wrestle my dismay into submission. "I'm sorry," I say, my voice almost normal now. "I had one drink with dinner, that's it. And then

I was walking home and *someone pushed me*. On purpose. A red Ford almost ran over my head."

"Okay. What model of Ford?"

"I . . . I have no idea. I just saw the grille. Maybe it was a hatchback?"

"And can anyone else confirm this?"

What the hell? I'm not claiming I saw aliens or . . . or devil worshippers in red robes. The cops believed *that* shit, but this guy is looking right at my scraped hands and wants more proof?

My knees start to burn and sting, then my eyes. I look down to see one leg of my jeans is almost ripped open at the knee. "Look at me," I moan.

"I can see that you fell."

"I was pushed. Why don't you believe me? I'm not lying!"

"Beth?" I whip around as yet another hand touches me, this one just grazing my shoulder before I twitch it away. Good Lord, it's fucking Mike again.

Stumbling back, I get distance from both him and the cop. "What are *you* doing here?" I demand.

"I'm, uh, eating dinner." He points to the street corner diagonal from this one. Two-person tables hug the wall of a terrible kabob place I never visit.

I'm suspicious at yet another unexpected appearance by Mike, but then a bright thought pops into my head. "Mike, did you see who pushed me?"

"Pushed you?" He looks puzzled until I hold up my hands, and then he gasps at the sight of the oozing blood and peeling strands of skin. "Jesus, are you okay?"

"I would be, but this nice officer here won't help."

"Ma'am, you've clearly been drinking. You need to move along."

"I had *one drink*!" I yell, immediately losing hold of whatever control I'd managed to grab.

When the cop reaches for the radio clipped to his shoulder, Mike touches my elbow gently. "All right. Why don't I stay with you and make sure you're okay? Can you walk?"

I don't want him walking me anywhere, but this policeman isn't going to help. Still, I give the man one last glare. "I want to file a report."

"Great," the officer says. "There's a form online."

As he rattles off the website address, I snap a pic of his badge, then turn to head home with Mike. I move only a few feet before I jerk to a stop. "I thought you said you were eating dinner."

"I was pretty much done."

I take a step back, then another, and Mike winces as he checks my expression. Yeah, I'm scared and pissed and wary. All of this wild shit started when I met Mike, didn't it?

He holds up both hands like he's dealing with a dangerous animal who might attack. Smart move, because that's exactly what I am. "Let's go back to my table, then," he says. "All right? Get a napkin for your hands at least. Right over there."

He doesn't touch me again, either because I'm scared or because he is. But when he edges toward the intersection, I follow, my mind a mess of roiling fear. Could it have been him? It could be anyone, even this man I swear I never saw once before I foisted myself on him. Yet I still trail behind Mike, afraid to walk alone. Afraid of what will happen the moment I move away from the crowds and turn onto a quiet path.

None of this makes sense, and my eyes flit from person to person, car to car, trying to find clues or warnings or sudden movements anywhere. Who could be stalking me? Who wants me hurt? And *why*?

CHAPTER 16

We cross one street, then the other. Mike gestures to a table, and I force my roiling mind to focus. Atop the table sits a plate with two empty kabob sticks and a pile of yellow rice. It could belong to anyone.

I jut my chin toward a white paper sack dotted with grease stains. "What's in the bag?"

"Um. A snickerdoodle?" When I raise one eyebrow and stare, Mike opens the bag and holds it toward me. I lean gingerly forward to look in at the pale, cinnamon-dusted cookie.

Okay. It's his table.

When I spin around to face the intersection, I can see the violinist, her arm a blur of bow work. The place where I stood is partially obstructed by the traffic pole, a road sign, and a garbage can. "What did you see?"

"Nothing, really. I heard a shout and looked up to see you talking to that cop."

"Hmm." If he was sitting here, there's no way he'd have time to spot me at the curb, cross two busy streets, and work his way through the crowd just to shove me into traffic. I'd only been standing there for fifteen seconds or so.

Unless he's secretly Usain Bolt, it probably wasn't him. Just another coincidence that he was close by. He does only live one block from me, and it's not like Santa Cruz is a huge city.

Maybe Mike is actually my guardian angel. An angel who hasn't gotten his wings yet and is also down to bone. That would really change the feel of *It's a Wonderful Life*.

I'm sinking here, I can feel it, my burning hands beginning to shake as my mind tries to process anything past the shock. "Mike?" I whisper. "Would you walk me home?"

He crumples the bag closed and is immediately at my side. My right knee hurts, but I try to hide the limp as I move stiffly toward our street.

"Do you want to go to a clinic?" Mike asks. "Those scrapes need to be cleaned out."

"I worked in the ER for years. I think I can handle it."

"The ER?" His head twists toward me.

Oh damn. Frazzled, I've forgotten myself and let down my guard. This is bad. My face burns, and the tears are back, trying to worm free. He knows I'm a liar now. Just like everyone has always known. I'm a freak, a loser, a psycho.

"I thought you were an accountant," Mike says past the rushing in my ears.

"Uh, yeah," I babble, walking faster, ignoring the way my knee throbs. Think, think. Come on, brain. "Well, um," I stammer. "I'd just met you, and I didn't know if you were a creep or not. Didn't want you tracking me down at work or anything."

"Oh. I see. Understandable for a hookup, I guess."

Relief shoves aside my moment of panic. I've covered that lie, at least. But poor Mike. I've really torn up his self-image. How the hell did I have a one-night stand with such a sensitive soul? "Sorry," I mutter. "I'm being careful because strange shit keeps happening."

"Like someone pushing you?"

"Exactly."

"There are other things too?"

We take a left on our shared street, and I look at him, not trying to hide the way I'm studying his face. He's not someone from my past,

I'm sure of it. "Where did you grow up originally? You don't have much of an accent."

"Ohio, near Cleveland."

Can I believe this man? He says all the right things, but that's exactly how a stalker would behave. I'd like to be able to trust my gut, but I don't trust anything about myself. What I can believe is that he's not the Flash or Superman, and there's no way he could have flown across that intersection and pushed me into the street. Right?

So I let a small truth free. "I got some weird mail the night you saw me in my driveway. I don't know who it came from, but they obviously know my address. There was also an incident with my job. Someone posted crap about my employer online, then tried to pin it on me. And now this."

"Wow. I'm so sorry. Do you have any idea who it is?"

"I really don't. Which is why I've been a little . . . prickly with you. It started around the time we met."

"Ah. That makes sense. I stood on the street pretending to be a dweeb who couldn't find the rental right in front of his face just so you'd approach me. The perfect setup."

I manage an actual laugh. "Exactly. You're wily."

"I am." Mike shoots me a look, his face getting serious again. "Hold on." He stops in the middle of the sidewalk and tugs his phone from his jeans. After a few seconds of poking and swiping, he hands it to me.

"What's this?" I ask.

"My work calendar. Go ahead and look through it. You can check my worksites, all my flights in the past month. Whatever you want."

"Mike, I've given you every reason to believe I'm a crazy woman. Do not give me access to your phone."

"Eh, I'm not scared of you."

I watch his open and honest face for a long moment and wonder if he's the nicest guy in the world or this country's greatest con artist. Then I take a full minute to scroll through his calendar, paying special attention to the flight he took here and the two-night stay in Cambria. If this is a cover, it's a good one. And seriously, look at his adorable face.

"All right." I hand the phone back. "You pass."

He tries to do a fist pump, loses his phone, and bats it into a bush with a frantic attempt at catching it.

"Tone down the fake-dweeb act. You're overdoing it."

Blushing furiously, he digs around in the manzanita bush until he retrieves his phone, and damned if I don't feel charmed. He seems like a genuinely good guy. Maybe, just maybe, he's on my side? What a strange feeling.

The warm fuzzies fade when we reach my house. I stop at the end of the driveway and stare at the dark windows. The crickets are just starting up their songs. The sky is fading from blue to orange, and the constant breeze has taken on a new chill. It's beautiful. And for the first time since I moved here, I don't want to go into my cozy little home.

Maybe that's a good thing, because I won't miss it as much when I have to move on. And I clearly need to think about moving on. I blink back more tears at the thought.

"Want me to head in first and check around?" Mike offers.

"Yes," I answer, but my feet are glued to the ground. He can check around all he likes, but I'll still be by myself when he leaves. I'll wake up feeling those hands on my back, and I'll be all alone in the dark with the old nightmares of looming monsters and probing hands. We stand silently for a long moment.

"Or," he finally ventures, "if you feel all right about it, you could come to my place and watch something. How about *Antiques Roadshow*? Wait, is that too nerdy?"

Yes. It's fantastically nerdy, and my heart twists with relief at the thought of it. Secrets in the attic. Beautiful little hidden secrets that never hurt anyone and now spread joy. "British or American?"

"British all the way. Uh, unless you prefer the American version." No, I need all that English calm tonight.

I stare at my door a bit longer. It feels safer to go home with him than it does to invite him in. There are too many pitfalls in there. He might discover one of the brochures from my mailbox or a letter with my full name on it. I didn't care what I might expose that first night, because I'd never see him again, but things have gotten stickier now.

I try to remember where I stashed the Liars Anonymous info, and I can't. "Could you wait here? I need to clean up my hands."

"Sure. I'll stand guard. You feel okay going in?"

I hesitate again. "I'll leave the door ajar. Come on in if you hear a blood-curdling scream."

"You got it."

Hiding the keypad with my body, I punch in the code and shove my door open without stepping in. I reach inside to slap the light switch up, bracing for chaos, but everything looks normal. So far so good. "I'll be right back," I call, making sure any stalkers inside can tell I'm not alone.

After that, it's easy. There's just the bathroom and my bedroom, and I turn on both lights before digging out the first aid kit out from the bathroom cabinet. I flex both wrists, and nothing seems sprained, which is good news, but God, the soap burns like acid when I wash my hands.

Cringing at the spots of blood left behind on my towel, I carefully blot the water off, then spray both palms with Bactine before placing my widest bandages over the scrapes. Once my hands are finally doctored up, I hurry to the kitchen to fill a baggie with ice cubes for my knee.

This is going to be one sexy evening! In that spirit, I lift my hands to show Mike when I step outside. "I know I rocked your world last time, but this isn't going to be one of those nights, so lower your expectations."

He blushes again, but that doesn't stop his comeback. "I think I've made clear I'm only putting out once a month, so lower *your* expectations."

"What about just hand stuff?" I ask, then show my palms again when he chokes on his own spit. "I'm kidding! Look at me! I'm the definition of no hand stuff."

Shaking his head, he smiles widely at me. "Glad you're back to your normal self, at least."

It's strange to think he already recognizes my usual personality. Vulnerability stretches awake inside me, and I want to shove it back into its box and nail the top shut and never be vulnerable with anyone again.

This isn't safe. None of it is. But I'd rather take the risk of catching brief feelings for this man than the danger of being alone when an unknown menace is stalking me. Mike is definitely the safer bet.

CHAPTER 17

"Beth?" The whisper tickles my mind, but I try to brush it away. "Beth, it's almost eight."

I'm lost and it feels nice. I'm floating and warm, dreaming of lying nude in the sun, everything peaceful around me as a nearby seagull pecks at a strip of bacon. Beret tosses the bird another piece. He's standing next to me, wearing his red beret, but he's naked otherwise, his body surprisingly buff.

"Beth!" he says, holding out a strip of bacon. The sound of Beret actually speaking wakes me with a start.

"Ah!" I pop up, my cheek wet with drool. "What?"

"Hey, morning glory," a man says. Mike stands over me, wearing a crisp button-down and jeans, a plate held in each hand. I let out a brief, hoarse scream before my brain catches up to remind me that I spent the night on his couch.

He grimaces and steps back. "Sorry."

Blinking owlishly, I look around and orient myself. I'm on his couch in his little one bedroom over the garage. Sunlight streams in through the east-facing windows, and the sheer curtains dance in a weak breeze. "Oh," I croak.

"I didn't know if you needed to get moving or not. Sorry to wake you."

"Oh," I repeat, still groggy. I wipe my cheek and feel a topographic map of his throw pillow pressed into my skin. Perfect. Maybe I'll chase this guy off after all.

"Bacon and eggs?" he asks, lowering the plate.

My stomach growls in response. "Thank you." He offers coffee, and I happily accept, even though he warns that he has no cream. I crave the caffeine too badly to care.

We weren't up late, but apparently I needed the sleep after this stressful week. I only remember two and a half of the *Antiques Roadshows*, so I must have drifted off during the third one. It had been really . . . nice. But last night feels far away, and now I wish I were home.

A cute turquoise blanket slides off my lap when I scoot over to make room for Mike. He joins me on the couch instead of making me stagger over to the tiny table in the kitchenette.

When I take my first bite of scrambled eggs, I moan, all awkwardness vanishing with a poof. "Wow. This is so good!"

"Thanks. It's a weird family recipe with a little cream of mushroom soup stirred in."

"Ew, that is weird. And it's amazing." The bacon is a bit chewier than I like, but I'm not complaining. To each his own, and even bad bacon is still good bacon.

We eat quietly, and once the caffeine hits, I feel less muddled and more thankful. "This is so nice, Mike. I didn't even make you coffee when you spent the night. I'm sorry I was rude."

"Clearly you'd already gotten what you wanted from me."

"True, but I still don't think I'm up for hand stuff this morning, if that's what you're angling for."

"Then put down the plate and get the hell out."

I almost blow coffee out my nose at that, but I manage to retain the last shreds of my dignity in the end. He grins at me like he's proud he made me laugh.

"I'm heading out in about thirty," he warns. "I can drop you off and make sure everything's good at your place, if you want."

"No, I feel better this morning, thanks. I'll be fine. I just got spooked."

"Is there a hospital here in town where you work?"

"I'm doing administrative stuff now, so it's mostly from home." It feels strangely thrilling to just drop the truth out there like it's no big deal.

We talk about the pandemic and burnout and what it was like to be on the front lines with people dropping dead in the emergency room every day. I can feel my tension rising at the memories and try to shake them off.

I made a lot of money as a traveling nurse during those years, but that also meant I was smack in the middle of the worst of the crisis. If I run from Santa Cruz, I'll likely have to go back to bedside nursing, and I don't think I'm ready to face that kind of trauma. Those name-calling, combative patients had reminded me far too much of being taunted on the playground. Then there are the gunshot wounds, more frequent and devastating every year. No thanks. I'll hang on to this remote gig as long as I can, but that doesn't mean I can stay here in my favorite town much longer. Not like this.

My mood plummets at the thought, so I'm thankful for the plate of comfort food on my lap. When we finish breakfast I stand to test my knee. There's a slight twinge, but no dull ache or throbbing protest. "Let me run to the bathroom, and then I'll get out of your hair." At least the thought of snooping in his bathroom cheers me a bit.

After locking the door behind me, I rush for the toilet, then find myself assaulted with a gold-framed mirror directly opposite. Yikes! I look like shit; half my hair is flat, and the other half has wrestled itself into a scraggly nest. Despite all my sleep, or maybe because of it, my eyes are slightly puffy. It might all add up to a sensual just-out-of-bed look if not for the tweedy texture of my left cheek. I rub hard at the mark and hope it fades soon.

I'm glad this isn't Mike's actual home, or I'd really have to doubt his sanity. Why would anyone want to stare directly into their own eyes as they poop? Is he haunted by this feature of his new place? Does it torment him every morning? I don't think we're close enough for me to ask.

Once I've carefully washed my bandaged hands and smoothed down my hair, I glance around at the countertop, but Mike is a pretty boring guy. There's sinus spray and toothpaste and sunscreen. A comb and toothbrush and floss. Like I said, boring. Which seems absolutely perfect to me right now. There's no straight razor or bondage gear or anything pointing to danger. Whew.

I rub my stamped cheek one more time, then emerge to find that Mike is already washing the plates. I retrieve my coffee cup from the living room for a last sip.

"Looks like a nice day," I say. "I think I'll walk to the corner later to ask some of the shops about cameras."

"That's a great idea."

I'd filed the report last night on my phone, not that there had been many details to contribute. Someone pushed me. I fell in front of a car. That was about it.

Maybe it *was* an accident. The memory is less visceral now, the feeling of the big hands on my back a fading memory. And the possibility that my brain is broken still hovers at the back of my mind. Am I crazy? My heart beats a little faster at the thought.

I have to be a little crazy, right? To live the way I do? To lie and run and hide? How would I notice if I tipped from a little crazy to a lot?

"Let me know what you hear from the cops," Mike says as he scrubs a frying pan.

"*If* I hear." I bring my cup over and place it next to the sink. "I'll leave and let you get to work. Or I can help dry. If you—" Everything freezes. My words, my breath, my heart, my thoughts. I stare so hard at the little red nightmare perched on the windowsill above the sink that my eyelids tremble.

Mike rinses the pan and slots it into the drying rack right in front of me. I want to step back, to cringe away, but my body has chosen freeze instead of flight, and it thinks if I stay still enough, everything will be okay. Mike won't be dangerous, I won't be cornered. And that damn red devil girl on his windowsill won't be aiming its beady black eyes at me.

She's smirking. I know it's just a toy, but I swear I see her mouth rise at one edge as her eyes narrow. She's mocking me for feeling safe with this fucking stranger I met on the street.

I hear a strange gurgle in my throat, and Mike turns to look at me. I slide one foot back, then manage to shift my body away from him, but I'm caught now.

"What's wrong?" he asks.

Everything, Mike. But you already know that. "You're the one," I grind out past clenched teeth. "You put that thing in my bag."

"What?" He follows my gaze and looks at the devil. "That thing?"

I keep backing up until my ass hits the table.

"I thought you left it for me," he says, shaking his head.

My purse is on the table, so I grab it and sprint for the door. When I bend over to slip on my shoes, I nearly fall into the wall because I'm trying to open the lock at the same time.

"Beth! Hey, what's wrong?"

"You put that thing in my bag," I growl. "That devil doll."

"No! What? It was on the stairs in front of my door when I got home the other night. I assumed it was from you since you're the only one I know here. What are you—?"

But I don't wait for yet another comforting explanation. Another goddamn gaslight about what's going on here. I charge out the door and race down the wooden stairs.

It's him. It all started with him, didn't it? He's always around. Always nearby. Always so much more fucking helpful and patient than any other man in the history of any one-night stand.

"Beth!" he calls from the landing, but he's too late. I'm gone. I'm flying, a knife stabbing into my knee with every step, but I refuse to slow down. I sprint into the street and race down the block toward the safety of my home. I was wrong to turn away from it last night. It's my refuge. My safe space. I should have gone straight home and locked the door against the world.

What the hell am I doing, trusting *anyone*? I know better, damn it. No one has ever rescued me from anything. I'm an outcast. I'm on my own and always have been.

"Hi, Liz!" Mr. Sanchez calls, but I don't even manage a wave before I dodge around a barefoot woman pushing a shopping cart piled with old blankets and boxes. I throw myself at my door and punch in numbers. It takes me three tries, but finally I'm in and slamming the door behind me. I lock it, then drag a kitchen chair over to shove it beneath the knob.

My stomach churns as I turn on every light in the living room, then hurry to the kitchen to do the same. I swallow hard to stop sickness from rising up as I grab a knife from a drawer before lunging to shove open the bathroom door. Nothing. I turn that light on too. Then I tiptoe toward my bedroom.

It's at the front of the house, which isn't unusual here. The backyard is another living area for most of the year, and no one wants guests parading through their bedroom to get outside. But it is a strangely vulnerable feeling, having a bedroom right off a busy street. What if someone saw the darkness in my place last night and broke in? What if they climbed right through the window and crawled under my bed?

I'm stalling, and my stomach only clenches harder, so I force myself to push the door open. I shove my hand into the dim room and sweep the wall until my fingers find the switch.

Click. Light blooms, and there's no one there. And yet . . . I crouch down in the doorway and peer under the bed. Still no one. I'm alone.

But I knew that, didn't I? I left my tormentor behind a few minutes ago.

I retreat to collapse onto my sofa, shivering from the cold, pungent sweat that coats my skin. I'm hot and freezing at the same time, and I can *smell* myself. This isn't the kind of sweat that comes from exercise or heat. This is terror. I've smelled it on patients so many times in so many hospitals.

I can't call the cops. Imagine me babbling about a stuffed animal and a man I went home with even though I thought he might have pushed me into traffic. I don't have any proof, and the most they'll do is roll their eyes. Assholes.

But I need to connect with someone. Anyone. And I only have one person.

I pull out my phone and text Tristan. I've heard his voice. I know he's not Mike or Frank. So I type out part of the story, leaving out this morning's scare, because it's too embarrassing to admit I went home with a stranger in the middle of being stalked.

I filed a police report last night. Someone pushed me into the street in front of a car.

Three dots appear immediately on my screen, and I sigh with relief that he's there.

Oh my God! Are you ok? I can't call right now unless you need me to make it happen.

No, I'm fine. Just spooked. About to jump in the shower and then I need to work anyway.

What happened? Are you hurt???

Not really. Just some scrapes. It could have been much worse, but I'll be ok.

Thank God! Who did it?

It was too crowded to see. Hopefully something will turn up. I swipe a hand across my sweaty face and cringe. I'm gonna get cleaned up. Talk later?

As long as you're sure you're all right???

My lips tremble as I smile. I just needed this moment of connection. To know if I reach out, someone will respond. And he did. I'm all right. Thank you, Tristan.

When my phone dings again, I'm bitterly grateful I never gave Mike my number, because I don't have to jump like a frightened rabbit every time I get a text. In fact, this time I melt, because Tristan sent me a shiny pink heart.

Silly to be so squishy about a tiny thing, but it's just . . . kindness. And my God, I need that right now. "You're okay," I whisper to myself. But am I really? No, I'm not okay. I'm terrified.

"No one can get in here, girl," I whisper. "You're safe." That's true. I'm home now, no longer asleep in an apartment with a man who might be stalking me.

Just to be safe, I open the feed of the doorbell camera next door. It faces the street, so I can see anyone walking past my house or hanging around on the sidewalk nearby. Someone flies by on a bike. Three cars pass. An unleashed dog trots toward a bush and lifts his leg. If Mike were crouching behind that bush, he'd have gotten peed on, but he's not hiding there, and neither is anyone else.

A painfully skinny guy in a beanie eventually walks by, his neck craning as if he's looking for that dog that just passed, but he keeps moving.

After a good three minutes of watching, I give my head a rough shake to clear it. Right now I need a shower and more coffee because I have a full day of work ahead of me. Which is fine. I'm locked up tight, and Mike can't get me in here.

God, could it really be him? His patient kindness actually makes a lot more sense as a stalker ploy than genuine care. It has to be an act.

But why would Mike do this? Who the hell is he?

I try not to think about how vulnerable I made myself last night. I need to calm my thoughts instead of ramping them up. I'll do my work, and then I'll head out to search for security footage from last night. *That* would be something I could show the cops.

Right now all I can say is "This person lied about who he was and slept with me." If that were illegal, I'd be in jail along with a good chunk of the population. My only hope for making him pay is getting him on tape.

CHAPTER 18

The hot spray of the shower feels like a cure for all misery. I brace my hands against the wall and bow my head to let water cascade over me until my skin feels too tight. The pressure in this old house isn't great, but the tiny bathroom traps steam and turns the air into a warm hug.

I scrubbed my entire body with a loofah and extra soap as soon as I stepped in, then washed my hair and soaped up again. My hands have stopped stinging, and now I finally feel clean. Still, my muscles refuse to melt out of their rigidity.

A low-frequency vibration trembles through my skeleton, some bastard child of dread and panic. I'm dealing with danger, yes. Someone tried to harm me. But more terrifying than that is the lack of control.

The lies I tell aren't for fun. They're meant to protect me. To control the uncontrollable: other people. I want to decide how they view me, what they know, what they'll never know. No one gets any part of me unless I volunteer it.

Isn't that how life should be? Shouldn't I have dominion over my one precious self? Otherwise I'm just a struggling animal surrounded by piranhas, nipping and nipping at me until big parts are torn away.

Why the hell is this happening now? Did I invite it by turning into the liar people in Fair Isle always named me? God, it was suffocating, growing up in that town where everyone knew the worst about me. And I couldn't even defend myself, because it was true.

I had lied and then lied some more. I'd put my tiny hand on a Bible and testified in court. I'd sent two innocent people to prison. I'd stood in church and repeated the fictional stories, then let myself be blessed for surviving it. I'd ruined the Hoffholder name and eventually dragged the May name through the mud as well.

A lot of people felt duped and foolish, my parents most of all. I might not have been a bad seed like Jacob, but I'd been an embarrassment whose mere presence reminded folks that they'd behaved terribly too.

It never mattered if things started to die down, if I'd gone weeks without anyone mentioning my past, because it would always come back. My freshman year of high school was the worst, because that year our tiny local theater chose to show *The Exorcist* for the last week of October. It seemed that everyone in my school snuck in to see it.

Hey, Exorcist, weren't you possessed when you were a kid? Was it like the movie?

Bet Elizabeth May fucked herself with a crucifix too!

Show me your tongue, Devil Girl. Let me suck it.

God. I'd finally escaped all that, and I've lived with such beautiful remove since my divorce. No one has glimpsed the whole of me in a long while, because I refuse to let them.

Now this asshole has violated that. Violated *me*.

I can't figure out why Mike would be involved, but more than that, I can't fathom why *anyone* would. I was five, damn it. I was *five*. I get that schoolkids can be cruel, but I'd thought—I'd fantasized—that I'd be safe as an adult. I'd held my breath and gotten through it, and once I left for college, I'd told myself I was free. Then it started up again in my own home, with my own husband.

Because I was that same bullied kid, wasn't I? Still dragging that injury, that weakness, that stench that let the animals know I was the easiest prey in the pack, as if I had a permanent "Kick Me" sign tattooed on my back. But of course it wasn't only kids who were cruel. Hadn't adults been incredibly cruel back then? Hadn't they been stupid and reckless and pushed into a panicked mob by spooky stories?

Because what should have happened back then, what did *not* happen, was when a few kids told insane, impossible tales about their time with the Hoffholders . . . this family who were not strangers—a family who'd been born in Fair Isle and had lived, loved, married, and worked there for their entire lives—a solid, reasonable investigation should have been undertaken. A calm examination would have disproved everything.

There were no missing babies. There was no blood-spatter evidence, no scars on the children, no mysterious cave. None of the photos or videos allegedly taken of ceremonies or sex acts ever turned up. There were no pigs on the Hoffholder property and no stone altar in the cellar. Mrs. Hoffholder's skin was not branded with the mark of the devil, and neither I nor any other kids bore physical evidence of violent sexual torture. Zero children had gone missing from the Hoffholders' care, and no parents had complained of even a hint of abuse.

So why? *Why* had the word of a five-year-old taken precedence over all evidence to the contrary? I realized the answer eventually: The world is an incredibly screwed-up place. Witch hunts have happened since the beginning of time. People are not naturally good. Conspiracies have always helped shore us up, promising answers to our most insidious doubts. Because the truth is that life is hard as hell, and we're desperate to know why. It's so much more comforting to blame Satan than to accept that chaos might destroy us for no reason at all.

I won't let this crap ruin my life again. I need to make a plan to leave. After work today I'll cruise the job postings for traveling nurses. Maybe I could land a stint somewhere quiet with no trauma center full of panicked patients.

But God, I don't want to go back to that. I want to keep my current gig, and if I do, I can't move far away. My company requires that I go in for team meetings twice a month. I could try to find another position as a documentation specialist elsewhere, but that will take time. Months maybe. I need to find a way to be safe in the short term.

I try to picture all the shops on the corner where I was attacked. If I can get security video with Mike in it, I can press charges. That will put a stop to whatever shit he—

My vision goes black. One second I'm staring at the gray tile of my shower, and then everything is gone with a snap. I cry out, reaching to press my palm to the wall and place myself in this impossible darkness. What the hell is happening now? My breath is bursting from me in high whimpers. I'd beg for help, but there's no one else here.

I hope.

The hot water turns warm, then cool. My hand slaps the tile as I try to find the faucet. When I twist it off, the disappearance of the pounding roar is another shock. A drip, drip, drip fills the new silence and reminds me that my other senses are working. I can hear and feel and even smell the scent of soap on my own body.

I've calmed down enough to realize I'm not blind. It's only that the lights went out. Still, goose bumps erupt over me. My body curls in tight to hold in the heat and my soft organs. "Shit," I bite out past the shivering. I need my phone.

My hands pat, pat, pat again, past the cold shower curtain that clings like something black and wet from the sea, something trying to wind around me and drag me under.

When I finally touch softness I yank the towel to me. I wish it were bigger. Wish I had a whole blanket to cocoon into and hide from whatever new threat is descending. What the hell is going on? Am I under attack? Because there are three bulbs in that light fixture, and they didn't all burn out at once.

A few seconds later, my fingers find my phone on the counter, and my vision flares back to life. "Oh, thank God," I wheeze.

That's when I notice that the bathroom fan isn't running. That's why the silence was screaming so loudly at me. My electricity has failed. Or somebody cut it off.

I grab the robe hanging from a hook on the door and shove my arms in. There's no thunderstorm, but maybe workers hit a line or a car crashed into a pole.

But when I'm reaching to twist open the lock, I hear something. The squeak of a door? I jerk my hand from the knob, then press my fingers hard to my mouth when a floorboard pops somewhere close by. There's someone here. There's someone in my house, and they've cut the power.

I hear footsteps, a thump. Another sound. A door closing? In that moment, I regret every scary movie I've ever watched, and I've watched quite a few.

Dropping to the floor, I make myself small and open my phone app to hit 911.

"911, what's your emergency?"

"There's someone in my house," I whisper. "I'm in the bathroom. The power just went out, and I can hear someone moving around."

"You're sure no one is home with you?"

Now that I have the phone pressed to my ear, I can't hear anything beyond this space. Cupping my hand over my mouth, I barely breathe my answer. *"I live alone. Please help."*

The woman confirms my street address and lets me know that the police are on the way. She wants me to stay on the line, but I'm desperate to know who's in my house, so I turn the phone to face me and navigate to the security app. Maybe one of the outdoor cameras caught something. Maybe—Wait. The video feeds transmit via Wi-Fi, and the router has no power.

Another squeak of a floorboard. My throat squeaks too.

"Ma'am? Are you still with me?"

"I'm here," I whisper. "Are they on their way? How long will it be?"

"Someone is en route right now, ma'am. Do you have a dog or a firearm or anything else we should be aware of?"

"No." I close my eyes, willing to give up the sight I'd been so desperate for a few minutes earlier. I breathe and listen and wonder if the bathroom door is about to explode open under the force of a violent kick. I try to stop the high whine leaking from my mouth before I realize the sound isn't coming from me. "I think I hear a siren," I whisper.

"Good. Once the officer is there, are you able to let him in?"

"No, I can't . . ." I swallow hard past the lump in my throat. "I'm afraid to go out there. But there's a keypad. The code is . . ." That's when I remember the chair I wedged under the knob. "No, that won't work. I put something in front of the door. But he can go through the back gate!"

I give her the code to the back keypad and hear her relay it to the officer. Hopefully that means he's nearby.

Breathing softly, I strain my ears for any hint of what's going on. Everything is silent now. Perhaps the intruder heard the siren and fled. Or perhaps he's standing stock still right outside this door, ear cocked and axe at the ready. Oh Christ, I can almost feel him now, the pulse of his heart, the whoosh of his breathing. The—

A hinge squeaks from the other side of the house, and I turn my head toward the sound, toward the promise of that distant back door. Is it the police? Please, please, please let it be a cop. What a sudden change of heart I've had about law enforcement.

I strain toward the wood, and I'm almost sure I hear the crackle of a radio.

"Ma'am?" I nearly jump out of my skin at the 911 operator's voice.

"Yes?"

"Officer Barlow is inside, can you see him?"

Just as she asks, a man's voice says, "Clear," and footsteps draw closer to the bathroom door.

"Just follow his instructions, and I'll end the call."

The knob jiggles right next to my ear, and I'm surprised I don't pee all over myself.

"It's me!" I yell. "I'm hiding in the bathroom."

The footsteps move past, I hear him yell, "Clear!" one more time, and then there's a soft knock. "Open the door slowly."

Cautioning myself not to fling my body out in my desperation to be rescued, I unlock the knob and carefully ease the door inward. A skinny white man in his twenties stares intently at me. The dark threat of a gun is pointed down at the floor and not at my face, thank God.

"Are you all right?" he asks.

I clutch the lapels of the robe tighter and nod. "Did you find him?"

"We didn't find anyone inside, ma'am."

I nod. "Okay, good. I was in the shower and someone cut off the power. I heard movement." When he backs away and motions me out, I follow him toward the living area.

"All right. What did you hear?"

"A door opening, I think. I could hear floorboards popping."

He nods. "Seems like an older home. I assume there's quite a bit of settling."

"Yes, but . . . it wasn't like that. There were footsteps. And the lights were out."

"Officer Che is checking on that now. I'm Officer Barlow." His gaze sweeps up. "Is there a resident upstairs?"

"No. It's an Airbnb. The last guests checked out—" The unmistakable sound of a footfall creaks from directly over my head. Officer Barlow and I both watch the ceiling as the steps move away from us toward the side of the house. "Um," I say just as the muffled murmur of a voice drifts down.

"Perhaps they overstayed their reservation?" he suggests.

"No. I saw them leave. But I don't own the house. Maybe someone checked in last night. Still, I'm confident that's not what I heard." Or I'm almost confident. Aren't I? What if I'm overreacting? Worse, what if I'm hearing things that aren't there?

The power flares back to life, starting the roar of the bathroom fan again as lights pop on all around us. It's far too bright now since I turned on every damn light in the place when I got home.

The cop's radio spits out some garbled message I don't catch, but it's followed immediately by a tap at the front door. "That's Officer Che,"

Barlow starts, but whatever he's about to say dies in his mouth when he spots the wooden chair wedged under the doorknob. The front legs stick out like they're flailing in panic. My heart falls at the sight, and I know exactly what he's about to ask.

"Ma'am, did you put the chair there?"

"Yes," I answer in my calmest, most reasonable voice.

"Because the power went out?"

"No. Um . . ."

He shoots me a look before striding forward to tip the chair and slide it away with a loud screech. When he opens the door, his partner, a young Latino, introduces himself by muttering, "Meter box."

Officer Barlow nods. "Want to tell me what's going on?" he asks, raising his eyebrows at me as he points to the chair.

My mouth goes dry. "Uh, sure. Someone seems to be stalking me. I was pushed into the street last night. There's a report on file." I give him the number.

"You know who pushed you?"

I think of Mike, but how can I be sure? "I didn't see him."

"Mm." His stare is steady and unreadable. "Were you hurt?"

"Not really." I hold up my scraped and healing hands. "But a car had to brake hard to avoid hitting me. Now someone cut my power."

He glances at his partner, who dips his chin in a nod but doesn't speak. "Right," Barlow says. "Looks like your meter box was switched off outside. Not an uncommon prank by bored kids. We've gotten at least a couple of calls this month. I assume you haven't secured it in any way?"

I feel my shoulders start to inch up. "I don't even know what that is."

"There's a main switch on your meter that allows for power shutoff during an emergency. The fire department needs access, but they can cut through a lock if you want to install one."

"Okay, well, someone definitely turned off my power, right? So it could have been a thief or a stalker walking around in here."

"Yes, ma'am, but . . ." He looks at his partner again. "You confirmed there's a guest upstairs?"

Officer Che nods. "The woman says she checked in last night. Were you not aware of that?"

"It's not my rental," I mutter. "But I heard footsteps *down*stairs. I live here. I know what people moving upstairs sounds like."

As if on cue, a floorboard pops and squeaks above me. Then another. We all look up and listen for a moment.

"The guest is a pretty big girl," Officer Che says, adding a healthy dose of fat shaming with his wry tone. "Probably a real heavy tread."

I can feel my face heating as I stare, my eyes burning to a desert as I study the wooden planks above me. "It didn't sound like that. And there have been other things going on. Someone tried to get me fired. Someone left a . . ." I want to stop speaking because it sounds stupid even before it leaves my mouth. "A, um, stuffed animal in my bag. And I think I know who it was."

Barlow clears his throat. "Sounds like you're feeling a bit spooked. Go ahead and get a small lock or even just a zip tie for the meter box."

"Isn't that illegal?" I cry. "To mess with someone's utilities?"

"It isn't legal, you're correct. You could install a security camera if you're concerned. But it doesn't look like anyone came inside. The back door was closed tight when I got here, the windows are locked, and . . ." He gestures to the chair again. "Obviously this door was too. Do you see anything out of place?"

I look around, blinking quickly to try to force some moisture into the dry blur of my eyes. "It looks okay. I think."

"All right then. Be sure to check your window locks again too. We'll file a report. In the meantime . . ." He hands me two business cards. One with his name on it and another with a phone number for local community services. "You should consider a protective order if someone is bothering you."

My heart falls. I have no basis for that, no proof of anything. I willingly spent the night at Mike's house last night, and there's no evidence he's the one who pushed me. Yet. "If you could just look at store security footage from last night. Please." I repeat the incident number again and give him the address where it happened.

I see the glance he exchanges with his partner, a glance that says, *Women, am I right?* "Sure. I'll check into it, ma'am. Please call 911 if you experience an emergency."

Not *another* emergency. *An* emergency. He's not going to check into shit, and I'm alone with this. Again.

CHAPTER 19

Once they leave, I slam the door behind them and scurry to my couch so I can open the security app. The three cameras come back online. The one next door shows the empty backyard patio, and then the front of that house via the doorbell cam. All clear. Even the cop car has vanished. Finally the doorbell cam of the upstairs rental flickers to life, revealing the empty wooden landing above my front door.

I'm normally very aware of anyone going in and out because I can hear the noise of the stairs that lead straight up from the driveway, but I was gone all night. After spying a saved file from forty minutes ago, I open it to see a middle-aged white woman entering the apartment with a shopping bag. That was before I got in the shower. She must have checked in while I was at Mike's.

I open the previous file and see that same person leaving the apartment about two hours earlier. She's wearing a pink windbreaker and a flowered sun hat in both videos. I can't quite tell her age, but she moves easily up and down the stairs, like she's not much older than I am. Forty-five or fifty, maybe. And yes, she looks chubby, but Officer Che didn't have to be rude about it.

The woman was inside the apartment when the lights when out, so it clearly wasn't her that cut the power, and why would she? She's just a guest I didn't see arrive, because I was busy yukking it up all evening with my stalker.

And now the police think I'm an overwrought bimbo imagining danger in every corner. What a fantastic twenty-four hours.

The floor creaks upstairs before I hear the patio door open above me, and the sound makes my shoulders slump. That must have been what I'd heard earlier. The normal movements of a guest above me had felt menacing because of what I've gone through. Because I *was* freaked out, wasn't I? Anyone would be. It's nothing to be ashamed of, it's just . . .

"Gah!" I pound my fist into the couch cushion.

I've been flailing, racing around in a panic, knocking shit over, and managing to slam myself right into danger. I need to gather my wits and stop making things worse.

Cool. I can do that. I'm a goddamn ER nurse. I eat trouble for breakfast. I thrive under pressure and take situations as they come. No more panicking.

When I glance at the clock, I'm shocked by how early it is. Just past 9:00 a.m., and I already feel like I've lived a whole day, and a long one at that. Despite all the sleep I got, I'm exhausted, and despite my shower, I'm covered in sweat again. Well, that's just too bad because I am *not* going back in the shower with visions of *Psycho* rolling on repeat in my head.

I need to work. That's the one thing I have control over at this moment. I'll finish all my files for the day and let my brain puzzle through this shitstorm in the background.

After brushing my hair and throwing on my warmest, coziest sweats, I settle in at the desk and keep the blinds closed for the first time since I moved here.

Of course, once my work portal is open, I find myself staring at it, zoning out.

I really need to order another security camera. Or two. I'll put one right over my front door and one at the back. Paying extra for expedited shipping, I place the order, then return to my work.

But . . . I need to do more research on the Hoffholders. Yeah. And Fair Isle. Is there something going on there that would bring all this up?

I start to open a new browser window, then stop myself. This isn't how Eliza May, nurse extraordinaire, does her job. "Stop," I order myself aloud. "Make a note. Do it later."

Okay, good solution. Sliding things around on my desk until I find it, I pull my notebook out and write, *GET SHIT DONE*, across the top in big letters.

1. Hunt down Jacob Hoffholder.
2. Research Mike.
3. Get security footage from the corner last night.
4. Install new cameras.
5. Kick ass.
6. Take back control, you awesome bitch.

Closing my eyes, I let out a long, soft exhale. This is all doable. I draw in another breath and let it out even more slowly. *Focus. Do your job. Seize the day.* Or something.

Still, I keep the security feed open on my phone to reassure myself, and it works. There's nothing suspicious going on.

The woman above me leaves mid-morning, her long hair swinging as she jogs down the stairs. I hope she's doing something fun. Visiting a sister or maybe even having a little seaside affair.

Normally I'd make a point of introducing myself in hopes of good gossip, but this stalker has ruined even that for me. I'm too unsettled to enjoy talking to strangers. But watching the cameras does comfort me a little. I'm still part of the world even locked inside. He can't take that from me.

Two hours later I'm lost in the depths of a tough childhood leukemia file when I'm startled by movement on the patio camera next door. Just a wisp of motion, there and then gone. The strangeness of it makes my heart beat faster, sending me right back to the anxieties of the morning.

What was that? I keep watching, squinting at the screen. I'm about to give up and look away again when a ghost trails through the very edge of the picture. "What in the world?" I mutter.

After I tiptoe toward the French doors, I slowly part the curtains to peek out. Damn. I can see only the privacy fence, of course. I'll have to go outside. But that's fine. I'm still hidden behind six feet of wood. No one will even know I'm there.

It takes a moment to work up my courage, but I eventually unlock the door and ease it open. Birdsong swells into my space, and a puff of breeze tickles me with the scent of roses. I've been missing out on such a lovely day.

This stalker is slowly confining me, chipping away at my life, my freedom. Just a few days ago, I was lounging out here like the queen of the patio, and now I've locked myself inside. An ember sparks to life inside me. A fury.

I charge out and put my face to the fence to look through.

For a moment, I see only the table and empty chairs, the folded umbrella and coiled green hose. There's no one there. I start to withdraw when that white phantom catches the edge of my vision once more. Is it a flapping pigeon? A gull? A ghost?

Squinting, I press my face back to the wood, staring, waiting. A thump behind me makes me jerk so hard I bump my nose against the fence as my heart explodes with panic. I whip around, hair catching at a splinter and popping bright spots of pain through my scalp as I raise my hands to shield myself from attack.

A fat orange cat sits primly next to a broken flowerpot I keep meaning to replace. "Jeeves! You scared the hell out of me!"

Jeeves blinks sleepily in answer. He belongs to a family several houses down and makes himself at home anywhere he pleases. Normally I'm thrilled when he comes to visit, but now I'm imagining how often he'll set off the alert on my new camera when it comes. Oh well. Not his fault.

When I put my eye back to the slats, a man is staring right at me from a foot away. "Ahh!" I shriek, stumbling back and sending Jeeves flying over the fence.

"Sorry!" the man calls. "I heard talking."

"Oh. Just . . ." Shit. I've been caught spying. "Sorry! Yeah, I thought I heard someone over there too."

"That was me! I'm John."

John? Like John Doe? But this John is Asian, and there weren't any Asian people in Fair Isle, so I can't imagine he has anything to do with my past. "I'm Bess," I offer, then I recover from my shock and clear my throat. "Let me know if you have any questions while you're staying here!"

"Are you our host?" he calls.

"No, just a long-term renter. But I'm happy to hand out recommendations on anything. Nice to kind of meet you!"

"You too. We checked in late last night. We'll definitely ask if we need help! Thank you!"

When I hear him move away, I put my eye back to the space and see white curtains billowing from the open door as John speaks to someone inside. The curtains. That was what I kept seeing. I've never noticed them flying around before, probably because I was never so on edge.

Another man appears, a white man in a wheelchair. He doesn't seem interested in me, because he says something low to John, and they both disappear inside.

Probably not my stalker if he's in a wheelchair. Or could that just be a cover meant to distract me?

"Lady," I mutter, "you really are losing it." Maybe the cops were right to blow me off. I'm making connections where there are none. After all, one of my most recent scares—the man banging on my door—had nothing to do with me. Maybe that same man cut off the electricity as petty revenge against Grigore. Could he even have been the one who pushed me? I gasp at the thought. My attacker could be a vengeful criminal who thinks I'm Grigore's girlfriend!

"Okay," I say, "that actually makes a lot of sense."

I pull out my phone to text Grigore. Someone cut off electricity to the house a few hours ago. It's fixed now. But could it be that guy who threatened you last week?

No, Grigore responds immediately. He's no longer in town. You ok? The house ok?

I nod to myself. I am okay. I really am. As confident as Grigore might feel, he can't be that sure about the guy.

Determined to get back on track, I make myself a sandwich and add baby carrots and grapes to my plate, half proud of myself for using my fresh groceries and half ashamed I'm eating like a second grader. But hey, it's cheaper than calling for takeout.

I use my lunch break to google Mike Brocus. The idiot let me see his last name on his calendar app, and I'm immediately grateful it's so distinctive, because everything that pops up has to do with his environmental work. He wasn't lying about that. There are even pictures of him at conferences, with his bio included.

He is from Ohio. He is a scientist. He does have a dog named Princess, because, even though no social media account reveals itself, I find Mike in a photo for a man-on-the-street interview in a Portland weekly. I force myself not to smile at the photo of him holding a scruffy brown dog. Princess.

After enlarging a work photo, I study his face. Could Mike actually be Jacob Hoffholder? He'd probably want to leave his name and past behind as much as I did. More, even.

Jacob was just a scrawny white boy with straight brown hair, and teenage Mike could likely be described that way too. But Jacob's ears stuck out more than Mike's. I remember that one feature. Still, after a growth spurt and thirty years of time passing? I guess I have no idea what Jacob might look like as a grown-up, but I could swear his nose was thinner, like a sharp blade.

God, none of this makes sense. Mike is a career scientist, so he wouldn't need to hire himself out as some sort of proxy stalker.

I sit up straight in my chair. What about his ex-wife? Could *she* be Lauren Jensen? Is he still in love with her? Maybe they divorced and he hates her so much he's transferred those feelings to . . . me?

"That's stupid," I say aloud. And it is. But even knowing I'm slipping deep into an illogical rabbit hole, I try searching for Lauren Jensen again. I can picture her face so much more clearly than Jacob's because I'd gawked up at her with awe for many weeks. And Lauren didn't disappear like Jacob did, so I even know what she looked like in high school.

I search for *Lauren Jensen Iowa* and ignore the hundreds of results to click the images filter.

Zap. A bolt of electricity sizzles through me when I meet Lauren's blue eyes in the third photo. "Oh my God," I whisper. There she is. Still beautiful. Still blond and lean, though her teeth are bigger and whiter, as if she got veneers somewhere along the way.

She's in her forties now, her face longer without the baby fat, and her smile seems to take up the whole width of it. Wow.

My heart twists. I hope that smile means she moved on from all this. But she'd always had confidence going for her. If she was bullied after the trial fallout, I never saw it. She'd already had school friends and a community identity *before* the scandal. She'd already carved a place for herself in our little town. Later on, people called her brave for being the one to step forward and admit the truth. She'd moved through the world confident and sure of herself, and the world had made space for her.

I'd had no identity yet, so one had been forced onto me. Maybe if my parents had taken me to an ethical psychologist when I was young . . . Hell, if they'd just talked to me, showed sympathy, addressed the giant elephant in our family room even once . . . but no. They'd been big believers in silence and sweeping discomfort under the rug. They were embarrassed, ashamed, confused, humiliated. So I was too.

I'd definitely been jealous of Lauren's embrace by the town. And so, so bewildered. But somehow I'd never been mad at her, even though she brought me into the entire fiasco. I think . . . I think I just turned all that hatred on myself.

And how do I feel about her now? Well, now I know she was a kid too, and Jacob manipulated her, maybe even sexually abused her. I was too young to be clear on the details. But really, we were all kids, and the adults were to blame.

Curious, I click on Lauren's photo, and it leads to a listing for a house in Des Moines that sold in 2018. Lauren Jensen was the real estate agent. After hitting the link for her information, I wait impatiently for her bio on her agency's site to load, but all that pops up is a 404 error.

Shoot. She must have changed companies. I go back to square one and add Des Moines to my search.

Lots of closed home listings appear, which makes me think she must be pretty damn successful. Of course she is. She's Lauren Jensen.

She certainly doesn't seem like a woman who'd be stalking me. And why? It was her lead I followed through this whole thing, even the recanting. Maybe I could contact her? The idea goes against every step I've put into leaving my past behind, but she might have more insight than I do.

I click on a listing from 2020, hoping it will lead me to a new agency and a phone number I can call if I feel brave enough. But it's the same company, so I click back.

That's when I see the obituary.

CHAPTER 20

A shock jolts through me, piercing deep and leaving an ache where it hits. "No," I whisper.

This can't be right. It's an obituary for one of her parents, or a grandparent, even. But that's Lauren's picture next to the link. It's different from her work photo, less posed and more dynamic. The smile is the same, though. That impossibly wide smile that promises good things if you get anywhere near her.

Hand trembling, I click on the link.

Lauren Grace Jensen, beloved daughter, 1980–2024

I cover my face, pressing hard until my scraped palms burn from the salt of my tears.

Why am I crying? I barely knew Lauren, hadn't seen her in decades, and this week is the first time I've really thought of her in ages. I haven't earned any grief here. Yet somehow I feel like I've just watched her die, like I opened my door and found her crumpled on the sidewalk.

I hadn't realized what a *glow* Lauren had been in my life until this moment. A faint hint of strange color on my horizon, always there and never noticed. Lauren Jensen and everything she set in motion was the first solid memory of my existence. She changed the course of my life so completely that I have no sense of who I was before her.

With my eyes closed, I can see her as she must have been: vibrant and laughing, driven and strong. And then I see that smile open into a scream as someone pushes her into traffic. For her, the car doesn't stop in time.

My insides go taut and trembling. I force my eyes open and shake my head. That didn't happen. That's not how she died, and this isn't about me. It was cancer or an aneurysm or some tragic accident.

I review the obituary carefully, but there are no clues there, no requests to donate to a medical charity or hints about how sudden her death was. She was survived by her father and an older sister, she loved her cat, and she was known for her nonstop energy and drive to always do more.

I'm wiping away a tear when I see an option to share memories. One click, and the page unfolds into a revelation: many, many comments from people who knew Lauren far better than I did.

Most of them share happy stories and remembrances of better days, but there's a thread of regret running through the comments too.

> I'm so sorry I wasn't there for her.
>
> We had to cancel plans a month ago, and I forgot to reach out again. I let Lauren down, and I'm struggling to deal with that.
>
> I can't understand what happened!
>
> We should have believed her.
>
> I wish I'd known she was suffering.

"Oh no," I whisper into the knuckles I've pressed to my mouth. Did she kill herself? That's the only explanation for a few of these posts. "Oh God, Lauren. I'm so sorry."

Another bolt of pain. This one settles in with the stink of guilt, so I can't imagine what her family and friends felt, people who actually knew her. What agony they must suffer. Even I wonder if I could have helped her if I'd reached out. We were probably the only two people in the world who could understand what we went through back then. Maybe the past finally caught up and she couldn't hold it at bay.

And if the chaos and guilt of the past might have been too much for Lauren, does that mean it's inevitable for me too? Did that seed of trauma grow in her until it overwhelmed everything else and sucked her under? Is that what's happening to me?

I scrub a rough hand over my face and scold myself. *This isn't about you and your overactive imagination. This is about her.*

"Poor Lauren," I breathe. I don't want to think about it anymore, so I close every tab in my browser and reopen my work window. Whatever I'm enduring, it's obviously nothing compared to the demons Lauren wrestled with. Maybe she didn't outrun the past. Maybe guilt and regret caught up to her in the end. But that doesn't mean I'm losing my mind.

I manage to ignore the anxiety beating at my soul like a moth for another five hours. By the time I finish work, my eyes are gritty and my back aches. But my day isn't over. I need to drum up the courage to leave my reinforced nest and track down surveillance video.

Clouds have moved in, and I can hear leaves rustling outside the window, so I dress for a chill, donning jeans and a gray sweater before I pull a knit cap low on my head. It's probably overkill, but I feel warm and armored and nearly anonymous.

I grab a small can of pepper spray that's been floating around in my junk drawer for years; then I check through the blinds several times before opening my door. All clear. I hear bass music from a truck passing and a group of kids on a trampoline, screaming like wolverines, but I don't spot anyone watching me.

After booking it out to the sidewalk, I turn right, away from Mike's place, then hang another fast right at the corner to get to a busier street.

The crowd is what put me in danger last night, but I won't make the same mistake again. No standing in groups and no waiting at the curb. Still, I know there's nothing more dangerous for a solitary woman than running a gauntlet of vehicles and shadowed doorways in a quiet neighborhood. I divide my time between scanning the sidewalk in front of me and snatching quick looks behind to be sure I'm not followed. I see nothing, not even a biker or someone walking their dog.

Only one person is a danger to me; the rest of them will help keep me safe, which is why I breathe easier when I make it to an area with other pedestrians. A glance around reveals no one I recognize, so I hurry toward the intersection where I almost died.

Once I'm on that corner—four feet back from the street—I examine the different storefronts, and hope fills me up. There are at least eight good choices as far as sightline. First I try the boba tea shop, but the young teenager behind the counter gives me a blank look and says the manager is in a couple times a week if I want to try again. Not hands-on, I guess.

Next, I hit up a surf shop, but I'm told their only camera is at the register. The pizza place is a chain, and the manager says he needs to get permission from corporate. The guy at the vape store shrugs and checks the cameras for me, but the exterior shot is aimed the other way and doesn't get anywhere near the corner.

My hope has blown away on the damp wind by the time I make it across the street to the sushi place. The hostess looks concerned when I tell her what happened, and she immediately rushes to get the owner. He's a frail old man who doesn't speak much English, but the hostess explains in Japanese what happened, and he eagerly waves me toward the kitchen, his hunched back a slow guide in front of me. He ushers me into a tiny office and pulls a chair next to his so I can see the screen.

"What time?" he asks, then immediately begins clicking around on a screen that shows three live videos. When he enlarges the front feed, my pulse leaps to a gallop. It's a perfect shot showing the exact spot where I stood.

This evening only one person is on the corner, a vape in one hand, a skateboard in the other. But after a few more mouse clicks, a dozen people appear like ghosts from last night. Another click, and the crowd swells even larger, and there I am, sprawled on the ground. The car slides toward my face, my head, my spread hands. Then it jerks to a stop.

The old man makes a distressed noise at the sight. My throat is a solid block, so my internal shriek doesn't escape.

"Oh," he sighs. "Are you okay?"

"I'm okay," I croak. "Thank you." I show him my scabbed hands. "Already better."

He backs up the feed a few minutes, and now I'm upright and squeezing past the busker's audience, my face a serene blur. If I was hoping for a clear shot of my assailant's features, I'm not going to get it at this distance. Still, I know what Mike was wearing last night.

Holding my breath, I watch as my head turns to study the lights of the boardwalk. My foot taps to the music. I look up. And then I'm flying.

Okay, not really. It's much less dramatic than it felt. I lurch forward, hands reaching, and then I'm down. "Can you back it up?"

I watch again, forcing my eyes away from the fall I want to view over and over again. Instead I study the faces and movement just behind me. I see something dark shift behind my head and focus on that. But in the video, when my head lurches and drops, whoever is standing behind me turns away at the same moment. I see sunglasses, a dark jacket, dark ball cap, maybe the edge of a black mask along his jaw. Two hands lower, a head turns, and then the person is absorbed into the crowd. Judging by the wide, sturdy shoulders, it's a man.

"Again?" the gentleman beside me asks.

"Please."

It's the same thing. The shove, the pivot, the vanishing. Now that I'm watching closely, I see a pale strip between his ear and the ball cap. Shaved head or blond hair, I can't tell.

I turn my eyes toward the edges of the crowd, waiting for this monster to shoot out on either side, but that doesn't happen. He must have walked straight back toward the ice cream shop and past the bar where I'd had dinner.

On the video, I'm helped up by the people around me, and the car hesitates before pulling away.

"Once more?"

"No, wait," I murmur.

People talk to me and then move away. I drift to the side toward an empty area. The police officer joins me. And then . . . then Mike materializes on the left edge of the video, right in the middle of the street, crossing from the other side. He's not wearing a dark jacket or hat, his hair isn't shaved or blond, and my assailant didn't move in that direction when he left.

It wasn't him. Whatever else might have happened, Mike didn't push me.

Heat starts in my core and spreads out from there. A burning humiliation over how I behaved this morning. And last week. And the day after we met.

It isn't Mike doing this. It can't be.

Shit. What had he said about the devil girl doll?

"Again?"

I'm so lost in thought that I startle at the man's question. But I nod and watch again for a dark hat and jacket. I glimpse the man just after I move to the curb to wait. He's following in my wake, which means I can only see the very edges of him behind me. Oh God, if he was following me then, is he following me tonight? My pulse speeds to a flutter.

"Can you save this," I ask, "so I can have the police look at it?"

He nods. "I'll send email?"

"Yes! Email me. And I'll send it to the police. Is that okay?"

"No problem," he answers.

I give him my email address, and he saves a good ten minutes of the file and sends it off. "Thank you so much. You've been wonderfully helpful." After hearing so many noes today, I have to blink back tears of gratitude.

As I shake his hand, I offer a couple of small bows and then make my way back to the street. A misting of rain drifts down, wetting everything while barely hitting the ground. Tonight this looks like a different town. A few scattered people hurry by, but all the outdoor dining tables are empty. I toss a regretful look toward Mike's lopsided metal table. He really had been minding his own business and eating shitty kabobs.

So who the hell pushed me?

CHAPTER 21

I know I should check with other businesses, but I'm overwhelmed after watching the assault and scared the stalker might be nearby. Maybe I'll try again tomorrow. Or maybe I can even get the police to do their jobs? Yeah, right.

Walking away, I feel paranoid on the sidewalk all alone, afraid I'll get snatched into a doorway or alley.

I spot two nicely dressed people walking through a familiar door on the next block, and I perk up and hurry toward one of my favorite places in all of Santa Cruz. After getting close enough to see into the huge front window, I nod. Perfect. I can keep my back to a wall and see anyone before they get near me while I gather my courage for the walk home.

Reading at 7:00 tonight! the board outside the door reads. The laminated printout of the book cover promises some sort of epic history tome, but I'll take anything. Bright chatter swells over me when I open the door.

It's a solid crowd for a book reading. People are beginning to fill up the rows of chairs in front of the lectern, but I scoot past them and find a spot in a back corner. I can see a huge area of the store from here, and there is nothing but a bookshelf at my back.

When someone circulates with tiny cups of white wine, I take one gratefully and settle in. It's such a relief to feel in control for a moment. I'm surrounded by life, by chatter, by smiling people who don't even notice me. The gray evening has darkened the scene outside the window prematurely, and I could be anywhere: New York, Seattle, San Francisco. Should I run to one of those places? Would I be better hidden in a bigger city, or more exposed? At this point, I'm not sure. God, I'm not sure of anything.

Soon enough, the couple seated in the back row of chairs starts arguing, and it's a welcome distraction from the dark streets waiting outside. The man and woman sitting two feet in front of me look to be in their seventies, but the woman's overly plumped lips and huge blond wig make it hard to be sure. "It's just not worth the expense," she says. "The kids will sell the house before we're even cold in our graves, and frankly, that could be any day now."

"Sure, but I'll use it until then."

She rolls her eyes. "You can walk as much as you want on the trails around here for exercise. Run at the beach. Why a home gym? Are you having another affair?"

Wide-eyed, I press my lips tight together to keep from gawking too openly.

The man growls low in his throat. "Jesus, Margaret, I'm too old for that shit."

"Men are never too old for that shit," she snaps back. "But you've probably aged out of your preferred sexpot range, so maybe it's not fun anymore."

The argument is strangely comforting. Everyone has problems. Everyone is struggling. And I'm still a part of this big, chaotic world.

"You can use it too," the man says. When his wife glances at him, he clarifies. "The gym."

"Oh good. I thought you meant your road-worn penis." I almost spit out my wine at that.

"I just want a rowing machine and a treadmill," he snaps.

"We live at the damn beach, Hank. Row in the water!"

When Hank huffs and starts to rise, I spin to face the shelf and fumble frantically for a book, all the while mouthing, *Oh my God, oh my God,* to myself. After a few seconds I peek over my shoulder and see Hank fifteen feet away, speaking with another man.

Margaret idly pages through the book being featured tonight, but then she glances back to meet my eyes. I don't bother looking away. I've been thoroughly caught.

Her gaze shifts to my hands, searching for a ring, perhaps. "Don't ever get married, honey."

"Oh, no worries," I blurt. "I love 'em and leave 'em."

"It's the only good way to do it."

"Thank you," I say primly. I put the book back on the shelf, toss my empty cup, and slide away to track down the wine bearer.

"Ellie?"

I crane my neck, looking toward the coffee/wine bar at the other side of the shop. I really hate to expose myself more by heading that way, but a real glass of wine would—

"Ellie!" A hand touches my elbow, and I jump. "How are you?"

It's only Hilda, the owner of the store. I'm surprised she could sneak up on me since she's wearing her usual fifty metal bangles. "I'm great!"

I give her a hug because she's a hugger, taking the chance to look over her shoulder and scan the bookstore once again. No one is watching, so I close my eyes and breathe. Hilda is only an acquaintance, but this is a moment of caring I really need. She's a great hugger. And when was the last time I was hugged? My God, I can't even remember. Four months ago when Mary at the hospital wished me a happy birthday?

"Good turnout tonight, Hilda," I say when she finally releases me. "I'm so glad I wandered by."

"It's a great day for a night in, isn't it? And he's such a good writer. Have you read him before?"

"I don't think so."

"Well, read this one. You won't regret it. Oh, let's get you a glass of wine!" She raises a hand to wave at a young man behind the bar. I almost whoop when I see him filling a full glass for me. Score!

"How's your book coming, sweetie?" she asks.

It takes me a moment to remember the story I'd spun for Hilda last year. I'm too frazzled to keep up with my personas. But finally it comes to me: I'm an aspiring novelist with a boring office job. "Oh, you know. Revise, revise, revise! I've stalled out at about ninety pages, so who knows if I'll ever finish."

"You can't fix what you don't write. You know that. Stop mucking around and put new words down. Everyone has a story to tell. I mean, you spent five years living in a Midwestern commune, Ellie! Who wouldn't want to read your take on a mystery novel?"

Who, indeed? I'd certainly pick up that book. And I sometimes wonder if I truly could be a writer. I'm great at weaving stories, aren't I? I give her another hug and try not to sink too desperately into her comforting softness as her bangles chime against my arms. "Thanks, Hilda. You're the best."

She gives me one last, lovely squeeze. "I'm going to organize a writing group at some point, I swear. You'll come, right?"

"I will," I promise, and I mean it. I'd bet the other members would be happy if I only talked about their work and never brought my own. It would probably be a blast. And maybe it would inspire me to try?

Ugh. No. The idea of putting creative work out there for mockery and critique makes me queasy.

But it doesn't matter. I need to make a plan to leave Santa Cruz. Tomorrow, I promise myself. Tomorrow when I don't feel like one more straw piled on my back will be the breaking point.

"How's your mom settling in at her new place in Florida?"

"Oh, she's great!" I lie. "Absolutely loving the heat."

"You're going to visit soon, I hope?"

"Yes, she's already found a little art museum she's dying to show me. I'll go in the fall, though. I prefer seventy-five over ninety-five any day. But she'll make lots of cool plans. I can't wait."

I don't think my mom has ever been to a museum. She has no respect for creativity, or "dillydallying," as she called artsy projects for school. And I don't think she'd want me to come visit either.

I went home for two weeks after my college graduation, and she just seemed confused over why I was there. *I don't understand why your apartment isn't ready,* she'd said twice, and what was hard to understand about waiting for the previous tenants to move out?

What she'd meant was *We're done raising you and you're an embarrassment. Go away.* She'd sounded nearly as bewildered by my occasional phone calls later in life. The greeting every time had been *Elizabeth? Is everything all right?*

Which is funny. Because it would never occur to me to call her for help. Not then and certainly not now. My parents are strictly "pull yourself up by your own bootstraps" in their beliefs. Hilda would offer me way more help if I asked. A bittersweet wave of affection for her washes over me. Or maybe it's straight-up pain. Whatever. We can't all be born into the right families, can we?

The boy finally brings the wine to Hilda, and she passes it to me. "You're coming to next month's book club, right?"

"I wouldn't miss it for the world," I lie. I know I'll be long gone by then. Will Hilda miss me? Will anyone?

Hilda waves at someone else and excuses herself, and I retreat back to my safe little hiding spot, my tummy aching a bit with regret.

Hilda's such a nice person. So many people here are.

I don't want to leave Santa Cruz. I've never had a network of almost friends in my life. They might not know me, not really, but I know them, and this time if I vanish like a ghost, I'll leave pieces of my soul behind.

We can't always get what we want. Sometimes we can't *ever* get what we want. But what if I want to stay and try? Is that even possible? I'm not sure, but for the first time in my life, I feel a strange, hard kernel of bravery lodge somewhere in my chest.

What if I simply decide not to run? What if I could find a way to stay?

CHAPTER 22

Hilda was right. It was a fantastic reading, and I buy the book despite its steep twenty-nine-dollar price tag. It'll be worth it if I can lose myself in the Napoleonic Wars for a few weeks, and honestly, maybe it'll help put my troubles into perspective.

Full dark looms outside, so I retrieve my pepper spray from my purse before stepping out the door. The street disappears into mist when I turn my head to check for anyone around. I usually enjoy the eerie trepidation that comes with fog, but today I don't want extra spookiness. Then again, it is a good camouflage.

Deciding to use it to my advantage, I take off at a jog. Anyone trying to follow me will lose sight within seconds. Fog swirls around me, and I suddenly thrill with the exhilaration of it, of feeling strong and wily again, darting through the night like a ghost. I feel slightly unhinged, which is more like myself than I've felt in days.

"Fuck off," I mutter as I run and run, my legs burning. I run for long minutes before I skid to a stop to pivot into a recessed doorway. I wait there, panting, pepper spray clutched in my hand as I anticipate seeing a dark figure walk past my hiding spot. Or is that hope?

A need for violence surges through me, blooming like a bloody rose. My mind plots it. Step out, spray him, take a picture of his wincing, crying face for proof, then punch his nose, kick his jaw. I know exactly what a broken nose and broken teeth look like, and for a moment I'm exhilarated by the thought of inflicting that amount of damage and no less.

But nobody comes. Have I lost him? My pulse calms and so does that rush of aggression. I'm probably not being followed at all.

Still I think about the way he slid up behind me at the corner. He'd come from the same direction I did, so was he at the bar with me? Did he watch as I chatted up Beret? Did he listen?

I feel exposed by the thought, which is silly. He already knows so much about me. But whatever he knows, he didn't hear it from my mouth or my heart, and I don't ever want him to.

After forcing myself to wait a full five minutes, I peek out and look around. A car drives by, the headlights sliding solid white tubes through the air before they're swallowed by the night. If he was ever here, he's lost in the fog now.

Smirking, I ease out of the doorway and disappear myself like the headlights. Disappear like the phantom I am.

I keep close to the buildings and slink along, just another weirdo on these streets.

Speaking of being weird, I should text Mike an apology when I get home. I want to ask what exactly happened with the devil girl. But after that, I'll cut off communication. First, to protect myself from his inevitable withdrawal after dealing with my bizarre behavior. Second, to protect him, because apparently my stalker knows who he is and where he's staying. I can't drag more people into this.

Relief pierces me at the idea of excising him from my life. Except relief doesn't normally pierce, does it? I shove the sharp pain away and walk faster.

A woman's face suddenly looms out of the dark, staring. I jerk to a halt, head pulling back as I cringe away. I raise the pepper spray as an afterthought, my body doing what it thinks it can to help, but the woman only watches impassively with blurry eyes and a mouth that's just starting to smile.

It's me.

My face.

On a flyer.

Stapled to a utility pole.

Below the color picture of my face are three bold lines of text: ***Have you seen me? I'm Elizabeth May, known liar. Don't believe a word I say.*** Beneath that my phone number is listed.

A cry bursts from my mouth, and I lunge forward to tear the flyer off the pole. The paper is soggy and slumps willingly into my hand when I pull it from the staples. As I'm balling it up, an alarm blares in my brain, and I whip around with a cry, sure someone is there. *Right* there. Waiting for me even after I lurked so triumphantly in my hiding place.

No, I seem to be alone on the street. *Seem* to be, because he could very well be watching from a parked car.

With another small cry, I break into a run and make it to the next street corner, but as I turn to move toward home, my face greets me at that intersection too, this flyer taped to a stop sign.

I yank it down and sprint. Only one and a half more blocks and I'll be home. But what does that even mean? There's no protection from this. My worst sin. My biggest shame.

I pass another utility pole, and there I am again. *Elizabeth May, known liar.*

A fingernail breaks when I rake my hand down this flyer before tearing it into three pieces. I leave two corners of it dangling and crumple the incriminating bit into my other fist. Another corner, another flyer, another face. I hate that face. I hate myself. And now I'm panting as I rip it from the stop sign and race toward safety.

But once my foot hits the cracked concrete of my own driveway, I don't run to my door. I can't, because from here I can see another flyer glowing in the dark ahead of me, the white standing out beneath a streetlight even in the fog. It screams at my neighbors that I'm exactly the freak I am.

Grunting like a frustrated bull, I charge down my block to the next corner and tear that paper off too.

"Oh God," I groan. "Oh God." They're everywhere.

I swing my head wildly, dizzy with this new assault. To my left I see the muted shape of a man halfway down the block, staring at something white on a utility pole. Staring at *me*. Is it him? Is it my tormentor?

I take off, even as some rational voice deep inside tells me to calm down, slow down. *What are you going to do, shove that man to the ground? Kick his face?*

Maybe. Maybe I fucking will, because I feel fully capable right now.

But I see the red beret then. The damp, matted tails of white hair. And before I'm even halfway there, I watch the back of his weathered hand reach up and tear the flyer down for me.

"Oh," I sob, slowing my headlong rush toward him. Beret turns at the sound, and I see another scrap of paper in his other hand, a second flyer, and that's what breaks me. He's trying to help.

I choke up, my feet slowing until I'm stopped on the sidewalk, trying to hold in sobs. "Thank you," I manage to get out. *"Thank you."*

I wish I knew his real name, but even now he doesn't speak a word. He only nods, his mouth twisting in a sympathetic grimace, and then he sets off toward the next street at a shuffle.

There's no going home now. If Beret is out here trying, I have to try too, even though I know it's hopeless. I can tear down every last flyer, and what will that help? These pictures of me can go back up as quickly as they come down.

Mike will see them. Mr. Sanchez. Esmerelda. Hilda. Everyone.

And where did this picture even come from? It's my current hairstyle, and the yellow shirt is the one I ruined with the smoothie. Did my stalker take pictures of me while I was shopping?

Shuddering at the thought, I circle the block so I can make my way closer to Mike's place without actually passing it. I pull down two more flyers, but by the time I get home I've passed several blank poles. Maybe between Beret and me, we got them all.

But what comes next? And how the hell am I supposed to live with it?

CHAPTER 23

Big surprise, I didn't sleep well.

I got the first text around 9:00 p.m. Is this Elizabeth May, KNOWN LIAR? 😂

At first, I was frozen with fear, but it slowly sank in that this probably wasn't the stalker. It was just some asshole who'd seen one of the flyers. I deleted it and blocked and tried to move on. But my phone rang half an hour later.

Though I didn't answer, a voicemail alert chimed soon after, and I couldn't stop myself from listening. *Hey, sexy. I like your picture. Why don't I come give you the railing of your life? You're apparently good at lying, so your man won't need to know. Unless you want me to pound you right in front of him. Would you like that? Would you—*

Grimacing in disgust, I deleted and blocked that asshole too. Why are there so many sick men in the world?

Damn it. Clearly Beret and I missed some flyers.

When I got the first dick pic, I made a deep dive into my phone settings and muted all unknown callers and texters. Things calmed down after that.

I managed to fall into a fitful doze around midnight, but something woke me at four. A door closing, perhaps upstairs, perhaps in my dreams, but I sat bolt upright in bed, heart like a rocket ship leaving Earth.

I tried to tell myself that my address wasn't included on the flyer and that Grigore's name is the only one on file for this property, but I knew there was no chance of falling back to sleep. I tried to watch *Antiques Roadshow*, but my mind kept wandering to awful things, including guilt over the way I treated Mike, so I gave up and opened my work portal.

Five hours later I've gotten most of my work out of the way for the day, and I decide I need to leave the house to search for errant flyers while the sun is bright. I don a big hat for disguise and some running shoes in case I need to bolt, and I set out.

One flyer flutters on the pole of a traffic light near the river, but that's the only sighting until I get to Front Street. I find one on a stop sign, one taped to the door of a closed art gallery, one on the side of my favorite pizza place. The ink has run on many of them, but that only makes my picture more grotesque, more horrifying.

Standing there in the middle of the sidewalk, I'm surrounded by businesses likely all equipped with security cameras that caught proof of this monster, but what can I do? Papering a lie everywhere might be libel, but posting the truth about someone? Yeah, no one is getting arrested for that. And there's nothing inside me brave enough to walk one of these flyers into a store and show it to a stranger.

No one will care. The cops haven't even responded to the video I sent of a man pushing me in front of a car. And I am a liar. I am.

My joints and mind creak, rusty with shock as I walk stiffly to the next corner. When I reach it, I turn to the big community board attached to a local theater. There I am, my face multiplied and peppered among the posters advertising band gigs and upcoming plays. A local run of *Splendor in the Grass*, an acoustic open-mic night next Tuesday, and, by the way, Elizabeth May is a known liar! All of it right there for the entire town to peruse at their leisure.

I'm not racing to tear them down anymore. I'm too numb and clumsy for that, too beaten down. But I trudge to the board and pull off one, two, three flyers. I'm reaching for a fourth when a hand touches my shoulder.

"Betsy?"

Whipping around, I press my back to the wall, ready for an attack. A figure looms, silhouetted by the sun, and all I can see is someone tall and broad-shouldered, a hand hovering close to me.

"Hey," the figure says in a soothing tone that could be kind or could be a trick to get past my defenses. But then they lean forward, and I see dark skin and a short fade, a nose ring and perfect eyebrows, and it's Violet, my favorite librarian.

"Oh!" I gasp. "Violet! It's you."

"Are you okay?" she asks.

My bark of laughter is so loud it startles both of us, and I guess that's as good an answer as any. Her eyes go to the last flyer left on the board, and she tips her head toward it. "I can only assume this is about that library book you claim someone stole from your patio last year."

Her smile is so kind, her eyes so understanding, that I find myself smiling back. But I can't see much through the blur of my tears. "I don't think that's it," I manage to rasp.

She nods. "Yeah. I was actually thinking it's some asshole man you pissed off. Am I getting warmer?"

"I . . ." Some of the suffocating tightness of my chest eases. I've been so wrapped up in actually being a liar that I haven't considered other people might see the papers as an assault instead of guilt. Not *me* as the freak, but the person putting this crap all over town. Maybe, just maybe, it's not as devastating as I think. Is that possible?

Violet reaches out to carefully rub my upper arm. "Do you have time to sit down? Get a coffee? Looks like you've had a rough fucking morning."

Oh God, it has been a rough morning and rough night and rough week. But I can only assume that Violet, Black and queer, has had rougher spells than I have in life, and faced more menace than this too. I can't put this dumb shit on her.

But she tips her head to the side. "Yeah, I can see you're considering that coffee. Come on. I'm buying." Just as I'm stepping away, she shakes her head, darts past me, and yanks the last flyer down. "Goddamn bullshit," she growls before balling it up and tossing it into the nearest trash can. I do the same with the papers in my hand, then follow her down the block to a vegan coffee shop that, as a dedicated carnivore, I've never been to. But at this point I'll drink the hell out of an oat-milk latte for Violet.

I've lied to her too, of course. She thinks I'm a vet tech from Texas with a romance novel addiction, and only part of that is true. I do love a good romance novel. And I could definitely be a vet tech if I wanted, since I've done a lot of the same procedures on humans that they do on pets. I'm not from Texas, of course, but I've lived there several times over the years.

Is that close enough to the truth? No, it's not. But I try to stuff my guilt down as we order our drinks and grab a table.

"So," Violet says as she sets down our coffees and finally takes a chair. "Is it an ex-boyfriend? Because this looks like some abusive sadist shit to me."

I fiddle with my coffee a bit, open it, stir it, put the lid back on, take a sip. "To be honest"—my heart winces as I say the words—"I'm not sure. Someone has been screwing with me for a week. Tried to get me fired. Put something in my shopping bag at the store. And someone pushed me into the street the other night. Now this."

Her eyebrows rise nearly to her hairline. "Jesus. A recent breakup?"

"No."

"Wow. Okay. So you're being stalked?"

I nod past the alarm of hearing the word aloud. "I think so. Yes."

"I'm so sorry. Well, I'm not one to tell somebody to run to the cops, but you should report this if you haven't already."

"I have. They're not taking it seriously."

Violet rolls her eyes. "Surprise."

"Yeah. *Huge* surprise."

"So it could be some random stranger? That's scary as hell."

I take another drink, then clear my throat, trying to decide what I should tell her. I want to let it out, but right now she assumes I'm not a liar despite the evidence plastered around town. How the hell can I give that up and confess that I truly am?

She cocks her head, gaze drifting to the window next to me. "Hm. You know, if their first step was trying to get you fired, maybe it's not a stranger. Maybe it's someone you work with."

"That was my initial thought too. But then . . ." Pressure builds inside my chest, pushing up, looking for cracks in my resolve. And God, there are so many. Who else can I talk to? If Mike wasn't lost to me before, he certainly is now. And honestly, I'm still afraid of him. Same problem with Tristan. He could be involved. It could even be Frank, but . . . if I say this to Violet, if I—

My mouth lets it free. "Someone left a stuffed devil in my bag, and in school, when I was young, they called me Devil Girl. Because I . . ." I hesitate, and when Violet's eyes are too curious, too intense, I look down at the hands clutching my coffee so hard that the lid is lifting off.

Screw it. I don't ever have to go to the library again, do I? And suddenly I don't want to be invisible anymore. Because if I'm invisible, no one will notice if something awful happens to me.

"If you've heard of the Satanic Panic?" I wait for her nod. "It was like that. I was at one of those daycares. There was a trial, and I . . ." My mouth is so dry it's hard to move my tongue. "I made up stories. I was really little, only five. But it stuck with me. Devil Girl, you know? So I think whoever this is, it's someone from my past."

I dare to look up and am absolutely gutted by the awful twist to Violet's mouth. The dawning horror. The shocked contortion of her face.

"I-I was sorry," I stammer. "It all came out a couple years later. I told the truth then. I swear."

"You were only *five*!" she says, her voice too loud, and I cringe away, glancing around. "Sorry," she adds quickly, lowering her volume. "They really called you Devil Girl?"

I wave a hand. "It wasn't, like, every day. Just schoolkid stuff. Certain groups of kids. The mean girls. The jocks. It was just what people thought of when they saw me."

"Jesus," she huffs, and when I'm sure her disgust isn't for me at all, I melt. I melt into tears that I wipe away and wipe again because they're slowly leaking out of my eyes and won't stop.

"Sorry," I mutter, using my coffee-stained napkin to dab at my cheeks. "I'm just tired."

"Tired of bullshit, probably. So it's someone from your past? From Texas? And they're *here*? That's messed up."

It is messed up. But she might not feel so sympathetic if she knew I still lie every single day to every single person. I'm not from Texas, I'm not who she thinks I am at all, so she'd name me a psycho too, just like my stalker. I know that. I *feel* that.

Violet leans forward, intent now. "Okay, so who was harmed back then? The daycare people? Did someone go to prison?"

Yes. Linda and Mitchell Hoffholder were both convicted in a joint trial, both sent to prison for a minimum of twenty-five years. Life had gone back to something approaching normality after that, with the added spice of the attention my parents and I got in church. My parents didn't believe in pride, but being proud of the Lord's blessing was a different thing. I'd been a little hero of Christianity, strong enough to fight the devil even as a kindergartener.

I'd stood in front of congregations and meeting halls, hailed as both a warning and a weapon in the fight against Satanists. I'd loved that part of it, soaking up the attention as only an outgoing child with repressed, nearly silent parents can.

The bad stuff had only validated my story further. The nightmares that tormented me had been proof of my suffering. My new skittishness at being touched? Just more evidence of how I'd been tortured. And I had been, hadn't I? Three different pelvic examinations, swabs of my throat to check for gonorrhea, a church "therapist" twice a month to flesh out the Technicolor details of my terrifying demonic assaults.

And my parents standing stoic and proud that their daughter was helping fight the devil. I was righteous and sturdy in a world filled with weakness.

"The owners of the daycare served time," I finally say, the words gravelly with shame. "A little over two years between arrest and prison. They were released when the convictions were overturned."

She nods, seemingly not even shocked by what I just said. "So both of them are obvious suspects."

"Yes, but the man is dead, and this isn't a woman. She'd be about eighty by now, so . . ."

"Someone else in the family? A kid?"

"Maybe. But their son was in on the accusations too. He started it."

"So he wouldn't blame you."

"No, but . . . the other witness and I recanted. He didn't. So maybe he's still angry that we screwed up his demented little plot?"

"Wow." Violet points at me. "There you go. He's your suspect."

Jacob Hoffholder. I nod, because that makes sense, doesn't it? He'd already been swimming up from my subconscious as I examined Mike's face for similarities.

That creep got what he wanted when his parents were arrested, and then we took that from him. Jacob Hoffholder is a much likelier suspect than Frank Doukas. And maybe a more dangerous one.

I press my hand to my stomach to guard the sudden, sharp ache. Coffee dances with the acid in my gut to form a choppy sea. I breathe carefully until the rising pressure in my throat passes; then I nudge my cup away.

This is why I don't talk about that time, why I don't even think about it. It's a leviathan hidden in the deep, always waiting to pull me under.

"I guess I'd better go do more research," I murmur, nearly squirming with the need to get up and rush home, where I can lock the door behind me.

"Let me know if you need help. Librarians have great research skills, you know."

Shit, they do. And if she looks up my name . . .

No, that doesn't matter. I've already revealed the basics, and exposure is no longer my greatest threat. Jacob was a troubled child who apparently turned into a troubled man, and if he's holding a grudge against me?

I jump to my feet, but Violet reaches for my hand. "Don't hesitate to come by the library if you want to talk. Let me know how you're doing."

"Thank you," I croak, my throat thick with gratitude and the deep ache pushing up from my heart. "That means so much." She listened like a friend. She took my side. And she wants to help. I'm nearly dizzy with the strangeness of that.

"And if I see anyone tacking up more flyers, I'll start filming, all right? Can I get your number?"

"Thank you," I repeat, then give her my number and add her to my contact list. After I thank her once more for the coffee and the brainstorming, I'm out the door and speed-walking down the street in an attempt to outrun my thoughts.

It doesn't work.

I was only seven at the time, so I don't remember a lot of the fallout from the investigation that helped overturn the conviction. I wasn't interviewed until Lauren had already recanted. But I remember the rush of relief when the investigator from the DA's office told me she'd heard the stories about the Hoffholders were made up. That Lauren was now saying she told me what to say. Was that true? Had Lauren pressured me?

A dam broke inside my tiny little heart. I'd felt like a strange shapeshifter for two years, uncomfortable in my own skin, but always starving for more approval and attention. That one prompt from the investigator popped me like a water balloon. I began babbling wildly, asking if I was in trouble, telling her I didn't really want to say that stuff, that the policemen said the Hoffholders did bad things and I had to help put them in jail. I only wanted to help save the younger kids.

I told the woman I possibly remembered pigs on a farm and maybe even candles, but there were no dead babies. There wasn't a cave. That I'd seen the devil but maybe just in dreams. That Mrs. Hoffholder did hurt me when I was naked, but that was because I turned on the sprinkler without asking, and when she found me dancing naked in the water, she paddled my butt. But also that I was scared of all those demons and caves and pigs and Satan, and I had so many nightmares. And then I just wanted to go home and never talk about any of this bad stuff again, because it wasn't true. It wasn't true, and all the stories scared me.

Not exactly a reliable confession, what with Satan and the pigs, but Lauren had already pointed them toward proof. She said she watched Jacob Hoffholder plant the only physical evidence ever found: a copy of *The Satanic Bible* and four black candles.

A new county attorney, a young man who'd gone to college and law school in Chicago and was seemingly unafraid of questioning the world around him, had ordered the physical evidence rechecked for fingerprints. The only prints found belonged to Jacob, almost as if his parents had never once handled *The Satanic Bible* in all the years they'd been performing cartoonishly evil ceremonies. Everything else fell apart. A social worker lost her job over some of the more leading interview sessions. A prosecutor was fired for withholding evidence. The county sheriff was eventually recalled.

Once the conviction was overturned and the Hoffholders sent home, I was forever known as a fantastical liar with a filthy imagination. My parents, burdened by this swift turn in the public's attitude, considered me damaged goods as well. Their stoicism turned to sour disapproval. And I turned to solitude.

Oh, a few holdouts in town still firmly believed that the devil had come to Fair Isle, and this reversal of witness testimony was only more proof of his devious ways. We moved from our Lutheran church to a smaller, stricter Baptist congregation, but it was never the same. My parents were no longer suffering heroes; they were just an embarrassment, and in the Midwest, that meant a lot of awkward exchanges and lost invitations from people they'd known their whole lives.

My mom and dad were disappointed in me, but I was disappointed in them too. We drifted along in parallel silence for most days, most years, until I grew up and ran to the farthest corner of Iowa for college. I would've run a thousand miles, but in-state tuition had me in a chokehold. Now I can run as far as I like.

Jacob Hoffholder. Could he really be my tormentor? The boy who started all the lies in the first place? It's time to find out.

CHAPTER 24

I'm so sorry, I type from my blanket cocoon on the couch. I know this is weird. But can you send me a picture?

Uhh . . . what kind of picture? Tristan follows that with a winky face, and I manage a shaky smile.

Of your face! I reply, adding the exclamation point and a laughing emoji so I seem playful instead of psycho. But the madness comes out anyway. With all this crazy stuff going on in my life, I just want to be sure you're . . . real. So could you send me a pic?

I cringe before I type the next part, but I know anyone can pull a picture from a search engine. The photos he sent originally could have been grabbed from any white-male dating profile in the world. I need proof that he's not Jacob Hoffholder. Real proof.

A thumbs-up would be too common, but . . . Can you give me a thumbs-down sign in it? To signal how stupid this is?

Silence. Because of course there's silence. Who the heck would want to play along with this sad game? He hasn't acted suspiciously in the nine months we've known each other. He asked about that hospital in Las Vegas. Later he was interested in switching up his career and asked questions about my new job, then told me he'd applied for a documentation position in Florida. He scored an interview two weeks later and asked if I'd be willing to call him to give some advice. He didn't get the job, but we've been texting ever since.

So yeah, Tristan is just a normal guy, and I'm the weird one again. Holding my breath, I wait for him to make an excuse, explain that he's busy. But then my phone vibrates, and the picture loads, and it's just . . . Tristan.

He's wearing a ball cap again, and I wonder if he's balding, but that fleeting thought vanishes as I study him. I can't see much of his eyes beneath the deep shadow of the brim, and he's making a goofy, closed-lip smile. As requested, he offers a prominent thumbs-down, and his looming hand blocks part of his face. But on his right, I can see that his ears definitely do not stick out in any prominent way.

He's not Jacob Hoffholder. Even in childhood, Jacob had those damn ears and a pointy nose much narrower than Tristan's. I blow out a long breath.

I hadn't realized the weight of the doubt sitting beneath my heart until this exact moment. Because Tristan *isn't* Jacob, and that weight leaving my body reveals a dark, deep shape of anxiety that had been growing there. He really is just a friend. My eyes are sweeping over the plain white wall behind him, searching for more clues, when my phone rings.

"Did I pass the test?" he asks.

"Yes!" I cry, still delighted. I'd told myself Tristan couldn't be my stalker, because he's in Florida, but how could I be sure? Maybe the stalker has planned this for months, slowly working his way into my world, building a friendship with me while pretending to be an innocent nurse in Tampa.

But no, Jacob is the only suspect who truly makes sense, and that means Tristan is safe to talk to.

"I didn't think it was that great a picture," he says, "but you sound happy."

"I'm so sorry," I immediately offer.

"Nonsense. But now I'm more worried. Does this mean things haven't improved?"

"No, they definitely have not improved," I say with good cheer as I prop my feet on my coffee table and stretch out. "Things are, in fact, pretty damn bonkers."

"In what way?" He sounds confused by my mood, but I'm embracing this bright spot because everything else is scary. Relief feels almost like joy at this point.

"May?" he prompts.

"Well!" I scramble to remember what I was telling him. "I finally found a video of when I was pushed, and the cops haven't bothered to respond about that."

"You saw the guy?" Tristan yelps.

"Not very well. He's hidden by the crowd."

"Still, that's some kind of progress, I guess."

"Yeah. But there's more. Last night . . ."

"What?" he snaps. "Did something happen? Are you okay? Why didn't you text me?"

I clear my throat, trying to banish the thick emotion gathering there. "It's just . . . kind of embarrassing. I didn't know what to say."

"About what?"

Shit. Am I really going to do this? Sure, everyone in town knows, but Tristan doesn't, and he never will unless I tell him. I decide on a half truth, which is progress for me, isn't it? I'm trying. "He put up flyers all over town. About me."

"What? That's insane. What do you mean by flyers?"

"He put my name and photo and my phone number on them along with a warning. Like, beware of this woman!"

"Jesus. That's so scary. And they're all over town?"

"Basically. I tore a bunch down, and a friend helped too. But I've gotten some creepy calls."

"This is not safe, May. Did you call the cops?"

I groan even though I appreciate his suggestion. "You know how I feel about that. They're not taking any of this seriously."

"But you need to get it on the record at least. Make them take it seriously. Show them the flyers."

I shake my head. "I threw them all away." Did I do that on purpose so I wouldn't have to talk to the cops again? Or was I just panicking?

"Well, call them anyway! You have to make them see what you're dealing with."

I can tell by the way his voice is getting louder that he won't drop this unless I make him. "Yeah. Um. Listen, I understand why you'd say that. I get it. But I don't want to deal with them."

"I really think you should," he presses. "You could be in actual danger. You need protection from this guy."

I want to snap at him, tell him to back the hell off. But of course he's only saying what anyone else would say. *Go to the authorities. That's what you're supposed to do.* He's right. And it's nice that he's worried. If it feels like he's trying to cut me open and examine my insides, it's only because I'm hiding things.

But I've spilled too many of my guts today. Got to hang on to a few vital organs.

"Okay," I say breezily, "I'll think about it. But I am being careful. I ordered more security cameras, and they'll be here tomorrow."

"Cameras. That's a good idea. But I'm worried about you being alone with all this pressure."

"I'm used to being alone. Traveling nurse, remember?"

"Yeah, but . . . Just reach out to me if you need to talk. Don't hesitate. I know too many people who carry so much on their own shoulders, and then . . ."

"I'm fine, Tristan."

"Yeah, sorry." He lets out a shaky sigh. "I'm overreacting. My brother . . . my brother killed himself a couple of years ago. And I didn't even know anything was wrong. I'm still . . . God." He sighs again. "Sorry, I'm still trying to work through that."

"Oh my God. Tristan, I'm so sorry!" My heart tears open a little at the grief in his voice. "I had no idea."

"It's okay. I don't really like to talk about it."

"I get it," I say. And boy, do I. "But if you ever do want to talk, I'm here."

"Thanks. I'm good. I just don't like thinking about you alone with this stress."

"I'm okay. You don't have to worry." I hate people worrying about me, because that means they're looking at me, seeing me. But beneath the deep discomfort, something sweet and painful lurks. Something that makes me want to reach out and hold him. Because he cares.

"Sorry to spring that on you," he says.

"No! Don't be sorry. But please don't worry about me. I'm having friends over to hang out tonight. I'm good, I promise."

When we get off the phone, I'm swamped by a wave of shame. Shame for lying to him, yes, because I don't really have friends and no one is coming over. But there's something deeper there. Something darkly familiar.

This feels like my childhood. Like the guilt that lived inside me for all those years, mixed up with a terrible yearning for connection. But the yearning could never overcome the sharp fear of people mocking me and calling me names.

"You're not a kid anymore," I tell myself. "And no one will . . ."

My words trail off because at this point, people really might laugh and call me names because of the flyers. But this isn't school. No one can force me to walk into a building every single day with my tormentors. When I sit alone at lunch now, it's because I choose to. People don't avoid me anymore, because I make myself interesting and confident. I'm in charge of my own life now.

"You sure about that?" I ask myself.

God.

A soft murmur interrupts my thoughts. Then a low moan.

Eyes popping wide, I sit up and twist my laptop around to get a better look at the security feeds.

Oh my. The other patio is suddenly right there on my screen, and I spot the wheelchair, facing away from the camera. The man in the chair has laid his head back, his face tipped toward the sky, and I can just see John crouched in front of him.

Another moan sounds, and I'm about to turn off the camera. But then John shifts, and I realize his head isn't low enough to be doing what I think he's doing. Hmm. Nope, not fellatio, but his arms are working. Working *hard* actually. Jeez, that is one hell of a hand job! Truly impressive.

"That feels so good," I overhear, and nod in chagrined agreement.

John shifts again, lifting one of his partner's legs in a move I haven't seen before. For a split second, I wonder if I should be taking notes, but then I watch as he runs a hand down the man's leg and digs his thumb hard into his foot, drawing another deep moan.

Oh. It's just a massage.

The man reaches out to stroke a hand over John's hair, and John looks up to offer a tender smile as he dips his head into the touch.

Tears sting my eyes, and I feel exquisitely guilty in that moment, much more guilty than when I thought I was spying on sex. That's odd, isn't it? That this love and vulnerability is harder for me to watch than something dirty?

I turn off the feed and refuse to think more about it.

I'm fine, just like I told Tristan. I'm used to being alone. And none of this madness changes that.

CHAPTER 25

Five minutes later, I'm still a little shaken by the murmured endearments and contented sighs I overheard. I'm happy for them, I really am, but my skin crawls with discomfort all the same.

I'll never have that kind of love or devotion, but I've never wanted it anyway. Well, not since my divorce. I might have had stupid dreams when I was younger, but I learned my lesson. I'm relieved not to leave my raw heart pumping out in the open like that, thanks very much.

I head for the fridge to draw myself an ice-cold glass of boxed rosé. I'm not going out to dinner tonight, because I can't summon the courage. I'm afraid of being followed, of course. But also . . . what if I walk out and find that the flyers have bred like horny paper rabbits? If that bastard put them up once, why wouldn't he do it again?

No, tonight I'll insulate myself with wine, reality television, and a frozen pizza. The outside world can go straight to hell, and so can the vegetables I bought at the store.

Of course the outside world almost immediately makes an appearance, refusing to be ignored. I'm just taking my first sip when someone knocks.

Frozen in the harsh light of my open freezer, I stare at the door, wondering if there's any hint of my presence through the adjacent window blinds. I won't answer it. I can't.

But what if it's the cops with an update? What if they've caught my stalker? I close the door as slowly as I can and refuse to even blink lest I miss something.

Another knock, and then a voice calls, "Beth?"

It's Mike! I mean . . . Oh no, it's Mike. My brief jolt of happiness twists into abject anxiety. I still need to apologize for thinking he might have pushed me. "Shit, shit, shit," I whisper.

After I hover there for a full minute, there's another knock. "I just want to make sure you're okay," he says through the wood.

I'm not okay, so there's no hope for him there. But I tiptoe closer and carefully lift a wooden slat one millimeter to peek through.

Mike is staring at the ground, his forehead creased with worry. He's dressed neatly in jeans and yet another crisp button-down, but his jaw is scruffy with stubble. When he lifts a hand to massage the back of his neck as if he's carrying around too much tension, I finally give in to my urge to apologize.

After a bracing breath, I open the door a few inches. "Hi."

"Hi," he answers, his expression still tight. "Are you all right?"

"Sure. Yeah. I'm great."

"Um," he says. I wait for more, but instead of speaking, he unfolds a paper. I know what it is, of course, and my insides clench like I've just spotted a tiger sneaking up on me.

Damn it all to hell. I really should not have opened the door, but now I'm stuck. "Crap," I mutter. "I guess I didn't find them all, huh?" I follow that up with a clearly fake hiccup of laughter; then I nod for some reason. I keep nodding, bobbing like a damn idiot.

"It was taped to the garage," he explains, "right by my stairs."

"Sure. Yeah." Inexplicably, I raise my wineglass like I'm toasting him. "So sorry about that. It's fucked up."

"Yeah, it's definitely fucked up." He waits a beat, obviously expecting an explanation. When none arrives, his eyebrows rise. "Want to tell me about it?"

"No, I do not, actually."

Eyebrows going even higher, he presses his mouth into a very flat line and stares until I squirm.

"Sorry," I say again, and there goes my stupid nodding head, bobbing away like I'm a funny car ornament.

Mike sighs as if he hates this as much as I do. "Look, Beth, there's clearly something very wrong going on here. And whatever this is, *whoever* this is, they know that we're . . . uh . . . acquainted with each other. So as much as I don't want to violate this bubble you've built around your life, I'm feeling a little threatened too."

This bubble. Like it isn't a highly fortified geodesic dome meant to survive a nuclear apocalypse. Still, he's managed to infiltrate it with guilt. Because he's right, isn't he? I have dragged him into this, whether I intended to or not.

I know Mike didn't push me, and I know he's not Jacob Hoffholder, but I can't invite him in again. It would be stupid to take that kind of risk right now.

But it's so nice to see him.

No, no, I scold my stupid heart or body or whatever feels so warm when he's around. No more exposing yourself *or* him.

I bet he's tried googling me already, but my name is simply too general. I've done it myself, and there are athletes, authors, politicians, scientists. My name was used in a couple of tabloid articles so many years ago that you'd have to dig deep to find it. I should end this once and for all, but he deserves something, doesn't he?

"We could go for a walk if you're not afraid to be seen with me," I offer. "I just need a minute to change."

"I've already been seen with you, I guess." He tries to cut the harsh words with a smile, but it's thin. "So a walk would be okay."

I stick my glass of wine in the fridge, put on a bra and a shirt that's not stained or wrinkled, and slip into my sneakers. Then I pause and look around to see if I've forgotten anything, secretly hoping if I stall long enough, he might give up and leave.

He doesn't leave. Mike is waiting at the foot of the stairs, his back to me as he stares out at the scraggly palm trees that line our street. I can still see the paper unfolded in his hand, and my mind races, trying to figure out what he must think of all this.

His mouth twists wryly when he turns to see me looking at the flyer. "I finally got your number, at least."

"Ha!" It's my first genuine laugh of the evening. "Joke's on you. I have all the dick pics I need now."

He winces. "Ouch. Really?"

"Yeah, though they weren't high quality. It's amazing what men will willingly put out there. Have to assume some of them are into humiliation kink."

"So . . ." He folds up the paper and tucks it into his pocket. I resist the urge to yank it out and toss it in a trash can. Barely. "I take it someone printed out more than one of these? It wasn't a note just for me?"

"I've found at least twenty."

We head to the corner, and I turn us toward the busier area near the river.

"I am sorry about pushing this," he says after long minutes of silence. "I really am. But I'd like to know if you're in danger, and frankly I need to know if I am too. Because this definitely seems like a dangerous ex-husband situation."

"It's not," I say. When I don't offer more, I feel him staring at the side of my face, and my cheeks heat.

"What's going on, Beth? I feel like I deserve to know."

Good Lord, I do not want to talk about this, and I have no idea how to deal with my squirming unease. I'm never self-conscious with anyone. Why would I be? It's all pretend for me. I don't care about first impressions or my body's flaws or my penchant for weird jokes, because I'm just acting out whatever part I've chosen for the day.

Maybe I can do that now too. Make up a completely fictional story. I start searching my brain for ideas, but my imagination fails me.

"How did you get that stuffed devil?" I ask.

"Like I said, I found it on the stairs up to my place, and I thought it was from you. You're the only one I know here."

I nod. Exhaustion is defeating all the shields I keep so carefully in place. I have much bigger worries than protecting my secrets at this point. Violet already knows, after all. And yes, I've apparently put Mike in danger.

"I have a devil toy too," I admit. "Someone put it in my bag at the grocery store while I was checking out. I freaked out when I saw it at your place, because . . ."

When my words fade away, he gestures toward a bench facing the river. It's close to an intersection and visible to passing cars, so I feel safe enough to sit. We stare down into the bushes and thin trees that hide the trail below. The water glints beneath the last rays of slanted sunlight.

It'll be dark soon, and I need to get this over with so I can get home and hide again. "I've never lived in one place this long," I start. "I move around a lot, usually twice a year. But I like it here, you know?"

"It's a beautiful place."

"It is. And everyone here is weird. Like me. Quirky or exploring or just . . . I don't know. I don't want to leave."

"And why would you have to leave?" I see him turn toward me, but I stare straight ahead, refusing to return his look. "Is this the part where you tell me you're a dangerous spy?" he asks, softening just a bit. He's angry and worried, but I can tell it's not in his nature to be harsh.

I smile at the sparkling water. I should have thought of that. It's a good story. "I wish this were an undercover situation. That would be so much cooler. Like, *exponentially* cooler."

He waits. I wait. I'm still hoping he'll give up.

Surprise, he doesn't, and his next guess nails it all down. "Who are you hiding from, Beth?"

Who am I hiding from? The entire world surges toward me, a tsunami of threat waiting to sweep me away. "Everyone," I answer so quietly I hope he doesn't hear it. "Or maybe just myself. I don't know."

"I don't understand. What are you saying?" He reaches up to rub his eyes, clearly losing patience.

So I stare at the water, at the leaves shaking in the breeze, at the jumbled makeshift shelters farther along the riverbank, and I tell him.

None of it really matters, after all. Mike will go back to his real life in a few months, and I'll move to a place where I'm once again surrounded by strangers, and all of this will be wiped away like it never happened. Like *I* never happened.

I try to convince myself the knot in my stomach is relief at the idea instead of doom, but I'm not sure anymore.

I let it out. All of it, or as close to all as I'll get. The story floods out of me, the Satanic Panic, the daycare, the police, the trial. I tell him that two years later it all fell apart and I became infamous among my peers as Devil Girl. I tell him about Lauren and then Jacob, who must be doing all this to me, because who else would care?

I tell him all of that, and the release of pressure feels nearly euphoric, like I'm purging that sickness after decades of keeping it in.

This is it. This is who I was. But it's not who I *am*, because I hold tight to that part and bury it even deeper. I don't tell him about the dozen different names I use, the lies I weave, the fiction I build around me every second of the day, because I just can't. I can't see that through his eyes. Surely he already thinks of me as erratic and crazy, and I refuse to confirm the truth of it.

"Jesus," he sighs when I eventually go quiet. "I'm so sorry that happened. It sounds . . . All that shit for your whole childhood? My God, I'm still haunted by having buckteeth, and those jokes went away after I got braces in middle school."

"Yeah, it wasn't great. But worse things happen to other people. Much worse things happened to the Hoffholders."

"That doesn't mean it wasn't torture for you."

"True. But I grew up and got out and moved on." *Liar,* my inner voice chastises. "I'm *fine.* I never thought it would come back, but now . . . yeah, it's definitely back."

"What do the police say?" Mike asks, and I try not to sigh with impatience. It's a perfectly logical question.

"I haven't told them about my past. Or about the flyers. They didn't seem to even care that I was assaulted. They didn't believe it."

"I'm happy to tell them about the flyer on my door," he offers.

I nod, but it turns into a shake of my head pretty quickly. "The police really screwed me up when I was five. They were part of it, Mike. They were so damn excited to hunt devil worshippers that they planted ideas in my head. The term *leading questions* doesn't begin to cover it. They terrorized me with stories that gave me nightmares for years. I thought I'd been raped by the devil. Can you imagine what that does to a kid?"

"No. I honestly can't."

I swallow back the acid rising in my throat. "Everyone who was supposed to help me made my life a living hell. I wasn't raped by Satan; I was raped by multiple doctors sticking fingers and instruments everywhere they could. Therapists terrorized me by calling me a liar if I told them something didn't really happen. 'Girls who lie are bad girls, Elizabeth. Are you a bad girl? Or will you tell us how they hurt you?' Then my parents would stand up in church and repeat everything while hundreds of people stared at me, picturing every moment in their minds."

I wipe a tear off my cheek and bury my face in my hands. "They took truth away from me. They took my mind, my memories, my voice. And now it's happening again. Everyone is looking at me. Everyone thinks . . ."

When he rests his hand on my shoulder, it's an anchor. I'm back in the present, on this bench, with this man, in my own body. I'm not a terrified little girl. I'm not a tortured teenager. "I'm so fucking sorry," he says, the words gritty with emotion.

Oh God. Has anyone ever said that before? Has anyone apologized to me? For so many years, I didn't think I deserved that. I wasn't a victim, I was a liar. A *perpetrator*. I just wanted to be forgiven. But I never got that either.

"Please don't . . ." I sniff hard and wipe a sleeve over my nose. "Please don't tell anyone about this."

"Of course not."

"Not even your ex," I say. "But I guess Princess is okay."

"She is a great listener."

I manage a strangled laugh. "All right, now you know what's going on. I can't imagine there's any danger to you. It feels more like he's trying to embarrass me, humiliate me, and boy, is it working. But I'm sorry you were sucked in."

He nods. "What's your next step?"

"I have no idea. I'm getting more security cameras. I tried to track down the other girl, Lauren, but she died last year. I think she killed herself. I guess neither of us really escaped it after all."

When Mike removes his hand, my shoulder feels too cold. I want it back, but I can't ask him for more. He's already being so kind. "So you haven't told the police about Jacob?"

"No. They don't seem to want to listen. At first I thought it was someone else. And even now I don't have any proof. But it has to be him. Only he and his mom are left, and even back then she didn't move around well enough to chase down the toddlers. It's him, but why would they believe me?"

We both pause to watch a squirrel beg us for food. It eventually gives up with a few angry chitters. "I can help try to track him down online," Mike says. "See if he's left any clues."

"That's really kind, but you don't have to help. It's enough that you listened. I'm sorry I've been so . . ." I dare to look at him, and he grimaces comically. "Yeah," I say. "Exactly. You showed up right when all this started, and I've spent days going back and forth about whether you could be involved. I've even wondered if you could be Jacob Hoffholder all grown up."

"Hm."

"An average white guy," I explain, then clear my throat. "Sorry, though. No offense."

"None taken, I think? Do I look like him?"

"Not unless you got your ears pinned back."

"Nope, I only had the buckteeth to deal with."

The sunlight is starting to fade to dusky yellow, so I gather the last of my energy and stand. "I'd better be getting back. I didn't get much sleep last night." A yawn rises right on cue, and my jaw cracks with the effort.

"All right. But I'll walk you home if you like," Mike offers.

"I'll take you up on that. And thank you for coming by. I meant to apologize yesterday, but I couldn't get up the nerve."

"Hard to imagine you not getting up the nerve for anything."

I flush warm at the compliment. "Eh, I'm a big talker, but I run from real trouble."

"Sure you do."

He's being funny, but he has no idea. "You don't owe me anything, of course, but . . . maybe you could check inside before I go in?" I cringe, but I still offer puppy-dog eyes of pleading.

He rolls his shoulders back and stands straighter. "Of course I will. Don't be ridiculous."

Aw. I wish this would all just go away, because he's such an adorable nerd. Or he's part of an elite tracking unit hired by a vengeful Midwestern guy with a grudge. People are full of surprises, so you never know.

But Mike is true to his word. He walks me home and sticks his head into every room while I wait in the doorway, my hands clutching the frame so hard my knuckles ache.

"All clear!" he calls. "You're sure you're good?"

I let go my grip and step inside. "Yeah. I'll barricade myself in my bedroom tonight and hopefully sleep like crazy. Then tomorrow I'll get my new cameras, and it'll be cozy as Fort Knox in here."

Mike hesitates a moment, then slowly raises his arms from his sides in question. I'm shocked by how quickly I fling myself into the hug. After revealing my worst moments to him, I'm surprised I don't want him to disappear. I *need* him to go, but I feel strangely attached to him now, and his arms are the coziest trap around me, pulling me into smooshy feelings.

Ugh. Gross.

But God, he's nice, and my soul is wide open and splayed out after finally telling my story. I squeeze him and inhale the clean scent of his shirt. "Thank you," I whisper before forcing myself to release him. I have to stuff these feelings back inside and stitch everything up.

After I lock the door behind him, I stand frozen for a long time, fighting the urge to call him back. It's so quiet now. Even the normal street sounds are hidden by my thumping heart.

I've always treasured my privacy, my solitude, and this asshole stalker is taking that from me. But I'm determined to persevere, so I retrieve my wine from the fridge, throw a pizza in the oven, and settle onto the couch for a few hours of coziness before I have to face a very long night alone.

CHAPTER 26

"Guh." The grunt pops from my throat like I've been punched in the gut. For a dozen heartbeats I'm stuck there in the doorway of my bedroom, my arm against the wall, hand on the light switch, lips parted.

There's no one in my room, not at first glance, anyway. But I'm locked in terror in the doorway, every cell in my body trying to retreat deeper inside as I stare at my neatly made bed. If I don't move, I won't be seen. If I don't move, this won't be happening.

Because my bed wasn't neatly made the last time I saw it. It was a riot of blankets and sheets, the aftermath of my restless night. It was a mess like the rest of my bedroom. Discarded clothes strewn in front of the narrow closet door. Clean clothes stacked on the dresser. A few crumpled Kleenexes on the floor where I'd missed the trash can.

I'm usually a little neater, but my life has been spiraling, and now it's all circling faster and faster around the sinking vortex that is my bedroom.

Someone made my bed. Arranged the throw pillows. Put away my clean laundry. Picked up the dirty clothes. Snapped the top onto the hamper and tucked it neatly into the corner. The tissues are in the trash. Even my books are stacked in a perfect line.

My body suddenly jerks free of its paralysis, and I stumble back, then yelp in horror when my hip brushes a chair. "No," I cry as I pivot on my heel and race madly for the front door.

I tug my phone out as I twist the locks open and surge into the cool night. If someone is out here waiting, so be it. We'll fight to the death while I scream bloody murder for help.

"911, what's your emergency?"

"I need help, please. *Please.* There's been an intruder." I rattle off my address, then answer the operator's questions. I'm not injured. I don't know if anyone is still inside. I'm waiting at the curb. I don't know if I'm safe.

"Please," I plead again, as my hands and jaw shake with violent trembles. How long was I sitting there alone on my couch before I went to the bedroom? Almost two hours? Was someone there the whole time? Were they watching? Are they under the bed or in the closet right this second?

I know Mike didn't do this. He was with me inside the house, and I watched as he stuck his head in the bedroom to check for only a second. He did his best. How was he to know my room was supposed to look like the aftermath of a gale-force storm?

Oh God. I should have asked him to stay. Should have asked if I could come over. Why didn't I just follow him home and beg for help? What the hell is this independent woman bullshit I've been leaning into?

I fucking *need* someone right now.

Something rustles in the bushes next to me, and I lurch away, even though I can tell it's the size of a lizard scurrying through dead leaves. Or a rat. Not a man, though. Not a monster. Right?

Headlights sweep around the corner and light me up, and I'm torn between relief and fear. Is it the cops or the stalker?

In the end, it's neither, just a beat-up station wagon sputtering by. The driver doesn't even glance at me, because a barefoot woman crying outside isn't some exceptional sight here. Usually I appreciate that live-and-let-live attitude, but tonight it's a terrible realization that if I do scream for help, I might not get it.

Teeth chattering, I wrap my arms around myself and turn in a slow circle, trying to keep my eyes on everything all at once. The car parked next to my mailbox looks empty. My car behind it looks empty too. Mr. Sanchez's porch light is bright, and I spot a flicker of motion from his television.

The corner of my eye blinks with light, and I swing wildly toward the flash of the police car approaching. It's so far away. The sirens aren't on, and I swear the car is moving in slow motion through the neighborhood. Waving my arms, I silently urge them to hurry, damn it, hurry.

When the car pulls up I'm relieved to see a female officer driving. Maybe she'll take this more seriously than the cops did yesterday.

I try my best to explain once the police are out of the car. "I went for a walk earlier, and I just realized someone was in my house while I was gone."

"All right," the woman says calmly. "You were robbed?"

"No. Or I don't know. But I just went to my bedroom, and it's . . ." I stumble over the explanation. "Everything is moved around."

"All right. We'll go clear the place and then have you come inside and explain."

I follow close on their heels until she tells me to wait at the door. A few minutes later they wave me inside and ask for the story. I stammer it out in a great rush. "I went for a walk with a friend this evening. We were gone for about thirty minutes, and when we got back he looked around the house for me because I'm being stalked. He checked every room and said it was fine. But I didn't look into my bedroom until just now."

"Okay. The bedroom looks pretty clean. What was disturbed?"

"That's the thing! It was a mess. I haven't cleaned up in a while. The bed was unmade and clothes were everywhere."

"Someone . . . ?" The woman's mouth tightens with disbelief. "Ma'am, you're saying someone cleaned your room?"

My face goes warm under her doubtful eyes. Then it goes hot. Yes, that's what I'm saying, and I know it doesn't sound reasonable, but none of this is reasonable. "Look, a bunch of strange shit has been happening. I was pushed into the street a few days ago, and I filed a report. Someone turned off my power. There's a record of that too because I called 911. Someone has been following me and watching me for days and making sure I know."

"And now they've cleaned your room."

The wry note in her voice pushes me from embarrassment to irritation. "I only make my bed on special occasions, all right? And after the stress of the last week, I haven't even put dirty clothes in the hamper. Someone did all that, and it seems they were going through my stuff too, because my clean clothes are put away. I didn't do that."

"Could it be your cleaning service?"

"I don't have a cleaning service, and if I did, they'd be working here longer than thirty minutes. Look at the kitchen. It's still a mess."

"All right, let's stay calm," she suggests coldly, like I have no right to be upset about this. She glances up. "Is that a rental upstairs?"

"Yes, an Airbnb, but I don't own it."

"So the cleaner for the rental could have accidentally come in here, right? I notice you have keypads. Maybe she started cleaning and then realized—"

"The cleaner doesn't have my code," I snap. "The police have been ignoring me all week. I'd like some actual help."

Her lip twists at my tone, but she shakes it off after she shoots her partner an exasperated look. "Okay, ma'am, you take a look around and tell us if anything is missing. I'm going to make a call, so just sit tight."

Half an hour later, I've checked everywhere and confirmed that my clean clothes are in the dresser. I've washed my hands, and I'll definitely need to wash all my clothes too. God only knows what that sick fuck did to them. And I'll put on new sheets. I feel grimy and violated and so damn scared.

While I'm explaining the security camera system to the officer, a white man in a sport coat appears in my doorway, and she looks up to nod at him. "This is Detective Heissen," she explains as the detective lifts his narrow chin in my direction.

"Oh, thank God." They're finally taking me seriously. I have a real detective to help, and relief crashes through me so forcefully that my knees shake.

He's my height, but his thin face and long legs make him look taller as I approach. There's something reassuring about the lines around his eyes, like he smiles a lot.

I reach to shake his hand and realize to my horror that I'm crying. "Thank you so much," I rasp. "This has all been a lot to deal with."

"Yes, ma'am," he answers warmly. "I can see that. I reviewed the complaints on file today. Want to tell me what's going on?"

"God, I wish I knew!" A shaky laugh rumbles out of me. "It's been way more than I reported too. Little things I wasn't going to call the cops about. Some weird mail . . ." I drift into silence.

"Can we have a seat?" he asks as he saunters forward to sit on my couch.

"Sure. Yeah." I take the chair across from him and lower my voice a bit. "I think I know who's doing this. It's a man from Iowa."

"Iowa? So it's someone you know?"

"No. I mean, yes. A long time ago. I knew him and his family about thirty years ago."

His eyes search my face for a moment. "When you were a kid?"

"Exactly."

"What contact have you had since then?"

"None. I left Iowa after college."

"Facebook, maybe? Instagram?"

"No."

His head tilts in question. "So this man you knew thirty years ago has traveled here to California to break into your house and . . ." He gestures toward my room. "Make your bed?"

I shift and cross my legs. Then uncross them. "It sounds bizarre, I know, but I think he's trying to freak me out. The day before I was pushed into the street, someone put something in my shopping bag at a store. Something that relates to our hometown. And to me."

"And what would that be?"

I ignore that question because putting a stuffed animal into someone's cart isn't a crime. "Did you see the surveillance video I sent from the sushi restaurant?"

"When you fell into the street?"

Every muscle in my back stiffens. "I was pushed. You can see in the video that someone—"

"The only thing in the video is you standing near the curb and then falling. Or perhaps there's another video that hasn't been logged? I didn't have much time to check."

"No, that's . . . that's all I could find. I was hoping the police would follow up after I finally found a business willing to share their video with me. The ice cream shop might have a better angle if you care to look." Two can play at this judgmental game. After all, I'm not the one failing at my whole entire job here. "I've been dealing with this on my own. I don't have unlimited resources."

"Neither do we." His elbows are perched on his knees, hands loose between them. I keep expecting him to get out a notepad and jot something down, but he only stares at me, his dark eyes intent, and I can feel my entire body tightening up.

He opens his hands in a plea and tries another warm smile. "All right. Why don't you show me what turned up on your security cameras tonight?"

"I can't. There's a doorbell camera for the upstairs rental, and cameras for the rental next door. There aren't any cameras in my personal space."

He nods. "And you're not the owner of these properties, but you have access to the camera feeds?"

"The owner doesn't live here, and I get a rent discount for keeping an eye on the rentals for him."

"And with all this going on, you didn't turn any cameras to point at your doors? It seems like you'd want to get some proof if you have a stalker."

Trying desperately to maintain my patience, I answer calmly. "In the past I wanted privacy. Obviously at this point I'm more interested in my own safety, so I've ordered more—"

"So someone shut off your power and you thought they were in the house. Someone pushed you into the street. And now your bed was made while you were out on a walk. But there's not one camera angle that would show who's breaking into your house or following you."

It's not a question, but I answer anyway. "That's correct. As I was trying to say, I ordered more cameras. They're supposed to be here tomorrow. I'll put them up as soon as I get them." I sit straighter, refusing to back down despite how ridiculous it all sounds. "There's more. Yesterday someone put flyers up around the neighborhood about me. My phone number was on them. I don't have film of that either, but I can show you the dick pics I got in response if you want proof."

He shakes his head with a grimace. "How about just show me the flyers instead?"

Shit. I can hear the words echoing in my head before I even say them. "I don't have any," I say quietly. "I threw them away."

"You threw every flyer away? You didn't keep one for evidence?"

"No!" I swallow hard, trying to tamp down the volume of my voice. "No, I didn't. I was really pissed off and even more freaked out, and I had to march all over the neighborhood in the rain. So no, I didn't keep any wet, torn-up flyers. I didn't think you'd help anyway."

"I see. And what did these flyers say?"

"They said . . ." Damn it. "They had my name and number and my picture so even strangers would be able to see who I was. And they called me a liar."

His eyebrows climb nearly to his hairline. "Are you?"

"What?" I ask, confused for a moment.

"Are you a liar?"

My attempt to hide my anger gives way, and I draw back to glare at him. "Why would you ask me that? I'm being stalked. I need help."

"I ask because this is serious."

I nod, agreeing with that, at least. "It *is* serious. Thank you for finally realizing that."

He bounces his fist on his knee a few times and sits back, still holding my gaze. "I'm glad you understand that this isn't a game."

"Why would I think—?"

"Because filing a false police report is a crime, Ms. May. Are you aware of that?"

What?

My jaw begins to shake again. The room feels suddenly cold despite that I can hear the heater whirring away. This asshole isn't here to help. He's here to make things worse, just like the cops have always made things worse for me. They believe what they believe regardless of the evidence. Or lack thereof. They have stories they like to tell themselves about who people really are and what the world is like beneath its scummy surface.

"I'm sure it is a crime," I say past cold, clumsy lips, "to file a false report. But I haven't done that, so why would I care?"

"It uses up a lot of resources," he continues as if I'd stayed quiet. "Pulls our attention off actual crime in the neighborhood. We take that kind of thing very seriously."

"Actual crime," I murmur.

"Yes."

His eye crinkles are a lie. They're not from joy and good humor; they're from glaring at innocent civilians or from squinting into the sun like an ignorant asshole. "One of the flyers was taped to my friend's place," I say with a tremble in my voice I can't hide. "He might still have it. I'll give you his number."

"Did this man see who left the flyer on his door?"

I stare dully at him for a long moment. "No," I finally say.

"Of course."

I snap. "This is going to look bad for you when I end up murdered, and reporters discover I begged for help and you did nothing. Could be a career ender, Detective Heissen."

"Reporters, huh? Interesting that was your first thought."

Rolling my eyes, I sigh. "How is that interesting?"

"It's interesting because our office has been made aware of who you are and what you're doing."

"What? What does *that* mean?" But I know, of course, and my gut is already sinking, sinking, until it's compressed into an impossibly dense mass in my belly. Devil Girl. A known liar. A psychotic life-ruiner. A freak forever and ever.

He cocks his head, eyes narrowing. "Ms. May, I think you'll find that we're not as gullible as a small-town police department in Bumfuck, Ohio."

"Iowa," I whisper, wishing I had the nerve to point out he's not even getting the basics right, so he clearly knows nothing at all. But I don't. I don't have any nerve left, just this horrible, growing terror. I'm truly alone, just as I always intended.

The detective raises his eyes to someone behind me, then tips his head in a signal. For a moment I can feel hands on me, grabbing my arms, pulling them behind my back for handcuffs. Then the vision pops and disappears, because the cop rounds the chair and hands something to Detective Heissen without even glancing at me.

My relief is short-lived. Heissen lays a brochure on the table. Letters spell out *Liars Anonymous* in vibrant font across the top. My heart drops. My skin goes cold. I feel set up. Abandoned. Betrayed.

"Ma'am," Heissen drawls, "everything you claim has happened to you is unverifiable, unwitnessed, easily faked, and somehow never puts you in any real physical danger."

"A car nearly—"

"It's almost," he interrupts, "as if you're constructing an elaborate hoax. Again."

"That's not my brochure," I whisper. "The stalker sent it to taunt me."

"In that case I'd advise you to lock your doors, set up those missing cameras, and contact a mental health professional, Ms. May." I hear the snide edge in my name when he says it now.

"I was just a little kid," I murmur. "There was no elaborate hoax. I was five years old."

"Be that as it may, you got a lot of attention and sympathy from that episode, and you're not five years old anymore, are you? You're certainly capable of coming up with"—he sweeps a dismissive hand in the direction of my bedroom—"whatever this is. It seems you move from community to community on a regular basis. Is that correct?"

I don't answer, because I know I'm already alone, even with him sitting right there. They're not going to help. No one is. Maybe not even Mike if this continues.

"Who made you 'aware'?" I ask. "Is there a record? Did he call? Was his name Jacob Hoffholder?"

Detective Heissen slaps his knees and stands. "If you want any information related to police records, you can file a request with the department. I'm not at liberty to discuss that at the moment, pending any charges against you."

I squeeze my eyes shut. Shake my head. Charges against *me*? There's that pressure again, as old and familiar as any childhood memory. *Tell them what they want. Be a good girl. Don't talk back,* from my parents. *If you don't tell us more about what happened, babies will die,* from the police. *Lying is what very naughty kids do. Are you a liar? Or are you ready to tell us about the bad things?* from the social worker.

Detective Heissen wants me to comply and make his life easier. But what about my life? My truth? Do I ever get to have that back?

"This isn't right," I say as he moves to the door. "I haven't done anything wrong, and you're refusing to help me."

"Noted," he says blithely.

The female officer brings over a report for me to sign. I read over what she's written, and I can't deny that it's accurate and sounds as ridiculous as they're making it out to be. I carelessly scratch my name, then stare at that damn brochure until they all leave. The brochure that tells them I don't matter. None of the cops wish me luck or encourage me to call if I need more help.

Once they're gone, I have no idea what to do with myself, because what if . . . what if it's possible? What if I did make all this up? If I'm losing my mind, if I'm actually going crazy . . . how the hell would I even know?

CHAPTER 27

That's what delusion is, right? I think something is happening to me even when everyone else denies it? There's no true evidence of stalking except little bits and pieces I could have planted myself.

What if the elaborate lies I've woven for so many years have finally closed in and wrapped me so tight I can't see out? Because what can I actually prove? I could have created that fake account online. Could've seen that toy devil in the store and grabbed it in a fugue state. I might have even lost my balance and fallen into the street. But the flyers?

I raise my head. If I did that myself, there would be evidence.

Snatching up my phone, I open my bank account. There haven't been any debits from a mail supply store or other place I could have made copies. I don't own a printer, so I didn't make them at home. I check my credit card statement just to be sure, and no, there's nothing there either.

I know I didn't make up the flyers, because Mike had one in his pocket. He read it, showed it to me, folded it up again, and took it with him. Unless Mike is a figment of my imagination too.

"Okay, come on," I huff to myself. "Don't be an idiot." Mike is real and so is everything else. I can't let some asshole cop's reality destroy mine again. I can't believe other people over my own memories. I have to be strong in a way I couldn't when I was so small.

Even then, I'd known I was lying. I'd *known* that. A young nurse is the only one I remember being skeptical. She'd pressed gently, hoping to prompt the truth, but a doctor had intervened and sent her out of the room. For months I'd wished I'd admitted the lies, but I'd thought Lauren's stories were true. That she needed my help. My fear had been real and large and looming, and the false memories had grown to nightmares in my mind. But I hadn't been crazy, and I'm pretty sure I'm not crazy now.

I check the tracking on my camera delivery and sigh in frustration that my order might not arrive until 8:00 p.m. tomorrow. Maybe if John and his partner go out during the day, I could sneak over and steal their patio camera. I'll think about it.

A glance at my phone tells me it's past 11:00 p.m. Mike could still be up, and I want to text him, but I'm terrified to reach out. What if he doesn't believe me?

I get up and grab a knife from my kitchen, then check every room, every window lock; I even check under my bed. When I feel nominally secure, I huddle on the couch, wrap a blanket around me, and text Mike.

Hi. Are you up?

I know it's too late to text Tristan in Florida, but if Mike doesn't respond—

Three dots appear, cutting off my desperate planning. Just like that, I'm connected again.

I am. I've actually been looking into some people online. You said that the other girl died a year ago? Lauren? Is her last name Jensen?

My body jerks with alarm. He probably knows everything about the Hoffholders. Everything about me.

But . . . of course he does. What the hell did I think would happen? He likely started researching the second he got home, because who wouldn't google such a juicy story as soon as they got a chance?

I sigh out a curse, and my head drops with weariness. I'm so damn tired, all my adrenaline washed away by disrespect and defeat. I feel like I could sleep for twenty-four hours.

And really, Mike knowing everything doesn't matter. Yes, I feel like I'm standing naked on stage with a hundred spotlights shining on me and a camera zooming in for a close-up, but I'll survive even if I'm used to skulking in the shadows.

That's her, I type back. Why?

I looked her up. Sorry. I was reading her obituary. She seemed like a great person. So sad.

Yeah. It is.

Did you notice that commenter named Audrey Echols?

I open my laptop and navigate back to the obituary. After scrolling through the comments, I find the one he means. We should have believed her.

I did see that, I text back. Why?

I'm just wondering what it means. Do you know her?

I shake my head. No.

Ok, sorry. My mind was churning a bit. Everything good over there? I thought you'd be asleep by now.

Me too, I answer. And I start to explain. I start to type it out. Remember when you checked my bedroom and it was nice and neat? Well, I didn't make my bed today. Someone broke in and cleaned my . . .

"No," I say aloud, wincing away from the awful things the police implied. Wincing away from how improbable it all is.

I delete the unsent message.

You should get some rest, he texts. But first . . .

A picture loads, the color a bit faded, but the faces still crisp. A little bucktoothed boy is holding a fish, his smile proud and wide, his legs stick thin. A young girl in a yellow bikini makes a face as she points at the fish. A man with his hand on the boy's shoulder has a more serious expression, though his eyes sparkle. His face looks startlingly like Mike's does today. It's his family, and they are definitely not the Hoffholders.

I melt with relief and affection. Awww. Little Mikey! Look how cute you are!

Gee thanks, he says, but he follows it with a blushing emoji.

Buckteeth and all! Hey, thank you for sending that.

And then I'm crying. Because it means a lot that he hasn't run away screaming yet, and even if he does, he was here for me tonight. That's something precious, isn't it?

I'll text tomorrow if I find anything else, Mike writes, breaking into my thoughts.

Thank you so much, I answer immediately.

I reopen the obituary page, but before I can take a look, my phone buzzes again. Expecting another text from Mike, I wince with guilt when I see that it's actually from Tristan. Look at me, juggling two men.

Hey, how's it going tonight?

I frown. Yeah, I'm not really cut out for dividing my attention. And I'm way too tired to tell Tristan the truth tonight. Lying is so much easier. I'm good. You're still up???

Couldn't sleep. I've been worried about you.

I'm fine.

Yeah? No more trouble?

Sighing, I shrug off the guilt and embrace the exhaustion. All good, I lie. Already in bed myself, actually. Long day.

He doesn't respond right away, and I feel bad, but I really am too tired to keep this up.

And now I hear voices outside. God. Please don't be anything. *Please.*

I open the security feed and immediately relax. The two guests next door are on their patio. Music plays softly, barely audible. They're on the outdoor couch, and a bobbing point of bright light makes clear they're passing a joint between them. It's not allowed, of course, but I've only tattled on guests one time. That wasn't really because they were smoking, but because they were rude, racist assholes who gave me a chance to ruin a small part of their day with an extra cleaning charge.

My phone buzzes. Got it, Tristan says. Let's talk tomorrow.

I turn down my lights, switch back to the camera feed, and stretch out on the couch. The men start singing along to an old Annie Lennox song, their heads close together, fingers entwined.

When I fall asleep, I dream of floating high above the world, the voice of Annie Lennox urging me higher.

CHAPTER 28

When I wake and discover I slept for a solid eight hours, I'm buoyant with relief. My back twinges when I shift on the couch, but that doesn't dampen my mood. I feel immeasurably better, and I haven't even had my coffee yet.

After grabbing a yogurt and throwing a piece of bread in the toaster, I start the coffee. My place smells glorious within minutes, and now I'm thinking about Mike again. After his texts last night, it almost feels like Mike and I are a team, and boy, that's a new feeling. Scary but kind of really nice? Interesting.

The warm cozies don't last long, though. I'm only halfway through my yogurt when I minimize the security feed on my laptop and the obituary page glows to life, waiting for me. Shit. Poor Lauren. It's the weekend, so the only work I have is digging into this, and I should probably get to it.

I return to the name Mike mentioned last night. Audrey Echols. We should have believed her.

Is it something to do with the Hoffholder case? That wouldn't really make sense . . . unless Lauren had changed her story again for some bizarre reason. I frown. Wait, *did* Lauren change her story again?

"Hmm." I open Lauren's old Facebook page. Her final post was three days before she died. Hit the town with my girlies. Thank you for getting me out of my own head! I love you! What doesn't kill us makes us stronger. Yes, that applies to tequila too.

It's a selfie of Lauren with two other women; all of them are blond and pretty and smiling. So odd how often groups of friends look the same. Same values and attractions, I guess.

Lauren is holding the camera in one hand and a shot glass in the other. She doesn't look depressed, but I know that means nothing. A lot of people are able to mask depression, especially in social situations.

I'm glad she was with friends before. I'm glad she wasn't totally alone.

Unlike you? that stupid internal voice whispers, but I ignore it and keep reading. Three weeks before her death, Lauren posted a new real estate listing. Just on the market! Check out that backyard!

But just after that post came a very brief request. Does anyone have a local attorney they can recommend? Or maybe I need a PI. 🙁

Before that, almost all Lauren's posts were home listings mixed in with pictures of her traveling or out with friends. One picture from six months before is Lauren standing near a white Lexus SUV with a red bow on it. Bought myself a birthday present!

There's only one other recent post that catches my eye. A reminder about how scary it can be to be a female real estate agent, along with a snapshot of safe practices when showing homes. Hmm.

I go back to the post about wanting a lawyer and read the comments, but all I see are exclamations or questions. If Lauren answered anyone, she did it over private message, as there are zero hints about why she suddenly needed a lawyer or a private investigator. Was something going on? I shiver as the question winds through me.

When my phone rings I'm excited for the chance to talk to Mike about this, but Tristan's name flashes on my phone. I guess we're just calling each other now. I'm a little irritated, but my guilt over blowing him off while happily texting with Mike last night has returned. "Hey, sorry about last night," I say as I answer. "I was super tired."

"I'm sure you haven't been sleeping well," he says.

"No, I really haven't. And last night . . ."

"Did something happen?"

"I don't know," I sigh. The shame is back. The discouragement. The fear about speaking the truth. I need to start looking for a new place to land. I can't live like this. And I'm a grown woman, so I don't have to. "I talked to a police detective," I say carefully.

"Oh, that's great! I'm so relieved. I've heard it's best if you keep at them. Squeaky wheel, you know."

"No, you don't understand. They don't believe me."

"Don't believe you about what?" he asks.

"All this craziness. Everything that's happening." My heart is racing now, just remembering that cop and his snide tone.

"They're probably being careful and, you know . . . official."

"I don't think so. The detective threatened to arrest me for making false complaints."

Tristan stays quiet for a long time, and every second twists my stomach tighter. I've planted the idea now. That I'm crazy, hysterical, lying. Or more likely, he was already thinking that and I've crystallized the concern in his mind. I was so worried about Mike that I forgot to worry about Tristan.

"Tristan?" I finally say.

"They think you're lying?"

Oh God. I cover my face with my hand and just breathe for a moment. I remind myself that he's my friend. And most people trust their friends. I can do this. I'm not a coward.

Actually, I am a coward, but I need to pull my shit together and face this.

"Yeah," I answer. "I haven't been hurt, I don't have proof. The detective basically said I'm doing all these things to myself. For attention."

"Wow. That's strange."

"I mean, maybe it's not so strange that they're being unhelpful. Police don't have a great historical track record for believing women, do they? He said/she said, and no one has even spotted the *he* in this story."

"I guess that's true. But you sent them video, right? Of the guy pushing you into the street? So they do have proof."

I clear my throat. "I did, but the person isn't super visible. I mean, I can see someone behind me in the crowd, I can see who did it, but the detective says it looks like I just fell."

"Oh."

That's it. Just *oh*. But that one, tiny syllable is dripping with meaning. Doubt and withdrawal and disappointment, I swear I hear it all in that one small sound. "He's there, though!" I protest. "In the video! There's someone behind me in a hat and dark glasses. He turns away as I fall. They can't do anything with such a vague image, so maybe that's the problem. They don't like being at a disadvantage, so they're putting it back on me!"

He clears his throat. "All right. Well, there must be something else you can show them."

That's the logical next thought, yes. That if someone has been stalking me for a week, I'd have a picture or a recording or *anything*. "No," I answer, and the quiet that follows is unbearable. "Someone broke in last night," I blurt out, but I immediately regret the words and remind myself not to tell him the intruder just . . . cleaned up and made my bed.

"Holy shit. They broke in? Through a window or something? That's terrifying. Were you home?"

"No. And I . . . I'm not sure how they got in. But . . ." I look toward my front door. "Actually, I need to call my landlord." I know it wasn't the cleaning people for the Airbnb, but what if someone did get my access code? I try to be careful about hiding my hand when I punch it in, but I'm sure I've let my guard down.

Did Mike see it? God, now I'm back to blaming poor Mike. Regardless, I'll ask Grigore if I can reset it.

"Are you okay?" he presses. "Did they steal something? Or Jesus, you weren't hurt, were you?"

"No, no, I wasn't here." I wave his questions away. "I need to go, but I do think I'm on to something. I think I know who it is."

I hear a chair squeal as he sits up quickly. "Really?"

"Yeah. I'll tell you more later, okay? I don't really want to talk about it right now."

He's quiet for a long time again. I've pushed him away, and we both know it. I switch my phone to the other hand and wipe my sweating palm on my pants. "I need to go," I declare loudly.

"Wait. Maybe this is all just—"

"No, sorry. I have to call my landlord. I'll check in later." I hang up, face heating.

Let him doubt me if he wants. I'm burning up with anger over his questioning tone, but I know it's not really rage. It's not even Tristan. It's humiliation. The cops know who I really am, and that's all I'll ever be. The nasty liar. The pathological freak.

I pull up Grigore's name on my phone and call him before I can second-guess myself.

"Elizabeth," he answers gruffly.

"Hi, Grigore! Sorry to bother you!" I always find myself chirping like a little bird around this guy, trying to offset his stoic cool.

"No bother."

"Okay, well, I just wanted to let you know that someone broke into my place last night. I'm fine, but—"

"A thief?" His flat tone perks up to more of a bark.

"No, he didn't steal anything. I wasn't home, but I've been having trouble with a stalker, so . . . yeah. I think it was him."

"A stalker!" His voice booms now.

"Unless it was someone looking for you again?" I propose.

I hope he'll say yes. That he'll confess anything that proves this break-in wasn't about me. But he offers a negative grunt. "No. Not possible. We came to an agreement."

"Oh. Okay. Well, I'd like to change the code on my locks and put up extra cameras, if that's all right with you."

"Yes! Of course! I'll come over at noon. I'll bring you gun. We'll take care of this."

"No!" I yelp. "I don't want a gun! I've never even held one. I've ordered two new cameras, so I just—"

"Noon," he barks before the line goes dead.

Okay. Noon it is, apparently. I'm not accepting any gun gifts, but I can't deny that I feel a shit-ton better about my safety now that Grigore is coming.

Still feeling brave after Grigore's support, I dare to take one more chance and text Mike. Did you find anything else last night?

Not much, he responds right away. On my way to a bookstore. Want to meet for coffee and talk?

Okay. Maybe I do have a team after all.

CHAPTER 29

It's Hilda's, of course. I really shouldn't be taking the risk of running into her with Mike in tow, but how can I resist? What's hotter than a cute guy who loves books?

We meander in silence through the shelves, working our way slowly toward the coffee bar.

I allow myself a secret smile when I see the romance endcap. The store's romance selection had been spotty at best when I first started coming, but I'd pointed out to Hilda that snobbery doesn't make money, and it was the highest-selling genre, so she'd started stocking a corner with new releases. Two months later, she'd thanked me for the bump in sales.

Hey, not all heroes wear capes.

"Ellie!" I hear Hilda call from across the store, but I'm ready for it and already have a plan.

I roll my eyes at Mike and shake my head before I whisper, "She calls me Ellie. She's a little eccentric, so brace yourself." Then I head toward Hilda with open arms. "Hilda! Happy Saturday. How's it going?"

We hug, and I introduce her to Mike, grinning when she gives me a thumbs-up in response. I keep my life so segmented that it's entirely novel to watch two people I know strike up a conversation. They quickly fall deep into the subject of narrative nonfiction together, and it's like watching a cute movie on the big screen, except I'm actually starring in it. I'm so fascinated that I don't manage to contribute to the conversation at all.

Despite the awful things happening, I bask in this small moment of joy. Mike throws back his head to laugh at something Hilda says, and she touches his shoulder flirtatiously. Watching it just feels . . . nice.

When Hilda holds up a finger and tells Mike she'll be right back, I whisper, "Isn't she great?"

"She is."

"She's always encouraging me to write a book. I don't have the heart to tell her I don't have the attention span for it."

"Oh, I bet you could do it," he says. "You have so much personality. And it's just one page at a time. Or that's what I always told myself about papers in grad school."

As much as I love stories, I suppose it's possible I could write one of my own if I really put my mind to it. "Maybe one day." At least if I started writing, it would remove one lie from my portfolio. And actually . . . I'd get paid to lie. To make up as many stories as I wanted. I really should consider the idea.

"I bet you'd kill it," he says offhandedly as he pulls a book from the shelf next to us.

Feeling shy all of a sudden, I turn from him to trace a finger over a spine as if I'm checking it out. As easy as it was to go to bed with Mike that first time, I almost can't imagine it now. Getting naked, being vulnerable, sharing my real self? Eek. I feel my cheeks go red at the mere thought.

Hilda returns with a book about deep-sea diving and presses it into Mike's hands before flitting off toward the register. It's easier to turn and look at him once he's flipped open the book.

"Well, you've got to buy it now," I say, laughing when he winces and nods.

"I'll never be able to show my face here again if I don't. Looks like I have a new book. It does seem interesting, though."

"Are you a diver?" I ask.

We chat all the way through the store and in the long line for coffee. I check my phone once we're stocked with drinks. "If I leave abruptly, it's because my landlord is coming at noon to talk about security."

"Oh, that's good. Sounds like a decent landlord."

"He's great. And interesting. And it's possible he's bringing a small arsenal, so I feel better already."

Mike raises an eyebrow but doesn't ask what the arsenal might be, which is another bit of proof he has nothing to do with this. Every little reassurance helps my nonfunctioning trust muscles get a little stronger. One day they might be repaired enough to dare putting a bit more weight on them. But not yet.

When we pass the short hallway that leads to the bathroom, my brain catches up to my steps and I stop, then back up and throw a glance toward the bulletin board. From this angle, I can't see much, but I know what I'll find if I walk deeper into the space.

"Hold on," I mutter.

Mike waits until he sees me stop at the wall of bulletins and local ads, and I'm too slow to reach up and grab the flyer before he joins me. "Shit," he says when he spots my picture smiling at him.

I yank it down, but this time I fold it carefully before stuffing it in my purse. "Sorry," I mutter, apologizing for a dozen stupid things, but also a little sorry I agreed to meet him here. Was one moment of strange happiness worth the humiliation?

Actually . . . maybe it was? Because Mike bumps his shoulder against mine and says, "Let's walk down by the beach," like we're in this together. Maybe if I don't scare him off again, I can risk getting naked and vulnerable in front of him. Once. Or twice. I hope so, because he's making me horny with all this adorable caring.

He disappears to pay for his book, and we manage to escape the store without further incident. It's cool today but not at all foggy, so we're joined on our walk by large groups of tourists carrying all manner of gear.

Mike lets someone pulling a beach wagon pass us, and I notice when he starts walking again that he puts himself closer to the curb. When we get to an intersection, I look for traffic about four times before crossing, even with the Walk light.

Once we reach the arcade that fronts most of the beach area, I point him toward the north end so we don't have to wind through crowds to see the water.

"This place is pricey," I say, pointing to a sprawling restaurant with a huge oceanfront patio. "But it's actually good. So if you're going to pay tourist prices right by the water, this is one you want to try."

He cranes his neck as we pass the outdoor seating. "I think I'll have to come back here for breakfast. Look at the French toast."

"I love the—" And then, of course, someone new calls my name. And by my name, I mean one of the many.

"Betty? Betty, hellooooo!" A man jumps up from a table and rushes toward us. I try to keep walking, but he darts for the gate and races out onto the walkway to intercept me. "Betty! It's Gerald!"

Shit. I can't see Mike in my peripheral vision, but I can *feel* him looking at me. How could he not? There are posters everywhere screaming at him that I'm a liar, and Gerald is the second person this morning to call me by a different name. *Another* different name.

This is why I try my best to stick everyone in their own compartments in my life. If I'd sexed up Mike and walked away forever like I should have, this wouldn't be happening. "Hi, Gerald," I say, my voice wobbling between friendly and cool, because I can't figure out how to play this, and also I've never seen Gerald with his clothes on. I'd expected style and verve, but he's just wearing cargo shorts and a faded T-shirt from a surfboard store, blending in with all the other retired men having brunch.

"My love," he coos. "Eighty degrees tomorrow, so I hope you're meaning to join us at the beach. Opal is bringing margaritas. I'm thinking of getting one of those giant sub sandwiches. You know what I'm talking about? They slice it up for you, so it's easy for a picnic."

"Uh, yeah. Sure."

"It's going to be a perfect beach party. You should come. And bring your friend too." Teeth a blinding white against his deeply tanned skin, Gerald turns his charming smile on Mike.

"This is Mike," I say woodenly as I reluctantly introduce them.

The men exchange pleasantries, and then I stand awkwardly for a moment before gesturing toward the water. "Well, we're off!"

Gerald's smile fades a bit. "Oh, of course. Sorry, I didn't mean to . . ." His hand waves helplessly. It must have just occurred to him that I might not want to tell my companion about my nude sunbathing. And sure, I'll take it. "Have a good walk," he finishes quietly.

I steer Mike toward the beach, and we keep walking. Mike will bolt now. He has to. Sorrow pierces me at the thought, but I set my jaw and ignore it. I'm a nurse. I deal with sorrow a lot. I'm still *fine*, damn it.

He eventually clears his throat. "Beach party, huh?"

In any other situation, I'd think Mike was angling for an invitation, and frankly I might even invite him. But I'm pretty sure what he's angling for here is an explanation. I can't offer one, because what the hell am I supposed to say? *Don't worry, I know it seems like I introduce myself with a different name to everyone I meet, but . . . Okay, yes, I do.*

Instead I laugh. "Yeah, it's quite a party if you like hanging out with retirees. Which I do. But I don't think I'll make it tomorrow. Too many stalkers and investigations. You know how it goes."

"Sure." The word sounds dragged from his throat, so I jump right in to change the topic.

"Speaking of, I think I'll reach out to that friend who left a comment on Lauren's obituary. It seems crazy, but . . . I've been thinking. What if Lauren was going through the same thing I am? Do you think that's even possible?"

He hesitates for a moment as if he doesn't want to change the subject, but when I glance at him, he sighs and gives in. "I was thinking the same thing. That's why I wanted to talk. If this guy is really stalking you over something that happened decades ago, then it's not a stretch to think he'd go after the other witness too, right?"

"Right. And if he harassed her for a while . . . What if no one believed her, and it all hit her really hard? Maybe she felt hopeless and dropped into a bad depression about it. I looked through her old posts, and there were a couple of hints."

"Like what?"

"Nothing super obvious, but she asked for help finding an attorney, and then she said, 'Or maybe I need a PI.'"

"A private investigator?"

"Yeah. She also posted a reminder to real estate agents about how to stay safe while working."

I've got him now. His brow is furrowed and his eyes distant as he tries to help analyze the situation. "When was that?"

"Last year. A few weeks before she died."

"Seems like she was worried about something."

"Yeah," I agree. "Or maybe she wanted a lawyer to write a will because she was planning her death. But why would she bring up a PI?"

"It is eerie."

"Anyway, I wanted to thank you for reminding me of her friend's comment. It helped point me back toward Lauren."

"Sure. Good thinking. Let me know what you find."

We stop to watch the Dream Wheel above us for a bit as the sea lions bark from the pier, and God, I wish everything with Mike wasn't so messed up. Even a few minutes ago I might have asked if he wanted to take a ride on the wheel and look out over the swimmers bobbing in the ocean, but now I'm afraid the alone time will make him bring up Gerald.

But maybe I should bring it up. Maybe I don't even have to lie.

I chicken out, and we cut through the amusement park to head for the back entrance. "How's your work going?" I ask as we weave through the crowds, hoping I can lull him into a happy state by asking him about himself.

And bingo, it works. Mike talks about his next trip down to Moss Landing and the analysis he's doing, though I can only nod as if I understand his research talk. I carefully guide us back toward our street before I've even finished my coffee.

It's just after eleven when we reach my driveway, and though I'm eager to return to my computer, I find myself suddenly blurting out the truth. It spills out because I've opened that door and now I can't get it shut again. The seal's broken or something.

"That guy. Gerald? He . . . I . . ." Then I just stand there, open-mouthed and flailing.

Mike throws me a line, though it seems to be covered in barbed hooks. "The man who called you Betty?"

Oh balls. There it is, almost as if it had been hanging between us this whole time. I croak out a weird noise, but Mike waits silently, not giving an inch. I know he deserves an explanation, but I hate him a little in that moment.

Still, more leaks out. "Elizabeth has a lot of nicknames," I blurt.

"I guess it does. Yeah."

"Sometimes people pick their own for me."

"Okay. But you told me you were Beth, and that's what I call you. It's beginning to seem like you've told other people other names. And claimed different careers too."

Shit. Oh no. Note to self: Sleep with a dumb guy next time. "You're right," I admit. "I'm a very private person. You probably know that about me by now. I like to decide who knows what about me." Too much truth! I veer back to the point. "But I told Gerald to call me Betty because of how I met him."

"Oh. Like . . ." He clears his throat. "Like a group setting?" When I lower my eyebrows in confusion, he adds, "Therapy?" with a significant look.

I think he means AA, though the cocktails I've shared with him would be a bad sign if that were the case. But no doubt it would be easier for him to forgive my falling off the wagon than being a compulsive liar. "No, it's not that. I met Gerald at the beach. But like . . ." I clear my throat and tell myself this is funny. It is. In fact, I would happily have revealed this as hilarious titillation a few days ago. But everything feels so different now, and I hate it.

"We met at a nude beach," I force out.

"Oh," he says. Then, "Oohhh!"

"Exactly. But also . . ." Shit, what's happening to me? "I do like to use different names," I say on a rush. "And I don't think that's wrong. I like to keep people separate in my life. I think that's okay. They're all *my* names!"

"Okay, but it is . . . odd," he says, which isn't the ideal response, but I can see by the vagueness in his eyes that he's still trying to process the nude-beach part.

"Maybe I'm just odd, then. But I know, for instance, that if Gerald mentions his friend Betty to someone I know, they won't connect the dots. My personal information is still private. And you understand why that would be important to me." I nod, trying to convince him. "Or if you were to tell someone we're dating . . ." Wait, that sounds worse. I should have steered away from his part in this.

"No one will know I'm dating you. I get it." He shakes his head. "You realize that doesn't make it less weird, right?"

"Yeah, I kind of caught on as I was saying it." I gesture sadly toward my door, ready to let him off the hook. Tristan didn't understand. Mike won't understand. Because who would? "I get it, all right? Maybe you could just glance inside before you go? Or—" I change my mind before he can say no. Because why would he want to endanger himself for me at this point? "You could wait here while I look around! I'll be quick. Thanks."

"I'll take a look," he says before I get halfway down the driveway, and I'm so thankful for how kind he is. He must have had nice parents. Parents that taught him sometimes people need help and that's okay.

When I unlock the door, he steps inside. I watch carefully as he moves around my space. "Looks good," he says.

"Thanks." I drift in and hover near the door as he skirts the couch and heads back to where I am. "My landlord will be here soon," I say, making clear he can leave with no hard feelings.

"Okay. That's good. Let me know how it goes."

Yeah, his tone is definitely cooler than usual. But I tell myself that's fine because I won't have to be brave about Mike anymore. And Grigore's coming to save me anyway, so good riddance.

Still, I feel guilty even pretending to think that part. Or disappointed. Or maybe just really, really sad.

CHAPTER 30

"I don't know anything about handling guns, Grigore!" I protest yet again. "Seriously. It's a very generous offer, but I can't accept. I wouldn't know what to do with it."

Grigore looks displeased. Actually, Grigore always looks displeased, with his bulldog head and a neck nearly as wide as my shoulders. All those muscles seem to pull his face into a permanent frown, but now he's actively scowling down at me.

"It's a gun." He's holding said gun by the barrel, gesturing toward me with the grip or whatever the handle part is. "You aim. You pull the trigger."

I hate guns. That tends to happen after seeing so many organs and faces obliterated by them. "I totally get that. But look at me. I'm weak. Someone like you would just knock the gun away; then I'd have an angry bad guy with a loaded gun to deal with."

"Hm. I suppose." Thank God we're finally getting somewhere.

"The cameras should be here in . . ." I check the tracking on my phone again. "Two to three hours. I'll set up an alert on the system to go off if anyone tries to get in. Then I can call the cops."

"The cops," he mutters disapprovingly, and I have to agree. "Maybe call me. I don't like them around."

Grigore tucks the gun back under his jacket and snaps his fingers. The associate who's been standing outside steps in to hand him something much smaller than a gun. Grigore wiggles his fingers, and the man places a second black metal object into his huge palm. They look like small tactical flashlights, maybe?

Grigore turns and extends his hand toward me. I stare warily. "Tasers," he says.

I'm surprised. "Those are Tasers?"

"Small ones for ladies."

Oh great. Sexism. But okay, yes, I am intrigued.

"You keep one in purse, one by bed, and electrocute any asshole who needs it."

Ooo, I like that. I reach out and gingerly pick up both of the surprisingly heavy tubes. "Hmm." I turn one over and see a switch. It's on, so I turn it back to off. "Do you think they'll actually do damage? Like, in a good way?"

"You want to test on Luca?"

"Nope!" I yelp, shaking my head frantically. "But thank you! Thank you, Luca!" I give the guy an awkward wave, but he simply retreats to the doorway, his somber expression never budging.

"The shock will stop him for a minute. Maybe more. Who is it? Ex-boyfriend?"

"No, just some random guy. It's been pretty scary. But then there was also that guy looking for you. Maybe some of it is just . . ." I wait for him to agree that he could be at fault for part of my trauma, but he only stares. "So . . . who knows? But thanks for coming over."

"Call me next time," he orders, and I completely agree. Grigore hasn't bothered trying to quiz me about whether I'm truly in danger. He didn't express doubt. He just jumped right in with some deadly weapons. I'd throw my arms around him if I thought I could reach all the way.

Funny to think that tiny Doina was Grigore's mother. But maybe she deteriorated to that delicate frailness. Maybe she was a badass warrior in her time.

"You tell me his name."

I could hem and haw about how I don't want this man injured, but I'm not that kind of girl. Jacob has tried to get me fired, tried to drive my community away, destroyed my sense of safety, and broken into my home to paw through my belongings. Hurt him, Grigore. Hurt him.

I give him Jacob's name and a vague description. He waves Luca over again, and they have a conversation in Romanian.

In the end, it takes only three minutes to reset both keypad locks. Grigore lets me choose my own code, then makes a note of it in his phone. I don't mind. Any landlord would have a master key, and there's no universe in which Grigore would slip silently through my home to make my bed and put laundry away. With or without the lock code, if Grigore wants in, he'll get in.

He offers the gun one more time, of course, and gives me a disappointed glare when I refuse. "Call me if you see this man," he orders, and I nod.

You bet your ass I will. We're going extrajudicial, baby, because I'm definitely not calling 911 again. Grigore even gives me Luca's number just in case. I feel warm inside. Cared for.

Luca speaks up in Romanian again, and his words clearly irritate Grigore, who barks something at him, but Luca seems to insist.

With a sigh, he flings a hand in the man's direction, shifting so Luca can move back inside. "He had an accident yesterday. You're a nurse."

His bodyguard raises an arm, and for the first time I realize there's a beige bandage taped to the back of his hand. I wave him toward the kitchen and turn the lights all the way up before carefully removing the dressing. His knuckles look a bit smashed, and there are ugly cuts raking down the skin toward his wrist.

"Ouch," I say.

"Ouch," Luca agrees.

I lean in closer and angle my head from side to side. "Did you put this through glass?"

"Yes," Grigore answers for him.

Ah. The kind of accident that involves punching out a window, perhaps to unlock a door. Got it. None of my business. “Hold on. I think I see something in there.”

After I grab my big emergency kit and some tweezers, I return to the kitchen and lean over his hand again. “This will hurt,” I warn as I pull on latex gloves. He doesn’t even tense as I pick at the edge of one cut until a glass sliver catches enough light for me to home in and ease it free. A fat drop of blood wells. “Ouch,” I mutter again, then check every other wound for glass.

I find one more speck of it, then pour a bit of hydrogen peroxide on the spots where the glass was stuck. I can tell by the soapy-clean scent of his skin and the clean bandages that the cuts have already been washed out, so I just smooth on a liberal amount of antibiotic cream and apply a new dressing.

A comforting buzz washes over me, and I remember how much I’ve always loved caring for patients. I miss it, but not so much that I want to race back to it. Maybe in a year. Or five.

“That should heal up a little better now,” I say, patting his wrist. Grigore translates for me, and Luca flexes his hand before giving a satisfied nod.

All right, our little gang is ready to rumble.

Having the strength of Grigore and Luca at my back has changed my strategy. I’d been planning to use the cameras defensively, to help me feel safe in my own home. But I can do better than that. I’ll get proof on tape, get some images of what Jacob looks like here in Santa Cruz, maybe even a picture of his current vehicle. Then I’ll go on the offensive.

That might mean hiring a PI, just as Lauren had planned. Or it could mean a simple phone call to my landlord and his friend.

It’s time to take my weird little life back.

CHAPTER 31

> Hi Audrey. You don't know me, but I knew Lauren Jensen years ago and just found out about her death. God, what a tragedy. I'm sorry for your loss. On the obituary site you said, "We should have believed her." I apologize for prying, but can I ask what you meant by that? I heard she was possibly dealing with security issues??? I don't know. Maybe I'm just reaching for explanations. Again, sorry to pry. Thank you for your time.

I check the message again, but it's still unread after twenty-seven minutes. Apparently Audrey Echols doesn't hang out online all the time, which is great for her. But I haven't looked away from my screen in about . . . twenty-seven minutes.

Since I'm on Facebook I return to Lauren's old page, and I'm surprised to see a brand-new comment beneath her last post. RIP, Lauren. I've been thinking about what you went through.

I click on his name, Dave DesMoines. His account is private, but the message button is available, so what the hell. My Facebook name is Elle Traveler and has little to do with my real life, so what's the risk? I send him a shorter version of the note I sent to Audrey, asking for any info he's willing to share.

Audrey still hasn't written back, and there's a good chance she'll ignore me and my intrusive question. If she does, I'll send another message letting her know a bit more. If I have to reveal that I'm going through something awful, I will.

Either I'm desperate or it's getting easier, but I still don't like it.

In the meantime I check my phone again and see that my delivery is close! Tired of being locked inside, I carefully peek out, then wander down to the sidewalk to stand in the sun for a bit. The warm front promising eighty-degree temps is obviously approaching, because the breeze doesn't carry even a hint of the cool Pacific Ocean today.

A naked beach party sounds wonderful, and I desperately need to lie around with a margarita in my hand and melt into the sand for a few hours, but how could I possibly let my guard down long enough to enjoy it?

Mr. Sanchez pulls up in his minivan, and I smile and wave at him. When he gets out of his car, I take a step forward to join him for a quick talk, but he only waves weakly before retreating inside. That's . . . really abnormal. Mr. Sanchez is usually a chatterbox.

Damn it. He must have seen the flyers.

Jacob Hoffholder has ruined things for me in Santa Cruz. I can't control anything now, and I suddenly hate it here. I hate that I have no idea what Mr. Sanchez thinks about me. Hate that everyone is telling an unapproved story about me in their heads now. I want my camouflage back.

Just as I start to retreat toward my apartment, I glance up to see a big white van approaching. For a split second I wonder if I'm about to be kidnapped, but the vehicle squeals to a stop on worn brakes, and the guy who jumps out barely looks at me as he rushes around to the back. He has no idea he's my hero.

Half an hour later, I'm patting myself on the back and jumping through the last hoops on my security feed to check the angle of the cameras.

"Perfection!" I crow as both cameras pop online. I installed one a little to the side of my front door so I have a fairly clear view past the wooden staircase. I can see my entrance area, the driveway beyond it, two windows, and even the sidewalk.

The second camera is on the back fence, facing my patio doors, giving me a full view of the rear of my house: doors, window, and the gate that leads outside. I've set alerts for any movement within fifteen feet, along with an alert if the cameras lose Wi-Fi connection because the power goes out.

Screw Jacob Hoffholder. I'm determined to outsmart his demented antics.

After checking to make sure it's off, I slip one Taser into my pocket, reminding myself to put it under my pillow when I go to bed. The other I turn on and slip between the couch cushions, though I place it on the side of the couch I rarely use so I won't accidentally Taser my ass when I plop down to watch a movie. On the off chance I ever date again, I'll need to remember to move that.

Whatever. The possibility of dating anytime soon is very, very low. It's sinking in that as much as I love this town, I'll probably pack up and flee the moment I can arrange a new job and place to live. Too many people know too much about me. But not quite yet. Right now I need Grigore at my back because I'm certain this stalker will track down any new address. I have to fight this asshole now.

But when this all calms down? I could move to San Jose, where the hospital group is based. I'm required to go in for meetings, so I can't flee the state. But what about my beach living? I suppose I could try Monterey for a few months. Not as quirky as Santa Cruz, but it has the ocean, and I could still commute to the hospital. Perhaps I could start over there. Make new acquaintances. Spread new lies.

My stomach burns at that thought, so I shove it away. I'll deal with my absolutely ridiculous life once I've shut down this stalker.

But now I still have a late afternoon to waste. The great news is that I can monitor all this from anywhere. I can't take one of my typical four-to-five-mile walks around town, because I don't want to spend hours looking over my shoulder for threats. But maybe the library?

Yes, the library. One of the best places in the world. I feel safe just thinking about it.

I take the quickest shower anyone has ever taken, pull my hair into a ponytail, and put on a sundress to cheer myself up even more. The bright yellow swirls around my legs when I swing my hips, and I feel immediately light and free. A ray of weird sunshine.

After I stuff my laptop, purse, and sweater into a retro beach bag, I slip on some cute sneakers for the walk and feel almost cheerful. Cheerful adjacent.

My phone is in my hand with the volume all the way up in case a security alert pings, and I have my Taser in my pocket, but I forget about all that after a few steps in the perfect sunlight.

Pigeons coo gently from a rooftop, gulls squawk in the sky, and someone is playing an accordion in a nearby backyard. My bubble is back, this sense that I belong here, and when tears prick my eyes at the thought of leaving, I blink hard and ignore the sadness.

I'm lucky to have found this place for a couple of years. It's been a home to me, a real home, and I can come back to visit whenever I like. Maybe I'll retire here. I don't have to give it up forever.

When I pass the animal shelter, I have to resist the physical pull to go in and spend time with the dogs. I can't put any animals in danger. If something happens to me, and a dog runs into a busy street . . . Then again, if Jacob is following me on a bike, Cocoa would tear his ass up.

Lifted by the thought, I make a mental promise to take Cocoa on as many walks as I can before I leave.

I spot Violet as soon as I open the library door and feel a rush of embarrassment that I told her about my past. I want to sneak by the desk while she's looking down, but what if she glances up and sees me tiptoeing by? Everything was so much easier when I was unrepentant. Now I'm a tortured mess.

"Hi, Violet," I whisper, hoping she won't hear me.

She looks up and stands immediately to come around the huge checkout area. "Hey, Betsy." I lean into her hug and close my eyes. God, she's almost as good a hugger as Hilda, and the scents of coffee and cinnamon drift off her clothes. I wonder what her house is like. Breezy and open? Cluttered and quirky? I feel a sharp pain that I'll never know, like I'm already saying goodbye to her.

"How's it going? Are you okay?"

"I'm better, thank you," I say, reluctantly pulling away. "I've got new security cameras up. The cops are being complete assholes, but if I get him on video, they can't keep denying it."

"That's so good. You look like a new woman today. And all this color!" She sweeps a hand toward my dress, and I give her a little twirl to show off. Her laugh sounds relieved, making my heart squeeze to think she was actually worried about me. I told you she was my favorite librarian.

"I haven't seen any flyers since yesterday," she says, "but I'm on the case, so don't worry."

"Thanks, Violet. You're so sweet to look out for me."

Sticky emotions lurch up and try to overwhelm me, so I hurry away toward the seating area in the far corner. This isn't one of the newer, airier branches, but it's the closest to my place, so I'm used to the cozy layout. I grab a table where I can sit with my back to a dead-end corner and open my laptop. Sadly, there's no mental space left to browse for books right now, but I promise the books I'll come visit them again as soon as I'm done visiting the dogs.

Those idle thoughts burst into panicked flight the moment I see I have a message on Facebook.

"Please, please, please," I mutter, as I click on Audrey's tiny, smiling face. And then my whole world goes black.

CHAPTER 32

This isn't like my shower trauma. I don't think I've gone blind, and the power isn't out. This blackness is just a brief stutter in my vision that's broken by flashing stars, and then everything clears and I'm rereading the first shocking sentence of the message from Audrey.

> Lauren was being terrorized, it was awful.

Terrorized. Terrorized just like *me*?

I pull in a deep breath, hold it, and start to read.

> I talked to her about a week before she took her life, and I'm so ashamed I thought she was being hysterical. I mean, maybe she was, but if I thought she was losing it, shouldn't I have been even more concerned instead of blowing her off? I will never get over the guilt. She said she'd been attacked and no one took it seriously, and look what happened.

Oh God. Oh God.

I write back immediately. What did she say happened to her? Was she being stalked?

Audrey is still online apparently, because my message is read right away.

Yes! That's what she said! A stalker! I try to wait patiently for more information because she's typing again, but my mind is racing a hundred miles per hour. Because Lauren was being stalked too. A new message pops up after what feels like an eternity.

> It started months before her death. She said she could FEEL that someone had been inside her house. She called the police but after the second time, they chastised her about leaving doors unlocked. But she said someone went in her patio door when she was out front weeding her flower bed! Nothing was stolen, so they basically told her to calm down and get a big dog if she was gonna be so nervous about living alone.

I can hear myself panting, and my veins feel like they're pumping pure adrenaline instead of blood. Can I call you? I ask.

> Sorry, I'm at work, not supposed to be on Facebook either, but what my boss doesn't know won't hurt him.

Okay. I nod and try to slow my breathing. So did this kind of thing keep happening?

> She got a security system and got super careful. Paranoid, really. She even stopped jogging. And then she said something really bad happened, but no one believed her. Even I didn't believe her, because it didn't make any sense. The police said it didn't make sense!

What was it? I respond. What happened?

I've pushed too far. She takes a few moments to answer, and all she says is It was never made public and she stopped talking about it. Her job put her on leave over this.

If I could only speak to Audrey, I could make her understand. I sympathize with her hesitance, though, because even now I don't want to put my experience in writing. But I don't think I have any choice.

I'm being stalked, I write. It's only been going on for a week or so, but . . . no one believes me either. Someone was in my house. They moved things around. The police think I'm making it up. I'm sorry, I'm just desperate for answers. After a quick glance around the library, as if that caution will mean anything, I hit send.

And I wait.

Why does the truth feel so damn vulnerable? What's the worst she could do? Grab a screenshot and post it on Facebook to make fun of me to a bunch of strangers? It's not even a logical fear, because most people would scold her for doing something so cruel. So what I'm really afraid of is that she'll think things about me I can't control.

I hate not having control. But good Lord, there are so many other things to fear now, I have to learn to let that go.

Still, it's the only thing I have, isn't it? Everything else is spinning around me.

A new message finally arrives. OMG I'm so sorry. That's just what she said! Things were moved around. She was sure of it! She said she found her car keys on top of her fridge. The police told her she'd obviously gotten distracted and left them there. But who puts keys on top of the fridge???

Every inch of skin on my body prickles with alarm. I try to throw a smile at a little girl who runs a wooden car over my table, but my lips twist into something that feels tight and awkward and ugly, like a snarling animal.

Are you in Des Moines too? Audrey asks.

No, I answer. That's the really scary part.

She reads the message, and there's another pause. I'm trying to think of other ways I can persuade her to share more, but in the end I don't have to. Another long message arrives.

> Okay, here's what happened two weeks before she died. Lauren said she was supposed to meet someone to show a house. She was inside straightening up a few things. The house was staged, you know? Vacant. And then she said out of the blue everything went black.

My stomach twists so hard I have to put a hand to my mouth to stop myself from being sick.

> Someone put a hood over her head and tied her to a chair!!! But then . . . that was it. Nothing else happened. She was there for like an hour before she managed to get free and call the police.

Holy shit. I think of that shove into the street. My tidy bedroom. The flyers letting everyone know I'm a liar. Then I think of the police detective's scorn.

What did they say??? I ask.

> They said she was lying! Why would anyone tie her up and just leave her there??? She wasn't raped or threatened. She didn't see him and said the guy didn't even speak to her. When I talked to Lauren she was so distraught, but I didn't know what to say either. Because why would anyone do that??? Was it just some bored teenager or something?

A bored teenager. Like the kind who'd seemingly shut off my power? The goose bumps are back, because this is just like my story. In fact, it's almost exactly the same.

I look around again, all my nerves screaming that I'm being watched. But I spy no one, and it only makes sense that I feel hunted, because I am.

Another message. They said she tied herself. Her hands were tied in front, not behind her. She obviously got out of the ropes once she wanted to, so she was barely restrained. Lauren tried to explain that she thought the guy was still there so she didn't even try to free herself for a while, but no one believed her. Her agency asked her to take leave or maybe she quit because she didn't want to show houses. I'm not sure. And then two weeks later . . . God. I'll never get over this guilt.

I'm so sorry. I have to type it out three times before my shaking fingers get it right.

Audrey can't seem to stop telling the story now. She obviously needs to get it all out. I mean, I don't know if she was lying and that's why she killed herself? Or maybe she did it because her life was falling apart and everyone blamed her for it? But why couldn't I just be there for her? Why did I care if the story was true or not??? She needed help, whatever was going on!

This poor woman. I try to calm myself and let my years of nursing experience take over. I can't begin to guess how many loved ones I've comforted over the years, and Audrey needs comfort badly.

I've worked with mental health patients, I type. It's so hard to nail down what's going on and what will help. Please don't blame yourself. If Lauren couldn't figure it out, how could you hope to from a distance? I'm sorry.

She doesn't respond for a long time. I picture her blowing her nose and trying to get her composure back under control at her desk. It's been a year since Lauren died, but this is obviously still fresh and torturously painful for her friend. She's likely spent months going over every conversation they had and, maybe more vividly, every conversation they didn't have.

Thank you, she finally writes back. If you're going through the same thing . . . maybe it was all true for Lauren too. I'm so sorry. I wish I could help.

Trying to blink back my own tears, I make my shaking hands type again. It helps just to hear this. I can't thank you enough for sharing. And I promise you what's happening to me is very hard for anyone to believe. I've even doubted myself sometimes.

Thank you, she responds. I have to get back to work. But please let me know what happens and if I can do anything. I hope you're safe.

I close my laptop and drop my head into my hands. He destroyed Lauren's life too. He cost her her job and stalked her and poked through her house and he *broke her*. He broke her so badly she killed herself.

This is too much. It's like a terrifying horror movie. But I've done what I can to protect myself, aside from hiring a damn bodyguard. Frankly, that might be my next step, because I bet I could get a good deal if I hired one of Grigore's associates. Maybe I'll ask if things aren't resolved soon.

But I have one advantage in this battle: I've been isolated from people my entire life. I've been alone since I was seven. Yes, he's been able to drive a wedge between me and a few acquaintances, but I have no true friends to drive away, no real connections to undermine.

He might try to get me fired again, and he might even succeed, but I could find a traveling nurse position tomorrow with an understaffed hospital system anywhere. Hell, maybe I should apply for a gig somewhere really far away like Guam.

Big words, I know, but I have to get past this rising horror somehow. Getting confirmation that this happened to Lauren should be affirming, but it somehow makes it all worse. Jacob already knows the worst that might happen from his sick little plot. He understands what ruining a life can mean. Yet here he is.

This isn't just revenge. This is obsession.

CHAPTER 33

I pop into a noodle place to get takeout, knowing I'll be glad I did once the nausea wears off. If I'm going to be huddled inside my locked home for the next twelve hours, I might as well have ginger chicken to console myself. The place is empty at this odd hour, and no one follows me in or even passes by the glass door before I leave.

Hurrying along toward safety, I'm only five minutes from home when my phone rings. When Violet's name pops up, I'm surprised. "Hey, Violet. Did I forget something?" I'm already patting my pockets. Yes, I'm looking for the phone that's currently at my ear.

"I'm sorry, Betsy," she says breathlessly. "I had five people checking out, and then a toddler threw up on the carpet, so I couldn't call earlier. Are you okay?"

"Sure, I'm fine." I check over one shoulder, then the other. "Why?"

"I saw a man leave just after you did, and I was worried he was following you."

Oh no. I look over my shoulder and speed up my walk until I'm nearly jogging. My bag bounces heavily on my arm, a reminder I can use it as a weapon. One good swing, and my laptop will smash his skull, at least a little bit. "What did he look like?"

"White guy, forties or fifties. He was wearing a black ball cap and dark clothes and had a big backpack."

Shit, that sounds like the man who pushed me, but it also sounds like a good percentage of people anywhere in the US.

"That's about all I got," she continues. "He came out of the stacks right after you went out the door, so I noticed. I've never seen him before, but I don't know everyone who comes in here."

"I don't see anyone around," I say, slowing down so I can spin in a circle to be extra sure. "And I'm almost home."

"Okay, I ran over to the door to see if he was right behind you, but he got into an old black pickup, so watch for that. I'm so relieved you're all right. I was afraid I'd call and you wouldn't answer and . . ." Her long sigh whooshes through the phone. "But you answered."

"Thank you so much for checking on me, Violet. Seriously."

"Sure thing. Come back soon so I know you're okay."

"I will," I promise. So that's three things on my post-stalker to-do list. Spend time with the shelter dogs, visit the books, and check in with Violet. That's if I manage to get rid of this asshole before I give up and move, of course.

I'm only two minutes from my place now, but I duck behind an oak tree and look around one more time. No stalker and no black pickup that I can see.

As eager as I am to get home, I still open my security app to check the camera feed first. It looks clear, no one in the driveway or even lingering on the sidewalk. There are four recordings. Three show a group of people with a dog who stopped to talk in my driveway. The fourth shows the woman upstairs walking up the steps toward her rental. No one has approached my front door or back patio or gotten close enough to set off a proximity alert.

Everything looks clear. The videos are so helpful that I'm wondering if I should order more cameras. If two are good, maybe six would be perfect. One on every outdoor wall and two for inside my home. Would that be overkill? Probably, but I'll consider it.

After one last look around, I jog home. A moment of panic overtakes me when I can't get in the door, my brain racing frantically like a hamster on a wheel before I remember there's a new code.

My heart is nearly beating out of my chest by the time I get inside, and it's stuffy as hell without any windows open, but I can't do anything about that. I can't even bring myself to turn on a fan for fear I'll miss the sound of a window breaking or a doorknob jiggling. Nope, I'll just go ahead and sweat it out.

I stash my takeout in the fridge for later and grab a knife from my kitchen. It's a rainbow-colored ceramic knife I bought just because the colors made me happy, but tonight I'm thankful for its wickedly sharp edge as I check my bedroom and bathroom and closets for anything I might need to stab. There's no one here.

"Clear!" I yell just to cheer myself up. Then I shove a chair under the front doorknob and tie the patio door handles together with an old charging cord to secure that too. I won't pass a fire inspection, but fire is a chance I'm going to have to risk tonight. I want to sleep and I want to stay alive, and a barricade feels like the best way to reach both those goals.

Now that I'm safe, I take off my pretty sundress and put on a T-shirt and a soft pair of shorts for my night in, careful to move the Taser to my shorts pocket. I'd love to start a good binge watch of a show as a distraction, but I need to listen for danger all evening. Tonight will be a book night for sure.

I'm in the middle of downing a big glass of water when my phone buzzes at my hip. It's a text from Tristan. How is it going? Better, I hope?

I'm honestly not sure! He followed me to the library today!

You saw him??? You know who it is?

No, a librarian spotted him as I was leaving. But I'm 99% sure it's a man named Jacob. I think I'll recognize him if I see him.

Wow. Are you okay?

Yes, I'm safe. Holding my breath, I pause to listen for a moment. The only thing I hear is distant birdsong. And I'm locked in my house for the night. I should be fine.

Did you get those new cameras up? How many? They're watching your doors?

My chin draws in automatically, the hair on the back of my neck rising at this very specific question. The question, yes, but something else has just occurred to me.

Lauren died a year ago. And I've known Tristan for *almost a year*.

Despite the still heat in the house, I shiver. It's only a coincidence. It has to be. But that doesn't mean I need to be stupid.

I stare at his messages until he starts typing again. May? Are you ok?

Everything's good. I just need to contact my landlord again. Sorry. I'll text later.

The phone trembles in my hand as I scroll back through our old messages, looking for . . . clues, I guess?

He knew when I was getting in the shower that time my power cut off. And maybe he was trying to mislead me when he called the Reddit impostor a woman. But other than that? We chatted a lot about work over the last months. Exchanged jokes and memes and small stories about our days. He wasn't digging for much.

Since all this started, Tristan has been the one insisting that I call the police and protect myself, and why would he do that if he was the stalker? Anyway, he can't be Jacob Hoffholder. He doesn't look anything like him. Except . . .

People can pay to have their ears pinned back by a surgeon or even get a whole new nose. What if Jacob grew up and decided to become someone else like I did?

I try another search for Jacob Hoffholder. There's the story from nearly three years ago, which I never want to read again, so I try an image search. Nothing helpful. The man is a ghost.

The article said Mitchell Hoffholder died in 2018, so I search for him, hoping there's some sort of memorial with family photos online. Nothing there either, not even a note about the service. No one wanted to celebrate him, it seems.

At another dead end, I stare at my keyboard. How would someone search for me if they were intent on finding out what happened to that girl involved in the trial? They'd search for my name, of course. Or search for my *names*. I sit up with a little gasp before I frantically type in *Jake Hoffholder* and slap the Enter key.

The name is so unusual that the search engine wants to correct it Householder, but there is one return for an auto-glass repair company in Cedar Rapids, Iowa. Holding my breath, I click on it. It's an old Facebook post from 2021 welcoming their newest technician, Jake Hoffholder. And there's a picture.

Oh my God, it's him. *Him.* Not Tristan, not Mike, but the cold-faced little boy I knew back in 1991. I recognize him instantly: the wide mouth and narrow nose and those goddamn ears sticking out beneath a branded ball cap. I'd forgotten his eyes, huge and green, with distinctive hooded lids. With one glance I know I haven't seen this man around me, not in this decade.

No, it's definitely not Tristan or Mike. It's not Beret or one of the renters or the gardener who comes once a week. I haven't made bad choices or trusted the wrong people, and for some reason, I want to weep with gratitude for that.

This is huge. Now that I remember exactly what he looks like, I won't let him get close.

Everything inside me loosens, some parts with despair, some parts with pooling dread. Every day has been an endless cascade of crises, and I feel like I'm sliding down a waterfall and bumping off rocks. My entire being is bruised all the way down.

Closing my eyes, I tell myself to regroup, take a deep breath and exhale all the stress, and then get up and finish my glass of water. Stay healthy, stay alert. In the end, I manage to exhale a bit, but I don't get up for the water.

My nerves buzz, and my limbs ache. Now that I've seen Jacob's face, I'm picturing what he's done.

The black bag over Lauren's head. The ropes around her body. The unbearable terror of waiting for what might come next and what horrible form the inevitable violence would take.

I can't imagine how frightened she was. How shaking and scared. And Jacob Hoffholder had stood there watching her, stifling his cruel laughter at her torment. I wonder how long he'd lingered. Had he—?

My phone trills with an unfamiliar chime. I jump as if my home has been invaded, then whine a little when I realize it has. *Patio alert,* my phone banner announces.

He's on my patio. The monster who did this to Lauren is *on my patio*.

I jump up, take a step sideways to flee, then take two steps the other way toward the curtains that cover the door. Once the initial wave of panic passes, I remember the new camera feed and open the app with a shaking finger.

The loading wheel turns, turns, turns, and I tell myself not to scream when I see him, not to give my location away. Just let the camera record and call the police or Grigore or someone.

But Jacob is a ghost. I can't find him when the feed opens to show my patio and the tightly closed doors. The only movement is a branch of dancing green leaves that reaches into the frame. He's too elusive, too good at this, always hiding at the edges. He got away with destroying Lauren, and he'll do the same to me.

Then there's a shift of shadow at the bottom of the frame, as if Jacob is sliding along my home like a snake. Or . . . more like the cat that steps out of the shade to sprawl on the bricks. "It's Jeeves," I say with a slightly hysterical laugh. Just the sweet orange kitty from three doors down, and his only nefarious intention is shedding all over me and stealing a snack.

The alarm sounds again.

I go into settings and stare for a long time. Should I make the alert less sensitive? Or change it to only "human forms"? What about monsters?

Shit. I choose "human forms" for now because otherwise I'll be torn from sleep by every cat, possum, or raccoon that wanders by. But I don't like it. This man is too damn shifty.

With one last longing look at the sleepy cat sprawled on the warm bricks of my patio, I close the app and make myself pick up the giant historical tome from Hilda's. I have to manage this constant panic or I'll crash so hard I might never recover. A little reading, a little dinner, one little glass of wine. And a huge, aching hope that this will all be over soon.

CHAPTER 34

I'm trying to go to sleep at a reasonable hour, but the woman upstairs seems to have the same idea. I hear her walking around the bedroom above me, likely going through her own bedtime routine, and every creak and thump has me watching the wooden planks of the ceiling like a deer tracking a stalking wolf.

After checking both my new cameras for the hundredth time and seeing nothing but a couple of moths swooping against the lens, I close my eyes again. A door bangs closed upstairs.

Shit, there's no use. It's only ten forty-five. I'll try to sleep again in an hour.

Sighing, I get up and pull the chair from under my bedroom doorknob. Despite my sheer exhaustion, the constant trickle of adrenaline has soaked into every cell at this point. I'm too jittery and jumpy to relax.

"That's what I get for trying to be responsible," I mutter. I'm still wide awake, and now I'm grumpy about it.

I switch on only the bathroom light before I flounce over to the couch, hoping the dimness will lull me into winding down.

Though I turn on the TV out of habit, I immediately mute it when the noise makes me wince. I need silence, but I'm desperate to feel part of the world, so I leave it on mute and put on a *Housewives* episode I've seen before. I can't follow what they're yelling at each other, but I like the light and motion as they make frantic gestures across a dining table.

Oh, who am I kidding? I'm sucked right in, so I turn on the captions and stare at the drama unfolding. Obviously, I love wild reality shows. They're like watching the worst guests right next door but without any of the inconvenience.

Five minutes later I'm completely absorbed in the table-pounding theatrics when my phone buzzes. My whole body jerks in alarm, but it's not a camera alert. It's a text. From Mike.

My heart leaps with stupid excitement before it remembers I've ruined things with him. Pessimistic maybe, but the actual text only confirms the lump of anxiety weighing me down.

Hey, could I come by tomorrow to talk?

Oh God, the old "we need to talk." Surely I haven't known him long enough for that kind of thing? But the dread gaining mass inside me says that I have. *This is just too much,* he'll say. *Everything is weird. I think it's better if we stop hanging out or—*

Yeah, yeah, I get it, I tell my spinning mind. The worst part is that his excuses won't even be excuses. They're all justified and logical and very real. Mike deserves a nice, normal life, and I'm definitely not nice and normal. I don't even want to be, so screw him!

Good. There's my anger.

Embracing the petty, I close his text without answering. I'm not going to issue an invitation for him to come over and make me feel like shit. He can muster that courage on his own.

Yeah, I think I'll go to Guam after all. It's something new, and any stalkers, old or new, likely won't have the resources to follow me. And there are probably lots of cute soldiers moving through, temporary residents like me. It'll be more of an adventure than an exile, really!

The pep talk fails, and my mood sinks even further. I've always been free to make my own decisions about where to go and when. That's the point of living this life. I don't owe anyone anything, not even the truth. I hold all the power in my own hands. Or . . . I did.

But I don't anymore. Damn this man straight to hell.

In my best effort to outrun the loneliness that's slammed into me, I open Facebook.

There's a message waiting, and I expect it to be from Audrey, so I'm surprised to see that the man who left that RIP message on Lauren's page has written back. I click through, hoping to find more information about what Lauren endured. A clue, maybe, to help me through this. But there's no clue, just another terrifying surprise.

An old photo of Lauren from her Facebook account loads quickly and immediately sears my vision. She's been defaced. Thick black *X*'s are drawn over both her eyes, and blue teardrops run down her cheeks, a horrifying juxtaposition against Lauren's wide smile. The arm she raised to wave at the camera has been viciously slashed with lines that are red as blood and jagged with fury. But the caption below the photo is what makes me drop the phone in horror.

There's only one cure for crazy, Elizabeth.

My phone clatters to the floor, and by the time I gather my strength to pick it up again, the sender's account has vanished.

CHAPTER 35

I should have forced myself back to bed when I started getting sleepy, but my terror kept me immobile, curled on the couch beneath my blanket, praying for the sleep that eventually, miraculously, took me under. Now I'm full of regret as I stretch one cramped arm and try to blink my heavy eyes open against the flickering light of the television.

It's too bright for my tired eyes, so I let them close again and tug the blanket higher. It doesn't matter if I sleep here or in my bed, and I'm so exhausted I can't believe I woke up at all. The whole world is pressing me back down into the cushions, and even my bones ache from the constant stress. I'm sure I could sleep right on the dang floor if I needed to.

Wait, what woke me up? Was it an alert?

My hand is curled around my cell phone, so I force my exhausted eyes open to slits to look. No alert, just my blank home screen. Thank God. I'm way too tired for this shit. Sighing, I shove the phone under the throw pillow and start to drift back into my dreams.

They were pleasant, I think. Something about a party. Maybe a wedding? There were lots of people dancing in headphones. A silent disco?

When the light from the TV goes black against my eyelids, it's a relief. But two heartbeats later, it's back from whatever break it took, and I shift my hand to shield my face so I don't have to bother finding the remote.

Floorboards shift and pop. I curl my body a little tighter into the cocoon I've created. If that woman is still awake upstairs, I've probably only dozed for half an hour. I could look at the phone again and pay attention to the time, but God, I feel half dead from all the stress.

And now I'm thinking about Mike again. And about leaving. About the million things I'll need to do once I make the decision to go. Look through job listings, figure out a housing budget, plan to abandon this amazing town and the happy, fake life I've made for myself here.

Shit.

My eyes flutter open and find the reality show still unspooling on the screen. They're all forcing smiles in this scene, pretending to have good marriages and good skin and good finances as they spend wildly to keep up with their friends. They're all liars just like me.

Is it possible I'm not as big a freak as I think I am? Most people tell white lies every day. Mine might be more gray than white, but they're not malicious. Are they?

Just as my eyes are drifting closed again, there's another shift in light. Another dark moment of relief.

My brain turns slowly and sends out a weak blip of a notice. That was a shape. Not a shift of light. It was something like . . .

Oh holy mother.

My eyes snap wide open, and there's a man standing in front of the television. A *man*, not a shadow, not a dream, not a figment of my imagination.

I'm frozen, all my muscles hard as wood as I stare with burning eyes at the dark silhouette. He's only a few feet away. Close enough to reach out and touch if I—

He's watching me. He's just standing there fucking *watching me*, and how is that possible? The cameras. The locks. They should have stopped this, but now I'm caught and he's right here and I am going to die tonight.

Is he a ghost? Is it Mitchell Hoffholder back for revenge?

The shape outlined by the television is wide and dark, like he's wearing a black devil's robe, and the nightmare of my childhood is back just like that. The candles, the chanting, the murdered babies, the blood running down the walls. I'm sorry I told. I'm so sorry . . .

Oh God, my heart has never beaten this hard, like a beast struggling to break out of my rib cage and survive this attack without the rest of me. It strains so violently it seems possible I'll croak right here before he even hurts me. Because he's not moving. He's just a black, hulking outline of a human. Maybe—

"I know you're awake," he whispers.

I choke on the dry air swelling in my throat. I should scream, but I can't draw a breath. Can't even unclench my jaw.

"Come on, little liar," he croons, and that sickly sweet tone is almost enough to make my bladder release, because even without the Satanist flashbacks, he's something from a horror movie. A monster who's been living in my walls, and now he's crawled out to wear my fucking face or something.

My throat pops open and I scream. This is my chance, and I have to take it. I scream, and my brain throws out mathematical equations about who might be near enough to hear. That woman upstairs? The guys next door? But as I try to fight my way past the blanket and the cushions, the intruder leaps, shoving the table aside to pounce on me. One of his knees lands directly on my thigh with an explosion of pain.

"Stop!" I yell, but his hand slams over my mouth, and I taste the copper of my own blood.

"Shut the fuck up, Devil Girl." His voice is still that terrible singsongy rasp, and I can't get free of my cocoon. The heavy grip of his rough, cold hand lifts for a second, but it's back before I can even suck in half a breath to scream again.

"Swallow," he orders, and I have no idea what the hell that means. Then I feel solid lumps on the back of my tongue before he closes his other hand over my nose.

He's poisoned me or drugged me, and I need to resist, so I hold my breath. But my pulse is a drum in my head and my lungs burn, and even though I buck beneath him, he doesn't budge. So I do the only thing I can. I give in and swallow.

Bitterness blooms from my tongue to my throat to my nose. One piece is still stuck, so I swallow frantically one more time, finally getting one hand free to grab his wrist. I try to claw at his skin but feel only cool leather. When he lifts the hand from my nose, air explodes through my nostrils, and I sob against his other palm.

"There you go," he says calmly. "Was that so hard?"

I gag, but the pills stay down. "What did you give me?" I try to ask against the glove. When he lifts it, I think he wants me to repeat myself, but when my lips open, he shoves rough fabric into my mouth. I choke again against the mildew smell that fills my sinuses. It reeks of darkness and dirt. The stench of a grave.

Eyes rolling wildly, I try to see something, his features, his expression, but he's facing me, away from the strobing television, a man made of shadow and glinting eyes. His shape looks more like a hoodie and less like a robe now, but then . . . then black fabric descends.

I'm blind again, but this time I know why. There's a hood covering me. Just like the hood pulled over Lauren's head, the hood they said she staged herself.

Oh my God. *Lauren.* This is what happened to her, but the important part is she survived it. I'll survive it too. I will. He's only trying to scare me and set me up to be a liar yet again.

The painful, twisted thump of my heart begins to ease at the thought. I try to draw a deep breath through my nose and let it out slowly. It takes a few attempts, and I cough against the tears and mucus, but I'm no longer panting like I'm halfway through a marathon.

I will survive this. I know I will, even when he strokes a gentle hand from the crown of my head to my neck, making quiet shushing noises that prickle every inch of my skin with goose bumps.

Yeah, my sanity might not survive intact, but I can get mental health help, even if that means trusting a therapist. I'll cross that bridge when I get to it, and I'll be so damn happy I'm alive to limp across. This is petrifying, but he's here to terrorize me, not to end me.

His weight still crushes my body, the pressure nearly unbearable against my bruised thigh. Now that I understand what's happening here—some sort of staged humiliation—I don't want to fight back and push him to violence. I only have to play along for a bit, and then . . . then he'll go. Right?

He won't leave any evidence behind. I know that from the way it played out with Lauren. There won't be video or a broken window, and I'll look like an even bigger liar. But *how*? How is he doing this?

He clambers off me, knee digging harder into my bruised thigh, and the pain snaps me from my thoughts as I squeal a protest.

"All right, all right," he murmurs in a near whisper. "Where's your phone?"

When he starts to pat me down, hands touching through the blanket as I cringe away, I remember the little Taser stick in my pocket.

Damn it. I don't want to use it if he's only planning to tie me up and leave me here, but I don't want him to find it and turn it on me.

Squawking, I twist from the hand that grazes my breast; then I knock the pillow off the couch to hopefully expose my phone.

The touching stops. I feel his arm reach past my hip. It worked. "Wouldn't want you alerting anyone," he says, and his words are actually *cheerful*. What a sick fuck.

But I'm going to make him pay. When I get out of this, I'm not going to call the cops. I'll call Grigore instead, and he'll set up a trap for Jacob Hoffholder, or he'll use his underworld connections to flush this asshole out of whatever hidey hole he's been using. Then Jacob will be sorry. Sorry for this, and sorry for what he did to Lauren. He'll be lucky if I call an ambulance for his broken ass.

I took a nursing pledge when I graduated, basically to do no harm, but oh well. He's not a patient, and he started it. That oath will be one more lie I told in my life.

His hand is suddenly a vise around my arm, and he jerks me roughly up to a sitting position before tugging to strip the blanket from me. It's wrapped awkwardly, and he grunts with the effort, but eventually the warm covering flies away.

"All right, come on," he grumbles. "Stand up."

Okay. This is the part where he makes me go sit in a chair so he can tie me up. I already know this, but my imagination is starting to get the better of me. What if he leads me to my bedroom? Or walks me out the front door and puts me in a car instead? My veil of calm is slipping away, and I'm frozen on the couch, unwilling to just obey.

He growls in frustration. "Get up or I'll shoot you."

He won't. I tell myself he won't because then there'll be a murder investigation, but what if he shoots me in the temple? That asshole Detective Heissen will stroll in, roll his eyes, and call it a suicide, probably while telling a joke about bitches being crazy.

Crap. I push to my feet and sway above my shaking knees, both hands outstretched for balance in my blindness. "Please," I try to say, but only a mangled grunt emerges past the gag.

I hear a screech of chair legs against the floor and nearly collapse in relief. I was right! He'll put me in the chair, and I'll play his game. Everything is going to be okay.

I don't resist, letting him grab my elbow and pull me forward until he swings my body around. The backs of my legs bang against wood, and the chair shifts against the floor again.

"Sit," he orders. I sit. "I'm not going to hurt you, so just relax."

He's confirming what I already know, and I should feel comforted, but something in his voice zaps me like electricity. It's such a vivid feeling that I have a brief fear I've electrocuted myself with the Taser.

But no, there's no pain, no cramping muscles, just this sizzling of my nerves screaming about a new danger. What is it?

Something soft and warm envelops me, and I frown into the black hood as the feeling tightens. I try to picture what's happening. When pressure squeezes my upper arms, I realize he's tying the blanket around my whole body, trying to restrain me without leaving any bruises.

Don't panic, I order myself. This binding will stop me from jumping up easily, but I'm hardly immobile. *Stay calm and lull him into a false sense of control.*

I hear him move away and strain my ears for his whereabouts. Is it possible he's leaving already? But no. His footsteps hurry toward my bedroom.

I consider trying to escape and rush for the door, but I hesitate too long, and he's back within seconds. Cool, smooth fabric like a bedsheet is suddenly wrapped around my legs. He winds it around and around before pulling it tight. Where are the ropes? Aren't there supposed to be ropes? Then again . . . this does sound even more far-fetched. *He swaddled me in a blanket, Officer. I couldn't get away!*

He probably learned from the last time and is improving his strategy. Damn him.

I feel the air stir as he rises next to me, and then he's moving away again, walking farther into the kitchen. Minutes pass. When I swing my head around, the world shifts and drags. I blink hard in the dark as my brain floats and turns as if it's loose in the fluid inside my skull.

It must be the effect of whatever he made me swallow.

I try to place the feeling, but I've never taken sedatives or . . . opioids? Whatever it is, it'll give the police one more incriminating sign to point to. *She took drugs and tied herself up, then claimed she'd been attacked. What a freak.*

"How are you feeling, Elizabeth?" he asks, and there's the electric stab of fear again, but this time I know what it is. His voice. I recognize it. I've talked to him before.

Oh no. No, no, no. This can't be right. I've seen his picture. It couldn't be possible.

But it must be, because the man who's crept into my home in the middle of the night to tie me up and torture me isn't Jacob Hoffholder. It's Tristan.

CHAPTER 36

Tristan is Jacob Hoffholder? No, the only way that's possible is if he got plastic surgery. Not just to pin his ears back, but to change his nose, even his chin. But why? It doesn't make sense. Maybe he just sent pictures of another man. Maybe he used AI.

Fuck, how did I forget about AI?

I try to shake my spinning head because that doesn't matter. What matters is I've been corresponding with this psycho for months. I flirted with him, I believed him, I let him see little glimpses of my life. Too many glimpses, apparently, because he tracked me down.

This whole week I was so paranoid about Mike, and I should have been looking much more closely at Tristan instead. God, what did I tell him?

I didn't give him much. I know I didn't, because I don't truly trust anyone. He did know that I worked for a hospital in San Jose, so he could have figured out my employer.

But how did he track me down in the first place? What breadcrumbs did I leave behind? When I'd left Fair Isle at age eighteen, I hadn't planned to eventually make Elizabeth Marie May vanish from memory. People had known I was leaving for nursing school. They'd printed our goals in the yearbook. But after that?

I squeeze my eyes tight against dizziness, trying to think. I met Tristan on Reddit when he asked about Las Vegas General Hospital.

He'd posted in several different nursing forums, and I responded along with a lot of others. We hit it off. Started chatting.

Elizabeth May. Nurse May. Las Vegas General Hospital. Oh my God.

My tiny groan is swallowed by the gag. It was that damn newspaper picture from the car accident! It had to be. One of my coworkers had helpfully identified me for the photographer as "Eliza May, ER nurse." Once Tristan started looking up Nurse May online, he'd found that picture. He'd put out bait. Then he'd tracked me down here, either with my nursing licenses or via background check or something. I'm well aware of how little privacy anyone has these days.

Damn it. I'd been upset about the photo at the time because of all the ways I try to stay invisible. My gut had known it was bad, just not this bad.

A huge yawn suddenly seizes my body despite my panic and fear. My jaw cracks with the effort, and I hear my attacker chuckle. "These things are good, aren't they? Fifteen minutes and bam! Are you nice and calm now?"

My brain is floating again, and my fear is smoothing out, the sharp edges sliding away. Another yawn takes me.

Whatever he gave me . . . I hope he didn't give too high a dose. If I start throwing up, I could die under this damn hood. Or . . . my respiration could simply slow until it stops altogether. *At least that would be peaceful,* my sleepy mind volunteers. In fact, if I go to sleep now, this will all be over when I wake up. Or don't wake up. Either way, I'll be past it.

I shake my head, and everything whirls. Suddenly there's movement, a shush of fabric, a flare of light, and my head is free.

"Peekaboo!" he crows.

I flinch from the bright light of the living room lamp he's turned on.

"Have you calmed down?" he asks. "Gonna play nice?"

Nodding makes the dizziness worse, but I try. I am going to play nice. I already had a plan, and now I'm too high to be scared. He'll do his thing, make his predictable villain speech, and then he'll leave.

Once my eyes adjust I blink owlishly around. He's already moved out of my vision, so the first thing I see is half a dozen pills on my coffee table. They look oblong and pinkish, and considering how quickly they brought me to this state, I'm guessing they're Ambien.

All right. I can survive Ambien. I think he gave me two, which is likely double the dose, but that's not lethal. Worst case, I'll sleep for a good long while and then wander around the neighborhood without pants on or something.

Unless, of course, he plans to slowly feed me the whole pile. God, I hope not. I have to assume those extra pills are a prop for the cops to find. *Look at the crazy woman, you can't trust her.*

My head dips a bit despite my attempt to control it, and I see the pink throw blanket wrapped tightly around me. My upper arms are immobilized, but my forearms are unrestrained, all the better to free myself later and raise police suspicion about the whole scene. It's all playing out just as I expect.

That tiny thread of confidence is keeping me strong, but when he walks past me and I finally see him in the light, all that confidence evaporates with a nearly audible poof.

Because he really isn't Jacob Hoffholder.

I recognize his face from the two pictures he sent, the broad cheekbones and ruddy skin. That part wasn't AI. He wears no ball cap tonight, so his short-buzzed blond hair is visible against a slightly sunburned forehead. He has dark-blond eyebrows to match the hair, and they don't look bleached.

When he moves back into the light, I startle, despite the sedative. His *eyes*. My God. Big green eyes with hooded Scandinavian lids. Just like Jacob's. But *not* Jacob's.

Still, I know this man. I recognize him. I squeeze my eyes shut until I see stars, trying to force my brain to grab the picture it sees. A picture, yes. That's it. Not from the selfies Tristan sent, but somewhere else. A photo on a wall. Formal and posed. And then my memory snaps into place with a hollow click.

I guessed the *wrong Hoffholder.* This isn't Jacob. This is a boy I never actually knew, but I saw his face in a school photo every time my mom dropped me off at daycare.

When I open my eyes he's standing before me, only three feet away. My gaze flies from his nose to his mouth to those unmistakable eyes. They're just like Jacob's, and I would have recognized them if he hadn't always kept them obscured in his photos.

I gawk up at him, still confused.

"Hello, Elizabeth," he says. "I'm Noah. Great to finally meet in person."

Noah. Is that familiar? A memory floats past on a gentle wave of Ambien. My mind reaches for it, but it's slippery as an eel, letting me touch it but not grab hold. Noah. Noah. I hear Linda Hoffholder saying the name, and I finally remember, not with a snap of recall but with a hazy brush of it. Noah is a brother. Jacob's *older* brother, a name I heard around the house. A boy I never met. But why would he be here?

There's only one answer, of course, and I nod a little at the truth of it. I ruined his parents' lives. Lauren and I both did, with the help of Jacob. And now this other son wants revenge. I suddenly find I'm not quite as dizzy now that my heart is beating faster.

"God, you're a real piece of work," he says, as if he's not the damn lunatic here, standing in the middle of my living room. "I talked to your neighbor," Noah continues as if we're having a conversation. "He called you Liz. I heard your new boyfriend call you Beth. The woman at the shelter calls you Lizzie! And you let me call you May? What the hell, Elizabeth? You're a mess!"

I stare at him, unmoved by his words. I know what a mess I am; he can't shock me with this.

"They were real nice at the shelter, though. Good place." He nods. Then he adds, "I'm thinking about adopting Cocoa," and those words hit me like a truck. My eyes immediately fill with tears at his terrible taunt. "Or maybe I'll just poison her. I could send a letter blaming you later. One last hurrah."

I panic at the evil in his promise and shake my head so hard that dizziness makes bile rise in my throat. If I'm sick now, I'll choke on it.

No. I won't die that way. Breathing carefully, I try to calm down and keep my eyes on him as he drops onto my couch.

Once I'm out of this situation, I'll warn the shelter about a stalker who threatened my favorite dog. They can take precautions and keep poor Cocoa safe. I won't let him hurt her.

"You really thought I was Jacob, didn't you? That's hilarious, because as much as Jacob hated you for years, he later became a Buddhist. So I guess you don't know anything about anything. He wouldn't harm a fly, literally, so that really does strike me funny."

His little soliloquy has given me the chance to calm further. My stomach and brain settle, and the flood of saliva from the nausea has moistened my mouth enough that I can work the fabric of the gag forward a bit with my tongue. I push and work until my tongue cramps. Then I push more and try to relax my jaw. A few seconds later, the rag falls from my mouth. I close my creaky jaw with a wince.

Noah jumps to his feet, but when I don't scream, he simply stands there. I'm not going to scream. I just want him to go. "I'm sorry," I croak. "I'm sorry about your parents." When he only glares, I stammer out, "I-I'm sorry they went to prison. I didn't understand what I was doing. I really didn't."

His bark of laughter rings out like a shot, and I jerk in fear. "That's what you're sorry about?"

"Yes," I whisper.

He nods. "Yeah. You know I was in college then. Wanted to be a large-animal vet. Cows, horses, pigs. That kind of thing. It's good money in a farming state."

I do recall some talk about college around his house, but I was only five. He wasn't there, so he didn't exist for me.

"Had to drop out," he continues. "Every cent of money in my family went to lawyers before the trial even started. We lost the farm. It was only a few acres, mostly pasture, but it would've been a good place to run a practice, do some boarding."

"I'm so sorry," I groan. "I never meant to hurt anyone. I swear."

"Intended or not . . . I had to drop out and help them. Had to watch my mother weep and my dad drink. I'd go to work every day, and when I came home, there they'd be, still weeping, still drinking. Until they were formally arraigned and locked up, of course."

My eyes are so dry they've gone blurry. I blink rapidly and try to think. My brain offers no help at all.

"And it was all so fucking ridiculous, Elizabeth. Satan? Sacrifices? They were Lutherans, for God's sake."

"I'm sorry," I try again, but he breaks into a bitter laugh.

"And my little brother." Another awful chuckle. "You know, the authorities let me visit Jacob once in foster care. The social workers were cloying and sympathetic, assuming I must have been abused too. I played along, because I wanted to get my hands on that little shit. I wanted to strangle him myself, but it was all supervised. So you know what I did instead?"

I shake my head, but he aims such a hot glare at me that I freeze.

"I sat there and listened to my little brother brag. His foster parents were taking real good care of him, he said. He lived in a big house in Sioux City. They gave him a brand-new BMX bike. And a Game Boy! I don't think I'd even seen one of those before. He had new parents, a new life. I was working twelve-hour days to pay for lawyers, and this pathological liar was a goddamn hero."

Just like me, I think, but even in my fuzzy state, I manage to keep the words inside.

Noah rushes past me and stomps through the kitchen. I hear the fridge open, hear a bottle cap bounce across the floor, and when he returns he's taking a long draw of a beer.

My dry mouth waters. I'm so thirsty that my tongue feels twice its size.

"Just like that," he says, eyes on the TV, where the women are lounging in a hot tub. Staring at his profile now, I dimly realize that Noah looks a lot like his father.

He tips the bottle toward the scene on the reality show. "They had a hot tub too."

When he glances at me, I shake my head. "What?"

"Jacob's foster family. He told me that later. After my dad died. It sounded like a life you'd see on TV. All those things other people had that we never had. He told me he would've lived a good life if he'd stayed there." He turns back to the television. "Do you remember the first time you sat in a hot tub?"

I do, actually. It was the day after my ex and I got married at the courthouse. We rented a room at a suburban Radisson for our honeymoon and swam like royalty in the outdoor pool the next day.

I drift for a moment, remembering how simple I thought things would be for us. The perfect, happy life I'd always wanted. That must have been what Noah had felt too. And Jacob. A yearning for a happiness that everyone else seemed to have.

My vision drags when I pull my eyes from the TV to look at him again. I'm starting to get it. Why he must hate all of us, the way we threw debris on the tracks and derailed his entire future. "I'm so sorry," I repeat yet again.

He nods, almost solemn now, but when he looks at me, his eyes burn. "Sorry you took my parents away or sorry you sent them back?"

"What?" I whisper again. "I don't know what you mean."

"You don't know. Exactly."

"No, I don't know!"

He nods. "That's because you just moved on with your life, didn't you?" Another swig of beer. "I loved my little brother when we were young. Watched out for him. Dad was hard on us, I won't deny it. I took the blame for Jacob when I could, because I knew Dad would be harder on him. Always was. But after the lies, the trial, the foster parents . . . Shit, when Jacob came home, I hated his guts, and I let him know. Shoved him. Smacked him. Told him he was a worthless piece of shit. Ignored the way Dad knocked him around."

His face twists, and he swipes a hand across his eyes. "Fuck."

"I'm sorry." It's all I can think. I'm sorry, sorry, *so damn sorry*.

"Oh yeah?" he grunts.

"I told the truth when I could," I insist. "I didn't understand . . ."

"Which truth was that?"

This again? My drugged brain stutters, and I just float.

He rolls his eyes. "The truth that my parents were nice, decent Lutherans who never hurt anyone? Or the truth that they were fucking monsters?"

"I don't understand!" I cry.

"I don't understand," he says in a mocking singsong. "*I don't understand!* No, you just don't *care*. I'm here for Jacob, Elizabeth. *I'm here for my brother!* All those years I hated his guts. After my parents went to prison, after they got out. I hated him. But when he was back home . . . Jesus Christ. How did I not see it?"

I'm slack-jawed with drugs and confusion and desperately afraid to say the wrong thing, so I watch and keep quiet.

He finishes the beer in one long draw before turning the bottle carefully in his hands. "My uncle let my parents live in a trailer on his land when they got out of prison. My dad had to work his fields for him. Earn his keep. And boy, he took it out on Jacob. Every damn day. And my mom just sat there and let it happen. Just like he said."

"Who said?" I ask before I can stop myself. My words sound slurred even to my own ears.

"Jacob. He said she never did anything to stop it."

"Stop what?" I plead, wishing I could raise placating hands. "What are you saying?"

"Ha. You sound just like Lauren."

Lauren. The reminder of Lauren calms me a bit. I should shut up and let him talk so he'll leave. And now I can tell the police exactly who it is. But something goes sour inside me. Something I can't put my finger on.

"Dad was always willing to give me a smack or two, but with Jacob it was different. Like he hated him sometimes. He dropped a fork on the floor? Smack. Speak with his mouth full? Smack. Called him a wimp and a pussy. That was before. But after . . ."

I frown and squeeze my eyes closed. I've almost got it. *Lauren.* She's the key somehow. When I force my heavy lids to rise, I realize Noah has moved closer. Speaking slowly, I pronounce my words as clearly as I can. "Lauren didn't tell anyone about you. I won't either. The cops don't believe anything I say anyway."

He winks. "Yeah, I made sure of that. And I made damn sure Lauren knew who I was before the end. I needed her to know exactly what she did. What both of you did."

The end. *The end?* What does that mean? "Is that why she killed herself? She felt so guilty?"

His laugh is full of real amusement instead of anger this time. "God, you're so stupid. But you've still managed to get yourself a nice place here. Sunny every day. Walk to the beach. Work from home. I've watched you swanning around like the princess of Santa Cruz. Must be real nice."

"It's . . . it's just a rental. That's all. I get a discount because—"

"Lauren was the same. Bragging on Facebook. Showing pictures of her beautiful life. Her fifty-thousand-dollar car. Her fancy condo. Three bedrooms and three baths for one fucking person. And look what Jacob got."

A ridiculous idea flares bright in my head. If I can alert Grigore . . . "I get a discount doing work for my landlord. You can call him and ask! I'm just a working stiff like you."

He doesn't even pause. "You know what really pissed me off, Elizabeth? She had a hot tub right on her back patio." Another terrifying laugh. "Can you believe that? Like she knew Jacob was watching and wanted to rub it in his face. Do you think he saw that on Facebook? Do you think that's why he killed himself?"

My heart stutters. My pulse flails like the wings of an injured bird.

Jacob is dead?

I shake my head in horror. He was alive a few years ago. But then? My brain shuffles around dates and events until they slide into some kind of line. The article came out three years ago. Tristan had said his brother died two years ago. And Lauren was terrorized a year after that.

Because Jacob had killed himself.

"He saw the life he could have had before she took it from him. With that foster family. A life with caring people who didn't beat him and rape him."

My heart drops, but my eyes snap up to meet Noah's. "What? None of that was true."

"Not for you, maybe. Congratulations."

I'm so confused. His words are a jumble grinding through the gears of my brain. I need him to stop talking so I can think, but he just keeps going.

"Jacob finally told me after Dad died. He made up all the Satanic stuff after he saw it in a magazine. That part was a lie. But only because he couldn't tell the truth about what Dad was doing to him. In a small town in the nineties, all the kids would have tormented him. Called him gay. He didn't want anyone to know. Ever."

Jacob? The room seems to recede with my shock. That sullen boy, stick thin and angry, hiding in his room. No wonder he'd been so cold and bitter. No wonder he'd known how to manipulate Lauren. Because he really was being abused. Raped. By his own father. Oh no. That poor boy.

"He just wanted to leave," Noah growls. "Wanted to go somewhere else. So he said they were Satanists, and it worked. He got away."

"Oh," I breathe. He hadn't been evil. He'd been suffering.

"He told me Mom knew and did nothing. She used up all her energy on other people's brats, and she didn't protect Jacob. I believed him, finally. Because I watched her ignore everything else. I did too, though, didn't I? I walked away from him when he was ten. And when he was thirteen. And when he was fifteen and they sent him back to live with us. I was his big brother. And I hated him instead of helping him."

"I'm so sorry," I say one more time, hoping he'll get it out of his system and just *leave*. But my eyelids are so heavy. Every time I blink they try to stay closed. I don't bother defending myself. "I get it now. I . . . I shouldn't have recanted. Your dad belonged in prison."

"He should have rotted there. But he's in hell now. I'll go back home and see Mom after this. I need to have a talk with her too, don't I? And that fucking foster mother who said she loved him and never once reached out again."

When he laughs, I almost laugh with him. Because he's leaving, thank God. He's going back to Iowa.

I slump and let the blanket hold me up. This will be over soon.

Noah moves past me again, and though I cringe away, I keep my blurry gaze on him until I can't crane my neck anymore. Past him there are shadows where there shouldn't be. A dark line behind the huge armoire that sits in the corner between my front door and the bedroom. I squint so hard I worry I'll strain my eyes.

It's a black, narrow rectangle as tall as the door to my room, but not in the right spot, and the armoire that sits there looks different. It's been moved. Pulled out. Or . . .

The room swims, and I gasp for air as if I'm going under.

Not *pulled* out. It's been pushed out. Because there's a door I've never even noticed behind the huge armoire. And those horizontal lines disappearing into the darkness? Those are stairs to the upper floor.

Noah hasn't been breaking in. He's been living with me for days.

CHAPTER 37

How did I never consider this? I must have registered the frame of the door at some point. And yes, now that I see it, I remember peeking behind a big tapestry in the upstairs apartment right after I moved in, where I spied a locked door.

At the time, I'd thought it was an owner's closet. Most short-term rentals have them. But I feel like an idiot now. Of course a two-story house has an internal staircase, and this freak has been using it to spy on me.

How often did he come in? Did he stare at me as I worked at my desk? Watch me as I slept? Hover over my bed and pant with excitement?

My flesh crawls. When I close my eyes I can see him watching. Then I see other strangers from long ago, gathered around to stare at me as my clothes are removed, my body held down, as the doctor touches me and hurts me, telling me to be quiet and not cry. The nurses were the only ones who were nice, which is why I appreciated them, but still they never stopped it.

Then all the people watching me in the courtroom: the judge, the attorneys, the press, the gallery, and, worst of all, the Hoffholders. But later, the glares, the eyes glittering with scandal once I admitted to lying. The whole town gawking. Everyone watching me, until I wanted to always, always keep myself hidden.

But Noah was with me even in the darkness of my own home.

Sickness rises again, and this time I have to swallow hard to keep my guts from spewing up. I force my eyes wide open so the visions from my past pop like a bubble. I pant through my nose until the worst of it passes, and I try to *think*, but God, I'm so woozy.

Surely this is almost over. Audrey said Lauren was tied up in a chair and left. So why isn't he leaving? Then again . . . I don't think she ever identified her attacker, so something isn't right. He hadn't spoken to her. Hadn't taunted her like this, yet he said he made sure she knew who he was in the end.

The end worms its way painfully through my brain, searching for a landing spot, but I can't think past the drugs. When Noah returns to the living room, grinning like a fiend again, all thought flies from my mind.

My pretty rainbow knife is in his hand.

"What—" I start, but he lunges for me. I buck back so hard the chair legs lift and teeter before smashing me to solid ground again. Before I can recover from that lurching shock, he's shoved the rag back into my mouth.

"You're right-handed," he says, even as his gloved fingers close around my left wrist.

I stare dumbly down at my own arm, my body trailing alarms that aren't quite registering in my mind. But when the knife descends, I buck again, trying to tip to the side for a moment's escape.

Noah presses his weight into my body, and I can't stop the knife, and there's a sudden sting. I'm already picturing the blood spouting and the pain growing, but . . . he pulls back. Only a tiny drop of blood wells. The shallow cut itches more than hurts.

What? I try to ask again, but it's just a strange, terrified moan.

"You're a nurse, so you know what hesitation cuts are, don't you?"

The air in the room swells and recedes, swells and recedes, and I think it might be time for me to pass out. I think I might like that.

Hesitation cuts? I think blearily. Yes, I know what they are. This is a good plan to make me look suicidal, isn't it? The drugs, the cuts, the ridiculous story. He's had a lot of time to plan since Lauren's death.

I stare down at the blood seeping out of my broken skin to reveal my invisible texture, the pores and creases and tiny hairs. It looks like art. Or like a river delta, somewhere where the soil is red. Texas, maybe.

Scowling, I order myself to focus. On Lauren's death. On her suicide. Because something looms over me, but I can't see the edges, can't find a hold.

When I drag my eyes back up to Noah, I find him smiling, proud and excited. He smells of cigarettes, which means he's been smoking in the upstairs rental. Wow. Grigore is going to be *pissed.* I almost giggle at the thought before I pull my attention back from its drugged wandering.

My eyes slide over the brightly colored knife still clutched in his hand like he's waiting for more. Then everything slams so firmly into place that I startle, making him jerk away in surprise.

Lauren didn't kill herself. He did it.

He can see the fear crash over me. I watch satisfaction bloom on his face as he nods. The Ambien can't protect me from this level of alarm, and I cry out in terror, a long, desperate moan.

Noah didn't want to leave any rope marks; that's why he used the blanket and sheet. He'll untie them and leave no evidence of restraint behind when he's done. When I'm *dead.* All evidence will point to a disturbed woman who wanted to end it all. A woman so confused and tormented that she couldn't be decisive even when cutting her own skin.

I'm still reeling when he grabs my left wrist again and darts in quickly for another cut, deeper this time, but still only a small notch. I hiss at the sting and press my feet to the floor to twist the chair away from him.

"I've already had to pay, you know," he says, his voice so sad that the hairs on my neck rise. "I didn't believe my little brother. I was dismissive. So cruel. I took my dad's side, and I lost my baby brother. You get that? I lost him. I failed him. And I live every goddamn day with the guilt of what I did. What I ignored. But what the hell have you lost? How have you paid?"

"Please," I try to beg past the gag.

He sneers at my grunting attempt, but then his face crumples into tears. "All you had to do was keep your stupid mouth shut!" With one shuddering breath, he gets control of himself and wipes his tears on a sleeve. "Jacob would have been fine where he was. He would've been good. Gone to college, maybe. Been able to have a relationship. But he was dropped back into pure hell because of you. He hated both of you for so many years. But when he couldn't hate anymore, he finally let go, found God or whatever he believed. But it didn't help. It didn't help!"

The sobs return, but he speaks past them, tears and spit dripping off his chin. "He lost everything. He lost his hope and his heart. Because of all of us. Now I'm repenting, I'm repaying. What the hell did you ever do to repent?"

I might beg for whatever mercy could be hiding in his soul, but the rag is stuck to my tongue, and I can't dislodge it.

"You and Lauren, my failure of a mother, that asshole foster mom. And me. *Me.* We all failed him, and it's not fair that we're still here and Jacob is gone. He's just *gone.*"

When he lunges in, I push with my feet one more time, shoving away, and the chair slides back.

"No one wants to help you now either," he says, the words rough and ragged and so, so raw. "No one believes you're suffering. Everyone just looks away." Those big eyes are red with some sickness that looks like sorrow.

"How long before anyone notices something is wrong, huh? You work from home. You have no family here. The cops think you're a problem. So . . . a few days? A week? Maybe the next guest upstairs will notice the smell."

I can see it. See *me*. The world moving around my little house while I stiffen, then soften, then begin to melt into rotting puddles. The flies will come. The maggots will sprout. And Mr. Sanchez will play with his grandson a dozen yards from me, none the wiser. John and his partner will check out and go home without a thought.

"I didn't find Jacob for two weeks." Noah's tears trickle down his flushed face as his expression slowly goes flat. His red cheeks fade to pale. He shakes his head. "Another indignity I didn't save him from. Another horror I fucking missed. But I promised him I'd make it okay. I picked him up and held him and told him I wouldn't let him down ever again."

Sympathy rises up in me like nausea. I understand now. I do. All the guilt and the love inside this man. But all I can see past the sorrow is me, dead in this chair.

Violet will try to call. Mike might come by. But then their days will carry on, distractions pulling at their attention, and they'll put me from their minds for another day or two before idly wondering about me again.

Even if somebody cares enough to call the police, I can already see the rolled eyes and the perfunctory knock on the door. I park on the street so guests can use the driveway, which means there won't even be a car to alert people that I'm still here. *Oh God, I'm still here. Please find me.*

I'm alone. I'm utterly alone. And no one is coming to save me.

CHAPTER 38

Another patch of my skin opens beneath the blade like it's eager to free my blood. As if it's been waiting my whole life to enact all those horrible stories I told when I was five.

I cry out in betrayal at how soft I am, how yielding. This time when I buck, one chair leg crashes down right on top of Noah's foot.

When I start to tip, I panic and throw my weight back toward him even as he barks and screams like an injured seal. I hope I broke something. I hope he limps for a year. A sad payback, but at least I'll have left a mark. I might feel a kernel of sympathy for this man, but I'm not willing to honor his twisted love by dying without a fight.

I need to reach the Taser. My wait-and-appease plan is no longer an option, and it's time to turn to violence.

I'm briefly thankful Noah planned for a forensic investigation and is concentrating so hard on my left arm, because that leaves me free to angle my right hand toward my pocket. My loose shorts have twisted, and the pocket is behind my hip now.

Noah has finally stopped shouting in pain, at least, but when I look up his fist is raised to hit me. I cringe away even as I try to pretzel my right wrist at an angle that can reach into the torqued fabric.

"Fuck," he barks, fist shaking with restraint. He can't hit me. He can't, because he'll leave a contusion and that will raise suspicion in an autopsy. Shit, I can't believe I'm actually pondering my own autopsy.

Before I can breathe a sigh of relief, he grabs a handful of my hair and pulls. I shriek against the gag and stretch my neck tall to relieve the screaming pressure on my scalp. I'm startled by the intense pain. The bullying I experienced in high school didn't extend to being jumped or punched. I might have been tripped or shoved every once in a while, but nothing had hurt this much.

I have been physically attacked in the ER, but I wasn't defenseless like this. I could fight back, and there were always coworkers nearby to help with restraint. This is a bright, unobstructed kind of pain, made more agonizing by my helplessness.

His grip eases. He lets go. My scalp throbs, and tears pour from my eyes.

It takes a few breaths for me to remember my mission, but I manage to work my fingertips into the resisting pocket. I lift my hip and slide deeper. *Come on. Come on.*

He's limping away from me, balancing his weight on his heel as he curses me for being a bitch, like I'm an asshole for trying to save myself from straight-up murder. Amazing the knots a violent man can tie himself into.

The pain he inflicted brightened my thinking, at least, and for a moment I'm not sleepy at all. I'm desperate and terrified and absolutely furious. He killed Lauren, and in just a few minutes I'll be his next victim if I don't get this goddamn Taser out of my goddamn—

There. My fingers brush the metal, warm from my body and still wrapped in the fabric of the pocket, but it's right there. I grip it with the tips of my fingers and try to ease it free. A centimeter. Then two. Then an inch.

But Noah is back, snatching up the knife from where he dropped it. His eyes are wet with new tears, and I feel a fierce pride that I hurt him as much as he's hurt me.

My fingers curl all the way around the Taser, and I slowly, slowly free it from my pocket. But before I can act on my plan, Noah strikes like a snake. For a split second, I think it's over. I wait for the blood and darkness. But he's only grabbed my left arm again. My right is still free, and I slide the Taser's switch on with one finger.

My brain wants to overthink it. Will it disable him or only burn? Will it shock me too? But as he leans to his bloody task again, I twist my body and shove up toward a few inches of exposed skin at his forearm. Then I press the fire button as hard as I can.

For a moment, I think the snapping sound is a misfire. He doesn't cry out. Doesn't respond at all, and the little Taser just . . . clicks.

But as the seconds grind past, I realize his lack of response means something else entirely. He's frozen, face a grimace and eyes bulging only inches from mine. A thick, phlegmy croak finally escapes his parted lips. My thumb aches from the pressure on the button, but I keep it up for a few more seconds before I release.

Noah tips right over and hits the hard floor with a fleshy thwap. I wish I'd heard a bit more bone in that, the sweet sound of a concussion, but he landed on his shoulder.

He's already stirring, already groaning, and I know this tiny weapon isn't strong enough to truly incapacitate him, so I take a deep breath through my nose, clench my jaw tight, and shove my feet hard enough to tip me right over too.

I land hard on top of his body, wincing as his hip bangs against my knee, and then I push the Taser against his back or maybe his shoulder, I don't care. I fire again.

The voltage doesn't affect me, thank God. That fear was still lurking in my brain, brought to the front by how much of his body I'm touching with mine, but I'm good. I'm good.

Noah is not good. Spit bubbles from his open mouth as he stares into nothing. A wheezing squeal whistles in his throat. I hope it burns like the fires of hell. I hope he's feeling every nanosecond.

I hold on until the clicking fades. It takes me far too long to realize the Taser has run out of power. I've wasted precious seconds.

Bracing myself for the unyielding surface of the floor, I torque my body and slide off him to crash to the ground. I'm stuck sideways in the chair, staring at the top of his head now. He doesn't move. God bless Grigore and his criminal habits.

I need to get free, and fast.

Now that gravity has pulled my entire body to one side of the chair, my right arm is trapped by my weight, but the blanket has stretched taut and exposed a gap along my left shoulder. I'm able to bend my arm in and wiggle it up through the space.

Yes! I've got one arm free. I yank the disgusting gag from my mouth.

When I brace my left hand on the ground, my arm smears bright-red blood all over the blanket, but I ignore it as I push up with all my strength to take the pressure off my right side. I pull until that arm is free too, then I tug the blanket around to get the knot in front of me. I desperately work my fingers into the tight twists of fabric until it's loose enough to work free.

The core muscles I so rarely use are beginning to cramp as I contort into a fold, trying to work my legs out of the loops of sheet.

"Ow, ow," I complain, but I bite back any other sound when Noah begins groaning.

He's still alive. I expect to feel relief, but instead, terror and fury slam back into my flesh as I drag myself farther from him. I need to get my legs out of this fucking tangle of cotton.

As I watch in horror, that bastard manages to turn his body from his side to his front. His next groan is more of a retching shout into the floor like he's an enraged, confused bull ready to charge. Now I'm in as much danger as I was before I tased him. He's alive, awake, and furious.

No! I kick and twist, pushing desperately at the sheet. One of my legs finally, finally tugs free. Then the other.

Noah flattens his palms against the floor and braces his hands beneath his shoulders.

He killed Lauren, and he'll kill me too. It's all he wants. All he's planned and worked toward for a year. It sounds like he'll target his mother too, and the foster mom Jacob lived with. A string of dead women with a connection the police will never discover. We'll be cold cases. Spooky tales told in the dark.

I don't want to be a dead woman nobody even remembers.

"Please," I pray, pushing to a half crouch as a rainbow of stars soar past in my distorted vision. I blink and blink until my gaze finally focuses.

The rainbow knife. The knife sits right between us, only two feet from his reach. And only a foot from mine.

Despite every cell in my body telling me to get farther away from this man, to run from danger like I always do, I summon all my courage to lunge forward. I grab the knife. I have it in my hand as he lifts his head, a long string of spit swinging from his brown bottom teeth.

His eyes radiate the death he promised me along with that terrible, mad love for his poor brother.

Holding his gaze, I raise the blade. Even then, he's not afraid. He knows I can't do it. I'm a woman. I'm a nurse. I'm a victim. I'm the girl who ran from everything and kept on running because I'm scared to face the world. I can't do it.

Noah growls, and I see in his glistening gaze that he still wants me dead. He pushes up to his knees.

That's when I remember. This man promised to kill Cocoa too. My sweet, ridiculous Cocoa. No. He's not getting away with this. I won't allow it.

It turns out that Noah's flesh is just as soft as mine. I drive the knife deep into his neck.

The ceramic knife cracks against a hard knob of bone, sending a faint shock up my arm to my shoulder. You're only supposed to use ceramic on boneless cuts, and now I've broken it off against his spine. But it doesn't matter. He's not glaring at me anymore; he's too busy turning those eyes desperately toward his own body as he reaches up to the blade sticking out of his neck. His fingers close over the beautiful rainbow, the twists of red, purple, blue, yellow so bright against his skin.

When he tugs, the knife comes free, and I'm surprised by the small dribble of blood. I expected a spout. We both look down to see that only the handle is in his grip. The edge of the blade—pretty green sliding into bright yellow and surrounded by gore—is still lodged in the side of his neck, stopping most of the arterial flow from escaping.

He drops the handle and reaches for his neck again, but there's nothing to grab hold of. Nothing to grasp. His fingers dig for a moment, hoping for purchase despite the slick red blood, but within a few beats of the pulse visible below his chin, his fingers slowly uncurl. His hand falls to the floor, knuckles rapping like he's politely knocking at the door of hell, and then the rest of his body follows.

He doesn't moan again, but bright-scarlet blood pours from his parted lips. His eyes are wide and pleading. He's still in there. He's not dead yet, but he's getting closer.

I'm on my hands and knees staring at him for a long time as I pant for oxygen. I can't get enough. The stars are back, no rainbows this time, just flashes of light that I have more trouble blinking away.

Once I manage to crawl to the couch, I'm able to pull my body upright, but standing was a big mistake. My stomach rebels with a sickening flip, and I stumble desperately toward the bathroom. There's not much in my stomach, but my body expels every drop of it in great, heaving sobs. Whatever pills were in there have long ago dissolved. I'm fully under the spell of the drugs, and when everything tilts, I grab the wall.

The cool tile supports me, but not for long. The bathroom slides up, and I slide down, and once I'm on the floor, I shut my eyes, and God, yes . . . this feels like heaven. My closed eyes and the cold floor. Yes. I need this. I need to rest. Just for a moment. Just for one moment.

And then I'll call the police. And an ambulance. Promise.

CHAPTER 39

Okay, I admit it. I slept for ten hours or so.

I'm honestly not sure what time it was when I passed out, but when I wake it's almost noon. If the ambulance might have helped Noah last night, it's . . . No, it's definitely not going to help now.

I stare down at the sickly white lump of him, my skin crawling. I've seen quite a few dead bodies in my career, but I've never gotten over how shocking the change is. Whether it's a soul or just energy, something important simply . . . leaves. Noah isn't a person anymore. He's a corpse.

And I killed him.

God, I'm scared. Not terrified, really, but filled with a white-hot coal of radiating dread. I killed a man and then slept half the day away, so this isn't going to look as simple as self-defense.

Still, I tell myself exactly what to do. Call 911, text Grigore for the name of a lawyer, explain to the arresting officer that it was self-defense, then shut the hell up and get ready to be ground into meat by a system that will hopefully spit me out sooner rather than later.

The metaphor makes my stomach heave because there's a distinct raw-hamburger smell rising up from Noah in the close confines of my locked home. A rotting sweetness that I have no trouble recognizing as old blood.

Cradling my cell phone against my chest, I back away. Parts of my body protest at the movement. My thigh, my shoulder, my knee, the tight sting of the cuts on my arm. But I keep backing away until I'm past the couch and near the patio doors. The smell doesn't quite reach over here.

"Call the police," I order myself in a desert-dry croak. But my hands keep the phone clasped tight.

I'll be detained. I'll have a good defense, and likely the police department will be embarrassed by the evidence—in the form of a corpse—that I actually was being stalked. I'll be able to point them toward Lauren's death. Still, there could be charges.

Whatever happens or doesn't happen, there will most definitely be a circus. That's a guarantee.

As an eager consumer of scandal, I understand exactly how delicious this story will be. A disturbed stalker, multiple police jurisdictions ignoring endangered women's pleas for help, a murdered blond beauty, and, the tastiest morsel of all, a call back to a wild tale of Satanic Panic and a gullible justice system. That story will be told over and over again.

And I'll be at the center of it all. My name, my history, my face plastered everywhere across the world. I'll never have control of anything again. Noah Hoffholder will succeed in ruining my life even from the grave.

I want to walk over and spit on him. I want to scream and cry and rage for the horrible story he told. Mostly I want this all to go away.

But I need to call the police.

Finally lifting my phone, I stare at the number pad on the screen. It'll take one second. That's all. One second to do the right thing. The smart thing.

Instead, I close that screen and open my security app. There's only one alert from last night, and when I click it, a video plays, showing Jeeves jumping down from the fence around 3:00 a.m. to sashay across my patio before disappearing from view.

There's no evidence Noah was ever here, and certainly no evidence that he came into my home and somehow ran his neck right into my favorite knife. But is there anything else incriminating here?

Raising my head, I look at the eerie black crack in the wall that leads upstairs. Suddenly afraid there could be more danger lurking up there, I tiptoe toward the door and peek past the angled armoire.

A length of heavy twine tied to one leg of the armoire disappears into the dark space beyond the door. When I bend to check the area beneath the wood, I see a small black lens attached to the underside of the cabinet. A camera. He'd been watching me.

"Gah." I shiver and wait for any answering sound from above, but I hear nothing.

With a last glance toward the dead body on my floor, I squeeze through the opening and into the stairwell. The open door at the top lets incongruously cheerful sunlight glow into the narrow space. At least I can see that the path is clear. The stairs rise steeply up.

I force my trembling legs to take each step. At the upstairs landing, I turn to move into the room I slept in during my first year in Santa Cruz. The bed is a rumpled mess. The big seascape tapestry that had covered this door has been tossed on the floor in front of the dresser.

Pausing, I hold my breath and listen for sounds in the apartment. There's nothing. No TV, no breathing, no creaking floors.

Where's the woman I saw on video? Did he sneak into her rental and take over the space? Kill her so he could get to me?

The noise of a car driving by suddenly swells, and I realize the front windows are both open. Noah likely listened to every conversation I had out there, with the police or Mike or even Mr. Sanchez. Then he'd watched me all day with the camera, firmly embedding himself right into the center of my life. Right into my home.

I can't decide if I should call out or just walk in. In the end, I can't bring myself to reveal my presence, so I step over the tapestry and slowly slide my feet forward, easing toward the open bedroom door and bracing myself to run if I find that woman waiting. Or if I see her body.

The living area is wide open and empty. A glance into the bathroom reveals that's empty as well. There's no one here.

I exhale what feels like five minutes of breath, and my entire body wilts with relief. There are empty beer bottles on the coffee table, and a dinner plate filled with blackened cigarette butts, but no weapons that I can see.

When I finally get the courage to move farther into the room, I spy a set of car keys on the side table near the door. The keys rest in a bowl shaped like an oyster shell, and next to that is a flowered sun hat. Next to the sun hat is a blond wig.

I turn in a slow circle, looking for evidence of another person, but there isn't even another pair of shoes, just a half-empty duffel bag and a pink windbreaker hanging on a hook. Was it only Noah the whole time?

After pulling my phone from my shorts pocket, I check the old recordings of the guest going in and out. I'd assumed it was a woman because of the pink coat and floppy sun hat, but there's only the one person. I can pick out the line of his jaw even though he kept his face tipped down.

No woman ever came through the front door. It was just Noah in disguise.

What had the cop said? *The guest is a pretty big girl.* I'd thought his tone was fat shaming, but he was being sarcastic about gender identity, not size.

Jesus, I feel so dumb. All it took was one cheap wig to lull me into a false sense of security. If I'd known there was a man here, I would have been on guard and suspicious. But his half-assed costume fully reassured me.

How stupid am I? Answer: so stupid it nearly killed me.

I shiver as I turn in a slow circle, picturing him up here listening and waiting, imagining how often he came down those hidden stairs and moved through my private rooms.

When I can't take it anymore, I head back down, the pit of my stomach dropping with every step closer to the corpse.

With each passing minute, I feel my chance to do the right thing slipping away. I just need to do it. Just call the police. Set the process in motion and stop thinking about it.

Instead I retreat to the bathroom to tie my hair back in a ponytail and rinse off the dried blood. Two of the cuts are barely visible. The deeper one looks like a cat scratch. All are beginning to heal. Hard to believe I look like I've had nothing more than a run-in with a stray. I take a few sips of water from the faucet to wet my parched mouth. After that I . . . just stare at myself in the mirror for a very long time.

I don't deserve this. Not for lies I told when I was five years old, and not for telling the truth when I was seven. I didn't deserve to be stalked, and I don't deserve to be exposed to the entire world when I'm the victim here. Every little detail laid bare, every lie revealed, and every choice I've made scrutinized in comment sections on online platforms across the world.

Intellectually, I've known for a long time that I didn't deserve all that shame as a little girl. But shame isn't logical. It's a parasite with no reasoning. It burrows in, leaving warped scar tissue behind along with endless larvae that carve their own paths, damaging new parts along the way.

Though I shudder at the imagery, that was how it felt. As if I were riddled with unhealed holes from the start, too weak to stand up for myself, too frail to fight off more damage. So I made a suit of armor instead.

And now, realizing that the people I hurt at the start were actually worthy of that pain? I don't know. It should make me feel absolved, but instead it makes everything clearer. I was only five. I didn't know anything about sex, or abuse, or rape. I never deserved any pain from the start. It wasn't my fault.

Jacob didn't deserve it either. Poor Jacob. Of course he was lost and angry. Of course he was acting out. That's what abused kids do. The authorities should have looked more closely, acted like the adults in the room. Lives were ruined because of their responses, not because of three kids.

And even Noah. God. I can understand that he wasn't pure evil. I get that the terrible knowledge of what happened to his brother warped him. But he made his cruel choices, he killed Lauren, and I can't help him now.

The brutal truth is that the police never helped any of us when we really needed it. Not back then and not now. Hell, the system ruined my life before I even had one, and I won't let it ruin me again. I refuse.

With a decisive nod, I hit the telephone icon on my phone, and I place the call I need to make.

CHAPTER 40

"What time did this happen?"

We stare down at Noah's body together, and the sight of it is somehow more terrible and more normal with two other people here.

"I don't know. Sometime between midnight and two or three in the morning. He . . . he drugged me. I passed out after I . . ." I gesture awkwardly toward the rusty wound on his neck.

Grigore nudges Noah's leg with the toe of his alligator cowboy boot, and I notice the body moves stiffly. Rigor mortis has already set in, and that will make this all the more difficult.

Clearing my throat, I gesture toward the open stairway door. "That's how he was getting in, apparently. Did he rent the apartment under his name?"

Grigore opens something on his phone and shakes his head. *"Nu,"* he says, then adds something more in Romanian before turning the phone toward me. The reservation reads Jane Black.

That's good. I think? No one will know he was here. "I know this is too much to ask. I know I should call the police."

Grigore lifts one shoulder in a casual shrug. "The cops sniffing around my business and asking questions? I don't like that. And they don't like me. But hey, the ocean is right there, and this guy's already dead. Also, I have a big boat." He glances at me as I gawk at him. I'm thankful, yes, but I'm still shocked. "Are you hurt?" he asks.

"Just bruised. Maybe a little woozy still. Your Taser did the trick, so thank you. If I hadn't had one in my pocket . . ." Oof. I don't want to think about it. There'd be a corpse here, but it wouldn't be Noah's.

Grigore brightens. "Ah, good. The Tasers work! And then you . . ." He draws a finger across his neck and nods.

"I mean, yes, but he was getting back up! I didn't just, like, *murder* him."

Grigore shrugs again. "Stand your ground," he says. Then he says something to Luca in Romanian.

I should be glad they don't care about the ethics of any of this, of course, because apparently Grigore's going to throw a dead body in the ocean for me. That's not something I should feel moved by, but I'm honestly touched. I asked for help, and he appeared.

"Cameras?" Luca asks with a gesture toward the door.

"I turned them off after I called you, so there's no record you're here. And he came in through the interior door, so there's no record he's here either."

He replies in rapid Romanian, and Grigore nods. "Good idea. Erase the last video of this guy going upstairs. If anyone ever asks, it looks like he left and never came back. I'll gather up his shit and store it. Like he's a customer who left crap behind in a rental. No biggie. It happens."

"He has a black pickup somewhere nearby, I think. The keys are upstairs. Should I . . . ?" I have no idea what to suggest, but I'd like to pretend I have something to contribute.

"We'll take it somewhere shady. Thieves will make it disappear like poof!" He nods and repeats, "No biggie."

Exactly how often has Grigore done this? No, I don't want to know. Right now I'm grateful to have a skilled criminal on my side, and the fewer questions I ask, the better.

"I'll pay you," I blurt out in such a loud voice that even Luca jumps a little. "I can take money out of my retirement account. Just let me know how much."

"Eh." He nudges the body with his boot again, though this time it's more of a kick. "For this scumbag? We'll make deal. You patch up my guys for the next year. How about that?"

I blink several times. "Patch up? Like from *gunshot wounds*?" Not that I haven't seen more than my fair share, but I can't perform surgery!

He says, "Eh," again. "It's Santa Cruz. Daly City. Monterey. Not so many gunshots, you know. Mostly stitches. Broken hands."

I want to protest that I'm not a criminal, except that I clearly am, so I keep my mouth shut.

"Hey," Luca chimes in, "you forget sunburn!" The two men burst into wild laughter while clearly making fun of someone named Sergei, though I can't understand the words peppered between guffaws.

Their explosive laughter is interrupted by a knock, and we all go quiet while exchanging wide-eyed glances.

"I turned off the cameras," I remind them in a whisper. "I don't know who it is."

Grigore nods toward the door, and I tiptoe forward to risk a look through the peephole, hoping whoever is out there won't notice the way my head blocks any light.

Damn it, it's Mike. I press a hand to my mouth to quiet even my breathing before I head back toward Grigore. "It's a guy I'm dating." But I correct myself. "Used to date."

Grigore nods, and we wait quietly until another knock cracks through the room. "Maybe he didn't hear us," I breathe, "and he'll just go away."

An hour passes as we watch the door. Okay, it was probably only twenty seconds, but it felt like an hour. I actually hear the scrape of Mike's shoe against sand as he turns away. But he only makes it as far as the closed window a foot from the door.

"Beth?" He calls through the glass and closed blinds. "Are you okay?"

Yeah, he definitely heard us. But he's worried about me, so my body doesn't know whether to go warm or be scared. He's just so nice. He couldn't deal with something like this even if I wanted his help. "He knows I was being stalked," I say softly. "If he heard your voices, he might call the cops or something."

"Just come to the door," Mike continues, "and let me know you're all right. I'll go away if you don't want to talk!"

We all look from the door to the dead body directly in the line of sight. "Better to call him," Grigore suggests.

I nod, but then think of a more convincing solution. "Hold on," I say, before untying the cord I wrapped around the patio doorknobs. I slip outside and quickly jog toward the side gate. If I call Mike, there's a possibility he'll suspect I'm being forced to comply, and I need him absolutely comfortable. There can't be a moment's doubt that today was very, very normal. Just in case.

Hopping from stepping-stone to stepping-stone in my bare feet, I move as quickly as I can toward the front of the house. "Mike?" I call before I even get around the corner to the driveway.

He jumps and spins toward me. "Beth! Are you all right? I heard people inside." He gestures uncertainly toward the window.

"Oh sure! I'm good. Great. My landlord is here. Again. He's, uh, fixing something! I was just out back. You know? Sitting on the patio!" I'm babbling, and my pulse is speeding out of control.

Is there any blood on me? I glance down at my gray T-shirt as casually as I can while my brain frantically spits out possible explanations.

Fuck. Blood on my sleeve. A thick smear. And some on the hem too. "Sorry," I say, brushing at it as if that will help any damn thing right now. And of course, his eyes move to the bloodstain. "Got my period!" I say with far too much pep. "It's kinda messy! But yay."

"Oh. Okay." His eyes flash toward my face then back to the rusty stain, then back to my face again. "Congratulations?"

"Yes! Ha!" Lord, I sound like a maniac, but the words keep coming. "It's always a relief! And hey, congratulations to you too."

"Uh, thank you. Yes."

"We're in this together," I joke for some ungodly reason.

His eyes widen, but he nods. "Absolutely. My responsibility too. I totally agree with that. Real glad you got your period."

"Yeah, great news. We dodged a bullet. I mean, I'm just kidding. I have an IUD. And we used a condom, which is awesome. But still . . . Woo-hoo!"

Jesus H. Christ. Well, the good news is, I've definitely replaced his memory of any strangeness at the front door with this bizarre conversation. *Mission accomplished,* I assure myself as if I said all this on purpose. In more good news, Mike is definitely a stand-up guy. Not that it will matter after this.

"I texted last night . . . ," he starts.

When he leaves it at that, I raise my eyebrows. I need to get rid of him, so maybe I should preemptively let him know there are no hard feelings. And honestly, I guess there aren't. He should run the other way. Breaking news: I'm not just a liar anymore; I'm also a killer.

Just over Mike's shoulder, I watch the line of a window blind lift, and I have to stifle a squeak as I gesture toward the sidewalk. "I'll check my mail while I'm out here. Gorgeous day. Nice and warm."

"It is really nice," he agrees as we stroll very slowly down the driveway. When a group of teens walk by, I cross my arms over my chest, hyper aware I'm wearing a thin T-shirt and no bra. But at least it's another good distraction for Mike.

When we get to the mailbox, I only stand there awkwardly, because I've realized I shouldn't open it in front of him. There could be a dead bird or a severed finger or a picture of me with a junior-high perm in there. I curl toward it, yank open the door an inch, then shut it just as quickly. All clear. "Slow mail day," I chirp.

"It's Sunday," he reminds me. Then we stand around looking at the ground some more. I'm afraid to open my mouth again, so I can't help him. He'll have to break off our friendship all on his own.

Turns out he's willing to face it head-on. "So . . . I've been thinking a lot about our talk yesterday."

Nodding, I close my eyes. "I'm sure. I get it."

"This has all been a little crazy."

"Right?" I force a laugh and open my eyes. "More than a little." He doesn't know the half of it. "It's okay," I add at the same time he says, "It makes sense."

I cock my head. "Huh?"

"After everything you went through as a kid. It makes sense that you'd want privacy."

"Yeah," I say. Then, "Really?"

"If the actions of others made me infamous and vulnerable for half my life, I'd be very careful about introducing myself to people. Or trusting anyone. I guess."

I stare at him, blinking back shock or tears or something. "Right. Yes. True."

"It's all been pretty surprising." He winces. "At first you were a good surprise, inviting me to dinner and then . . ."

"The sex?" I suggest.

"Yes, that. I'm just a middle-aged science nerd who works too much and has a dog named Princess, and I'm not super forward about dating, so . . . yeah, the sex really came out of nowhere."

"Surprise," I whisper, and throw in some quick jazz hands. He flashes me a pained smile.

"But then," Mike continues, "this whole situation got surprising in a different way."

My jazz hands fall away. "Yes. I'm really sorry I dragged you into this chaos. You're a nice guy, and I've taken advantage of that."

Now he frowns. "I guess."

Right. Men don't like being called nice guys. I'm juggling a bit too much to tiptoe around the male ego. But now I wish he'd get it over with and say goodbye, because my eyes are burning again.

"I just needed time to think," he says.

"Of course you did! I'm a ridiculous person. I just . . . God, I felt like I had everything under control, and suddenly everything was out of control." I blink hard, determined not to weep. "But you were kind to me when I needed kindness. I'll never forget that. You helped me get through this."

Mike frowns. "Is it done? Did something happen?"

Oh no. I shoot a panicked glance at the door hiding the man I killed hours before. "I . . . I don't . . ." After that spiel about periods and pregnancy, all my words seem to have dried up. "I . . ."

"Oh. I see. It's *done*," he says. "We are. I understand. I pulled back. Things just got so . . ."

"Weird?" I suggest.

"Yeah. But even if . . . You can text me anytime you want to go for a walk. Or if you're feeling nervous about that asshole stalker. All right? I'm sorry I made things awkward."

"You?" I yelp, grimacing when he winces. "You definitely didn't make things awkward. That was all me. Me and my ridiculous life!" I laugh, and I mean it, but I still have to turn away and wipe my eyes. "But it's time for me to move, I think." It's time. I know it is. But maybe I just want someone to ask me to stay. Just to hear those words before I go.

"Move?" He glances around at the street. "But this town won't be the same without you."

"Oh, don't worry, there are plenty of weirdos waiting to take my place. It's Santa Cruz."

"Hm."

I laugh to keep it light. For me or for him, I'm not sure. "Time for a change of scenery. Will you take Cocoa for walks when I'm gone? You have to watch her around bikes. And squirrels. She's just so—" And then I burst into tears.

"Oh." I hear him sigh, and I hold out a hand to stop him from hugging me, though everything's too blurry to be sure of his intention. But if he hugs me, I'll lose it completely. I'll wail and sob and possibly confess.

"I'm fine!" I gasp, adding to my list of lies. "I'm fine. Sorry. It's just been a lot." I'm not actually sure why I'm crying. But it really has been a lot, and there's more to come. I still need to get back inside to deal with the *dead body in my house*.

"Okay, but . . ." Mike starts to reach out, then hesitates and drops his hand. "I don't want to leave it like this. I could text tonight. Make sure everything is good? Maybe we could walk Cocoa together before you go. You can give me all your pointers on how to make her happy. Deal?"

I sniffle, trying not to cry harder when I realize I'm saying goodbye to him while I'm red-faced and snot-nosed and my boobs are jiggling around with every hitching breath. And then there's the corpse waiting for me when we're done. "Thanks," I squeak before I spin and walk toward the side of the house to escape back to the patio. "Bye!"

I guess I've made a decision. I'm leaving.

I can't move far if I'm going to be part of Grigore's criminal empire for a while, but I can't stay here. I need to shove Mike into the past, and I can't live in a murder scene. If there's any chance ghosts exist, Noah is definitely going to stalk me for eternity. He hated me so much already.

I slip back through the patio doors, shut them tight, and wipe my face. "All right. Tell me how we get rid of the body."

Time to pull off the biggest lie of my life.

CHAPTER 41

"We don't have to cut anything up, do we?" Both men turn to look at me, and I squirm a bit under their focus. "I know I'm a nurse, but . . ."

"Better to leave it all together," Grigore says. "People throw parts in. Big mistake. Instead of one chance of washing ashore, now you have five or six."

"Ah, of course," I say, trying to hide my horror with a thoughtful nod. "Makes sense." I manage to stop myself from shouting, *How many people have you killed?* because I don't want to be a murderer *and* a hypocrite. Maybe he just gets rid of dead bodies for cowards like me.

This could be the end of your life, I tell myself very carefully inside my own head. This could be the mistake that ruins everything. And I still have time to change my mind.

Okay, this *might* ruin my life. But reporting it to the police *will* ruin my life. At least this plan gives me a fighting chance.

It's not that I don't feel bad about wiping Noah's existence from the face of the earth. He loved his little brother. He still has a mother. Maybe he even has friends. But Noah is the one who chose violence. Frankly, he'd still be alive if he'd minded his own business and gone to therapy, but he chose to murder Lauren instead.

"The rug isn't big enough," Grigore is saying. "You have a tarp?"

I frown for a moment before perking up. "I think I do." I bought it during my last move because it was raining like crazy when I left Austin.

After racing for my bedroom closet, I dig around on the top shelf until I find the folded tarp and drag it free.

This is my last chance. Once we move the body around, all innocent explanations for delay fly right out the door. Am I really going to help dump a person in the ocean and lie to anyone who asks about him, including the cops? Yeah, I think I am.

"Found it!" I shout.

I've been training for this my whole life, haven't I? I can lie to anyone about anything. So yes, I'm going to dump this dead body and lie for the rest of my life. This is a lie I've chosen. A lie to make my life bearable. And I can live with that.

"Can you go in the boat with Luca?" Grigore asks.

"Me?" I squeak, feeling guilty even as I say it. This is my problem, not Grigore's.

"It looks better to see a man and woman together. Like a date. Instead of two big guys."

"Like a date," I repeat, and Luca gives me a thumbs-up and a wink. "Sure," I agree, though I'm already feeling seasick.

Grigore snaps out the tarp, and before I'm ready, the men are lifting Noah's body. They drop him a bit more roughly onto the black plastic than I would have, but I know it doesn't really matter. What would be the point of showing more respect when they're going to—no, when *we're* going to—roll him over the side of a boat and send him to the bottom of the sea to be eaten from the inside out?

Okay, that's enough. I breathe shallowly through my nose and try to stop my brain from sending up morbid images of crabs scuttling out of human openings.

"Luca, back the Navigator in. Bring it close. Elizabeth, take that painting on the wall. To block the neighbor's view."

His calm confidence is settling my nerves. If he's not worried, then I don't have to be. We've got this.

"No talking outside," he orders both of us as Luca slips out the front door.

I wrestle the bright coastal painting off the wall, and when Grigore opens the door, I find the SUV already in place and the liftgate rising. After swinging the painting sideways, I make it through the door and wait on the far side of the vehicle, doing my best to hold the frame at the ideal angle to block the view.

Only a few seconds later, the men haul out the rolled bundle and slide it into the Navigator. It looks very much like a dead body to me. I can't even imagine what else it could be, frankly. An extremely lumpy and heavy rug inside a tarp? Come on. It's clearly a person.

But it's done. Grigore takes the painting from me and lays it over the body. Once the hatch lowers . . . Wow. It looks like we're just transporting household crap.

"Liz!" a tiny voice calls.

I jump and spin, my heart thundering a path all the way up to my throat. I watch Mr. Sanchez's little grandson carefully check both ways before running across the street.

"No!" I scream as I race to meet him. "Roberto, you're not supposed to cross the street without your grandpa!" And where is he? Was he so busy watching us load a corpse into a truck that he lost track of his grandson?

I swivel my head back and forth, searching for him or any other witness. But when the screen door clangs, I realize he's coming out the front door. "Berto!" he yells, and I take the little guy's hand and scurry across the street with him, hoping to keep everyone far away from dead bodies.

"Mr. Sanchez," I pant. "Hi."

"Liz," he says a bit coolly as he leans down to pick up Roberto.

"Listen, I want to apologize if anything strange happened. I've had a stalker, and he's causing problems for me, but . . ." I clear my throat. "I think he might have spoken to you? The police are watching for him now, so hopefully he'll back off."

"A stalker?" he asks skeptically.

"Yeah. He actually broke into my house last week. Pretty scary. You probably saw the cops here."

"Oh. Yeah. Okay, I'll let you know if I see him again. He said you were a bad lady. A scammer."

I rub a hand over my head, not having to fake my stress. "I'm sorry. I'm not a scammer, I promise. I hope this guy won't be back, but I'm going to move anyway. Just in case." The grief is back. But at least Mr. Sanchez gives me a small smile.

"We'll be sad to see you go. Don't leave without saying goodbye, all right?"

"I won't." I wave at Roberto, who's giggling against his grandfather's neck. "No crossing the street!" I order, which makes him dissolve into peals of laughter for some reason. Kids are funny.

When I leave, I'm followed by the sound of stern Spanish from Mr. Sanchez as he points at a car driving by. Roberto is the first baby I've been around long enough to see grow into a wild preschooler. He's already talked about kindergarten and going to the big-boy school. But I won't get to see that now.

I'm crying again, but I only murmur, "Let me get dressed," to Grigore as I head straight for my door.

When I emerge wearing old joggers and a dark long-sleeved T-shirt, Grigore nods at me, then gives me a thumbs-up when I tug an old baseball cap low on my head. "I'll take care of things here," he says. "Luca knows what to do."

"Thanks." I point toward the armoire. "There's a camera under there. I assume there's video on his phone."

"I took the phone from his pocket so it wouldn't track him out to sea. We'll delete the videos and destroy it. A new guest arrives in three days, and hey! Everything gets normal again."

Just like that? Is it truly this simple to make a man disappear? I suppose when he's already living as a stalker, that makes everything easier.

If Noah's digital trail can be unraveled, it will show him checking in to the rental under a fake name, then sneaking in and out for days wearing a wig and hat before his phone eventually winks out.

He's clearly lived an unsteady life since the death of his brother. It would be no surprise at all if a man like him vanished. He simply moved on. That makes more sense than him living in the walls of a vacation rental, stalking a stranger, then making a casual return to society. Doesn't it?

"Leave your phone," Grigore orders as I reach for the door. Right. I probably shouldn't be tracked out to sea either. I toss it on the table and rush outside to join Luca.

"Ready?" I ask as I climb in and close the door, ignoring the deep ache in my bruised thigh. He nods and rolls down the driveway to the street. Where a cop car sits. Waiting.

Fucking hell. Every organ in my body lurches as if I'm in freefall. I *am* in freefall, dropping to my ultimate doom. Why didn't I just call 911? Maybe the story wouldn't have exploded. Maybe they wouldn't have even arrested me. I might have—

"Smile," Luca orders.

"What?"

"Smile! Ha!"

When I turn to him, I see his teeth clenched in a grin. He raises his eyebrows, urging me not to be stupid, so I laugh too, though it sounds like a wheezing bark.

"Date night!" he says. It's early afternoon.

But I nod and swing my head back toward the street to find the cop car isn't actually waiting. It's rolling past my property at a very slow crawl.

I lock eyes with the driver and see the female officer who was here during the last call. We stare at each other. I nod and give a small wave, but she only watches flat-mouthed as the car inches by. Her eyes shift to Luca, then back to me.

If they hadn't been so quick to dismiss me this time, I'd think she was watching over me, suspicious of this large man driving me somewhere. But I know she doesn't give a shit, so I just wait. And I'm right. Eventually, the car rolls past and keeps going.

"Holy mother," I murmur. "I think I peed a little."

"Huh?"

"Nothing." And then Luca pulls out, and he actually turns in the same direction as the police car! This man has nerves of steel, because I definitely would have made the most suspicious choice and sped in the opposite direction. Wow. My eyes nearly bug out of my head when we come to a stop behind the cops at the next intersection. But when they turn right, we turn left, thank God.

My heart rate has nearly returned to normal when we hit the highway, but when I ask where we're going, Luca answers, "Moss Landing," and I'm convinced we'll run into Mike there. At which point I'll have to awkwardly explain that I'm on a date with a huge younger man who doesn't speak much English and is definitely not hauling around a dead body in a tarp.

I guess I'm okay with it, though, because a few miles later my head lolls to rest on the window, and soon after that I fall asleep, not waking up until a door slams shut.

"Where—?" I start, but I see dozens of masts swaying against clouds, and I know exactly where we are. Still, I look around in dismay, because the masts are several hundred feet away. Luca is walking away from the vehicle, and we're in the middle of a decrepit seaside lot.

He unlocks a tall chain-link gate and pushes it open just far enough to drive through. The fence guards a complex of rusting old metal buildings.

I'm now very aware that I don't have my phone, no one knows where I am, and my hot date is very much a criminal.

"Luca?" I ask with deliberate calm when he opens the door and gets back behind the wheel. "Where are we?"

"Boat," he answers simply.

"The boats are over there." I point toward the huge harbor and boat yard across a span of water.

"Private dock."

Yeah, that's what I'm worried about. But he's right, of course. How would we get a body to a boat in a public harbor? I hadn't even considered it.

We ease through the gate and drive around to the side of the largest building, hiding ourselves from the street. I can see a crooked dock now and three fishing boats tied to it.

I'm suddenly realizing what sort of crime my new Romanian family is involved in. They're clearly bringing in product from offshore.

It's drugs. I'm in a drug gang.

Just for a year, though. Then I'm going straight.

CHAPTER 42

Criminal activity or not, it's so peaceful on the water that I can pretend this is a date. I stare in wonder at a bobbing group of fat seals as we speed past.

The wind cools the sweat I worked up as we loaded the boat, and sunlight glitters with impossible beauty against the water. If this were really a date, it would be a nice one, but the body of the man I killed bumps against my feet to remind me that this isn't a joyride.

We're far enough out that I can't identify any details of the shoreline aside from the twin smokestacks of the Moss Landing Power Plant. Santa Cruz and all my worries are a blur far to the north.

Well, not quite all of them.

Luca cuts the engine. I stare across the sea for a moment longer, listening to waves slap at the hull. I wish we could sit here for hours while I convince myself, but Luca reaches for the tarp and begins to open it.

"Uh," I grunt. "Do you need to do that? Can't we just throw him in?" I don't want to see Noah again. Ever.

"No. No cover. The fish will eat."

Right. Yeah, that image is not helping my nerves. But suddenly the tarp is open, and Noah is aiming his half-closed eyes right at the cloud-dappled sky. I blink down at him. His gray, stiff features are grotesque now, but I can somehow see the teenager in them. The posed school photo of a boy who wanted to be a vet. None of us should have suffered through this. I want to weep for him, for Jacob, for Lauren. I want to weep for myself. But that will come later.

"Turn," Luca orders. I hesitate until he draws a short-bladed knife and leans over the body.

"Oh!" I yelp as I twist around to stare back toward shore.

"Will make him not float," he says as a ripping noise cuts through the soothing sounds of nature. A terrible smell burps up behind me.

"Oh God," I pray, trying not to picture what he must be doing. Yes, I'm a nurse, but this is way outside the bounds of treating living bodies.

But when he says, "Okay," I turn and see what he's done. Noah's shirt is cut open, and a long, bloodless wound tears through his abdomen. He definitely won't float.

Nurse or not, I wouldn't have been able to do that. I want to thank Luca, but I'm afraid I'll be sick if I let my jaw unclench.

"Okay," Luca pronounces again before he tosses his knife overboard. "Ready?"

Am I *ready*? No, I don't think I am. But I nod numbly and rise to brace my feet in a wide-legged stance against the rocking boat.

I see the handle of my rainbow knife lying in the folds of the tarp beside Noah and lean over to pick it up and toss it into the water with the other knife.

When Luca bends down to grab Noah beneath his arms, I hesitate. The blade is still inside his neck, jammed into his bone. And my blood is on the blade too. How long would that preserve DNA evidence inside his body? Long enough to point right back to me?

It's possible.

"Shit," I growl. "Hold on. He cut me with this knife first. I should probably . . ."

Luca sits back with a magnanimous wave of his hand, and I reach toward Noah's neck.

Holy moly. Am I really going to do this? But I have to. I can't worry every day that he'll wash ashore and bring my DNA along with him. Even if the fish eat most of him away, if the knife is lodged in his spine . . . No. I have to do this.

The wound is cold and sticky when I touch it. If I weren't a nurse, I'd probably hurl over the side of the boat, but I'm used to cleaning out cuts and debriding wounds, and I try to keep my eyes locked on those few square inches and pretend this is work. I do miss having a pair of gloves, though.

"Shit," I mutter again as I dig my fingers in deeper, the blood like cold jelly sliding under my nails. I'm just starting to shudder when I finally get a tiny hold on the broken blade. I grip it one more time and try to tug. The wound grips back, holding the knife in place.

"Here."

I take a rusty pair of pliers from Luca's hand and get back to work. When the blade finally pops free, I brace myself for more blood, but nothing emerges. It's just a black-red hole leading to his death.

I throw both the sullied rainbow blade and the pliers into the deep. When I look down at my thoroughly bloodied hands, I wish I could toss them in too.

We've drifted farther out, and I picture a trail of colorful murder implements rocking peacefully against the sand fathoms below.

"Come on," Luca says, snapping me from my daze. "But take off shoes."

Right. There are always news reports of feet washing ashore still encased in shoes. I nod and pull off one sneaker, then the other. Noah's big toes stick out of holes in both his socks, and for some reason I reel back at that reminder of his humanity.

Noah was a person. His brother's death might have twisted him into such damage that he'd become a boogeyman, but he'd had a real life. He'd loved and lost. He'd been a son and brother. My mind spins, but I toss the shoes into the ocean and try not to give up and jump in myself.

I can do this. "All right," I whisper and grasp his ankles tightly. "One, two, *three*."

I heave as hard as I can, but Luca still bears most of the weight. He hauls Noah's shoulders up to the rail, then shoves him over. The feet fly from my grip as the body drops into the water with a violent slap.

When I look over, Noah is drifting down, his eyes still staring up at scuttling white clouds as his face gets smaller and smaller. And then, just like that, he's gone.

I lurch against the railing. Luca's surprised exclamation follows me as I lean down to shove my hand into a rising wave to wash off the blood. But the wave falls away and leaves me dangling a foot above the sea. Bloody water drips from my fingers in scarlet bubbles, and the boat rocks, and the waves shimmer, until finally the meager contents of my stomach rebel.

When I vomit, Luca laughs. "You bring more fish!" he says approvingly. The image doesn't help settle anything, and I vomit again.

"Here," Luca says, offering a pail on a rope that he's dipped into the ocean. I plunge my hands in and scrub desperately; then he tosses the dirty water down the outside of the boat to rinse off my sick.

The ride back seems interminable, and I huddle low in my seat, trying not to think about Noah Hoffholder's toes sticking out of his socks or the crabs picking at his neck or the awful way he tried too late to help his little brother.

In the end, I'm only sick two more times.

CHAPTER 43

Luca drops me off a couple of blocks from my house after explaining that Grigore was picked up and everything is done. Being able to trust these men, to lean on them, has been a comfort I've never had in my life. But I'm still incredibly relieved that I'll be alone in a few minutes, so I can cry or freak out or curl up in a ball with no one watching.

It's strange to take such a normal walk though my neighborhood after the trauma of the last day. Strange to wave at a neighbor with a hand that had been stuck in a dead man's neck a mere hour before.

But the bizarre normalcy is offset by the silent farewells I make along the way. This might be the last time I see Joy, the carefully sculpted white poodle who always greets me from behind her white picket fence. Or my favorite olive tree decorated with programmed lights that change color to reflect every individual holiday, no matter how obscure. Or even the little fairy garden that's slowly falling apart on the corner just before my street.

When my neighbor Carol stops to tell me about a debate over a new city council proposal, I manage to carry on a reasonable conversation, though I remember none of it once I'm two steps away. My mind is trying its best to go into standby mode. I just have to make it back to my place. I'll retreat to my bedroom and lock the door against ghosts until I can reassemble the energy I'll need to find a new place.

If I can afford it, Monterey might be the best bet while I work off my debt to Grigore. But maybe San Jose would be more—

I freeze, my feet skidding over sandy concrete as my body jerks to a stop. My brain flares back online, throwing out panic and chaos as it tries to decide whether I should hide or run.

Four houses down, Mr. Sanchez stands in his driveway, talking to the last person in the world I want to see here today. Even worse than just talking, Detective Heissen finally has his notebook out, and he's jotting down whatever Mr. Sanchez is saying. A hell of a time for him to pay attention.

This is bad, my stupid brain squeaks, the least helpful warning in the world. Yes, it's bad. Because apparently Mr. Sanchez did see something today. Perhaps, after hearing I was sketchy, he was watching me through his blinds. He might even have been using binoculars, because that's what I would have done.

It looked like a dead body, he'd say, and I'll try to protest that it was just a rug and an old painting I was getting rid of, but that won't explain the bloodstains on the floor, will it? And under my nails? There's no way the seawater washed away all of Noah's DNA.

I take one step back, thinking I'll flee, but I don't even have my phone or purse. I have no money, no keys, no nothing. That moment of doubt is my downfall. Detective Heissen looks up and spots me.

His eyes narrow. His jaw tightens. He can see that I'm about to run; I know he can. But where would I go? How would I even disappear when he's only eighty feet from me?

This is it. I'm done. It's all over.

Heissen turns from Mr. Sanchez and crosses the street toward me. I inch reluctantly forward.

"I'm sorry, Liz!" Mr. Sanchez calls out, and I want to cry at his simple message of regret for turning me in for murder. He really is a nice guy. "Sorry!" he calls again as he walks toward his house, and I lift my terrible hand to absolve him. No one wants a cold-blooded killer for a neighbor. He did the right thing.

"Ms. May," the detective says.

"Yeah." My voice is dull and hopeless. I need to get it together, to fight this, but I don't know how.

"We need to talk. Perhaps we could go inside to speak privately?"

So he doesn't have enough for a search warrant yet? Nice try, asshole. "The last time I invited you in, it didn't go well for me." I walk past him so I don't have to meet his eyes. Then I take my time opening my mailbox and peering inside again.

The stalling helps nothing. My brain is still spinning in mad circles and throwing out panicked screams instead of ideas.

"I apologize for that," Heissen says, trying to butter me up now that he wants to search my place for murder weapons.

"We can talk here," I mutter, giving up on the mailbox ploy to turn toward him, arms crossed and eyes drifting to the side so I don't have to meet his gaze. I can feel my face heating up as I picture him clapping me in cuffs in front of the neighborhood.

"We got a tip," he says, and yeah, I can feel the tip watching from inside his house right now. I keep my face as blank as possible.

He flips open his stupid notebook. "A woman was picked up on a drug charge a few blocks from here. Lucy Crake. She's hoping to make a deal."

"Lucy?" I murmur. The woman I give a few dollars to on occasion? I glance down the street, wondering if she was camped out near my place this morning.

"She threw out a few lines to get our interest, and she says a man paid her boyfriend forty bucks to turn off your electricity."

"Huh?" I gulp, totally dumbfounded.

"I drove her by to confirm this was the house. She said the man who paid was in his forties, maybe. White guy. Blondish hair."

Holy shit. *What?* I stare dumbly at Heissen.

"I talked to Mr. Sanchez over there, and he described encountering the same man a few days ago."

I glance toward Mr. Sanchez's house, then back to look the detective dead in the face. "Really?"

"Do you recognize the description? White, average height, mid-forties, short blond hair?"

"Uhh . . ." What am I supposed to say now that they're finally taking me seriously? Twenty-four hours ago this would have been great. If he'd told me yesterday, I would have called 911 this morning to yell, "We got 'im!" But now? Oh no. Now I really don't want them looking for Noah Hoffholder.

"Ms. May?"

"Sorry, this is quite a shift."

"Yes, I apologize about last time. We didn't have much information to go on."

His stupid half apology finally breaks through my confusion and props me up with a little anger. I straighten and cross my arms even tighter. "I don't recognize that description. It could be almost anyone."

"Yeah, it's not the most helpful. But I went back to look for more video from that first incident."

How is this happening? Why is he only now doing this? Now, when it's way too late to help anyone? A strangled noise sticks in my throat.

"It was, uh, too late at a couple of places," he admits. "But I did get one other angle of the guy walking away. Looks like a white male with a bit of weight around the middle, but we couldn't make out much more than that. He was wearing a black hoodie and a face mask."

Heissen is lucky I'm hiding a murder, or I'd read him the riot act about waiting too long to gather evidence. Now I'm grateful he didn't get a good look at Noah, but I glare to keep up the act.

He clears his throat. "You said you know who's doing this?"

"No. I don't."

"But you said it was a man from Iowa."

Sweat prickles under my arms as waves of panic cascade through me. *Now* he remembers I'm from Iowa? This is an unmitigated disaster, and I'm going to prison for sure.

"No, I . . ." I snatch at the first thought that springs to mind. "I was just freaking out, making connections that weren't there."

"Oh?"

I tap into my decades of lying experience and grab a thread. "The guy I suspected is married to someone I know, and she posted pictures of them in Hawaii last week. So I was wrong. No one came from Iowa to harass me." I manage a quick gulp of laughter at the absurdity of the idea. "Obviously. I guess I was panicking."

"You're sure?"

"Yeah, and that man doesn't have blond hair, anyway. So."

He glances toward my front door. "Did you get those cameras?"

"Yes! They worked well last night. No problems. All quiet on the Western Front!"

When he frowns, I curse myself for always being such a damn weirdo. Can't I be normal for once?

"Sure," he finally says. "Would you like me to take a look around your place for any vulnerabilities?"

He really wants to get inside. It might be that he's trying to appease me after his threat to arrest me, *the victim*. Or it could be that the patrol officer told him about strange activity at my place this morning. Regardless, there's a bloodstain on my floor.

"No thanks. I'm good."

He casts one more look at my door as I raise a quick hand to swipe at the sweat on my forehead. "Well," he says, "please give us a call about any suspicious activity. I apologize for the confusion last time."

The *confusion*. God, I'd love to tear him a new one. Instead, I say, "Thanks," and stare at him until he nods.

"I'll be in touch," he adds, and I can't tell from his tone if it's a promise or a threat. When I don't respond he finally gives up and strolls down the block toward a gray sedan.

I wait until he's in his car before I hurry to my door and punch in the new code in record time. I slip through, slam the door shut, and . . . gasp in surprise.

Everything has been cleaned up. Everything. The pills, the cigarettes, the beer bottles, the blanket. They're all gone. I have no idea what the bloodstain looks like because the royal-blue rug has been moved toward the kitchen, and the table and chairs now sit on it, a bit too close to the living area.

The room smells of bleach and other cleaning agents, but that's offset by the piney scent of a green candle burning on my kitchen counter. I'm definitely not allowed to burn candles here, so whoever Grigore called to clean up must have left it.

I'd like to check upstairs too, but the armoire is back in place with the door shut behind it. If I meant to stay here, I'd ask Grigore to add a dead bolt, but . . . that's not happening. I have to leave for so many reasons.

Why does that make my heart twist? Why do tears spring to my eyes? I've always left. It's what I do.

Within a few weeks of moving, I'm usually plotting my next location, looking through rental options and prices, plotting out the sights I'll see in my next place. Months before I ever leave, I'm ready to go. I never have a real home, and that's the way I want it.

But this time? This time I haven't scouted locations or searched out rentals. Not even for Guam. And I've known for days that I would need to move, and do it quickly.

"It's time to go," I order myself. "No more stalling."

But I only take two steps toward the laptop on my coffee table before I veer toward the kitchen and my phone instead.

The screen lights up with alerts. There's nothing from Grigore, likely because he's avoiding leaving an evidence trail. But there's a missed call from the Santa Cruz Police Department, a voicemail from Violet, a reminder about a pedicure appointment on Tuesday, and some texts from Mike.

I listen to Violet's voicemail first. "Hey, Betsy! Just checking in. I had a bad feeling last night, which is really silly, I know. But I figured it wouldn't hurt to make a quick call. And hey, come by Tuesday if you want dibs on new releases. I won't be putting them out until noon, so if you get there early, I'll let you have first choice. Text me if you get this, all right? Bye!"

Pressing my lips tight together, I let the tears roll down my cheeks. She's so thoughtful. And kind. And cool. If I weren't such a freak, maybe we could have been real friends. That won't happen now, but I still text her back with a promise to drop by on Tuesday. I should have a few plans in place by then, so I can give her the news that I'm leaving and make my goodbyes.

I can get my pedicure, head to the library, then go out for a nice lunch, maybe stroll down the beach. I can live just how I want to live in my favorite place for one more day. To pretend I belong. Pretend it's home.

I'm sniffing back tears as I open Mike's texts. At the sight of the last message, the sniffles turn to weeping. It's a close-up picture of two smiling faces. One is Mike, grinning into the camera. The other is Cocoa, her tongue lolling happily out as Mike presses his cheek to her silky brown ear. They're both adorable dorks, and I love them for that.

Love? my brain screeches. No, not deep, long-term love, but I at least have a terrible crush on both of them. And God, it hurts to feel that. It's a pain I haven't felt in a very long time.

I took Cocoa out for a walk as ordered, Mike had texted. We had a terrible time together as you can see. Boy, this girl really hates bikes, doesn't she? Good thing there aren't many bicycles in this town. Haha. She says she misses you.

I sink into a chair, drop my head into my hands, and sob over the terrible mess I've made of everything. But at least this time, despite this huge, pulsing lie I've added to my life, I know I've done the right thing. And when I finally get out all my frustration and sorrow, when I raise my head and look around, I feel lighter.

Most of the guilt, the guilt I've hauled from town to town, from decade to decade, the guilt I've hammered into armor and held between me and the world . . . it's gone.

I take a deep breath. I let it out. And for the first time in my life, I feel free.

CHAPTER 44

One month later

I unlock the dead bolt of my new place and pull against the sticky frame. After a few hard tugs, the door finally flies open, letting in a warm, flower-scented breeze. I make it halfway outside before I remember I need to carry a physical key for this rental and hurry back to dig through my purse.

My place is the smaller end of a duplex that used to be a single-family home, so my door is actually on the side, and the "kitchen" obviously used to be a mudroom. It's only a studio, but it has a fenced backyard, so I snatched it up as soon as I saw it.

Keys in hand, I carry the things I've piled near the door to my car. Just as I'm slamming the trunk, a bike flies past, startling me into a yelp. I'm staring after the man when the metal fence behind me rings with a clang. Suddenly there's a clatter and motion, and I'm nearly knocked off my feet by the force of the dog that clips my leg.

My heart leaps into my throat with terror. "Oh no," I murmur, and then I take off at a full run, my sandals slapping the sidewalk.

"No, no, no," I pant, each syllable shot from my lungs with a footfall. "No!"

A car screeches to a stop right beside me. There's shouting. I don't pause, not even for a second, though I do dare a glance back over my shoulder toward the man now sprinting toward me. I hear his footsteps pounding even quicker than mine, and I do my best to push into a higher gear.

Up ahead, the bike rounds the next corner instead of crossing the street, thank God. The footfalls behind me are catching up, but I keep pushing, hoping to gain ground.

And then he flies past, his running shoes carrying him faster than my sandals can. I slow down to gasp gratefully, bending over for a moment to try to catch my breath.

"Hey!" I hear Mike yell. "Stop!"

A few moments later, I can breathe a little better, and I do my best to run again.

"Gotcha!" Mike shouts from somewhere ahead.

I round the corner, nearly skidding into a light pole; then I let out a little whoop of joy. Mike is sprawled on the grass with the dog in his arms, his grip tight on her collar as she tries to wiggle free.

"Cocoa!" I call, doing my best to sound stern instead of relieved before I collapse to my knees and add my hand to her collar. "I've got her."

"I might be too old for this," Mike pants.

"I definitely am. I think she's figured out how to lift the latch on the gate. I'll have to add a bungee cord or something."

"Smart girl," he says, and I preen for a moment before realizing he's talking about Cocoa.

After brushing off my green knees, I push up to my feet and tug her to my side by the collar. "Silly girl. I was just about to get your leash and free you from your prison."

"Hello, by the way." Mike leans over to give me a kiss before I start to work my way back to the house in an awkward hunch. "It's really good to see you."

Now I am preening. "It's good to see you too." I reach up for another kiss, then straighten with relief when Mike hauls Cocoa into his arms. She finally gives up her vigil for the dastardly bike rider and licks Mike's face like she's missed him even more than I have. "How was Big Sur?" I ask.

"Cold. Foggy. I'm ready for some sun."

"Oh, I bet you are, mister." His blush makes my heart soar.

Once we've trudged back to my house, I grab Cocoa's leash and snap it on before she can escape again; then I wait for Mike to find a new parking spot that isn't blocking a driveway.

Once he's parked and locked up, we walk three blocks down and knock on the door of a pretty pink-and-white house with a similar layout to my old place. One apartment downstairs and one up, but this one has a full backyard instead of a patio.

When the owner opens the door, I give her a grateful hug as I squeal, "Playdate!"

Violet hugs me back quickly before moving on to the dog, who's whimpering with happiness to see her. I'm playing second fiddle to everyone today. "Cocoa!" she coos. "How's my best girl?" Cocoa's butt nearly wiggles her right off the stairs. I get it. Violet's pretty great.

My question about Violet's home was answered a couple of weeks ago when she invited me over. Her place is light and airy, but it's also a little cluttered with knickknacks and photographs. A lovely combination that's like nothing I've ever had for myself. When you move every six months, you don't accumulate much of your own.

A tiny bark sounds, and Cocoa howls while trying to tug me straight through the house.

"He's already outside," Violet says as if I needed another clue, but her voice stops Cocoa from pulling, at least, as she tries to curl her entire body around Violet's legs.

"Sorry. I should have brought a fur roller for your pants." I cringe, but Violet only laughs as she scratches between Cocoa's ears. Another small bark is the magic spell that frees her, and this time I let Cocoa lead the way to the back door.

I barely have my hand on the latch when she shoves her way through with an excited whine that transitions to ecstatic barking as she and Chompers chase each other in circles beneath the palm trees, one big brown blur and one tiny mottled one. It's true love, and I'm glad they're spayed and neutered, because I do not want to know what their offspring would look like. Or how that process would even happen, frankly.

"Chompers!" I call out, but he only has eyes for Cocoa. Second fiddle again. Oh well. Family is complicated.

In the end, I couldn't leave Santa Cruz. I tried. I researched apartments in Monterey. Then in San Jose. I toured a place that I really liked and paid the application fee.

But when I got the email letting me know I'd been approved, I had a panic attack. It was the first panic attack of my life, despite all the trauma I've suffered.

My heart was telling me not to leave. Telling me to *stay*. For once in my life, to just *stay* and let my roots continue to grow in this sandy, sunny soil. Who knew I had roots? Not me, not until I tried to yank them up.

So here I am, being brave and taking a stand. I watch as Cocoa and Chompers slow their circular race and trot to a corner to sniff something interesting. I leave the two lovebirds alone and head back to my own blossoming romance.

"Where's Jess?" I ask as I sneak my arm around Mike's waist for a little squeeze. Jess and Violet are the old married couple of this group. They've been together three years.

"Working. But you'll see her when we drop off Chompers on Sunday for that wine-tasting tour. Thanks again."

"No need for that. I'm thrilled with this arrangement. Chompers is all settled in?"

"Yep. It took him a couple of days to work through his anxiety, but now he realizes he's the favored prince of our castle, and he's truly full of himself."

I blink back tears. "Oh God, I'm going to cry again. I'm so happy you went to meet him."

"You're even sappier than Jess," she says, but I can see her own eyes are damp too. "Go on. Get out of here. Enjoy your date, kids. Don't stay out too late."

Everything makes me cry these days. Everything is just *so much.* But I manage to control myself as I hug Violet one more time before Mike and I depart.

As soon as we get back to my place, Mike grabs his bag from his car, and then we're off, driving down the hill toward the ocean.

We listen happily to music until we're past the edge of town and the vista opens up. "Everything was fine this week?" Mike asks, grabbing my hand.

"It was great. Good weather every afternoon."

"And the stalker? Still no reappearance?"

"Nope," I squeak. "Nothing. I'm pretty sure he's long gone." It's not quite a lie, is it? He's well and truly gone.

"That's good. I always worry about you when I'm out of cell range. But maybe the cops finally starting a real investigation scared him off."

"Maybe! Or he gave up when I moved apartments."

"And that detective? Still no word from him? No follow-up?"

"Nope. Nothing. No news." Again, it's not quite a lie. There's no news because I didn't tell Detective Heissen I was moving, so he has no idea where I am. He stopped calling after I ignored his first three messages, and I know Grigore hasn't had any contact with the guy.

As far as Heissen knows, I've disappeared from Santa Cruz. Unless I run into him at the grocery store or something. If I do . . . well, I don't need to lie to him, just give him the cold shoulder.

I'm trying my best to give up my fabrications, after all, especially with Mike. I've even tried consolidating my worlds. I told Violet that after the scare with the stalker, I decided to change up my life a bit, and I asked her to call me Beth instead of my old nickname of Betsy. The women at the shelter still call me Lizzie, but I signed everything as Elizabeth and told myself that was a kind of transparency.

And the biggest step of all? I found a therapist. Hard to believe, but I'm starting to like her. Maybe even trust her.

Still, she's two towns over in Aptos, so I can keep her separate from the rest of my world if I decide it's too much to handle. But I'm making progress. I told her all about my past, but more important, I told her about my present.

Well, not the murder part. I'm not stupid.

It was my strategy of lying about everything that was so terrifying to lay bare. But she didn't seem shocked or disturbed, and she taught me a neat trick right off the bat. When I feel pressured or panicked or vulnerable, I should take as long as I need to think how I want to answer questions. The pause lets me step back from my initial impulse to always use a lie for protection. It helps me consider how much truth I feel safe revealing. Or at worst to say, *I'd rather not discuss that right now.* Hell, I've even used that one on Mike.

Full admission: I've seen him more than six times, and it's only been one month. It's a dangerous risk, but I've decided to jump in. Or to wade in slowly and safely, at least. He'll be here for a few more months, and then we'll see what happens. It's just dating, my therapist assures me. We can stop at any time.

But honestly, Mike is too good to keep tucked into a safe compartment. And too good to abandon. In fact, he's pretty fucking great.

Still, this is scary stuff. To make myself vulnerable. To reveal bits and pieces even as I'm just learning them about myself. I hardly know who I really am, after all. Some of my parts are still stuck in that little girl from so long ago, still buried under the mess I made of everything.

Do I still want to be a nurse? Do I want to try writing? Would I ever want to attempt marriage again? Am I mature enough for a long-term relationship? How could I know?

My therapist assures me I'm not crazy and that I'm fully capable of having a healthy relationship if I work at it. So here I am, working at it. And trying my best never to lie about anything more serious than whether the new tan lines around his eyes from his sunglasses are noticeable. (They're pretty bad, but please don't tell him.)

There is that one big lie, of course. That giant, rotting falsehood. That wall has to remain in place, but it's hopefully more of a low fence between us than a fortified palisade. Hopefully. Still, as the highway curves closer to the ocean and I look out at those dark-blue depths, Noah Hoffholder looms in my mind with the size and weight of a tall mountain. He promises that I'll never really be normal and never have a fulfilling life, especially not with a man like Mike.

How could I? I'll drag a corpse along behind me for the rest of my years, and my future freedom is no longer a guarantee.

But when I turn from the dark reminder of the sea, Mike is grinning at me, delighted and joyful. And I have to stay in this area to be on call for Grigore for a year, so why not just . . . try? The doors are open. I'm not a trapped animal, and I don't have to keep thinking like one.

"What?" I ask Mike, sneaking another look at his smile.

"I'm just happy to be on a date with you."

"Oh, is that right? I thought maybe you were more excited about the destination."

"Bullshit. It's all about the company."

"Yeah, that's what I meant, actually."

He chortles like a delighted schoolboy.

"It took you long enough to ask," I say as I pull onto the narrow parking strip above the dunes. "I was beginning to think you'd forgotten."

"Are you kidding? How could I possibly forget? I think about it at least once every day. But I was trying to be a gentleman."

"Well, kind sir," I say as I open the door to a gust of salty breeze, "are you ready to show that dignified ass to the whole world?"

"Maybe not the *whole* world," he answers, but he leaps from the car and practically jogs around to the trunk to retrieve the chairs and bags. "But definitely to a few people on this hidden beach."

I grab a big bottle of sunscreen from the glove box and join him, and we take off at a run, leaping and laughing our way down the warm sand of the steep hill. For the first time in a month, I smile at the sight of the deep-blue waves and think nothing but happy thoughts.

Because no one's future is guaranteed, but mine might look more promising than ever. Instead of living a hundred different small lives, maybe I can live one big, bright one.

About the Author

Wall Street Journal bestselling author Victoria Helen Stone, author of the runaway hit *Jane Doe*, writes critically acclaimed novels of dark intrigue and emotional suspense. Her work includes *Follow Her Down*, *At the Quiet Edge*, *The Last One Home*, *Problem Child*, *Half Past*, *The Hook*, and the chart-toppers *False Step* and *Evelyn, After*.

Victoria writes in her home office high in the Wasatch Mountains of Utah, far from her origins in the flattest plains of Minnesota, Texas, and Oklahoma. She enjoys gorgeous summer trail hikes in the mountains almost as much as she enjoys staying inside by the fire during winter. Victoria is passionate about dessert, true crime, and her terror of mosquitoes, which have targeted her in a diabolical conspiracy to hunt her down no matter the season.

For more information, visit www.victoriahelenstone.com.